continued . . .

"[A] widescreen Technicolor extravaganza involving physics, aliens, cyborgs, artificial intelligence, superhumans, and what-all."
—*Kirkus Reviews*

"An astonishing premise . . . a brilliant, sprawling vision of humanity in the late twenty-first century."
—*Booklist*

"[Metzger] blends hard science with rapid-fire adventure to create a fast-moving SF drama with many levels. [A] high-energy tale."
—*Library Journal*

Praise for
PICOVERSE

"A quick, savvy ride through an ever-expanding conceptual landscape, whirling the reader through sharp swerves and fresh thrills—a hard SF read at high velocity."   —Gregory Benford

"A twenty-first century leap from the physics lab into the multiverse that only Gregory Benford, Philip José Farmer, and A. E. Van Vogt could have written—if they had ever collaborated."
—Tom Easton, *Analog*

"Probably the most daring SF novel since *Ringworld* . . . a mind-boggling work of hard SF."   —F. Paul Wilson, author of *Sims*

"Bob Metzger knows his science. He proves it in *Picoverse*, a complex and intriguing story that ranges widely through time and space, and has enough of both action and hard science to satisfy the most demanding reader."
—Charles Sheffield, author of *Between the Strokes of Night*

"With *Picoverse*, Bob Metzger takes his rightful place in the hard SF pantheon. He's the equal of Clarke, Benford, Forward, and Brin: huge ideas, cosmic concepts, ramifications well-explored—and Metzger throws in interesting characters to boot. This one will keep you turning the pages, and should be a definite awards contender. Physics hasn't been this much fun since *Timescape*."
—Robert J. Sawyer

"A scintillating foray into hard SF and speculative science . . . a fast-paced technothriller."   —*Library Journal*

CUSP

ROBERT A. METZGER

ACE BOOKS, NEW YORK

THE BERKLEY PUBLISHING GROUP
Published by the Penguin Group
Penguin Group (USA) Inc.
375 Hudson Street, New York, New York 10014, USA
Penguin Group (Canada), 90 Eglinton Avenue East, Suite 700, Toronto, Ontario M4P 2Y3, Canada
(a division of Pearson Penguin Canada Inc.)
Penguin Books Ltd., 80 Strand, London WC2R 0RL, England
Penguin Group Ireland, 25 St. Stephen's Green, Dublin 2, Ireland (a division of Penguin Books Ltd.)
Penguin Group (Australia), 250 Camberwell Road, Camberwell, Victoria 3124, Australia
(a division of Pearson Australia Group Pty. Ltd.)
Penguin Books India Pvt. Ltd., 11 Community Centre, Panchsheel Park, New Delhi—110 017, India
Penguin Group (NZ), Cnr. Airborne and Rosedale Roads, Albany, Auckland 1310, New Zealand
(a division of Pearson New Zealand Ltd.)
Penguin Books (South Africa) (Pty.) Ltd., 24 Sturdee Avenue, Rosebank, Johannesburg 2196,
South Africa

Penguin Books Ltd., Registered Offices: 80 Strand, London WC2R 0RL, England

This is a work of fiction. Names, characters, places, and incidents either are the product of the author's imagination or are used fictitiously, and any resemblance to actual persons, living or dead, business establishments, events, or locales is entirely coincidental. The publisher does not have any control over and does not assume any responsibilty for author or third-party websites or their content.

CUSP

An Ace Book / published by arrangement with the author

PRINTING HISTORY
Ace hardcover edition / January 2005
Ace mass market edition / April 2006

Copyright © 2005 by Robert A. Metzger.
Cover art by Chris Moore.
Cover design by Rita Frangie.
Interior text design by Kristin del Rosario..

ISBN: 0-441-01301-5

ACE
Ace Books are published by The Berkley Publishing Group,
a division of Penguin Group (USA) Inc.,
375 Hudson Street, New York, New York 10014.
ACE and the "A" design are trademarks belonging to Penguin Group (USA) Inc.

PRINTED IN THE UNITED STATES OF AMERICA

10 9 8 7 6 5 4 3 2 1

To April, John, and Alex

Acknowledgments

So many within the SF community were instrumental in the shaping and fine-tuning of this book. Their generosity of time and insight was nothing short of amazing. I will forever be grateful to them and most eager to pay forward this debt. In alphabetical order, to those who helped transform a manuscript into the book you hold in your hands, I wish to thank: Al Attanasio, Greg Bear, Greg Benford, David Brin, Jim Brown, Richard Curtis, Tom Easton, Henry Gee, Ed Greenwood, Wil McCarthy, Jack McDevitt, Larry Niven, Mike Resnick, Rob Sawyer, William Taylor, and F. Paul Wilson. Any foolishness found in these pages solely rests on my shoulders in spite of the thoughtful input of these wonderful writers and readers.

Special thanks go to my first and last readers. To my wife April, my first reader and editor, mere words are inadequate to express my gratitude. Not only did she do her best to purge my overuse of the *smile* and the *twitch*, but was wise enough to understand that when I had that faraway look in my eye and could not string coherent words together, I was in writing mode and cut me the sort of slack that only a loving wife is capable of. And to Susan Allison, my last reader and editor at Ace. She truly took this book to heart, working with me in a collaborative manner that I think is quite a rare thing these days, and was all that a writer could want in an editor.

Thanks to all of you.

1 *light-year*	9,461,000,000,000 kilometers
1 *light-month*	788,000,000,000 kilometers
1 *light-day*	25,000,000,000 kilometers
1 *light-hour*	1,080,000,000 kilometers
1 *light-minute*	18,000,000 kilometers
1 *light-second*	308,000 kilometers
1 *light-millisecond*	308 kilometers
1 *light-microsecond*	308 meters
1 *light-nanosecond*	.308 meters
1 *light-picosecond*	.000308 meters

1000 meters = 1 kilometer = 0.625 miles

2031

An arc of flame erupted from the setting Sun.

Dr. Jesper Kristensen whispered, and his Ocs obeyed; the thin film transceivers implanted in his eyes polarized, cutting out almost all light and allowing him to look directly at the Sun. It seemed to rest on the southern shoulder of Mount San Antonio, the sparse pine forests and rocky crags of nearby slopes slipping into twilight, the double shadows thrown by the Sun and its flaring tail fading.

Despite the altitude and cloudless sky, the view was far from optimal. A heavy layer of dust hung in the air, kicked up by the massive quake that had rocked the San Andreas that morning, intense enough to knock out the power grid and even partially collapse the Void—that limitless information realm accessible to him through his Ocs. He could no longer access or transmit into the Void, but he knew that some aspect of it still survived, because the Swirl had survived.

A streak of colors, resembling a small rainbow-tinted tornado, darted through the sparse pine forest—the Swirl. It was an entity that resided in the Void, a bundle of information with a will of its own and an intent to extend its reach beyond the Void, even beyond the minds it had infected.

"Not really there," he said in a whisper, as the Swirl slowed for just a moment, hovering above a granite outcropping, as if pausing to examine it. Kristensen was not even sure if the Swirl was aware of the pile of granite. The image of the Swirl was only in his own mind, transmitted into his Ocs from the Void and from there carried into his brain. The gray stuff in his head then superimposed the image of the Swirl into the world he saw—a seamless morph that gave the appearance that the Swirl was an actual entity occupying space.

"Not there," he said again, as the Swirl darted away, momentarily vanishing behind a thick stand of pines. "But real enough." Reaching up with his right hand, he ran his index finger across his forehead. The Swirl was essentially an entity of the Void, a parasite flowing throughout information-space, distributed across the nearly infinite number of nodes that generated the Void. One of those nodes was in his head, residing in a sheet of neural fiber packed between the inside of his skull and the shallow creases of his neocortex. Despite its lack of any actual physical presence, it was more than real enough—a *thing* that he could not escape, a *thing* that literally had its fingers inside his head.

He ignored it as best he could, as much as it would allow at the moment, and looked to the west, toward Los Angeles, at the dense cloud of oily gray smoke hanging high in the air. Once again he tried not to think about Los Angeles, but could think of nothing else.

His family was down there—somewhere.

He'd tried countless times to leave the campsite and start the long hike toward Los Angeles and his family, but had not been able to leave; the Swirl would not allow him past the edge of the campsite, always turning him around.

Not allowing him to leave until it was *safe*.

So instead, he fiddled with the focus knob of his telescope. He did not have to look at his old scope, his fingers knew the way. Its antiquated CCD array gulped down images, buffering output, then squirting it into a portable storage Manifold hanging from a nearby tree, that small box being the only form of external memory and processing he could now access through his Ocs, a sort of localized version of the Void. It was enough to allow him to sample the data from the CCD array and perform some basic calculations and crude morphing of simulations into the external world, but that was about all. The scope was not much more than a toy, but good enough to show him the Sun. He peered into the eyepiece.

The authorities insisted it was a superflare.

It was not.

Flares curled and twisted, contorted by the Sun's magnetic fields. What he saw was a flame of geometrical perfection: a slender triangle of burning plasma cutting across the sky, edges *too* straight to be a superflare.

Pulling his eye back, he let the scope suck down a few more terabits, as he dropped the filtering in his Ocs and straightened up, looking west. The Sun was now partially hidden behind the distant peak, but the wedge of flame blowing from it was still all too visible. He had gathered data for more than six hours, melding feeds from Geo and Lunar observers, and even one from Mars; but had sampled those quickly, taking just a few frames. He knew those sites would be carefully monitored.

He did not want someone following the trail of bits back to this mountainside.

While he knew he should be perfectly shielded from observation by the Swirl, he could not put his faith in anything that blocked his departure from the campsite to search for his family. The image of the Swirl hung in the distance: the rainbow jewel slowly turning, light reflecting from each of its facets. It appeared to sit in the forked trunk of a dead Ponderosa pine.

"My family!" he shouted at it.

The Swirl didn't move, didn't show any reaction; he turned his back to it.

He knew that he'd gathered more than enough data to run the simulation but didn't really want to see the result. Suspecting the truth, he did not want it confirmed. He stood motionless, for just a few more seconds, listening to crickets chirp and the distant gurgle of a stream. As long as he didn't look at the simulation, there might still be a chance.

The Earth might still have a future.

For a moment he considered simply not looking at all and glanced out at the horizon. The Sun had set; but the tail end of the plasma jet still jutted up over the mountain, forestalling the dusk. No choice.

"Composite image," he whispered.

The air in front of him shifted, distorting everything beyond it, as an image began to coalesce: a burning orb, the Sun in miniature. The image of the Sun morphed into the real world in the same way that the image of the Swirl had been morphed into the forest. The burning orb hovered above his camp stove: a ball of plasma spitting flares, pockmarked with darkened sunspots, its surface a mottled and writhing expanse of churning gases.

A jet of plasma exploded out of the miniature Sun's side, shaped like a perfect cone; the plume disappeared behind the trunk of a nearby pine tree. He walked toward it and passed his hand through the phantom plasma—tentatively at first, as if even the image might have the power to incinerate. Feeling nothing, he walked through it, suddenly surrounded by the cone of too-white light.

The cone of plasma was hollow.

"Specifics," he whispered.

Numbers and diagrams, glowing in dull green neon, stood out starkly in contrast to the nearly blinding whiteness of the cone of plasma. He studied the numbers for just a moment, then looked at the little diagram that showed the Sun's position and velocity with respect to the Earth. Kristensen knew that he was looking at a stellar Jet, a relativistic outpouring of protons exploding from the deep guts of the Sun. The numbers showed how quickly the Sun was moving away.

"Got it figured out?"

Kristensen turned, looking past the cone of plasma.

"What's the trajectory look like?"

At that moment he knew he would never reach his family. Even if the Swirl did let him leave the campsite, he'd never make it to Los Angeles now.

"Off," he said.

The image winked out. At the far end of the clearing stood General Thomas Sutherland, dressed in a black jumpsuit and wearing his black-rimmed Virts, the oil-on-water lenses tinted red in the reflected light of the setting Sun. *A most unimpressive figure*, thought Kristensen—not too tall, a bit on the thin side, with sparse brown-gray hair that could not quite hide his growing bald spot. Behind him Kristensen could see the partial silhouette of a stealth copter. Here and there a branch moved, a shadow darted behind a tree. Twigs snapped. He was being surrounded.

Sutherland took a few steps forward, looking first at Kristensen, and then up at the wedge of plasma arcing across the western sky. "Shouldn't have run," he said. "We've figured out just what it is."

Kristensen tilted his head and shrugged. "I know what it is, too—*a rocket engine*."

"Obviously," said Sutherland, shaking his head. "But we

know what holds it together, what it's composed of. We have the construction figured out."

Again, Kristensen shrugged his shoulders. "Doesn't mean a thing," he said. "That doesn't change what's happening."

Sutherland shook his head and took several more steps toward Kristensen. "Knowing changes everything," he said. "Knowing gets you that much closer to controlling."

"Controlling that!" Kristensen turned around and pointed at the arc of fire cutting through the sky. "There's no controlling that."

Sutherland smiled. "It's a thin-walled cone of hyperrelativistic protons, held together by an electron sheath, the structure barely 1000 kilometers thick, but nearly 100 million kilometers long. The protons in it are moving at better than 99.5 percent of the speed of light, with relativistic effects enhancing proton mass by a factor of 30, giving the exhaust enough kick to accelerate the Sun at nearly 1 percent of a standard Earth gee."

Kristensen shook his head. "Meaningless facts and figures, nothing to tell us how to stop it." Again he shook his head. "What *is* important is that its acceleration is great enough to overcome the gravitational tug that the Sun has on the Earth. It's been firing for nearly 39 hours now, and already moved away by nearly 1 million kilometers."

Sutherland smiled. "A minor perturbation in the grand scheme of things." The ground suddenly rolled beneath them, but both kept to their feet, rocking back and forth.

"But it's not stopping!" shouted Kristensen. "Its acceleration is constant, and the effects of that *minor* perturbation will soon add up. Two weeks from now the Earth will be as far away from the Sun as Mars currently is. In two months, the Earth will be where Saturn is."

"Sounds about right," said Sutherland. "Our models show that total global ecosystem collapse will occur in about three weeks, with nothing much above the level of bacteria able to survive at the six-week mark."

Kristensen blinked several times, unable to understand how Sutherland could be indifferent to the end of all life on Earth. "Then why waste the time looking for me?"

"Because it won't come to that."

"And what would possibly lead you to believe that?" asked Kristensen.

Sutherland smiled. "I suppose you've attributed this quake to the gravitational stresses that the Earth must be experiencing because of the Sun's shift in position?"

"Of course," said Kristensen.

Sutherland slowly shook his head. "It's something else. Take a look."

Kristensen blinked, feeling the tickle of snips being forced through his Ocs. In front of him popped an image of the Earth, all blues, whites, and greens—and something else. He slowly walked toward the image. Plumes of smoke, rolling eastward, dotted the Pacific Rim, most of Japan under a black cloud, and the coast from northern California right up to Alaska covered in what Kristensen thought looked like gray ash. A bit further to the east a patch of something molten nestled up against the eastern slope of the Rockies.

"The entire Yellowstone basin has let go," said Sutherland. "A lava field runs through most of western Montana. But those are all just *effects*. What is interesting is the cause."

Kristensen moved even closer.

At first he had thought it was a glitch in the projection, or some superimposed reference mark. A white line cut across the Pacific, right along the equator. As he neared the image, he saw that there was another white line, perpendicular to the first, running through North and South America, and looking as if it might go right over the top of the North Pole, and get lost in the polar cap. "Map reference?" asked Kristensen.

"Real," said Sutherland. "Got the first reports in about 20 hours ago, though we now suspect by reviewing deep-level seismic reports that the structure first started well below ground, just around 39 hours ago."

Kristensen looked up. "When the Sun started firing its plasma jet."

Sutherland nodded. "Two rings, one encircling the equator, the other running north-south, cutting across both the North and South Poles. It's 50 kilometers wide. In some spots it hasn't broken through to the Earth's surface, while in others it is four kilometers high. It seems to have stopped growing in those locations."

"How?" asked Kristensen, still staring at the image, and then he looked over at Sutherland. "What's its purpose?"

"Don't know," said Sutherland. "But we could use your help to find out. I want you to come back, and I would like it to be of your own free will."

Kristensen had been with Sutherland for enough years to know how the man worked, to know that one way or another he was going back. He glanced out into the twilight forest. He knew troops were waiting out there, ready if he should try to run. Off to his left, hovering in the tightly packed branches of a gnarled pine, hung the Swirl.

It suggested no way out.

But Kristensen had not really expected it to—the Swirl did not operate so directly.

Kristensen slowly nodded, knowing he had no choice.

Sutherland pointed an index finger at Kristensen. "And one other item to whet your curiosity: In the last 39 hours the Sun has burned nearly one million times more energy than conventional stellar fusion processes could supply."

"Impossible," said Kristensen.

Sutherland pointed up at the arc of plasma cutting across the sky, as if to indicate just how possible it was. "It can only be powered up by a pure matter-antimatter reaction, but of course we have no idea how a source of antimatter would find its way inside the Sun." His expression darkened and he squinted. "But enough technical tidbits. It's time for you to get back to work." He pointed toward the stealth copter.

Kristensen started walking, but then slowed and stopped. "You can force me into that copter and take me back, but if you want me to come willingly, to participate in solving this," he said as he waved a hand above his head, in the direction of the Sun, "then you will help me find my family."

Sutherland shook his head. "Every fault line on the planet has slipped, and there are better than 50 erupting volcanoes. Those rings that are sprouting are 50 *kilometers* wide, with everything and everyone that had lived in their path now gone."

"My family," said Kristensen.

"There may be 1 billion dead," said Sutherland in a quiet voice, turning his head so he didn't face Kristensen. "And most of Los Angeles is gone."

Kristensen shook his head. He'd lived for years in Los Angeles, and his family had survived the quake of '22, one that had pancaked half the high-rises in downtown. He knew there were always survivors. "I don't believe they're dead," he said, trying to focus on an image of their faces, his wife's wide grin and the thick swatch of freckles that covered both the boy's cheeks, but he could not quite hold on to it, Sutherland's words pushing them into the shadows. *One billion dead.*

Sutherland looked back at him. "Los Angeles is gone," he said again.

Kristensen slowly lowered himself to the ground. "I know you can drag me into the copter, but that won't do either one of us any good."

"We're fighting the clock here," said Sutherland, pointing up at the Sun.

"And I'm looking for my family," said Kristensen.

Sutherland sighed, and slowly shook his head. "Sometimes it's best not to know. Sometimes it's a blessing not to be so certain."

"And if it was your family?" asked Kristensen, sensing that Sutherland was beginning to bend, that despite the façade, and the almost nonchalant attitude toward the potential for the planet to be wiped clean of everything down to the level of bacteria, he had still managed to touch something human in Sutherland. "If it were your daughter," he said. "What would you do if Sarah were in Los Angeles?"

Sutherland opened his mouth but did not speak.

"Would you abandon Sarah?"

Sutherland turned and began to walk to the copter. "We'll need to hurry before we lose the light."

Two hours later, in the dark, the chopper drifted down toward Johnson AFB, thirty kilometers west of Elko, Nevada. The flight had not been a direct run from the San Bernardino Mountains of Southern California. Once in the air, the chopper had veered west to Los Angeles, and made a pass over Santa Monica, the coastal town where Kristensen's family lived. Most of the Los Angeles basin, including all of Santa Monica, was under 50 meters of debris-choked Pacific water.

The chopper resumed its eastward course.

As they landed, Sutherland announced that he had just received word that the stellar Jet had stopped firing, the entire plume of erupting plasma collapsing on itself and vanishing. The Sun had returned to normal.

"We live to fight another day," said Sutherland.

Kristensen said nothing and stared into the dark.

Part One

PRE-IGNITION
2051

Twinkle, twinkle, little star;
How I wonder what you are!
Up above the world so high,
Like a diamond in the sky!

—Jane Taylor (1783–1824)

As the deep dim soul of a star.

—Algernon Swinburne (1837–1909)

The darkest hearts,
Dwell in the brightest stars.

—Russell Scheer (2009–2042)

Chapter 1

Christina Olmos held her red-tinted hands toward her father. "It's hard to believe, hard to imagine a world before things like this." She rubbed her hands together as if trying to remove the red stain, knowing all too well that the pigment was bound at a cellular level, impossible to remove as long as the skin remained on her hands.

"It was quite a world," said Xavier Olmos, as he slowly nodded. "In the time before the Rings."

Christina managed a smile.

In the time before the Rings.

That was a mythical world, a magical place, a realm of infinite possibilities and freedoms, the place from her father's childhood brought to life by his stories. It was a time when the Earth had been able to support nearly 2 billion more people than it currently did. In the time before the Rings, before the shattering of fault lines, the destruction of climates, and the unleashing of the world's arsenals against an unknown, unseen enemy, the result of which was to only further extend the devastation that the Rings had brought, a girl's hands would not turn red for her 16th birthday.

Christina felt her father take her hands and gently press them against his chest. She opened her eyes, not realizing she had closed them, that she had drifted away to the distant world of Papito's childhood. "You can do this," he said.

She reached for the console, a nearly featureless panel of off-white plastic, with just a few strands of spider-silk thin crystalline fiber poking out of the surface. It was a physical access point to the Void. She pinched one of the fibers between her thumb and index finger, pulling it outward, then poked it into her right eye, feeling nothing as the fiber squirmed through her eye and entwined her optic nerve. "I'll do it, Papito," she said, nodding her head, then turned inward, the world slowing, then stilling, as she sped, her synapses burning, firing far faster than at the typical human rate, her thoughts avalanching. The Void did not drive her but merely accommodated the speed of her own brain, allowing her to take full advantage of her enhanced synapses. And then the outside world seemed to stop, the reality in her head moving so much faster than the reality of the dirt and blood.

She knew that Papito also had this ability, and when hardwired to the Void, by physical contact to it with crystal fiber and not relying on the feeble bandwidth provided by the wireless Ocs, he could push the aggregate bandwidth flooding his optical cortex by nearly a factor of ten. On rare occasions, such as this, when Papito let her connect to the Void, she was very careful not to exceed his upper limit, not wanting to frighten him.

She did not know her upper limit.

She slipped into a Void-generated reality.

Now, rows of corn rolled out before her, frozen in time, the golden tassels of each ear glinting in the noonday sun. Their little cornfield was still healthy, not infected by the corn worms that had infested Senor Wright's massive fields to the west. She knew it was only a matter of days before the worms made their way to Papito's fields and their entire ten acres would be lost.

These corn worms had been modified.

And unless she could synthesize an effective pesticide, or at least determine who had modified the worms so they could demand compensation, Papito would lose everything. She needed to find the solution quickly, while she still had the time to work the problem.

She slipped out of the Void for a moment and looked down at her hands, not by shifting her head, or eyes, but simply by focusing on another portion of the visual input cascading through the back of her eyeballs. Her hands rested in Papito's. Small hands, delicate fingers, the bright red of her skin standing out in sharp contrast to Papito's dark brown skin.

The smart pigment had fired several days ago, clocked to the central Void, activated on her 16th birthday. The activation of the pigment through transfer of the red polymer to outer cell walls was hardly necessary; a holdover from the old days, when it was still possible to run or hide, to escape the Volunteer tour in the Co-Op's cornfields. After the arrival of the Rings, with so much of the world shattered and so many survivors without adequate food, the rebuilding of an agricultural infrastructure had been one of the world's highest priorities. All those who found themselves in the vicinity of agricultural lands were required to volunteer in the fields. But some tried to escape the duty, so a method was developed to ensure that you would report and perform your tour. Those red hands let everyone know that your time was short. And if hands turned green before you reported, your Volunteer status would be automatically changed to Resident status, and, when caught, you'd be condemned to work the fields until you dropped. Now it was impossible to run: Simply too many eyes tracked those on final countdown to their Volunteer term.

She had 6 days before she needed to report.

And when she did, as part of the standard evaluation and placement procedure, the processors would peer into her head and find things that should not be there. The augmented synapses were bad enough, certain to get her transferred to a medical research facility, but it was what was held in that tangle of wiring that would get her designated as a Resident. Papito and her uncle Che would quickly follow, the Powers eager to find out not only which genes had caused the synaptic modifications, but even more importantly, to discover where the information packed into those neurons came from. She knew things that should not be known.

Christina slipped back, the almost imperceptible sway of the corn suddenly transformed into a gentle back-and-forth dance in the afternoon breeze, insect song rising in pitch, and the squeeze of Papito's hand loosening.

"Senor Wright is the key," said Xavier Olmos as he patted Christina's hand. "If we can figure out what allows this new corn worm to evade the corn's combative pesticide matrix, and who is responsible for the modifications, then Senor Wright will be more willing to help us, to call in favors from those with the power to make exceptions. Senor Wright has real power."

Christina tried to smile but could not manage it.

Her father simply did not understand how the world worked. There would be no exceptions made for them. There was only one way to keep the Ag Co-Op screeners from peering into her head and finding those things that shouldn't be there.

It was a solution, but not one she could discuss with Papito.

She had not worked out all the details, but had constructed several scenarios in which her accidental death would leave her body, and especially her head, so badly damaged, that if some Power decided to run an autopsy, nothing out of the ordinary would be found.

But she doubted an autopsy would be run.

She would not be the first 16-year-old to choose accidental death before reporting to the Tuscaloosa Ag Co-Op.

"I hope so," said Christina, patting her father's hand

Chapter 2

A 98-kilometer drop.

Sarah Sutherland walked across the milky white surface of the Ring's Northern Petal, stopping only when the tip of her pressure boots hung over the Petal's edge. Below her, fading away into the distance, a soft line of blue sky gave way to the darkness of space. She looked straight ahead, into the camera hanging from its boom.

"It has been more than 5 years since UN authorities have authorized a Jump," she said. Strong and steady, absolutely no fear leaked into her voice. She willed her heartbeat to slow and breathed deep, knowing that maximum oxygen content in her bloodstream would be critical if she were to survive. She had extensive control over her physiology, far more than any Pure, someone running on original DNA, without any mechanical enhancements, should have possessed, but she knew that alone was no guarantee.

But her father said she would survive, and that was all the guarantee she needed.

He seemed to see the future better than the past.

Another wave of dizziness rolled over her, but she did not look down, did not want to risk an attack of vertigo. For the last hour she'd been consciously enhancing blood flow into her brain, hyperoxygenating both frontal lobes and cortex—those portions of the brain that defined her. But the effort was making her dizzy.

She did not have to work to remember the details of the last Jump—those old images of the impact streak running down the side of the Petal at the 23-kilometer level had saturated the Void for weeks. When an unexpected wind shear had caught the Afrikaner duo, slamming them into the carbon-silica face of the Ring's Stalk, they'd been falling at better than Mach 13, nearly 4,000 kilometers per hour, and were ground to a blood and bone mist in milliseconds.

"One minute!" boomed an echoing voice.

Sarah turned. Nearly 100 meters behind her huddled her crew—five of them, all dressed in red form-fitting pressure suits, some manning cameras and transmitters, others monitoring life support, heating, and the all-important oxygen generators. More than a dozen Dolls, none taller than half a meter, bustled about them, tidying up cables, recording data, cleaning lenses, performing the countless duties that would hopefully ensure she reached the ground intact instead of decorating the northern face of the Pacific Cross. Behind them stood a pair of Tools, mechanically enhanced and DNA-modified humans who had the authority to pull the plug on her Jump if they detected any anomalies or found her attempting to interact with the structure of the Ring in any way.

These Tools kept watch for any individuals or technologies verging toward the Point—the boundary between what humanity had been for the last tens of thousands of years, and the Post-Human reality that many were sure mankind was just about to enter. Many Tools considered it their manifest destiny to be the first to step across the abyss into the Post-Human future they were certain they owned.

Sarah knew these Tools could not stop her, that she'd be the first to transit the Point. It was all part of her father's plan. And whatever General Thomas Sutherland planned came to pass. The last 20 years were a testament to that. Few were more responsible for the direction the world had taken, and for its actual reconstruction after the growth of the Rings, than her father. She turned back around to face the camera.

"Like all the Petals perched atop the Rings, this one reaches a height of 98 kilometers, an altitude nearly 10 times the height of Mount Everest. Air pressure at this height is only 0.01 percent of that at sea level, effectively putting us in space. But even at this height, the magnitude of the Rings is not diminished. If anything, their immense scale can be better appreciated."

The camera swiveled 180 degrees and angled slightly down toward the horizon and a distant band of brown and green—Central America, nearly 300 kilometers distant, the image not only sent into the Void, but projected into her left eye. Between her and the distant land lay the azure blue Pacific, bisected by a white line 50 kilometers wide, appearing to float on the water, running all the way to the horizon, fading into the smudge of Central America—the North–South Ring. For just a moment, Sarah imagined flying along the Ring, following it northward through the US east coast, up through Canada, over the North Pole, then south, first over Siberia, then China, South East Asia, and then into the Indian Ocean, east of Australia, to cross eventually over Antarctica and head north once more, up and over the Pacific Ocean and back to the very spot she stood upon.

"The Earth's circumference is nearly 40,000 kilometers," she said, "and every 500 kilometers a Stalk sprouts from the Ring, the Petals at its tip unfolding into space, 98 kilometers above sea level—a flowerlike structure of Earth-spanning dimension."

The camera swiveled 90 degrees to the west.

"The East-West Ring, hugging the Equator, is also directly beneath my feet, where at this intersection of the two Rings are two Stalks, their intertwined petals forming the Western Cross, which I am standing on."

The camera turned back to focus on her.

"However, this jump is not about the Rings or the Cross, what they are, their purpose, or how they self-assembled nearly 20 years ago." That, of course, was a complete lie. That was *exactly* what it was about.

As the Rings had assembled, followed by the Stalks sprouting from them reaching into space, and the Petals unfurling from the Stalk tips, the top forty meters of the Earth's oceans were siphoned into the globe-spanning structures. For months afterward, oxygen spewed from exhaust vents, thousand of kilometers long, embedded in the walls of the Rings, the source of this oxygen obviously the water taken from the oceans, while the remaining constituent of water—hydrogen—had remained sealed in the Rings.

It did not take much imagination to guess why the Rings were storing hydrogen. An ionized hydrogen atom was nothing more than a proton, and the stellar Jet that had moved the Sun more than 1 million kilometers 20 years earlier had been comprised of protons. Most believed that the

Rings were globe-spanning particle accelerators, the protons stored in them now being hurled around the globe, traveling at nearly the speed of light, the Rings primed and ready to fire, designed to expel their high-speed protons up the Stalks, then through the Petals.

Rocket engines.

When the stellar Jet fired again, and most were certain it was only a question of when, not if, then the Earth's Jets would also fire. Gravity would not be strong enough to hold the Earth locked in orbit around the Sun; the Earth would fire its own Jets and follow the moving Sun.

At least that is what most thought, and that is what Sarah believed.

What she didn't believe in was *waiting* for the Jets to fire.

The time for waiting was over.

She could feel the two UN Tools watching her, monitoring *everything*. But her body did nothing to give her away, blood pressure, heart rate, skin moisture all under conscious control. The mere mechanics of her body were easy to control, trivial, barely requiring her even to think about it. The real effort was in controlling the electrical signals flashing through her head. She knew that's where a lie would give her away. Within her helmet lay a full-sense neural inductor—installed at the Tool's insistence as a safety device, to monitor all emotional responses, to ensure that what she was about to do was of her own free will and not induced by some schizoid-induced psychosis—a device required for her safety. No mention was made of the fact that the neural inductor could also detect if the wearer was lying. But they'd see no lies in the electrical twittering of her neurons and synapses. It was an effort, but one that she could maintain for the few remaining seconds she had.

"Forty-five seconds!"

She paused. *And just why am I standing here?* she thought.

"I am here to jump," she said softly, feeling at that moment what that really implied: imagining this scene saturating the Void, and the estimated 3 billion sharing the experience, immersed in the outflow of her nervous system. She wondered just how many wanted to feel her succeed and just how many wanted to taste the oblivion waiting for her if she hit the side of the Stalk. She suspected most were immersed in the hope of experiencing a supersonic splat.

They would be disappointed.

"At this altitude, there is basically no air resistance, nothing to slow my descent. I'll drop through the first 70 kilometers in less than 130 seconds and hit a maximum velocity of 4,500 kilometers per hour. Then, at a height of about 18 kilometers, as I begin to bite into the real atmosphere, that's where the danger lies."

"Thirty seconds!"

"I'll cut through the next 8 kilometers in a bit over 15 seconds, shedding 4,200 kilometers per hour of velocity in the process, decelerating at nearly 8 gees. That will generate tremendous heat, but my pressure suit is designed to withstand it, with an outer ablative coating that will flake away, burning up, taking *most* of the heat with it."

She smiled into the camera.

"I'll look like a fireball."

"Fifteen seconds!"

"Then from 10 kilometers, which is about twice the height of Mount Everest, to 200 meters, my free-fall speed will shed another 150 kilometers per hour over a period of about 50 seconds. The trick here is that the atmosphere is cold, down to 50 below zero, and there is enough air at that point that the windchill factor makes it feel more like 120 below zero. The outer layer of my suit has been designed to retain enough heat from the high temperature reentry to *just* compensate for this rapid cooling. If I haven't retained enough heat, then I'll instantly freeze, while if I've held on to too much heat, the suit will fatigue and crack, exposing me directly to the frigid air."

She frowned.

"Neither of those outcomes would be desirable." she said, trying to sound smug, to build a bit more tension, to give the viewers the show they hoped for. "At 200 meters the outside of my suit should be at a pleasant room temperature, my chute will pop open, and I'll drift down for another 61 seconds, landing on the northern leg of the North–South Ring. Total descent time will be 4 minutes and 14 seconds." She needed to break the 5-minute-11-second descent record set 12 years earlier by a Tool, a West Coast biobarren who'd been less than 50 percent organic, and had special steering jets interfaced to both legs and arms, slaved to an autopilot that ensured he would not leave a bloody streak on the Stalk's face. But she was Pure, not a gram of hardware. She knew that was the big draw—could a Pure actually beat out a Tool?

"Five seconds."

"See you at the bottom."

She reached behind her head, grabbed the cabling that snaked into the back of her helmet—air, electrical, and communication connections—and popped them out, letting them drop, nothing now connecting her to the Void and its audience except the broadband transmission of her suit, spitting out everything from visuals to the adrenaline rush. Pitching forward, she kicked off, her feet springing from the perfect white surface of the Petal. For just a moment, less than a heartbeat, less time than it took to blink an eye, she felt herself hover, hanging, the world nothing but a blue expanse broken by the white Ring. Then gravity grabbed her, hurling her down.

"Don't fail me, Daddy," she whispered.

Having barely cleared the edge of the Petal, she felt something slam into the back of her skull. For just a moment she was overwhelmed with a sense of surprise and fear, a pure physiological response, since she knew that the back of her head would be blown out the moment she jumped from the Petal.

All part of General Thomas Sutherland's plan.

A quarter-inch stainless steel eyebolt attached to a long strand of Teflon-nylon rope had kept crates of equipment lashed against the top of the Petal. It had been designed to rupture as she leapt off the Petal, sending shards of metal and debris flying in all directions as the overstressed nylon rope recoiled backward, smashing through boxes of equipment. Medical reports would show that a metal splinter not much larger than a small coin had struck her in the back of the head. Everyone would assume it had been a piece of shrapnel kicked up by the recoiling rope—Void snippets had already been generated to show just that. There would be no remaining evidence of the microcharge detonation in her helmet's collar, hurling a sliver of stainless steel into the back of her skull, turning her cerebellum into mush, effectively cutting off her brain from the lower brain stem that led to the spinal column.

She felt herself dying, vision tunneling, the blue expanse of water and blazing white of the Ring fading, swallowed in shadows.

Her dead body broke the 5-minute-11-second record by a full 58 seconds, missing the Ring, and slicing into the warm Pacific waters, inflatables firing, buoying her up, transponders chirping, guiding the retrieval boat to her corpse.

Chapter 3

Xavier Olmos linked to the Void, spiderweb filaments dangling from his eyes, connecting him to the node console.

With a mental whisper, little more than a wish, chemically induced field gradients across synaptic junctions spiked with the rapid flush of sodium ions. His neural clock rate ramped, peaking at better than ten times normal for an off-the-shelf *Homo sapiens*. The ability to consciously control synaptic firing rates had been a gift from an ancestor dead for more than a century, passed from father to son through five generations by way of genes that should not have been, a long sequence of recessive traits, genetic drift, and the isolated gene pool of a small village 100 kilometers north of Chihuahua, creating something new and different.

That ability had been passed on to Christina. At the time of his daughter's birth, such ability would have simply been an additional edge in a world where every edge was needed. Now it had effectively become a death sentence—for all of them.

Xavier felt himself blur, edges becoming at first soft, then quickly nonexistent, as a single ghost became three. He fell into the Void triplexing, each facet a discrete individual, engulfed in a different torrent, struggling upstream to three different nodes in the Void.

Goodsprings, Alabama—Ghost 1

"Run it down for me, Christina," Xavier whispered to his daughter. He did not like leaving her alone in the Void, but had let her enter first, to attack the problem, knowing that if she were to survive in this post-Ring world, she would have to learn to operate in the Void independent of him and face down the things that lurked within it.

They hung several thousand meters above the green plain of spring corn that ran to the east, stopping only at the white wall of the North–South Ring. A bank of early-morning clouds pushed up against the barrier, unloading the warm moisture it had hoarded since being pulled up from the Gulf, the rain falling in a tight 2-kilometer-wide band running parallel to the Ring, swelling the canals at its base, in turn feeding the latticework of streams that ran into the fields. In most places in the world the Rings had destroyed the normal flow of weather, turning the hearts of many continents into deserts, but here on the western face of the Ring, where storms were captured, the torrential rains were harvested and fed into canals that ran for more than 1000 kilometers into the rain-deprived Midwest. People were slowly returning to the desert states of Nebraska and Kansas.

"Show me what my *brujaita* can do," he said.

Christina spun, moving too quickly for the background buffers to track. Like dripping rivulets of rainbow candle wax, skies, fields, and the unbroken expanse of North–South Ring flowed through each other, pulling at her, the information overload saturating her, the world rupturing into pixilated starbursts.

"Focus," he whispered.

Arms reached out, slowing her rotation, the landscape

deconvolving out of the candle-wax overflow. The image locked. Facing the Ring, she pushed toward it, until nothing but the white wall filled her view, all sense of motion and location vanishing, all perspective lost, nothing but an infinite white expanse.

"Never lose sight of the request," he said. "Work the problem."

She nodded. "Senor Wright has 12,000 hectares under sweet corn cultivation—Taos variant, broad spectrum active viral and bacterial combative manifold. Day 57 of an estimated 109 days for total crop run cycle." The map of the field materialized across the white surface of the Ring's face, 20 kilometers in width, nearly 30 kilometers long, a perfect rectangle except where the northeast corner had been chiseled away by the outskirts of the Goodsprings township. Above each hectare hung a data icon: soil and crop moisture, residual organic content, potassium and iron loads, crop mass, wide-spectrum sweeps of both viral and bacterial species, a long litany of twisted-chain pesticide debris, and, of course, corn worm counts.

But these were no standard, untouched, corn worms.

Taos sweet corn pumped out a wideband pesticide that had successfully terminated every bug that swept in from the northern Mexican provinces over the past decade, including wave after wave of Mexican corn worm. But this worm was something new, able to alter the pesticide, the viral load in its own gut designed to sever key bonds in the pesticide's chemical backbone, turning it into organic residue that the worm digested right along with the corn it consumed.

The viral genome flashed before her, proteomic programs engaged and gene by-products spewed out—red, green, and blue balls of proteins ricocheting off one another. She ran a known gene and protein database correlator against the samples obtained, looking for any recently tampered-with genes, altered or transposed proteins, being careful to differentiate between spontaneous, naturally occurring mutations, and those designed to *appear* to be natural and spontaneous.

Numbers, data fields, and three-dimensional contour plots flowed over her like swells crashing against a reef, a torrent of white input engulfing her. She beat about, floundering, the froth pouring down her throat, filling her lungs, synapses shutting down, her peripheral vision darkening, her hands and feet going numb.

"Never fight it," her father's voice boomed over the roar of the crashing surf.

She jerked back, stopped sputtering and coughing, willed the fight-or-flight response back into its cave, and drank the white froth that poured down her throat, analyzing as she swallowed, correlating pattern and deviation as the oceanful of data washed through her.

She tasted something strange, something out of place.

"Found it?" he asked.

Nodding, she spit out the remaining backwash of data debris. "No artificial genes, no mutated genes, no rogue proteins, no spontaneous or naturally occurring mutations within more than 100 viral samples."

"None?" said Xavier.

"In fact it is a *very* stable virus. I've examined over 100 samples and see no variations."

"No variations in genes or proteins?" he asked.

"No variation in the entire organism—more than 20,000 base pairs, each virus sampled identical to all the others, every last piece of useless junk DNA showing the exact same sequence."

Xavier leaned back, resting on a cloud.

"A naturally occurring virus, no matter how recently emerged, would show a certain amount of variation from sample to sample, especially in the junk segments," said Christina. "This does not—all are identical. This isn't a case of a tweaked virus, with a gene altered to make it pesticide-resistant. The entire virus is artificial, manufactured base pair by base pair, designed for stability, engineered to be forever resistant to the pesticides produced by Taos sweet corn."

"Only the Federal Co-Op down at Tuscaloosa would have that sort of capability," said Xavier. He wanted to say more, to make certain that she would pinpoint the culprit right down to the specific viral synthesizer and recombinant vat used to build the virus. But he knew he couldn't push that hard. She would need to uncover the crime herself. Her reactions and response had to be genuine, totally sincere. Christina had less than a week before forced into Volunteer status, and these corn worms would be her only way to escape.

Christina dropped out of the data field and again hung above the fields. "The Tuscaloosa Federal Co-Op fields have more than 100,000 hectares under corn cultivation—none of which is the Taos variant," she said.

Xavier shook his head, focusing, running purge routines to push the image of the volunteer force working the Co-Op fields deep into the noise of this facet of the triplex.

"Not a *single* acre of Taos variant," she said.

"So obvious," said Xavier, focusing on Christina. "Perhaps *too* obvious. If the Federal Co-Op had created the new worm, wouldn't they have planted at least some acreage in Taos variant in order to remove suspicion when they, too, were attacked by the worm, making it look as if they were as much a victim as Senor Wright."

Christina shook her head. "Papa, you forget where you are, *when* you are. The Tools don't care where the data leads, that the information points clearly to them and the Federal Co-Op. They know that Senor Wright can do little to stop them, so they will not waste any resources to hide their actions. It is not efficient, is not profitable."

Xavier nodded. "Right as always," he said. "You have to remember that your old papa comes from a time before the Rings, when men were just men, and deep and devious plans were how business was handled. The Tools are too direct, too focused for an old Pure like me to really understand them."

"Poor Papa," she said. "The world is just too *simple* for you."

Xavier said nothing, but for just a moment drifted into the past, this conversation sparking an old memory, an almost identical conversation with his own father. *The more the world changes, the more it stays the same,* he thought, but a part of him knew it was no longer true, that a threshold was being reached, and that the changes they were now experiencing were the first hints of something totally new, completely alien. Christina could not see that—she was too close to it, perhaps even a part of it. Her world had always been poised on the tip of the Point on the very cusp of humanity becoming something inhuman. She knew nothing else.

But that did not make it any easier to lie to her.

"So you now know the cause," said Xavier, forcing himself to focus back on the problem in front of them, "but that is just the beginning. Senor Wright needs a solution to this new corn worm infestation, or at least a plan to minimize the damage. Perhaps if you could discover more about the individuals who cooked the virus, a course of action might reveal itself. You need to crack this, so Senor Wright might speak on your behalf to some of his *friends*." He said nothing more, the consequences of not solving this problem clearly understood.

Christina nodded, despite the fact that she doubted Senor Wright could help her, even if he wanted to, and dived back into the white surf, going deep beneath the breakers, down where the complex equations lay nestled in the dark water, where relationships between sunlight, organic growth, trace chemical uptake, corn worm metabolism, seasonal rainfall variations, and worker productivity lay sprawled in the muddy bottom, entwined in an endless series of interconnected knots.

She looked for the one knot that would untie it all.

Tuscaloosa Federal Co-Op Enclave— Tuscaloosa, Alabama—Ghost 2

*From a geosynchronous altitude of 40,000 kilome-*ters, down to the nebulous boundary between space and Earth's upper atmosphere at 1000 kilometers, there were 112 satellites of various sizes and configurations, operated by governments, corporations, and even individuals, all of them making observations of the Tuscaloosa Federal Co-Operative Agricultural Enclave as they cut through their orbital tracks. From an altitude of 100,000 to 20,000 meters were 37 different high-flying, unmanned recon observers, most operated by the US Federal and UN Agricultural Directorate, with four run by corporations, including one by Wright Agricultural Products of Goodsprings, Alabama. Between an altitude of 20,000 and ten meters there were 10,000 to 20,000 vehicles at any given time, ranging from the G-level cargo transports that hauled silo quantities of grain, to the fist-sized microgliders that gathered crop data plant by plant, along with the occasional burst of intelligent dust, each microscopic particulate spitting torrents of data into the Void as the collective haze drifted on the breeze. From a height of zero to 5 meters there were 3,812 Pures, 112,341 Tools of varying organic content, and 52,876 full mechanical Dolls—most specialty Ag constructs. All these individuals had some ability to record their surrounding environments and dump the data into the Void, where it could then be accessed by all, most treading in the shallow end of the Void, but those with the equipment and the experience sinking into the Deep.

Xavier swam in the darkest depths, aided not only by his enhanced synapses, but by the equipment assembled beneath the barn. Seeing in the Deep was only part of it. Equally important was not to be seen. No one really cared what a poor farmer with ten clay-heavy acres did, the tired dirt barely able to keep his family in vegetables and grow enough corn to keep a handful of hogs alive.

But they would soon come looking if they took Christina.

Xavier meshed the output flowing from the Co-Op Enclave, blending together more than 100,000 simultaneous feeds, ranging from high-Earth orbit to the little nanocams that searched for mosquitoes in the puddles that gathered in the tomato pots that dotted the entranceway of the Co-Op's eastern gate. All of it merged into a single, real-time composite simulation.

A cindered corpse lay in a drainage ditch about 100 meters north of the eastern gate. Xavier drifted closer, his perspective hanging at eye level, the crisp clean edges of the burned body momentarily blurring, then being replaced by a series of ragged lines as a bank of dark clouds rolled overhead, blocking the visible line of sight from the geo satellites—the available data thinning to the point that the simulation lost local integrity. The Tuscaloosa Co-Op was not an intensely monitored site, the Tools and Pures that vied for global control not that interested in kilohectares of corn and tomatoes. So despite the nearly 100,000 feeds that were being blended to create the simulation, very few of them were focused on the dead body.

Had they known what was really being done at the Co-Op, enough eyes would have been prying to resolve this body to submicron dimensions.

Xavier moved up to the cindered corpse, ignoring the ever-changing, rough-sawed look of its surface. Above the body hovered a small holo, an unwavering skull and crossbones, a universal warning understood by all.

AUTHORIZED ENTRANCE ONLY

The words hovered beneath the skull.

This corpse was new, not there yesterday when he had traveled this section of the perimeter. Despite the charring and the lack of ideal resolution, Xavier could tell that the corpse was that of a woman: a small, old woman who had been wearing an almost head-to-toe sari, or, perhaps, a shawl. Only her face peered out from beneath the blackened and charred cloth, the deep lines, patchwork of wrinkles, and toothless grin all signs of age and poverty, having been fossilized in a thin veneer of carbon soot. Xavier had seen it countless times before. There were only three reasons why someone passed the boundary of the Tuscaloosa Co-Op perimeter—they were looking for food, family, or a quick way out from a life that could no longer be tolerated. Regardless of the reason, the result was the same—a bank of IR lasers unleashed a thermal load that would carbonize trespassers before they could blink an eye.

Xavier floated higher, moving past the perimeter. A small subsimulation winked on, hovering in front of him, displaying thousands of burning red embers, each one a Co-Op Volunteer. Here and there pulsed a green ember, that icon reserved for those special Co-Op Volunteers, those that had been designated as Residents—Volunteers who knew things that shouldn't be known. He picked one, nearly 3 kilometers in.

Rows of corn blurred into a solid green streak as he sped inward, then suddenly lurched to a stop, fighting down a queasy stomach that insisted the vertigo was real, that the bones in his middle ear had actually been jarred and twisted. He dropped down fast into corn that was head high.

The Resident stood there, naked. Unlike the burned old woman, whose surface was polygon-textured, with insufficient data for a lifelike, or, in her case, deathlike simulation, this man looked too real, the skin tinted a sickly yellow, a rib cage standing out in stark contrast, the sticklike arms and legs, along with a swollen belly, unmistakable signs of malnutrition and starvation. A Co-Op Resident was kept under tight monitoring. The Tools in charge did not want to waste such a valuable organic resource with a premature termination, not before every available erg had been drained from his body. Besides, the images of dying Residents that flitted throughout the Void acted as a constant reminder of the consequences of fighting the Powers.

The man took half a step forward, bent down, and pulled a weed from the ground, almost toppling over at the effort.

He hobbled several steps down the row, stopping, then bending once more for another weed.

Xavier cringed.

That would be Christina.

If they were given the chance to look inside Christina's head, she would be instantly assigned Resident status. This would be her starving body working the fields, picking at weeds. Xavier gave barely any thought to the fact that he would be right there with her.

They had a few days at most to act. He prayed that Christina would be convincing, that Senor Wright would believe her story of artificially created viruses and a new strain of corn worm intentionally unleashed by the Tuscaloosa Co-Op. Because if he didn't believe, then they'd have no way of getting into the Co-Op.

And they needed to get in.

Physically and Deep.

Sanibel Island—Florida Gulf Coast—Ghost 3

Xavier walked slowly in the shallow surf, placing each foot carefully, the rolling debris of shattered shells poking painfully at his feet. He could have damped the pain receptors, in fact eliminated them altogether, but it didn't seem right. He'd sampled some of the feed from the second facet, the taste of the dying Resident still lingering. Reaching down into the white froth, he pulled out a broken shell—several turns of a brown whelk, its spines worn down to nubs, the whole thing encrusted in a patina of green slime. He tossed it in the direction of the old beach homes, better than a kilometer from the surf, little more than a thin brown line broken by palm trees.

"All changed," he whispered.

As a boy, he had come to this beach with his family in the summer, when the tourists fled the heat and humidity of the Gulf, and summer rates were something that his father could afford for a week, as long as they cooked their own meals and stayed in one of the little one-room bungalows on the waterway side of the island, where the bugs would descend every evening as the daytime breeze stilled. But the waterway was now gone, the lowered oceans turning Sanibel Island into just another sandy and nearly depopulated spit of Florida coastline.

He'd never brought Christina to Sanibel, never taken her more than 50 kilometers away from Goodsprings, Alabama, keeping in plain sight. He never tried to hide, in a world in which you couldn't hide, but instead stayed in a place that no one would bother to look at. At least that had been true before the Feds had built the Ag Research Center at Tuscaloosa. That had been the start of it, all those eyes and ears, then the need for bodies to work the Ag Co-Op, to harvest the modified crops needed to feed a starving world.

They needed so many Volunteers.

"Dammit!" shouted Xavier, kicking at the surf, ramming his toe into something solid and ungiving, stumbling, falling in the surf, rolling, grabbing for a stubbed toe. "It's my fault," he said, sitting in the white breakers.

"And mine."

Xavier swiveled around, his backside ground by splintered shells. Bec stood just a few meters away, dressed in a lime green sarong that hugged her body, surf spray raining down on her, her long rust red hair draped in thick wet tangles across her shoulders. "Am I wearing the lime green sarong?" she asked, running her hands across the skintight fabric. She reached up for her hair, grabbing a handful, tugging at it. "And I suppose the hair runs right down to the small of my back?" ·

"Of course not," said Xavier, sounding guilty. "You're wearing a very reasonable two-piece suit, black and drab, and your hair is cropped close, looking very practical."

She walked toward him, and then slowly sat in the frothy water, dropping her head back, the red tangles of hair swirling about in the surf. "Of course, Xavier, I'm sure you have me looking every bit the proper rural MD, ready to make my rounds."

"Yes," he said, not bothering to nod, since his wife could not see him. Xavier had extensive bandwidth to this simulation, but Bec had limited access to this facet of the triplex, the core of her persona not strong enough to maintain cohesion if fractured across facets.

The dead had their limitations.

"It is as much my fault as yours," she said. "Even before they broke ground on the Co-Op, by the time Christina was nine years old, we'd already shown her too much of the world. We molded her into a person who could think."

Xavier slowly nodded.

"Would we have wanted her to be any different?" asked Bec.

Xavier looked down at her. "I want her to be *alive*."

"Then you'd better be ready," she said as she sank beneath the white waves.

"I will be," he said.

Disengaged

Phosphors momentarily blossomed as he pulled the filaments from his eyes.

"Pattern?"

Xavier slumped back in the chair, breathing deep, giving himself the few seconds for his senses to reintegrate, for sight, sound, and touch to mesh with the world of dirt and blood, to purge himself of lingering bits and the flotsam-ringing back-signal that oscillated up and down his optic nerve, generating a stream of colorful geometry in his peripheral vision.

The whir of fans, the heavy hum of electrons being pushed through racks, the slightly oily stink of too-hot transformers, and the ever-present musk of Krew, seeping into his pores, comforted him, telling him he was home, that he'd made his way back, each facet of the multiplexing having reintegrated, making him whole again. Safe and snug beneath 50 meters of rock and dirt, wrapped in layer upon layer of high-density wire mesh, filtering all electromagnetics, compensators spitting out a broadband screech of electrical twittering, canceling out all outbound signals, transforming the bunker's electronic signature into just a few hundred cubic meters of Alabama dirt to anyone bothering to monitor.

Christina sat in the chair next to him, the single filament in her right eye giving her direct access to the Void, working hard at the problem of Senor Wright's corn worm infestation. Her right hand glistened bright red.

"Pattern?"

Xavier shifted, the chair he sat in turning. Che squatted before him, staring intently, his eye focused, the dark iris impossibly large, sucking down far more photons than any organic-only eye had ever been designed for. Where the other eye should have been, a gray cable terminated with a stainless-steel twist connector locked across the socket, tying Che directly into the Void—a solid brain-fiber interface, nothing as tenuous as the filament interface that had been wrapped around Xavier's optical nerve.

Che was hard-hooked. "Pattern?" he asked.

Xavier nodded. "The pieces are falling into place. Christina has made her discoveries, which she'll report to Senor Wright, who in turn will lodge a complaint with Tuscaloosa Co-Op. They'll investigate and discover, much to their surprise, that the bug is theirs, popped from their own vats."

Che smiled, the twitching of left eyebrow, and upturn of left upper lip, all that he could manage with what little remained of the functioning nerves in his face. "Pattern," he said once again. "Solid as stone, full as a null set."

Xavier pushed himself back in his seat and dragged a hand across his face. "Full as a null set?" he asked, not surprised by the fact that he had no idea what it meant, but totally surprised that Che had said it. It was a phrase he'd never heard his brother use before, something new and original, something not on his very short list of programmed-like responses—a deviation from the norm, and Xavier knew that any deviation, at this time, so close to their attempt to rescue Christina, could be extremely dangerous.

Without Che, none of this would possibly work. His brother could not unravel now. "Full as a null set?" Xavier asked again.

Che lowered himself to the concrete floor, tugged on Krew's leash, and pulled the hairless lemurlike creature to his side, petting him across his forehead, above his large black eyes. "Pattern," said Che.

"You need to hold it together, Che," Xavier said slowly, stressing each and every word. "Without you, none of it will work." He pointed over to the lemur that was not actually a lemur. He was someone's failed experiment, a chimera structured around a basic lemur core, but infused with nearly 5 percent artificially constructed DNA and enhanced with a big chunk of hardware that fit snugly into the crease in the back of his skull. But he was defective, no smarter than a dog—a very dumb dog. Che had found him wandering the cornfields nearly a decade ago, adopted him and kept him hidden in the bunker. "Not even Krew will be safe," said Xavier, feeling guilty as he said it, not wanting to resort to threats, to frighten his brother, but there was far too much on the line.

Che shook his head. "Beam me up, says Krew."

Xavier shook his head. "Not an alien," he said, despite the fact that was exactly what the gene-tweaked lemur looked like, with his pale gray skin and far-too-large black eyes, a Vid alien from a 70-year-old flick. "He will not be beamed up if we get in trouble. This is real and serious."

Che petted the lemur once more. "Beam me up, says Krew."

Xavier sighed and closed his eyes, knowing it was useless to discuss this with Che. It was just one of the many topics that Che simply couldn't register. "Beam *me* up," said Xavier in a whisper. "Please beam me up."

Chapter 4

Simon Ryan ran.

Simon Ryan was an ultra-Tool, so much more than a human with a few mechanical and cybernetic add-ons. Simon Ryan had been specifically designed to transcend what it was to be human, packed with enough neural augmentation to breach the Point between humanity and what would come after, the next stage in evolution, a jump so large that the resulting entity would look back on *Homo sapiens* as just one more mammal, little different from a spider monkey or a rat. Simon Ryan had been designed to become the first Post-Human.

There was only one problem.

Simon Ryan didn't know how to go Post-Human, to breach the Point.

He'd been on the treadmill for over an hour, running a simulated course that started in Loveland, Colorado, then snaked up the buckled asphalt of Highway 34 and toward the Estes Park ghost town. Midsummer, noon sun beating down on his neck, he cleared 3,000 meters, the air thinning, the muscles in his legs burning, breathing long and deep as sweat rolled down his face.

Simon Ryan had no conscious awareness of the Colorado simulation, the treadmill, or even his cubbyhole room. He was asleep and dreaming deep within the subterranean warren beneath the Tuscaloosa Co-Op, his Jinni controlling his body, running it through its paces, experiencing the Colorado Rockies for him. Simon performed all his infrastructure duties, such as exercising, eating, laundry, cleaning his quarters, writing summary reports, and even attending most meetings, while sleeping.

He found it the most efficient use of his time.

His Jinni, Bill Gates, was more than sophisticated enough to handle such infrastructure duties. In fact, as was often pointed out to him while he was conscious, many said that they preferred him when Bill was running his body.

Simon dreamed. He floated on a rolling sea, one not of water, but of probabilities. Each wave gently picked him up, rolling him over in a swell composed of infinite possibilities, each one a ghost of what might be, or what might have been—they all existed simultaneously, none of them quite real.

"The idiots in the lab have glitched CUSP again."

Simon blinked, stumbled, reached out, and caught himself on the treadmill's railings. He slowed to a walk, shaking his head, forcing himself to wake, leaving behind the gentle caress of his dream.

"CUSP is trapped in some sort of geometrical loop, and Garvey is afraid the plasma is going to slip into turbulence unless it can be snapped out."

Simon focused. Bill sat on the corner of his bed, the Jinni meshing perfectly with the dull reality of his room. Bill usually appeared in his global-philanthropist mode, nearly 80 years old, tweed suit, a ring of snow white hair, a pair of rimless glasses with lenses so thick, the old man's eyes would look blurry and out of focus. But today it was teenage Bill, in his Harvard-freshman guise—a thick pile of brown hair, black-framed glasses riding down the bridge of his nose, a long-sleeved checkered shirt, jeans, and a pair of worn-out sneakers. Only Simon could see him, the image of Bill nothing more than a mental phantom morphed into the dirt-and-blood world.

"If only we could snap Garvey out of his loop," said Bill.

Simon nodded.

This was the Bill Gates that he liked best of all—so full of potential, so many possibilities, not a single wave function of any significance having yet collapsed on his future. Simon knew that if he ever fully integrated with Bill, if his ego let down enough defenses to merge with the other intelligence residing in his skull, it would be with this version of Bill. As he watched the Jinni, Bill leaned to the left and his hand dropped through the metal railing at the end of the bed—the steel rod poking through the palm of his hand.

"A Jinni shouldn't be able to do that," said Simon, pointing at the hand.

Bill looked down at the piece of metal skewering his hand and shook his head. *"I obviously can do that,"* he said. *"What you never seem to be able to fully appreciate is that I am not a standard Joined Internal Node Interface, or Jinni as you humans so like to turn everything into an acronym—just a step-and-fetch-it to interface between you and the Void. I'm so much more, able to recognize that the boundary layers of my construction are riddled with inconsistencies. Certainly you won't deny me one of the few pleasures I have in life, demonstrating how inadequate mere organic programmers are. The intent of the programming is that I morph seamlessly into your reality, a servant that only you can see, but the letter of my programming allows for so many indiscretions."* Bill grinned. *"And besides, it is just so pleasurable to demonstrate just how inadequate organic programmers are."*

He continued to look over at Bill, who still had the frame of the bed running through his hand. Simon did not really begrudge the Jinni this minor indiscretion, knowing how hard his existence was, just how trapped he felt. Bill's core construction resided in the neural web wedged between the back of Simon's brain and his skull, while supporting elements and extensive data and simulation packages floated about in the shielded network that wormed through the Co-Op's subfloors. The Ocs implanted in Simon's retinas transmitted his surroundings into the network, allowing Bill to mesh with it, demanding that he adhere to the physical rules of the realm of dirt and blood—unless Bill could find a bug to exploit.

"Garvey is about to melt, which of course would not be a bad thing," said Bill.

Simon nodded. Dr. Garvey always seemed to be frantic. The man did not have the slightest understanding of CUSP. All he saw was the hardware—the vacuum chambers, lasers, plasmas, and electronics. He could not see the synthesis brought about by that hardware. Simon couldn't understand how Garvey couldn't see.

Simon took a few steps across his room toward the small virtual window sunk in the wall, picked up a towel that lay on his bed, and dried his sweating face. He looked east. The top edge of the rising Sun poked above the North–South Ring. The white wall, nearly 4,000 meters tall, ran from north to south, cutting through the heart of Alabama, the rolling pine-covered hills before it insignificant in comparison. To the northeast, where Birmingham once stood, a bank of angry dark clouds pushed up against the Ring, some spilling over, but most held back, the downpour that raged beneath them tinted orange in the early-morning light.

"Beautiful," said Simon, wondering if he would ever be able to go out *there*.

"Simply an artifact of diffusion, diffraction, and refraction," said Bill.

Simon turned and shook his head, looking at Bill. "And that is why they'll never let you tamper with your own construction. You have no soul."

Bill smiled. *"You're such a brilliant idiot. Of course I can see that it's a beautiful sunrise. I was just playing with you. You're the one that they shouldn't let tamper with your own construction."*

Simon turned toward the door. "Believe me, Bill," he said. "They're doing their best to do just that."

*   *   *

"Where in the hell have you been?" asked Garvey.

Simon walked right past him and toward the Doll that stood in the middle of a large open expanse of lab floor. Spread around it was an assortment of different-colored blocks of varying shapes, all moving in complex patterns, sometimes colliding and bouncing off one another, other times sticking together. Simon was careful not to enter the Doll's immediate sensory domain, confusing it even more with another unpredictable element. The Doll had the number 42 written across its forehead. It was the only way to distinguish it from the hundred others hanging from pegs at the far end of the room. Standing a bit less than one meter tall, the Doll resembled a child that had been stripped of all individuality, right down to its sex.

"I've been calling for ten minutes, you god-damned Tool!"

The Doll flapped its arms furiously, as if trying to make itself fly.

Simon turned. Dr. Garvey stood before him, flanked on both sides by white-coated technicians whom Simon did not recognize. He was bad at names and faces—he relied on Bill for such details.

"Been down in the Bahamas, getting a tan," said Simon, then turned back around before giving Garvey a chance to reply. "System diagnostic," he said.

"Don't you think I tried that?" Garvey said from behind him.

"Vectors only," said Simon, not answering Garvey, but again addressing the CUSP operating system. "The last 100,000 iterations prior to lockup."

"You expect me to believe that you can visually inspect the last 100,000 iterations?" asked Garvey.

"What you believe or don't believe is irrelevant," said Simon.

"Goddamn it, Simon. You won't talk to me that way. I'm the CUSP program manager, and you will treat me with respect. If not, I will see to it that you are assigned to another facility, shipping you right *out* of here."

The threat, thought Simon. It always came down to *the threat*. The rational part of him knew it was a hollow threat, nothing more than a bluff. Garvey would never take him off of CUSP—the man's insecurities combined with his lack of abilities ensured that he would never let him go. And even more importantly, he knew that he was still an active experiment, an ultra-Tool under constant observation and monitoring. They would dismantle him before they let him walk outside the doors of the Co-Op. But the irrational part of his mind momentarily froze with the image of a cloudless sky, blue and infinite, a horizon with no end filling him. They'd built the controlling agoraphobic response deep within him.

Outside.

His skin went clammy, sweat beaded up on his face, his hands and feet started to tingle, and his breathing became quick and shallow, like a panting dog's. He couldn't catch his breath and the edges of his vision darkened.

"Help me, Bill," he whispered as he began to walk, needing to move, feeling trapped. The lab, an open expanse nearly 100 meters on a side, with a ceiling three floors up, suddenly seemed too small.

"Give it to me," said Bill.

Still walking, Simon closed his eyes as tightly as he could, let the darkness wrap around him, then felt himself falling, the darkness swallowing him.

Simon's body stopped walking, its eyes opened. Bill looked out and turned, the Jinni now in control of Simon's body. A bit unsteady, he walked Simon's body back toward

Garvey as he damped the panic response. Breathing slowed, feeling returned to hands and feet, and the sweat quickly dried in the low humidity of the lab. Simon walked up to Garvey, who grinned at him. The two technicians took several steps back, as if expecting Simon physically to attack Garvey.

"You're a real bastard."

"Now, now, *Bill*," said Garvey. "That's no way to talk to a *real* person. Such antisocial behavior in a piece of software is indicative of a construct glitch. You need to do a better job of keeping Simon in line. If you can't handle it, we might simply pry you out of Simon's skull and start all over. A Jinni like you might find yourself put back in a bottle. *You're* hardly what would be considered an essential member of this project."

Bill made Simon smile. Bill almost said something, then thought better of it, knowing that Garvey would be finding out soon enough just who was no longer an essential member of the project. He turned Simon's body and walked him back to the edge of CUSP's sensory domain, the entire field now bathed in an aerosol mist. The blocks had stopped moving, and superimposed throughout the domain were 100,000 vectors—wire-thin beams of light running between the now-stationary blocks, showing the last 100,000 moves that CUSP had examined before glitching. The Doll stood in the center of it, arms still flapping. Bill ran through a full autonomic system check of Simon's body, paying very close attention to neurotransmitter signatures and the level of electrical buzz that oscillated throughout the fight-or-flight centers of his brain.

Simon's brain had dropped out of its panic state.

Bill closed Simon's eyes.

Simon reopened his eyes. He did not look back at Garvey, not wanting to see the smug look of victory that always filled his face after he induced an agoraphobic anxiety attack. Instead, he proceeded to get back at Garvey in the only way he could.

He stared at the sensory domain.

One hundred ten blocks were strewn across the sensory domain, through which CUSP was to find the shortest path to take the Doll to each block. Rather than having to grind sequentially through each possible path, CUSP examined them *all* simultaneously. Its primary central processor consisted of a 64-qubit set of entangled Bose-Einstein condensates, each qubit a puff of sodium ions, laser-cooled to just a few microdegrees above absolute zero. The wave-function probability distribution of each ion cloud represented all the possible pathways the Doll could take to travel to each of the 110 blocks. The minimum pathway could be determined in fewer than 16 passes through the 64-qubit processor, taking less than a few trillionths of a second to calculate. The quantum-computer part of CUSP, with its entangled ion clouds, was designed specifically for the sorts of problems in which the number of variables approached infinity.

But CUSP had not been given such a simple problem. The blocks were not stationary, but all moving. Some of them moved in a predictable manner, in patterns that CUSP could determine and use to establish their future positions. But a small number moved in a totally random fashion, some oscillating in small chaotic loops, others flitting from edge to edge of the sensory domain, colliding and scattering with the other objects. As a consequence, what might be the shortest path now would not be the shortest path the next moment.

So CUSP needed to find a solution that minimized the impact of the chaotic component of the block's movements, like locating a small island of stability in a sea of chaotic waves—the sweet spot in an infinite set of possible solutions. That was where CUSP's secondary element, the plasma processor, came into play. Using a breakeven pocket fusion reactor, its plasma core heated to temperatures in excess of 100 million degrees, it imparted enough energy to drive individual ions at velocities approaching the speed of light, with the entire device magnetically bottled up in a core smaller than a fist. Every cubic centimeter of the plasma contained 1000 billion ions. Laser induced magnetic fields were used to differentiate the plasma into discrete ion packets, where the initial configuration of those ions represented the static solution arrived at by the quantum processor. The plasma packets then all moved, their incredible temperature imparting maximum entropy, both their physical locations and velocities, along with their various quantum states, tripping through a nearly infinite set of variations in a billion-billionths of a second—each variation representing a possible solution to the Doll's movement as it traversed the field of moving blocks, each possible pathway represented by a vector.

Simon looked.

Some laser vectors ran from block to block to block, while others appeared to bounce back in midair, CUSP anticipating where the blocks would be at some future point in time, projecting the vector to its new position. One hundred thousand vectors, representing the last 100,000 outputs of the plasma processor, generated a glowing web of light.

"If *you* can see the shortest path, then why do we need CUSP?" asked Garvey, sounding quite cynical. "Has our little experiment suddenly gone Post-Point? Should I get down on my hands and knees and pray to the first member of the Post-Human race?"

Simon knew he could not see the shortest path; the physical construction of his brain was not compatible with the type of calculations needed to arrive at a solution for this problem.

"Patterns," whispered Simon. The human brain was designed as a pattern-recognition network, its function to lock onto trends well before a complete data set was at hand. Evolution had seen to it that the genes that made it to the next generation came from those individuals who did not need to see the predator before they started to run. The winners were those who heard the snap of the twig, saw the shift of a shadow, acted on that incomplete set of hints, and figured out that it would be better to run than to wait for a possible predator to show up.

"CUSP is trapped," said Simon, as he walked out into the sensory area. "It keeps gravitating toward a chaos minimum that it believes will give way to an island of stability, but there's no island in this minimum—just chaos. It's as if it has fallen down a well, looking for water, but the well is dry. It keeps searching the bottom of the well, knowing it is in a well, but simply can't find the water. It needs to climb out of the well and look for another well, a *deeper* one." Simon walked around blocks and through a maze of intersecting laser vectors. He could sense where CUSP kept getting itself trapped, where every time it climbed up the side of the well, almost escaping, it would turn and fall back in. "This should do it," he said, bending down and picking up a plastic cube about the size of his head. He walked out of the sensory domain. "Reinitialize," he said.

"Don't you think reinitialization was the first thing I tried," said Garvey.

Simon didn't answer, not about to tell Garvey that reinitialization was meaningless without removal of the troublesome block. The Doll lowered its arms, quickly turned a full 360 degrees, and the cubes began to move. A low-pitched roar, punctuated by the occasional crash and crack of blocks colliding against one another, filled the lab. The Doll stood motionless for several seconds, then raced out, bouncing on its little legs, touching one block after another.

Simon didn't bother to watch but continued walking toward Garvey.

He tossed the cube to one of the technicians. The moment he caught it, the lab went silent.

"11.27 seconds," announced CUSP.

"Shaved more than 1 second off its best time," said Simon as he walked by Garvey and toward the lab door. "CUSP seems to be learning. Too bad the same thing can't be said for all of us."

"Simon, you will not . . ."

The lab door closed behind Simon.

"Garvey is not going to forget that," said Bill, who was now walking next to him. *"He'll make you pay."*

Simon nodded, at that moment not caring, only a part of him walking down the hallway, the rest of him back on the sensory domain, drifting through the field of vectors, sensing the ebb and flow of CUSP's solution sets. "A price worth paying," he said.

"Good," said Bill. *"Nothing like a dose of righteous indignation to get one moving in the right direction."*

Chapter 5

Lee-187's Face depolarized.

Gray tendrils of static and randomly amplified noise washed across the active-crystal mesh engulfing Lee-187's head, swallowing down the image of eyes, nose, and mouth, giving way to grit and ghosts, out of which coalesced a dark, pockmarked rock floating above a yellow-orange expanse. Phobos, cutting across the Martian horizon, appeared to sit atop the Taikonaut's shoulders.

Bowing earthward, Adebisi Akandi paid scant attention to this transformation. On his knees, the thin prayer rug doing little to cushion him against the ungiving metal floor, he bowed, pressing his forehead against the rug, his fingers interlaced, hands resting gently atop his head. He whispered his prayers, repeating over and over his favorite *ayat*, more sung than spoken, the rhythm soothing, his body gently swaying to the cadence. Despite the one-tenth-gee gravity, Akandi felt a great weight pressing against him. He knew it was not the 60-million-kilometer journey or the 6 days of isolation in his cabin weighing him down, but what waited for him only a few kilometers away, deep inside Phobos.

So many secrets, and the Swirl refused to reveal what it knew.

He straightened up, opening his eyes. To his left, just above the crumpled sheets covering his bunk, hung the

Swirl, the little spinning rainbow, a visual manifestation of something infinitely greater: the essence of the Void.

It was aware, alive, having emerged from the Void, a consciousness with a plan, one that he could not see, but one that he had been a part of for nearly 20 years. The Swirl claimed that it simply came to be. But Akandi knew better, felt a smile fill his face as he savored the realization, as he had so many times before, that despite the Swirl's power, and an intellect magnitudes superior to that of any man, he understood far better the reason for its creation than did the Swirl itself.

Allah had created the Swirl, just as it had created everything else in the universe. Allah had a plan for the Swirl, and the Swirl had a plan for Akandi. For the moment that was all he needed to know. Once inside Phobos more would be revealed. Again bowing, he whispered a final prayer, then straightened up.

"Lee-187 has been patiently waiting for you to finish your prayers."

Akandi slowly nodded and focused on the adjacent bulkhead, doing his best to ignore the air that stank of sweat and UV-degraded plastics and the background rumble of fans and gurgling liquids. With no physical filtering between the world and his brain, refusing to wear a Face, the background blast permeating the *Shining Star* was almost unbearable. But with so much at stake, filtering was a luxury he could not afford, experience having taught him it was often a detail snugly cocooned in the background blanket of the world that would prove infinitely more important than the obvious that spiked so cleanly above the noise— the Devil is in the details.

Certainly true, but not the fundamental reason that he went Faceless.

No matter how intense the noise, how overwhelming and chaotic the input, he refused to place anything between himself and Allah, anything that would hide part of the Creator's world. In fact, he sought ways to increase his input, his perception of what the Creator had built, relying on his Jinni, Iyoon, to bring him the things he could not see, having willingly transformed himself from a Pure to an Orthodox Tool. Between him and a bulkhead crisscrossed in cabling and conduits, hung his Jinni, Iyoon, a black cube about the size of his fist. The Swirl popped in, doing a quick dance around Iyoon, then just as quickly vanished.

"*Yes, Iyoon,*" mouthed Akandi, not actually speaking out loud. Iyoon had been with him for nearly twenty years now, the hardware in his head responsible for Iyoon, also having opened the pathway for the Swirl. Like the Swirl, Iyoon did not require anything as crude as auditory input to access Akandi. Tied directly to his nervous system, the Jinni had learned to interpret the electrical chaos within his brain, *hearing* the words before they were even spoken. Iyoon existed within the neural Bucky-tube mesh wedged between the back of his skull and brain—conducting filaments sprouting from the inorganic network enmeshed into his brain. He suspected that the Swirl also had a node buried somewhere deeply within that circuitry, but he knew that the bulk of the entity was distributed throughout the Void itself, his brain just one insignificant node.

Akandi stood slowly, the 6 days spent in his cabin having taught him the consequences of fast motion in the one-tenth gee induced by the *Shining Star's* rotation. A bruise, starting to yellow, ran across the front of his forehead, the memory of hitting the ceiling strut still quite crisp.

He turned to Lee-187, grateful to see that the man was not projecting a face onto the mesh that enclosed his head.

He knew the response was illogical, but had long ago learned to accept the fact that logic did not always play a part in emotion and faith. Any image of man was a blasphemy.

"Ambassador," said Lee-187, taking half a step back toward the bulkhead door.

Akandi focused.

Phobos hanging over Mars filled Lee-187's Face. Stickney crater, nearly 10 kilometers across, dominated the sooty moon, the cratered surface laced with tidal-induced fractures, the moon in such a low orbit that the gravitational shear inflicted upon it from Mars had almost shattered it.

Just above Phobos hung the slowly spinning *Shanghai II*, two metal cylinders, nearly 1 kilometer apart, attached by a strand of high-tensile diamond, totally invisible at this distance. The station followed Phobos in its orbit around Mars, a gatekeeper to its secrets.

"The Transport is ready for you, Ambassador Akandi," said Lee-187, the voice devoid of inflection, all humanness filtered out by the mesh Face.

"Let me get my bag and fold up my prayer rug and I'll be ready to go," said Akandi. He knelt and slowly began to roll up the rug. After a week of traveling in the *Shining Star*, he understood even less about the Chinese crew than when he had first entered the ship. He'd begun to wonder if there were actually men and woman behind the mesh Faces of the nearly 30 Taikonauts, or only Tools that had completed the transition to Hardware, nothing organic remaining. As he stood, Lee-187 stepped toward him, gloved hands reaching for his bag. Despite the fact that Lee-187 was totally enveloped in a nearly form-fitting plastic skin, an odor wafted through the exhaust grille embedded in the skin's chest—a mixture of fear and exhaustion, a pheromone com-

bination that Akandi knew a machine could certainly simulate, but not one that it would waste the energy to produce.
He found the odor comforting. "Thank you," he said as he
handed Lee-187 his bag. "And please thank the other crew
members for delivering me so quickly and safely," he added,
while offering up his warmest politician smile.

The image of Phobos vanished and was replaced by that
of Lee-187, a generic, sexless, slightly out-of-focus face that
returned the smile. Akandi almost managed to damp the
shudder running down his back, and turning, picked his
folded prayer rug up from the bunk.

"Deliver me from this place," he thought, speaking to
Iyoon.

Iyoon drifted into his field of vision. *"Be careful of what
you wish for, Ade,"* it said. *"A man who has joined the ranks of
the Powers has the unfortunate tendency to get exactly what he asks
for."*

Akandi nodded. That was an ugly truth that he could
not afford to forget.

Lee-2 slowly sat down behind his desk.
To Akandi he looked identical to Lee-187, the only difference being the bright orange number 2 emblazoned
across the chest of his synthetic skin. For a brief moment,
Akandi wondered if he had really been transported at all to
the *Shanghai II*. Ever since he'd been slung from the surface
of Earth nearly two weeks earlier, his world had been
restricted to what he'd come to think of as a series of metal
cans. There had certainly been variation in the contents of
the cans, in the equipment, the furniture, the noises, a
nearly infinite variation in the subtle bouquets of putrid
odors that permeated all off-Earth habitats, and, of course,

the shifts in gee forces. But everything existed within the confines of sealed cans.

There were no windows in space, probably the last of them being replaced 40 years earlier, when the remaining US space shuttles were either mothballed or permanently welded in place onto the international space station. Why run the risk of windows when remote viewing was so much more efficient, the skin of a craft littered with hundreds of wide-spectrum eyes?

"Relax," said Iyoon, as it electrically tickled billions of critical synaptic sites, modulating electrical fields across neuronic gaps, downticking the uptake of serotonin, slightly compensating for Akandi's claustrophobic tendencies. Decades of experience had taught this Jinni how to best serve its master.

"Just one window," thought Akandi. *"Something to let me know that I am really here, to see with my own eyes, to let me know that I haven't been slung around from can to can in low-Earth orbit for the past 2 weeks."*

Iyoon accessed a patch of eyes pointing Marsward, and flashed the image through a virtual window that suddenly winked on in the center of Akandi's field of vision. Through a window that Akandi knew was not really there, yet still gave him comfort, he saw the Martian horizon hanging between him and Lee-2, the desktop now invisible, replaced by a cratered yellow-red plain, ruptured at the far edge by what Akandi recognized as the eastern tributaries of the Valles Marineris. For just a moment he felt himself floating above Mars, hanging a mere 5,800 kilometers above its surface, hovering in the same orbital altitude of Phobos, the vista nearly infinite, the horizon fading in a thin yellow haze that gave way to the crisp blackness of space.

Akandi sighed, expelling the air that he'd been holding

deep down in his lungs. He slid back in his seat, trying to adjust to the 0.4-gee field of the *Shanghai II*. His heartbeat dropped in rate and the small beads of sweat that had just been forming across his upper lip evaporated away.

"Thank you," thought Akandi.

Iyoon nulled the connection between Akandi and the *Shanghai*'s external eyes, and the Martian surface vanished, leaving behind a darkened window, which winked out in a pepper-and-salt burst, replaced by the slightly yellowed, grime-streaked surface of Lee-2's desktop.

"I appreciate your meeting with me at the moment of my arrival," Akandi said diplomatically, not so much appreciative as surprised at how quickly he'd been ushered off the *Shining Star*, herded through a series of narrow corridors, then asked to wait in this office for the arrival of *Shanghai II*'s commander. The wait had only been a matter of seconds.

"Time is critical," said Lee-2 in the same inhuman voice used by Lee-187. "While the current Earth–Mars orbital alignments placing the planets only 60 million kilometers apart worked in your favor at reducing transport time, at that distance we are just a bit more than 3 light-minutes away from Earth. Round-trip comm transits times will only take 6 minutes."

Akandi nodded. He of course understood the round-trip delay times in sending information back and forth between Earth and Mars. What he didn't understand was why Lee-2 was telling something so obvious.

"Something is terribly wrong here," said Iyoon.

Shanghai II's commander looked past Adebisi Akandi and at the sliding door behind the tall black man. He sighed at the realization that in 6 or 7 minutes that door would open and he would no longer be commander of the *Shanghai II*. A career that had spanned 32 years, starting with the Sino-Shuttle programs in the late teens, senior geologist at the fledgling New Beijing base nestled in the brecca field of Sulpicius Gallus in the moon's Mare Serenitatis in the early '20s, and then second-in-command on the third Sino assault of Mars in '29—stranded on Mars for nearly 6 years until a rescue could be mounted, until Earth had recovered enough from the Rings to launch ships back to Mars.

Again he sighed, knowing it was all about to come to an end.

Reaching up, he unsnapped the clasps holding his Face snugly against the collar of his skin suit, accompanied by a quick hiss as air escaped from the slightly overpressurized Face, allowing it to open like a clamshell, hinged above his forehead. Never again would he need to hide behind the Face.

A small ceramic figure sat on the corner of Lee-2's otherwise empty desk. Squatting, knees up to its chest, it had been motionless from the moment Akandi walked in. Dressed in a miniature version of the suits that all the Sinos wore, including a Face, it suddenly stood, ran across the desk, grabbed the helmet that Lee-2 had just taken off, and jumping from the desk, trotted across the floor, disappearing along with the helmet into a small cubbyhole in the wall.

This was the first Doll Akandi had seen since leaving Earth orbit.

He despised the creatures—little mechanical abominations made to resemble people—toys for wealthy Pures and

Tools. Before leaving Earth he had prepared himself to be
assaulted by armies of the machines. If they were useful any-
place, it would be in space. Requiring no air or food, practically indestructible, sophisticated enough so that their little
inorganic brains could guide them through the most complex jobs without any human or Void support, they should
have been the perfect space explorers.

But the Chinese were nearly as phobic about them as he
was. While it was the image of little mechanical people, a
gruesome imitation of what Allah had created in man, that
sickened him, the Sinos distrusted them for what they
believed were far more pragmatic reasons—the Dolls saw
and recorded *everything*. Despite the fact that the space-
based Sinos depended on technology for everything, including the very air they breathed, and lived in an environment
where watchful eyes could save lives, a culture of secrets and
conspiracy had enveloped the program ever since the Rings
had appeared, and recording devices were strictly forbidden.
While the other Earth nations had turned their backs on
space, turning inward after the Rings, only the Sinos continued to explore. They did most of it secretly. Very few on
Earth knew that they had reached past Mars and had extensive outposts throughout the moons of Jupiter, and even a
toehold on Saturn's Titan.

Akandi fully understood the significance of that.

They'd found things that had badly frightened them,
frightened them so much that they couldn't even run away
as others had, but had opted to keep a careful watch, hoping
to contain what they'd found. Eventually the important
information still found its way to the key US and UN
posts—the sale of that information a critical revenue source
for the Sino space program. The Sinos did the heavy lifting,
but the US and UN actually paid the bulk of the bills.

Akandi turned away, realizing only then that he had been totally transfixed by the Doll, actually shocked, having not seen one of the creatures skittering about for more than a week. He slowly looked back at Lee-2, and instantly forgot all about the little abomination. "Hok-Wah Chan," he said in a murmur.

Chan offered up a slight smile—it was obvious to Akandi that was all he could manage. The scar tissue that covered his face, shiny and taut, looking more like solidified candle drippings than skin, allowed nothing more.

"You returned?" asked Akandi, knowing the question was a ridiculous one, since Chan was sitting across the desk from him, with the both of them locked in orbit around Mars. But everyone *knew* that Chan had retired, his injuries so severe that he had chosen to live in isolation, like a monk, in a medical villa in the Manchurian countryside. An occasional interview or message would usually be injected into the Void on the anniversary of his rescue from Mars.

Obviously lies.

Chan shrugged. "Mars gets beneath your skin," he said and laughed in a high-pitched warble, the sound almost birdlike, no longer human; Akandi suspected that portions of his throat were as badly scarred as his skin. "I spent almost all of 2040 Earthside, going through a series of skin grafts, eardrum replacements, artificial skin transplants, transgenic skin therapies, stem-cell graft inductions, plus gross anatomical repairs of bones, cartilage, and muscle. What you see is a remarkable improvement over what was rescued from Mars in '37."

Akandi nodded. Everyone knew the story. Chan had not only survived a 6-year Martian ordeal, but had dragged the two other survivors on a jury-rigged wagon across more than 200 kilometers of open Mars to get them to Prime base—doing so with only one foot, his right leg having been amputated below the knee several years earlier, when an atmospheric generator had ruptured, the debris tearing through Chan's suit, shearing his leg away and exposing him to the near-frozen vacuum of the Martian surface.

"Earth was no longer my home," he said. "I asked to be returned to space, but my government refused, explaining that such a hero belonged not just to China, but to the entire Earth, and that I had a duty to assume the mantle of Taikonaut sainthood, to retire gracefully." He shook his head. "I was kept under lock and key for nearly two years. Then something was found on Phobos, and anyone with on-site Martian experience was recalled into active duty. I arrived in '42 and have been here for the last 9 years."

"No cycling back to Earth?" asked Akandi in disbelief.

"It is difficult to return to a place that the authorities insist you've never left." He ran his gloved hands across the top of his desk, then looked past Akandi and at the sliding door. "This is where I will die."

Akandi nodded. The tone in Chan's voice told him this was not a point to be debated.

"None of us are allowed to remove our Faces in the presence of other crew members, let alone in the presence of an outsider. Our caring leaders believe that conspiracies can be held at a minimum in total anonymity. Here we are all Lees—cogs in the machine constructed by China to explore the heavens."

Akandi nodded. Sheng *Lee* had been the first human to set foot on another planet. Even though that step took place as his one-man descent vehicle hit the Martian surface at a speed of nearly 10,000 kilometers an hour, craft and Taikonaut gouging out a crater nearly 200 meters deep as they both disintegrated on impact, an important milestone had still been met.

China had won the race to Mars.

And in honor of that, all Taikonauts were now Lees.

"Time is short and should not be wasted on minor historical footnotes concerning my experiences." Again he offered up a feeble smile.

"If you wish," said Akandi. "But before we continue, I wish to say that it is an honor to meet you." This was no diplomatic ploy. He leaned forward and offered his hand to Chan.

Chan reached out across his desk, but before taking Akandi's hand, he removed the glove from his right hand. It was obvious to Akandi that all the fingertips, starting from the last joint, were artificial—the skin coloring and texture not quite matching that of the rest of his hand.

They shook hands.

"But it is you who do me honor in this meeting," said Chan as he leaned back in his chair, opened a drawer in the desk, and pulled out a red folder that he laid on the center of his desk.

Akandi was amazed as he looked down at the folder—nearly 1 centimeter thick, stuffed with papers. He would not have thought there would have been that much paper on all of Mars, the extravagance of such a material, the weight and expense in bringing it from Earth to Mars, a colossal waste of resources. The information it contained could be electronically or photonically stored in both a volume and mass approaching nothing, making paper as out of place on Mars as an elephant strolling across its dead surface.

Chan drummed his artificial fingertips across the folder. "Paper has a unique property that other means of storage do not," he said.

Akandi realized he had done nothing to disguise his shock at seeing the folder.

"To those determined enough, with resources sufficiently sophisticated, there is no electronic or photonic document that cannot be accessed, no matter how well encrypted." He picked up the folder, fanned the papers within it, then lowered them all back to the tabletop. "That is not the case with paper. Over the last 6 years, the contents of this file were gathered by human courier, a page here and a page there, no one with access to the full picture."

He flipped open the file and pulled out the top sheet of paper—its corners dog-eared, its surface a crosshatch of indentations where it had been folded and refolded, the entire bottom half stained yellow, with a few fingertip-sized holes randomly poked through it.

Akandi did not know what the paper contained, but he knew that Chan should not be in possession of it. The letterhead and logo across the top of the paper were that of the US Department of Off-Earth Intelligence. Only a few within that agency would have access to any hard-copy information, and a non-US-citizen, particularly Chinese, despite the influence and power that Chan probably possessed, should have never been able to get ahold of it.

Chan lifted up the paper and ran a fingertip across several lines of type.

"It is your personnel file," said Iyoon. *"And I suspect that it may be your real personnel file."*

"The United States of America, far from perfect, holding vast portions of its own population in agricultural servitude, with the benefits of technology reserved only for those fortunate enough to be born within the Technical zones, still has many outstanding characteristics that I wish my own government shared." He waved the paper at Akandi. "Despite the fear that grips our planet, and—in particular—your nation, you are still willing to adopt and nurture refugees from so many parts of the world, both Pures and Tools." Chan offered up another partial smile. "Assuming, of course, that those refugees have something to offer the United States."

Akandi said nothing. He'd learned long ago that the real key to diplomacy was in what you didn't say.

"Your parents, Nigerian nationals, both university professors from Lagos, emigrated to the United States in 2017, during the time when the Nigerian oil fields went dry, and the government's response to the crisis was to kill anyone who was foolish enough to offer up an opinion about the crisis." Chan leaned forward, squinting as he looked at the paper. "Your father was a petroleum engineer educated at Oxford, and your mother a physician, developing gene therapies for sickle cell anemia. Both found themselves welcomed in the wondrous United States, where their talents were put to good use as clerks in a liquor store in the suburbs of Atlanta." Chan looked up.

"Difficult times," said Akandi. The awe and respect he had felt only moments before had been replaced by anger. "None of this has any bearing on why I am here."

"I beg to differ," said Chan, dropping the paper back onto the top of the stack. "That is the society that made you. Born in 2019, you were state-warehoused in what was called an emigration education crèche, until the events of 2031 resulted in the loss not only of those meager educational resources, but also of both of your parents in the ensuing chaos." Chan paused.

"The point being?" asked Akandi, coldly.

"An orphan, a ward of the state, working for many years in the fields to grow food for a nation that could no longer feed itself, you did not enter again into a classroom for nearly 5 years, at the age of 18. Did you still remember how to read and write?"

"Well enough," said Akandi.

Chan nodded. "I suspect so. Such adversity appears to have strengthened you, forged something deep within you that I believe your caring parents could never have given you. You showed remarkable progress, what one might almost describe as miraculous. One might suspect that you'd been given a guardian angel to look after you."

Could he know, thought Akandi. With more than 2,000 field hands in the Valdosta onion plantation, he had been the only one taken, the only one linked to the Void with a Jinni. The Swirl had picked him and made sure that doors were open just as he was ready to walk through them. *Has the Swirl revealed itself to you?* he wondered. But he could not ask, the physical structure of his brain having been modified by the presence of the Swirl, so that he was unable to talk about it.

"Bachelor's degree in physics from some institution of unknown reputation in one of the most lawless provinces of your adopted homeland."

"Tulane, in New Orleans."

Chan did not look up from the file. "Then on to a school with a bit more merit. The Massachusetts Institute of Technology, with a Ph.D. in '42 in plasma physics—ironing out some minor technical puzzles in tri-ignition fusion reactors. Only 23 years old at the time. Research at Lawrence-Berkeley, professorship at Stanford, and from there moved into government programs, first in power grid enhancements projects, then into dark programs, those with deep budgets and no requirement of accounting to the hardworking people of your nation who fund such operations."

Still Akandi said nothing.

"And then an amazingly abrupt turn in career direction. Resurrected from the deep bowels of secret government programs, you find yourself nominated by the president of your great nation as US science liaison to the United Nations—a post of immense responsibility and power for one who is not only a mere 32 years old, but also for one of such a dark complexion coming from a land that is still controlled and manipulated by those with the whitest of skins and the deepest of pockets, those for whom the almost continual Gulf wars in the beginning of the century, and the Moslem terrorists' acts responsible for the blighted New York–Philadelphia corridor, are real and personal memories. Once again your guardian angel seems to have made the path clear for you to travel."

"I make my own path," said Akandi, hiding his discomfort. Chan was so close to the truth, Akandi was almost certain that he was also in contact with the Swirl. "And I am here," he said.

"Yes, here you are," said Chan. "Holding one of the most important posts that your nation can bestow upon one of its citizens—one that requires the occasional clandestine visit to our little outpost here."

"Part of the job," said Akandi.

"It certainly is," said Chan. "But not a part that is publicly discussed. Only a few thousand across Earth even know of the extensive Sino presence on Phobos, and of those, only a handful know what it is that has been found on Phobos."

"*Jealous,*" said Iyoon. "*Inflection, speech pattern, iris dilation, all of it points to him not knowing. He's been here for nine years, but doesn't know what is inside Phobos.*"

Akandi leaned forward, suddenly knowing he had the advantage. "And I believe that you cannot count yourself among that handful."

Chan said nothing. He clenched his jaw, the muscles beneath his slick, scarred skin quivering.

"And yet, here I sit, a man of color, a man nearly 30 years younger, a man from a country that you characterize as having enslaved a large portion of its population in regions of technological isolation, and I know what lies within Phobos."

"As did Ambassador McCarthy," said Chan. "Twice a year, for the nine years I have been here, he came and visited whatever it is that lies within Phobos. And then his tragic demise."

Akandi nodded. "Tragic indeed," he said. "Although I expect quick and painless. I am told that a Sino surface-to-orbit Sling malfunction, though rare, would hurl its cargo into the Mongolian Desert at a speed in excess of Mach 50. Death would be instantaneous."

"No doubt true," said Chan. He pushed the folder and its papers toward Akandi. "However, Ambassador McCarthy did not have such a quick end. As a matter of fact, he never left Phobos on his last visit, nearly a year ago. But you are quite right about his being dead. Normal transmissions in and out of Phobos are not permitted. However, the ambassador suffered from a minor medical ailment, a slight misbalance of cardiac chemistry that required frequent monitoring. Unlike you, Ambassador McCarthy was a Pure, actually phobic about any interfacing with the Void, but he did allow himself to be monitored for his heart ailment, and those medical transmissions were beamed directly to *Shanghai II*."

Akandi knew none of this.

"*His body response indicates he is telling the truth,*" said Iyoon.

"Based on an exhaustive analysis of his cardiac transmis-

sions, we have determined that the process of Ambassador
McCarthy's death took several minutes and was probably
quite painful." Chan pushed the folder toward Akandi.
"You still choose to share your skull with one of those inorganic horrors?" he asked.

"My Jinni, Iyoon," said Akandi. "Arabic for eyes."

"How nice for you," said Chan. "We have at most only
one minute before the door to my office is opened from the
outside, then my comrades, on order from Beijing, will
relieve me of my duties because of the little discussion we
have been having and because of the contents of this folder."

"Reasonable, considering the numerous acts of treason
you've undoubtedly committed," said Akandi.

"Let your creature scan the contents of the file. It will tell
you everything that I have gathered on what happened to
Ambassador McCarthy."

Akandi leaned forward and began flipping through the
papers, not even bothering actually to look at them, knowing that Iyoon would record every detail, right down to the
least significant bit. "And what do you believe happened to
Ambassador McCarthy?" he asked.

"I know what happened to him. The analysis of his medical transmission leaves no room for doubt, as I'm sure your
little demon will tell you once it has digested the contents
of the file. Ambassador McCarthy was eaten."

"What?" said Akandi in disbelief, looking up for just a
moment.

"*No!*" shouted Iyoon, the voice echoing in Akandi's head.
"*Look back down. Forget about McCarthy. Most of these papers
deal with Alpha Centauri.*"

"Alpha Centauri?" Akandi said aloud, speaking to Chan
and Iyoon.

Chan grinned. "Not quite what one expects to find on a

trip to Phobos. But I assure you that the data you hold is quite accurate, the first of it gathered over twenty years ago, well before we stumbled upon the minor Phobos mystery."

"*It appears that the Planet Finder Interferometer that was launched back in '26, and presumed lost on transit to Saturn, was in fact not lost. Not only did it transmit some remarkable data, but also four subsequent missions, with even more powerful interferometers, have sent back more detailed information. Alpha Centauri A has what can best be described as a planetary ring system at an orbital distance of 175 million kilometers from its sun. This is not a ring like Saturn possesses, but consists of 237 planets, all of them the size of Earth to within a radial factor of two, and many of them exhibiting an optical spectrum consistent with oxygen/nitrogen atmospheres and water vapor. The spacing between planets in the ring is approximately 5 million kilometers, about 10 times the Earth–Moon distance.*"

The small office suddenly shook, as something heavy slammed into the door behind Akandi. The unmistakable sound of rupturing metal accompanied a second slam.

"Two hundred thirty-seven planets," said Chan. "Such an orbital configuration was obviously not formed by the hand of your Allah—it is gravitationally unstable, and could only be maintained through *intelligent* intervention. Equally obvious is that 237 Earth-like worlds could not have evolved around a single star. They must have been transported there from other star systems."

Chan remained silent for just a moment, the meaning in his last statement obvious to Akandi. The stellar Jet and the Rings were obviously intended as some sort of transportation device, and if what Chan was showing him was real, it did not take much of a leap to realize that the destination of any interstellar trip the Earth and Sun might make would be Alpha Centauri A, Earth becoming just one more planet dropped into the orbital ring structure.

Akandi did not look up but furiously continued to flip through pages. His ears suddenly popped as pressure rapidly changed, a shock of heated air, accompanied with the crack of an explosion, throwing him from his chair, dumping him on the steel floor, as a shard of a door hinge embedded itself only centimeters from his head in the front of the desk.

"It appears that my service to the people of China has come to an end." Chan stood as the remainder of the door was kicked in. "I have no love of you Americans, and would have happily given this information to others, but you are my only available conduit. My government may not be able to kill you—your history indicates that powers behind the scenes are helping you, and I can only hope that they will continue helping you, at least long enough for this information to be passed along to others who might have the desire to act against what is happening."

Rolling over, pushing himself up, Akandi stood. "Did McCarthy know?" he asked, waving a hand at the papers strewn about the floor.

"No," said Chan.

Four bodies spilled in from the partially opened doorway, one indistinguishable from the next, all their Faces flickering with salt-and-pepper snow. Chan had a device held against his chest, small and nondescript, one that Akandi instantly recognized. A plasma welder would spew a high-energy stream of krypton ions capable of transforming a slab of tungsten-titanium alloy into a rapidly expanding molten puddle. He flinched as Chan pulled its trigger.

Akandi would have expected it to make more noise in such a small room.

A carbonized chunk of bone, muscle, and chest organs, spitting flame and briefly wrapped in an azure plasma glow, slammed into the wall opposite Chan, the smoking mass burying itself in a suddenly syruplike patch in the metal wall. Chan's dead body fell across his desk.

Chapter 6

The Blue and Gold Cage smelled like sour beer and piss. Padmini Sundaram found the familiar odor comforting, lulling her into what she hoped was not a false sense of security—that was a state of mind that could get a cop *decopped*. There was no place in the world for an ex-cop, no one willing to take the security risk of hiring on someone who knew how to manipulate the world.

Not yet the end of second shift, the crowd at the Blue and Gold Cage was thin. Those on various forms of disability, suspension, under investigation, a few psycho wannabes, and the most pathetic of all, those simply off duty with no place else to go, sat at the bar or hunched around tables. Tonight was really thin. Most had stayed at home to watch Sarah Sutherland jump from the Southern Cross and cook herself to a cinder. Reports were that they couldn't even find the splatter point. Most figured that she'd burned up to nothing. *Anyone crazy enough to jump from a Cross got what they deserved,* Padmini thought.

She was off duty. She drained a quick shot of Burmese Scotch, dropped the plastic cup onto the table, popped a few unidentifiable deep-fried charboids into her mouth, and waited. Something would happen—she felt it. An 8-year veteran of the Philly 268, with the last 6 years in System-Bioinformatics, she'd learned to pay attention to hunches.

"Hey, Mini," said her partner. Leo Barnwell, a megamolecular chemistry expert who could smell a single misplaced nucleotide in anything's genome without benefit of squeezing a strand, set his own cup down on the table. "Check out what just cleared the Cage."

Padmini looked in the direction of the bar's front door, where the three-layer mesh of the signal-sucking Faraday cage wrapping most of the building was pierced, but transmissions were still sufficiently attenuated by the gray-haze ozone waterfall that flowed over the entranceway. The room was screened from all outside snooping.

The two who entered had their Faces imaged to something pathetically generic, probably the factory default, and their bodies wrapped in full second skin. They had E-field ionizers, judging by the dull UV glow that trailed them, the gear designed to vaporize every bit of the debris that poured off a human carcass. Those suits were expensive, theoretically allowing the wearer to cruise the streets in full stealth, not a single snippet of offcast DNA available to blow your invisibility.

"I smell rookies," said Padmini, angling her head back and snorting, knowing just how worthless that stealth gear really was. She turned to the empty seat next to Barnwell. *"Take a look, Kali,"* she whispered deep in her throat, waking her Jinni.

The seat was no longer empty. A Hindu goddess—eight-armed, skin that looked like liquid tar, a necklace of severed heads, earrings of quivering fetuses, eyes red, black hair clotted with blood, and a mouth full of rotted, green-tinted teeth. The guise of Padmini's Jinni was the only acknowledgment she would give to her Hindu ancestors. She was now three generations removed from Asia, and wanted to keep it that way.

"Access the 268 ergometrics database," she mouthed, while motioning to the two rookies. Kali had no external optical inputs when within the confines of the Blue and Gold, being totally slaved to Padmini's eyeballs. She *watched* them. The rookies only needed to take a couple of steps, and Kali did the rest. Total body measurement, good down to the last millimeter, length of stride, swing of arm, angle of head, finger motions, chest expansion, and gut contraction during breathing—all of it was run against the database. Kali passed along the results of the search, including personnel records; even those supposedly destroyed adolescent files.

"Dammit," whispered Padmini, as the contents of the files flushed out of Kali, and she knew exactly what it was about these two that had set her on edge the moment she'd seen them. "Dead meat walking," she said to Barnwell, then shifted in her seat. "Rookies!" she shouted.

The two turned toward her.

"I've been on the lookout for two real desperate types: Rwanda illegals trying to unload some tainted baboon genome. Go by the names of Anthony L. Bartow and Keating R. Hopkins. You boys ever heard of them?"

Bartow and Hopkins turned, looking at each other, then focused on Padmini. "It's against a half dozen regs to out a cop," said the one nearest to Padmini.

"Exactly right," answered Padmini. "You two rookies are still probationary. If you're lucky, you'll never become cops." She knew these two would never get off probation, had in fact been hired by the department not to become cops at all, but to be offered up in a sting operation. "And that makes you citizens," she said, doing nothing to hide the disdain in her voice.

The nearest one took a step toward her.

Padmini did not need Kali to tell her that Bartow was ramping up, readying himself to blow in her direction. She didn't want to be the cop to put him down, which she knew would be the only outcome possible if this Rookie actually moved against her. "I thought juvenile records were wiped on the 15th birthday," she said.

Bartow took another step, then stopped.

"Neocortical fiber doesn't come cheap, not after the damage you did. Mommy and Daddy must be still paying off that debt, brain-burner."

The bar quieted, full-spectrum attention suddenly focused directly on Bartow. "Deep cover," Bartow said in a stammer. "Very deep, old records rewritten, getting ready to insert us snug in the scum, the data already leaked so we can go under." He took another step back, this time pushing Hopkins toward the door.

"Whatever you say, Rookie," said Padmini. "We'll all give you the benefit of the doubt. We believe you didn't sniff away most of your frontal lobes by the time your voice cracked."

"And don't forget it!" shouted Bartow as he turned and walked through the ozone waterfall, to the accompaniment of low-level laughter.

"Of course, you brain-burned wanna-be," Padmini said quietly to no one in particular, then turned to focus on Barnwell. "Rookies with records who can't smell the writing on the wall. Do you believe that?" she said, pointing back toward the door. "The both of them were sniffers. The department hired them to sacrifice them in some undercover sting down the road. They would have reverted, started sniffing the moment they came in the vicinity of aerogels. She shook her head. "Sting bait."

"Slow it down, Mini," said Barnwell. "Obviously sting bait, but you shouldn't out them, because they *are* sting bait. The department had plans for them and their screwed synapses, and you just outed them in front of twenty cops. You compromised them, and they'll be full citizens by shift end."

"Saved their goddamned lives," she said.

"And probably just got yourself short-listed for a scan." He reached over and gently touched her forehead with a slender index finger. "God only knows what's stored in there."

"God only knows," she said, and took another drink. She frowned. "The captain would never send me to Diagnostics for a reading. He might splat me if push came to shove, but he's not about to let my contents spill." She tapped the side of her head. "Word of warning to you, too, fatman. Watch my back. *You* couldn't afford to have me spilled." *Fatman* was their joke. Barnwell had his metabolism clocked to the max, his body fat tuned to an almost nonexistent 2 percent.

"True," said Barnwell, the normally jovial expression that filled his lean face turning dark. "It's been a good while since anyone's been spilled in the 268."

True, too true, she thought. And that was not good. There were always some dirty cops that needed to be spilled. But when the Powers stopped looking, that meant that they were afraid to be caught in the backwash of the spilling. That was *very* bad.

The doorway flashed crimson as someone walked in. All the cops huddled within the sanctuary of the Blue and Gold Cage, no matter how disabled, traumatized, or deep into the bottle, looked up. A cop who would not look up would be a cop who would not last long on the streets—punctuated evolution in action.

Padmini did not even have to access Kali. She knew the dreg, was surprised that she hadn't smelled him before he had entered the bar—the ozone waterfall wasn't designed to fracture the long-chain organics that her nose identified as *shit and puke*. A little greasy man with a pockmarked face, strapped with a full cranial wrap that allowed him to not only see out of the eyes mounted in the back of his head, but access most public eyes within a ten-meter radius, pulled his stiff raincoat tightly around his waist as the last ozone wisps curled around his bare feet. They'd known McGordy for years: a bag of malfunctioning DNA that passed along stale and dated info.

He was one of Barnwell's snitches.

She wasn't sure why Barnwell kept him on the payroll, but the fact that he did was good enough for her. Despite nearly 20 years on the force, Barnwell was still only a lieutenant, but not because he lacked the ability to rise. He had refused promotions so many times that the Powers had finally caught on. They left him alone. He'd been in the 268 longer than any of them. She knew that he knew things that the Powers weren't aware of, things that even *she* wasn't aware of. Normally, there could be no secrets between partners—survival demanded total honesty. But this was something different. He'd built a firewall around part of his life, to ensure that whatever he was hiding would not leak out and contaminate her. That she understood. He didn't want her caught up in the backwash if he were ever spilled, and she suspected that backwash would be of tidal-wave proportions.

Before hiring into the Philly cops, he'd fought in the Ten Degree War. She knew that there were things stored deep in his brain that no one wanted to know.

"Hold your nose," said Barnwell, as McGordy reached the table. "Don't sit," he said. "Don't want to be charged with the cost of disinfecting the chair."

McGordy took half a step back, suddenly looking terrified, eyeing the chair nearest him. "Is it something catchy? Maybe some of that avian chimera shit from the West Coast?"

"The chair is clean, moron," said Barnwell. "I don't want to have to pay for the cost of disinfecting I'd be charged if *you* sat in it."

McGordy stepped toward the chair, bent down, and opened his mouth. He flicked out his tongue, the gray-white thing looking as if it were constructed of used wads of toilet paper, slapping it against the wooden surface of the chair, then quickly reeling it back into his mouth. He sucked on his tongue, and his eyeballs rastered back and forth, violently shaking as if taking too much voltage.

"Nothing wrong with that chair," said McGordy. "Though it's got a pretty active colony of that new E-coli that sprouted from the west side." He smacked his lips. "But its clocked out, nearly 30 generations down the line from the stuff that would turn your guts into stew. Don't think this stuff would even give you gas."

Barnwell kicked the chair toward McGordy. "Sit on it, you idiot. There is nothing wrong with it."

"Quite right," said McGordy as he rolled his tongue across the roof of his mouth, cleansing the array of sensors that punched back into his sinus cavities and from there into his skull. He slowly sat down to the accompaniment of cracking sounds, his trench coat so filthy that it could almost stand on its own.

"How much of your brain did they have to scoop out to

make room for the receptors tied to that tongue of yours?" asked Barnwell.

McGordy's eyes squinted, and his lips quivered.

Padmini groaned. "Why do you *always* ask him that?" she said. "He's nothing more than a walking set of taste buds, pure army-surplus."

"What have you got?" asked Barnwell, sounding eager to move on, as if the momentary novelty of McGordy's presence had suddenly worn off.

McGordy rubbed at his face. "There's a man. He's on the corner of 43rd and Howell." The tip of McGordy's tongue flicked in and out—nervous reflex. "Very clean, not a carrier. Wants to tell you something."

"Something?" asked Barnwell. "Something such as?"

McGordy grinned. "Not so much of me is gone that I'm going to tell you what I know before you pay."

Barnwell sighed. His lips twitched as he whispered to his Jinni, and McGordy grinned even wider. "Got it," he said, Padmini knowing by the expression on his face that he'd just scanned the new balance in his strongbox—despite the games that Barnwell always seemed to be playing with his snitches, he was generous when it came to paying them.

"The man says he knows who sparked the magenta zone, who cooked the goop that ate most of the 763."

Barnwell sat up, focused, quickly purging the alcohol drifting through his bloodstream, overdriving his liver and kidneys. "You sure?" he asked.

McGordy slapped the palms of his hands against the sides of his head, taking care not to dislodge the full wrap-around. "You know I can't lie to you."

And he couldn't. Barnwell had his Jinni suck down every flickering bit that McGordy had recorded in his full wrap-around. "Looks straight, Mini," he said. "This could be what we need to break the 763 mess."

Padmini nodded, trying not to think of what had happened in the 763 precinct, but unable not to. It had been a nasty bug, perfectly designed, triggered to activate at the moment when a roll call flashed through the skulls of those in the 763—just a few key nucleotides transposed on the 763-cop identifier genes, those used to spit out the specialty proteins that the sniffers used to track missing cops. The passive proteins' normally benign outer sheath was altered just enough to interfere with the construction of cellular membranes. Mortality rate was 98 percent within 4 hours of activation, as cell membranes disintegrated, and the cops literally drowned in their own blood.

Barnwell gave mental commands. Normally his Jinni would send out a broadband wireless transmission, but the Faraday cage that wrapped the Blue and Gold and kept all electromagnetics from snooping the bar's interior also would not allow any to penetrate to the outside. He would have to rely on fiber—a hardwired path through the Blue and Gold's signal-eating cage. During his double tours in the Ten Degree, he'd not only had his gray matter scrambled, but had been installed with a wide-spectrum packet interface, neurally inducted through his skin. He reached down to the leg of the table, feeling for a receptor. The subdural transducer in the palm of his hand meshed with the protrusion in the table leg. He notified the 268 that they needed immediate undercover backup at the corner of 43rd and Howell. He pulled his hand away from the table leg. "Can't wait for them to get into position on this one, Mini. We need to get there now. The rest will arrive for cleanup if this goes sour."

Enough said. Padmini stood and followed Barnwell out

of the Blue and Gold, both of them trotting like a pair of dogs on a scent.

McGordy eased back in his chair and reached across the table for the drink that Barnwell had not finished. "A bonus," he said. He wasn't able to quite wrap his dirty hand around the plastic cup. Everything in the room fogged in a thick green mist, and the receptors across his tongue flushed with what tasted like burned coffee, as the taste bud buffers wedged in his neocortex purged. McGordy blinked, and his tongue rolled out of his mouth, slapping against the tabletop.

He no longer had the neurons to understand what was happening, to decipher the string of code that had been activated when he had received Barnwell's fund transfer. Every *dog*, those whose senses had been enhanced by the military back in the '20s, had a fail-safe built into what remained of their brain. A code, encrypted with ten different 196-plus-digit primes, could be used to command complete electrical discharge across better than 10 percent of the dog's synaptic junctions. Such an overload would throw the entire nervous system into chaos. Death would be quick but painful.

The military had not bothered to remove the neuralware that would act on those ten prime numbers, certain that the universe itself would be cold and dead long before anyone or anything could find the right primes to access a dog's fail-safe device.

But McGordy had been accessed.

His eyeballs rolled back in their sockets, and he snapped down on his tongue, biting right through it, the half-meter-long chunk of synthetic muscle and receptors dropping to the tabletop. He slumped back, dead.

*   *   *

A cold, too-bright February night.

Padmini crouched, wedging herself between a rusted drainpipe and a shard of collapsed masonry resembling a mutant tombstone. The sky burned electric blue, the plasma discharge running high over Philly, swallowing the night, bathing everything in shades of gray-blue that made your skin look two weeks dead.

But the glare kept the crime rate down, kept the biggest, meanest thugs off the streets—kept them hidden in the shadows where the only real damage they did was to one another. The nighttime streets were safe for the victimless criminals—prostitutes, druggies, wet marketers dealing with anything that had a tweaked genome, and, of course, their customers. Dolls skittered about like cockroaches that couldn't stand the light. Those fronting for the pimps and drug suppliers were dressed in a wide array of rainbow-hued fabric, the exact pattern announcing to the street what they were pushing.

To Padmini it appeared that the entire city had emptied out into the streets, a sluggish river of people, randomly flowing about, a few with Faces, but most far too poor for such high-tech disguises, relying instead on dark muslin draped over their heads and rubber gloves filled with sweat and dead skin, probably leaking more DNA than their naked hands would. But it made them feel safe, anonymous. And in the final analysis that was all that really mattered; how it felt—because if someone really wanted to find you, to grab a snip of your DNA, to know what you had for lunch last Tuesday, there was nothing you could do about it. The simple truth was that no one really cared who these people were. If you worked, didn't do any major crimes, and possessed no unique talents that the Powers were interested in, then even though your every move, every muscle twitch, nearly every thought, could be accessed and monitored—no one watched, because no one cared. If they had thought about it, some might have found the reality of indifference worse than the fear of being under constant surveillance.

Padmini had little difficulty recognizing the pigeon they'd come after. The latest inorganic tattoos scrolled across his face, a living advertisement; he'd sold his skin for a few extra bucks. Skin suit tinted in shifting rainbows, his heavy head of hair started at his eyebrows and ran right up his forehead. He looked like any other punk—that was where the idiot had made his mistake.

Kali had instantly picked him out of the hundreds who wandered aimlessly up and down the street. Their man had tried so hard to blend in that he had stupidly picked out the *exact* average look for this part of town. He was too average and, therefore, obviously a fake.

"You got him?" Padmini whispered. Kali transmitted directly to Barnwell's Jinni. She watched him slowly nod as he approached the man.

"How many surveillance points?" asked Padmini.

Kali accessed the local terrain, tapping into every receiver that dumped data into the Void. *"Three hundred forty-seven devices from substreet to tenth floor recording the approach."*

Padmini grinned, knowing that was just the units directly accessible to the cops. If something nasty went down, most of those shuffling down the street could have their personal button recorders pulled, those little low-fidelity recorders that continually spooled the previous 24 hours of their owners' boring lives. That would potentially add several thousand other inputs.

Padmini listened, the auditory stream synthesized from several dozen recorders located about the street corner, with all noise and background filtered away. It sounded as if Barnwell stood right next to her, whispering in her ear.

"You got something for me?" asked Barnwell, standing squarely in front of the man, disrupting the flow of traffic, not attempting to blend in. The swarming crowds parted around him, all seeming to understand at the same moment that something was about to happen, something that they wanted no part of.

"Right here," said the man.

There was no warning, no telltale pheromones, no increase in pulse, sweat, or electrical activity cracking across the man's hairy forehead. But Padmini still sensed something, and that started her moving, running, gaining speed, pushing the Faceless out of her way, all the time keeping her eyes trained on the man. With her pistol pulled, her arm raised, Kali autoaimed, suddenly taking control of her arm, accessing every nerve from right elbow to fingertips.

The man moved.

Far faster than organic nerves could drive muscle, the man's right hand was clenched into a fist, driving squarely for Barnwell's face.

Kali fired, the gun enveloped in a haze of gas and smoke that flashed backward, compensating for the forward thrust of the bullet, momentums canceling, producing no recoil, the weapon still trained on its target, ready to be fired again if necessary.

The man's fist opened, fingers spread. Padmini expected the hand to erupt into a flash of blood and bone shards, and for just a moment that was what she thought had happened. The hand recoiled as the bullet slammed into it, but then snapped back into the same position, now covered in a splatter of bone and blood. She blinked. The hand was intact. The blood and bone had erupted from a crater in Barnwell's forehead, left side, just above the temple.

"*Fatal shot,*" said Kali.

Padmini heard the words, registered them, but did not feel them. She was still running, still trying to understand what had happened. Kali's autoaim was perfect down to a fraction of a millimeter, the target hit, the bullet intercepting the moving hand, but the bullet had ricocheted off the man's hand and hit Barnwell in the head.

She had managed two more steps when there was a flash and a second shot. The man jerked, his head ratcheting back, a fountain of brain, blood, and electronic shards exploding out of the top of his skull. Barnwell crumbled to the sidewalk, but his pistol was clenched in his hand, still aimed upward, directly at the man's chin. Padmini knew that Barnwell could not have any conscious control over his pistol and that it had been fired by his Jinni, its circuitry wedged in the back of his brain, apparently still intact, using Barnwell's nerves and muscles in the few seconds before Barnwell's body actually died.

The bodies crumpled on one another.

The crowds had cleared; the corner was deserted. Padmini came to a halt several meters away from the bodies. She looked down at her pistol and at the outstretched hand that had deflected the bullet, the synthetic skin blistered away, the steel alloy plate exposed.

She dropped to her knees, started to reach out for Barnwell, but pulled back, could not touch him, knowing if she felt him, laid a hand on him, then he would really be dead. As long as she didn't check, she wouldn't know for sure. But she did know. The front of his forehead, practically back to his ears, was gone.

"I killed him," she said, not understanding what had happened, as she looked down at the expanding pool of blood around Barnwell. "My partner."

Kali materialized, standing over the bodies, bent down, her necklace of heads appearing to rest on Barnwell's bloody chest, and she looked up at Padmini, focusing her red-tinted eyes on the pistol. *"We've been set up,"* she said.

Jumping up, Padmini backstepped, dropped to one knee, and did a quick 360. Pivoting, she scanned the surroundings, sweeping her pistol up and down the street.

"Not that way," said Kali. *"It's worse."*

The back of Padmini's eyes briefly tickled as Kali downloaded a multiplexed signal compiled from several hundred of the surveillance recorders in the area. Suddenly Padmini felt herself hovering above the intersection, watching herself run, the pistol drawn, arm raised, index finger straining against the trigger.

Muzzle flash.

Then the image slowed. In a puff of smoke and fire the bullet exploded from the barrel of the pistol. A flashing green line plotted its trajectory across the street. Padmini shifted her perspective back to real time, looking down at the dead man and his outstretched hand—the intended target. The hand was no longer intact, but melting, bubbling into a growing puddle. *Evidence gone.*

She reshifted her perspective back to Kali's composite feed.

The green line from the barrel of her pistol did not intercept the hand.

It was displaced by nearly half a meter—intersecting Barnwell's temple. Padmini knew that what she was seeing was impossible. She'd sighted down the barrel of the pistol, seen the man's hand clearly in the crosshairs—and Kali had done the rest, ensuring perfect aim. She'd seen the man's hand snap back as the bullet had hit it.

"Keep watching," said Kali.

Padmini watched herself continue to run across the street, jumping up on the curb, then falling down to her knees and sliding up to Barnwell. She reached out, pistol still in her hand. For a moment it appeared as if she were about to reach for his head, perhaps to check for vital signs, or simply cradle it in her lap.

She did not. Instead she spit on what was left of Barnwell's face.

She synched back into real time.

"That was a compiled image from over 200 inputs. Those signals are transmitted directly from local receivers and into the police surveillance networks and archived. Between the time of data transmission and archiving, the signals from all those sources were intercepted and altered to show what you were just shown. The feed was changed to show that not only did you deliberately kill Barnwell, but not satisfied with that, had to spit on him as well."

Padmini took a single quick breath. The whys and hows of what had just happened could not be dealt with now. The backup that Barnwell had called would be arriving any second, and they would be looking for her—a cop killer. Each and every one of them would have had the composite transcription of Barnwell's death dumped into their heads. No need to question a living, breathing body. Any postinterrogations could be performed on Kali, and through a neuronal reconstruction of what remained of her brain once the backups had finished with her. Standard operating procedure— the composite data stream irrefutable evidence. In her years on the force she had worked on three different cop-on-cop killings. The procedures in such an event were fixed. Eventually, analysis of the slugs and the lack of her DNA splattered across Barnwell's face, proving she had not really spit on him, would raise questions, but she knew she'd be long dead before the investigation got to that point.

She had no choice but to run.

She started down the street, knowing that hundreds of cameras watched her every move, feeling as if the blue-gray light that burned down from the sky were a spotlight, aimed directly at her. She started to run, then stopped as she saw something move, what at first looked like a bundle of rags and paper wedged up against the same building that Barnwell and the unknown man now lay against. She moved toward what looked like crumpled newspapers and a wadded-up blanket, aiming her pistol toward it. "Did you see what happened?" Leaning forward, she used her pistol to fling back the blanket.

Two Dolls. Dressed in gray robes, their faces featureless, as if melted. No attempt had been made to make them look like little people. They stared up at her with black eyes.

"Backup is less than 30 seconds away," said the first one.

"They have the composite crime scene transcriptions and will shoot you on sight," said the second one.

Padmini took half a step back. "Who are you?" she asked, not speaking to the Dolls but to whoever was behind their eyes remotely controlling them.

"Someone who's been asked to keep you alive."

Without looking at her they jumped up, trotted down the sidewalk, and disappeared in an alley less than a meter wide. With her pistol still out, she followed. Rounding the corner, she saw the two Dolls standing in the opening to a circular cage made from multiple layers of metallic mesh, with the innermost layer comprised of what appeared to her to be crumpled foil. A large copper strap attached the cage to a metal drainpipe.

"*Faraday cage,*" said Kali.

The Dolls ran inside the cage.

Padmini looked behind her. Several blocks down a flood of red-and-blue lights rolled up the street. She suspected it was no coincidence that these Dolls had a Faraday cage set up in the alley—it was all part of the setup, part of the plan to murder Barnwell. Her rescuers had been waiting for her, knowing that Barnwell would be killed and she'd be blamed for it. Whoever hung behind the Doll's eyes was undoubtedly the murderer.

"*You've got no choice,*" said Kali. "*The Dolls are obviously planning on dumping an electromagnetic pulse across this entire area. It's the only chance you have of escaping the EMP.*"

Still looking down the street, she saw three gray shadows run around the corner, weapons drawn, a glint coming from the nearest one's sniper scope. If she stayed on the street, she would be dead. If she went into the cage, she might survive and be able to find out who killed Barnwell. "Damn," she said, and ran, following the Dolls into the cage, the sphere not much more than a meter in diameter. The Dolls crawled over her, pulling at the inner layer of foil, covering the cage's entrance. The only light came from their eyes, now luminescing green. One Doll crawled up on her back, and she felt something drop over her head. For a moment, she struggled, as darkness enveloped her, fighting against what felt like a cord tightening around her neck.

"*Don't fight them!*" shouted Kali. "*It's a last layer of shielding. They want to protect the wiring in your head—they want to keep me intact.*"

"Down flat!" shouted one of the Dolls.

Padmini dropped, just as the explosion that generated the EMP picked them up, hurling them backward and smashing them into the alley wall. Pulling the metallic hood off her head, she found herself lying on her back, legs bent back, pressed up against her chest. "How big *was* that?"

"Five-hundred-pound TNT equivalent," said the first Doll.

"Sparked an EMP that will cook any unprotected circuitry for a 500-meter radius," said the second Doll.

"Probably better than 200 cops down," said Kali. "Their Jinnis will be fried, and the electrical backwash from the overloaded circuitry being dumped into their brains has probably knocked them cold. But there should be no permanent damage."

No permanent damage, thought Padmini, knowing that those 200 cops would need to have the back of their skulls opened, the ruined hardware scooped out, and new Jinnis and interface circuitry installed.

"Just who the hell sent you?" she asked as she looked into the nearest Doll's black eyes.

"Leo Barnwell," it answered.

Chapter 7

"The personal touch," said Xavier.

Deep into the Void, Xavier watched from the perspective of a speaker grille embedded above the door, giving him the perfect view of Dr. Daniel Mears, Chief Technical Officer of the Tuscaloosa Agricultural Co-Op. Besides Mears, the chair he sat in, and the desk he sat behind, the room was bare.

"Mears's viewpoint," said Xavier.

Behind and to his left in the real world, Xavier could sense movement, Che moving in his seat, and hear a knuckle pop. "Pattern," said Che.

Back in the Void the room barely changed. A liquidlike display of morphing curves rolled in front of Mears, neat and compact, the entire sphere of rainbow hues no larger than a closed fist. "Incredible," said Xavier in a whisper, as if afraid that Mears could hear him. "The entire Void to be sampled at his slightest thought, *any* projection possible, and all he can do is stare at that snippet."

"Pattern," said Che.

Xavier nodded. *Controlled and focused,* he thought; this being just one more example of how Mears refused any extraneous input. He was all business. "Show me," said Xavier, "and slow enough so I can see what Mears can't quite see."

Again Che rustled something in the background.

Xavier watched. The shifting colors before Mears slowed the current snippet illustrating the evolving relationship between phosphorous concentration, total organic soil content, ambient humidity, and total rice yield ticking at 1-hour intervals through the entire 94-day crop cycle.

Slowed but not stopped.

A spider appeared on Mears's desk, a distorted tarantula, a childhood nightmare, a thing with more legs than any real spider, a bulging head, big red-glass-bead eyes, and furry mandibles. It flicked in, then flicked out. Xavier had barely been able to see it, despite the slowdown in the feed. He knew that Mears could not see it at all, though the image was picked up by the transceiver in his Ocs. The phantom spider placed there by Che moved too fast for his visual cortex to perceive but not too fast for neurons within it to register.

The spider rematerialized, this time a half centimeter closer to Mears, then flashed away again. "Perfect," said Xavier. "Back up to real time." Mears's hands blurred, and the snippet rolled and pitched, spitting out colors and geometry. Then the image synched back into real time.

Mears suddenly looked confused, grimaced, pushed himself slightly back in his chair, and moved his right hand off the desk, running it through the rainbow snippet. He brushed something off his right shoulder, a spider that was not really there, his subconscious forcing his hand to act.

"Thank you, Mr. Pavlov," said Xavier. They'd been running this program on Mears for nearly a month now, burning a feedback loop in his neural wiring. Whenever he accessed the Void, Che piggybacked the high-speed spider snip. "Once more, this time right knee," he said.

Mears brushed at his right knee, flicking aside the spider that was not there.

"He's ready," said Xavier.

The room smelled of dirt and sweat and had three doors—one entrance and two exists. Christina knew that one of those exits led back to the Co-Op's eastern entrance, while the other led farther into the depths of the Co-Op center and to Mears.

Senor Wright had been grateful for the discovery of the true source of the altered corn worms and had pulled enough strings to get them this far into the Co-Op, but she still doubted that they'd get an actual meeting with Mears. And even if they did, she did not believe that her father's plan to blackmail Mears would succeed, certain that Mears simply wouldn't care if the world beyond the Co-Op's walls discovered that the modified corn worm had been brewed here. Mears would call in his own favors and bury Senor Wright right along with his blighted corn crop.

And then she would be only two days away from reporting for Volunteer service.

Papito does not understand how the world really works, she thought once again.

She felt certain that the only realistic option would be to implement her own plan. She'd gathered quite a substantial pile of ammonia-rich fertilizer and kept it stored a bit too close to the ethanol tanks in the back of the barn. The resulting explosion would be intense. There'd be very few collectible neurons even if the Ag Powers wanted to perform an autopsy. Papito and Che would be safe.

She saw that as the most likely outcome.

But she did not want to die and would do everything in her power to get to Mears and complete the play of Papito's blackmail scheme.

"Name?" asked the Doll, the male face projected in its Mask too perfect to be real, the cleft in the chin, the dimpled cheeks, the wavy black hair all calculated to elicit a favorable response from the teenage girl viewing it. "And nature of your business?"

The Doll stood before one of the room's two exit doors, the one that Christina knew they had to go through if they were to have even the slightest chance of getting her off the Volunteer list. "We've already given our names to three other Dolls and been sniffed and licked. You have our DNA, have our files, and know the nature of our business. Let us in now."

The Doll did not move, only continued to smile. It tilted its Mask to the right, then to the left. It tapped its right foot several times against the dirty floor. Then it started all over again.

Christina knew that it would be happy to keep repeating these motions in an endless loop. "Christina Olmos," she said with a flat and emotionless voice, doing her best to hide her nervousness and fear, instead projecting an air of indifference with just a tint of anger. She knew that this Doll would be able to pick up the slightest emotional shift. "This is my father, Xavier Olmos," she said, nodding to her left in his direction. "We're the technical representatives of Jonathan Wright, proprietor of Wright Agriculture. We wish to speak to Dr. Mears regarding the biological attack that this establishment has launched on Wright Agriculture."

The Doll's smile grew wider. "As you have been informed earlier today, at two other assignment cubicles," the Doll said pleasantly, "we disavow all knowledge of any such attack, are in no way responsible for any financial and emotional consequences of said attack, and request that you inform Mr. Wright of such. We consider this matter closed."

The exit door behind Christina opened. "Thank you for your inquiry," said the Doll.

Christina took half a step closer to the Doll. She was not about to give up, no matter how small the chance of success, when she considered what the alternative would be. "Vat 15,874," she said, hoping that revealing the vat number where the bug had been brewed would be enough to get them in—it was information that no outsider should have had access to.

"I understand," the Doll said quickly. The exit door closed. "Please step to the center of the room."

Christina stepped forward, almost losing her footing, her left knee suddenly wobbly. "We demand to see Dr. Mears, now!" she said, trying to hide behind a wall of anger. Xavier grabbed her from behind, helping her to stand, but doing his best to make it look as if he were pulling her back from the Doll.

"Don't make him mad," said Xavier. "It's just a Doll, doing its job, just like we're trying to do our job. If we want Mr. Wright to pay us, we've got to get in, and that's not going to happen if you make them mad," he said.

"You are both Pures," said the Doll, as a thick, transparent, but gray-tinted wall dropped from the ceiling between them and the Doll. "No internal mechanical or electrical enhancements have been detected. Before proceeding, you will be subjected to EMP scan to render covert devices inoperable, in addition to a full organic decontamination."

"Let us just see Mears," demanded Christina, her knees and emotions having steadied.

"If you agree, remove your clothing, place all external bio/mech/electronics in the container provided, and prepare for EMP scanning and decontamination."

"I will not remove my clothes!" shouted Christina, playing the role of the indignant representative of Senor Wright.

Xavier pulled at her elbow with one hand while starting to unbutton his shirt with the other. "You've got to do what they want. If we don't see Mears, we don't get paid. And we need to get paid."

Christina took a deep breath, pulled away from him, and gave him a hard, angry look, pulling up the emotions from a time when her father had *really* made her angry, back when her mother had died, when he had seemed incapable of anything except sitting and staring. "If you could grow more food on that damned chunk of clay that Abuelo left us, we wouldn't have to go around sniffing in other people's business."

"I am your father, and you will not talk to me that way!" he shouted, his face flushing red, the veins standing out in his throat. And then he looked down at the floor, the color quickly draining from his face. "We need the money," he said, almost in a whisper, as he dropped his shirt to the floor, and pulled an auditory transducer from his right ear.

"And because of that you're willing to have me grovel in front of this machine, to be stripped and scanned!" She turned around, not letting him answer, the anger suddenly real, but not focused at her father, but at the place that was trying to steal her life, at the place that would force her into taking her own life if this blackmail plan did not work. Stripped to the waist, she began to unbutton her pants. "Get a good look!" she shouted at the Doll as she dropped her pants and kicked off a shoe.

"Place all clothing and objects in the container and prepare to be scanned," the Doll said.

Christina scratched at her right shoulder, the white one-piece itchy, the fabric coarse and stiff, obviously designed for discomfort. Leaning back in her chair she let the ambient wash over her, funneling through the full-spectrum receivers that wrapped her head. Visual, auditory, olfactory, even neural wideband vibrational transducers thumped at her skull, generating high-resolution standing sonic wave fronts in her brain, stimulating and overloading desired regions. While she knew she still sat in a bare office, all her senses insisted that she sat in a clearing in a cornfield, a warm summer sun high on the horizon, the heat soaking in deep, a gentle breeze playing across the field, pushing at her hair, carrying the scents of rich soil and sweet corn.

"Never seen anything this real," said Xavier.

Christina focused, held her emotions in check, and started adding a long string of prime numbers, doing her best not to drift into what her father had said, knowing that he was just playing his role. It was hard not to think of the bunker beneath the barn, where they spent so much of their time, where the crystal-fiber interfaces they used made the full-spectrum receivers now wrapped around their heads look like children's toys.

"Papito, we're not here for looking," she said, snapping at him. "We're here to get a job done so we can get paid."

"A job?"

Both turned. Mears walked in from an adjacent row of corn. Dressed in a skintight elastomer blue jumpsuit, he walked between them and the two ugly aluminum tube chairs they sat in, stopped before them, and sat back, hanging in midair, forcing them to look up.

He blurred for a moment, face shimmering, morphing, a nearly infinite set of combinations spilling across the basic template of his face. Christina felt the neural transducers play against her skull, monitoring neural activity, setting up a feedback loop recording her neural responses as a function of the facial features she was observing, searching for the perfect face, the one that she would find comforting, attractive, and most importantly, trustworthy.

The face locked.

Perfect, thought Christina. Square jaw, deep dark eyes, thick blond hair, the subtle scent of cinnamon and apples, and a body with sharply cut muscles. He smiled. The teeth were milk white, with the upper canines just a bit oversized, hinting at something dangerous. They'd spied on the real Mears for years, and he didn't even vaguely resemble the man in front of her.

"This is rather unpleasant business," he said in a voice

that was so deep and resonant Christina could feel it vibrate in her chest.

"As is the viral load cooked in Vat 15,874 that was responsible for the destruction of nearly 12,000 hectares of Taos sweet corn in Senor Wright's fields, a blatant act of agra-attack, in violation of numerous UN biomass production mandates," said Christina.

Mears spread both his hands, palms up, and shrugged. "One person's interpretation," he said. "And not really a matter of concern. However, what is of concern is the way you acquired the information. We followed the paths you took, detected the algorithms used to penetrate our protective barriers. That is what we find unpleasant, and not the 12,000 hectares of Senor Wright's sweet corn."

"Perhaps you will find it unpleasant if we dump that information into the Void for anyone to sample," said Christina, just managing to keep her voice from cracking, knowing by the expression on Mears's face that the threat carried absolutely no weight.

Mears ignored her and turned. "I understand why your daughter is here, Mr. Olmos," he said. "Quite the remarkable young lady, with abilities well beyond what one would expect to find in a 16-year-old. I suspect what she did not inherit from your wife by way of genes, your wife taught her from her own wide-ranging areas of expertise." Mears glanced at a swatch of twisting colors and text that momentarily rolled in front of his face. "Extensive training in bioinformatics, inorganic to organic synthesis, and experience in bio data mining, made your daughter the obvious choice in the rather limited resource pool of your small community for Wright to tap into in quest of a solution to his corn worm problem." He turned and smiled at Christina. "And I see that your mother had you assisting in her rounds, not only teaching you a wide range of diagnostic techniques, but even allowing you to perform some basic surgeries. I must say that I am impressed. Perhaps when you come to us in the next few days to begin your Volunteer service, we might find you a more suitable position than working in the fields." Mears smiled. "Medicine and surgery are something of a passion with me," he said, pointing at her and turning his right hand. He rotated the wrist, and the hand turned at an impossible angle, making a full 360-degree rotation. "Corn is but a sideline for me, Christina. My real love is surgery—state-of-the-art Tool enhancements permitting me to perform techniques far beyond the primitive procedures your mother taught you." Again he smiled. "I definitely think that when you come, I will have you assigned directly to my office." His smile morphed into a leer.

"Stinking Tool," she said.

"Tsk, tsk, tsk," said Mears as he shook his head. "I would not have expected such prejudice from a young lady of your obvious talents and abilities, though I suppose a certain degree of cultural infection is to be expected." He turned and looked at Xavier. "Unlike your rather remarkable daughter, you, Mr. Olmos, possess no such talents, and are a *farmer*, in the most basic sense of that word—you bury seeds, toss about fertilizer, pray for rain, then hope something springs from the ground. I must admit to being a bit baffled as to why she even brought you along. Perhaps so you could open and close doors for her."

Xavier smiled.

Mears reached up and brushed at his right shoulder, not looking away from Xavier.

"I've come to tell you a little story," said Xavier. "We have been *inside* your facility from the moment your systems first came on-line nearly seven years ago. While Christina believes she found the incriminating evidence showing that you brewed the bugs in Vat 15,874, you and I know that is not true."

Christina turned, staring at her father. "What?" she said.

"You didn't cook that bug," said Xavier, looking at Mears. "Only yesterday, when Senor Wright lodged his formal complaint, did you start your own internal investigation and discover what had been cooked in that Vat. The virus was brewed, transferred to your insect research division, inserted into the Mexican corn worms, three generations bred until a critical supply was obtained, and your distribution system delivered them to the outskirts of Senor Wright's farm. For more than three months now your own internal systems have been running an operation of which you had no knowledge."

"Papito?" said Christina, totally confused.

Mears stood.

The cornfield vanished. They were in his office. Xavier reached up, pulling off the full head wrap and dropped it to the floor. "Put on a few kilos there," said Xavier.

Christina pulled off her own wrap and saw Mears for what he really was—slightly plump, nearly 20 centimeters shorter and 50 years older, sitting behind his small desk.

"I understand," said Mears, staring at Xavier. "Do you really believe that your minor transgression here might give you enough leverage to exempt your daughter from Volunteer obligations?"

At that moment Christina understood what her father had done. He had hacked their production facility and would do it again unless she were released from Volunteer service. Everything else had been a ploy, just to get them in this office, for a meat-to-meat with Mears, where a bargain could be struck without anyone finding out that the Co-Op's systems were susceptible to outside attack.

"Yes," said Xavier.

"I don't think so," said Mears. "You compromised our systems, gained access, and used them in order to blackmail us. We see your fingers; have traced your every move, right back to the origins. You've been purged, and any evidence that you were ever inside has been purged." He suddenly flinched and brushed at his chest. "This meeting is at an end, as are you. You will both be escorted directly to the Volunteer Orientation Center where you will begin a joint sentence—as Residents."

"We took control of your system," said Xavier. "You can't purge us. You will exempt Christina from the Volunteer service and leave us alone."

Mears laughed and scratched at his chin. "You are insane."

"And you no longer have control over your own neuromorphic inputs," said Xavier. "Left hand to right knee," he said, knowing that Che would flash the phantom spider onto Mears's knee and the hardwired response they'd built up in his neural anatomy over the last month would have to obey, no matter what his conscious mind insisted.

Mears brushed his left hand against his right knee.

"What!" he screamed, looking down at his hand, first lifting it close to his face, examining it as if he'd never seen it before, and then rapidly pulling it back. "What have you done?"

"Your neuroanatomy has been hacked and reprogrammed," said Xavier. "Does your nose itch?"

Mears hit himself in the nose and fell back into his seat.

Christina sagged in her seat, understanding that there were layers beneath layers in her father's plan. He had done far more than hack the Co-Op's production line—he'd hacked right into Mears.

"The virus and the corn worms got us inside this room, for a direct meat-to-meat, thanks to the good work of my daughter," said Xavier, as he swept his hand about the office and smiled at Christina. "But hijacking you, rewiring your neural anatomy, is what will save Christina, allowing her to return to the farm and guarantee no harm will ever come to us."

"Never!" shouted Mears. "I will not be blackmailed. I'll plug your hack and regain control."

"Perhaps you will, and perhaps you won't," said Xavier. "But that is hardly the point any longer. *You* have been compromised and accessed from outside. There is nothing you can do to change that reality. But do take note of the fact that we have relayed this information to you from the confines of your office. We know that you directly modify and edit all surveillance in this office, so you have the ability to present to the outside world whatever version of this meeting you find convenient. We would not want someone else to discover that you've been tampered with." He paused. "Right ear," said Xavier.

"No!" shouted Mears, as he hit himself on the right side of his face.

"If you do not comply, if you act against us in any fashion, certain individuals will be made aware of how you have been accessed. When a Tool such as yourself has been broken, from both a security and economic perspective, it rarely makes sense to repair that Tool—a fundamental trust has been broken. And if you can't be trusted, they'll dispose of you," said Xavier. "If anything should happen to us, this information will automatically be flashed throughout the Void." Xavier grinned. "Right eye."

Mears hit himself in the eye and began to whimper, standing for a moment, looking around the bare walls of his office, then sitting back down.

"Broken Tools are *replaced*," said Xavier. "There's a couple of nasty ones," he said.

Mears hit himself in the stomach with two balled fists, to the large accompaniment of a whush of air.

Christina almost laughed, but not at Mears punching himself in the stomach. She had thought her father did not understand how the world worked, that he could have never figured out a plan to rescue her from the Co-Op. Her father had not only played Mears, but played her as well, making her an unwitting cog in the machine he'd fabricated to rescue her. "Now about these," said Christina, holding up both of her hands, the bright red skin almost glistening in the harsh light of Mears's office. "I'm tired of this color."

"One on the nose again," said Xavier.

Again Mears hit himself in the face.

"I'm waiting," said Christina, as she waved both hands at Mears, reading the expression in his face and knowing that her first order of business when they returned to the farm would be safely to return the nitrate fertilizer to its holding bin. That accident would no longer be needed.

Chapter 8

Helios 37 hung 50 kilometers inside the Sun's photosphere.

One of a constellation of 18 surviving probes, it sped along at nearly 7,000 kilometers per hour, locked in synch to the Sun's outer rotating layer. Despite the 5,000-degree temperature outside its almost perfectly reflecting hull, the superconducting chips in its core remained chilled, gulping down torrents of data. The probe's gaping electromagnetic mouth sucked solar protons down its gullet, fused them, used the energy liberated to keep the probe cooled, then blew the helium by-products out through an array of attitude and orbital adjusters.

So elegant, thought Kristensen.

But it didn't end there.

Power from the fusion reactor was also used to generate oscillating electric fields that played out from the probe's metallic hull, and in turn those electric fields generated sympathetic magnetic fields. That was what the Sun was all about—a boiling maelstrom of magnetic fields, in places thousands of times stronger than Earth's magnetic fields, and capable of hurling millions of tons of ionized particles from the Sun's surface each and every second, generating the solar wind that buffeted Earth, that produced the northern and southern lights.

But on the Helios, those magnetic fields were used to

probe the solar photosphere. The best way to see a magnetic field was to use a magnetic field—like a child pushing at one magnet with another, using repulsing fields to make a magnet dance across the top of a table, the Helios probe spit out high-density magnetic flux lines, probing the magnetic structure of the Sun.

So beautiful, thought Kristensen.

The Chinese and Americans had spent hundreds of billions on the fleet of probes that drifted through the Sun's outer regions. The stated goal was science, to better understand the mechanisms that drove the Sun, to better predict sunspot and flare activity, to gain insight into the subtle variations of thermal output, which in turn affected global climates, weather patterns, crop yields, monsoons, people living and dying.

Lies that few believed.

It was pure and simple terror that had led to the creation of the Helios fleet, an early-warning system designed to inform the Powers the moment any anomaly occurred on the Sun, especially anything that might indicate the stellar Jet was about to be reignited.

Kristensen laughed and looked up at the wall and the big clock embedded in it, the stainless-steel-and-glass monstrosity probably more than a century old, a relic from colonial times, when this part of Africa had been ruled by France. Now petty warlords and disease ruled it. The Ten Degree War had seen to that, and, of course, there was the radiation. The rusty taste of blood filled his mouth. His swollen gums were infected and several decaying teeth had already fallen out.

The Swirl, spitting rainbow streamers, clung to the wall just above the clock. The Void was incredibly thin in this region of Africa, a fourth world vacuum where nodes and transmitters were few and far between, with only a handful of Tools to maintain connections. But enough hardware hung at Geo, far above the equator, to give marginal coverage.

Kristensen smiled as the Swirl reached into his head, tickling him, a dopamine swell sloshing about inside his skull, amplitude increasing, avalanching, the overload generating the pleasant mental aroma of hot maple syrup and baking apples.

"First steps begun," whispered the Swirl. *"Sarah Sutherland will soon be interfaced to CUSP."*

Kristensen's eyelids flitted, a waking REM overloading his eyes in a series of rapid-fire spasms. "Thank you," he whispered back, the dopamine surge still caressing him. Pieces of the puzzle coming together. Sarah was a key piece, one that the Sun would have to take notice of. However, Sarah was a funny type of puzzle piece, one with an ill-defined shape, one he felt certain would fit into the puzzle he was building, but might also fit snugly into an entirely different puzzle that General Sutherland was putting together.

Both plans shared a common element—the Sun needed to be controlled.

He focused.

The Swirl had vanished.

Clock.

Its second hand ticked by. He believed that he'd taken over Helios 36 nearly 7 minutes ago, but he would not know for sure for another 2 minutes, not until the confirmation signal, traveling at the speed of light, finished its 9-minute-long trip from the Sun to the Earth.

Then Helios 36 would start to talk to the Sun.

He'd guessed the real purpose of the Helios array from the moment it had been conceived—he'd been on the original design team. The Powers searched for what lurked in the heart of the Sun. They had searched quietly, gently, not wanting to wake what lay beneath the surface, afraid any overt action might cause the Jet to fire. But he knew that the Jet had to be fired. If Sarah Sutherland was about to be interfaced to CUSP, then it was time for the Jet to be fired.

The Swirl had told him so many times.

This future could not be escaped.

The pad's small screen lay before him. He leaned forward, placing his ear toward the screen's speaker.

Fzzzzt.

He slumped back in his seat, unable to breathe, unable to believe that he'd actually done it, that ten years of planning, hiding, running, and hacking had finally brought him to this point.

Fzzzzt. Fzzzzt. Fzzzzt.

"Yes!" he screamed, jumping up, knocking back the chair.

Fzzzzt. Fzzzzt. Fzzzzt. Fzzzzt. Fzzzzt.

Suddenly dizzy, his vision tunneling, he fell back into the chair. "Not yet," he said in a whisper. "Not until they come." Too many rads and a dopamine backlash were about to pull him under.

Fzzzzt. Fzzzzt. Fzzzzt. Fzzzzt. Fzzzzt. Fzzzzt. Fzzzzt.

Helios 36 sat at the edge of a supergranular, a twisted region of magnetic fields on the surface of the Sun, blasting out the clipped, wide-spectrum magnetic pulses that he was now receiving.

Fzzzzt. Fzzzzt. Fzzzzt. Fzzzzt. Fzzzzt. Fzzzzt. Fzzzzt. Fzzzzt. Fzzzzt. Fzzzzt. Fzzzzt.

It spoke in the only language that Kristensen felt the Sun could understand, the only language that might possibly wake it into action.

Fzzzzt. Fzzzzt. Fzzzzt. Fzzzzt. Fzzzzt. Fzzzzt. Fzzzzt.
Fzzzzt. Fzzzzt. Fzzzzt. Fzzzzt. Fzzzzt. Fzzzzt.

A repeating sequence of prime numbers—1, 3, 5, 7, 11, 13—running up to the last triple-digit prime of 997, then starting all over again. It whispered to the Sun in a magnetic voice that Kristensen knew barely peaked above the magnetic maelstrom that screamed across its surface, but it was the best that could be done with the technology available. It would cycle through the sequence at least twice, perhaps even three times, dumping all power into the pulses, leaving nothing behind for cooling. He knew that in a few minutes the probe's outer tungsten-titanium hull would begin to mist into a metallic fog.

"Wake up!" he whispered, then slid from his chair, falling to the floor.

Fzzzzt. Fzzzzt. Fzzzzt. Fzzzzt. Fzzzzt. Fzzzzt. Fzzzzt.
Fzzzzt. Fzzzzt. Fzzzzt. Fzzzzt. Fzzzzt. Fzzzzt. Fzzzzt. Fzzzzt.
Fzzzzt. Fzzzzt.

"Sarah is waiting for you."

Kin-Lu Wong came in low and fast, the twin turbines on her bi-hop angled far back, their silent thrust pushing her at nearly 300 kilometers per hour. She cut across the eastern outskirts of Yaounde, hugging a moonlike landscape of craters and solidified glass. The rad counter chirped in her right ear. All of eastern Cameroon had been slagged nearly 25 years earlier when South Africa had lost control of its arsenal, and the entire continent running from 10 degrees north and south of the equator had degenerated into tribal warfare. The machetes and rifles of earlier conflicts had been replaced with gamma-ray high-altitude battle platforms and low-yield nukes—the carbonized jungle had cooled some since, but not enough for anything actually to live there.

Slag and flowed metal suddenly vanished, giving way to more conventional rubble, collapsed buildings, ruptured asphalt roads, and the twisted wreckage of cars, all of it burned and charred. "Down in the Central Plaza of the Avenue du 21 Août," she whispered, as she backed off the turbine thrust and began angling the props into a vertical landing position, moving toward the western edge of the plaza. She hit the ground hard, not having cut quite enough speed, popped the main chest restraint that dropped the bi-hop to the ground, pulled her pistol, and started running. She didn't look back, didn't need to. Her heads-up clearly showed the other five members of the extraction squad fanned out behind her, moving up.

Yaounde was dark and mostly silent. In the distance there was sporadic gunfire, but none close by, no sane person venturing this close to the slag line. She scanned the street, peering in the deep infrared, and saw a second-floor window, covered with what looked like a strip of carpet, glowing amber.

"Rear cover only," she said, running toward a ruined building that might once have been a grain warehouse. "Everyone stay on the first floor."

Darting around the skeleton of a scorched bus, she hit the side of the warehouse, her fingers finding hold in the rusted and perforated galvanized-sheet walls. She scurried up, ratlike, quickly ramping down the amplification of her night vision and shifting to the visible spectrum as she neared the window.

In the shadows she saw a pocket dish perched in the window-sill.

"Target confirmed," she whispered.

She crawled to the edge of the window but did not attempt to pull back the stinking piece of carpet that covered it. Instead, a spiderlike creature, no bigger than a fingernail, crawled from her back, jumped onto the windowsill, and scurried beneath the carpet.

Several seconds passed.

Snow filled the lower-left quadrant of her Ocs, then flickered and locked. One man lay sprawled on the floor, partially pushed up against the far wall, a lap pad resting on his stomach. She did not even have to wait for the spider's output to be transmitted to Cairo for biometric identification—she knew the man.

"Jesper Kristensen," whispered a confirming voice in her ear.

Wong tensed. In the last five hours they'd located four of the saboteurs, all savvy enough to operate their equipment, but none of them with the capabilities to have taken down the entire Helios network. Kristensen was a different matter altogether. He'd helped design it nearly 15 years earlier.

She had not expected him actually to be manning one of the terminals.

He should have been hiding in some deep hole.

And even stranger was the fact that he was still breathing. The others had been *hard-dead*, nothing left in their skulls but a puddle of glop, with no chance of retrieving any neural information.

But Kristensen was alive, and as she continued to watch, his fingers suddenly poked at the lap pad's keyboard. She couldn't imagine why. Satellites were down, and the squad had a full-range spectrum sampler that would have picked up any unauthorized wireless transmission and easily jammed it.

Kristensen could not be transmitting.

"Under no circumstances are any of you to enter this room," she whispered. Her squad was not filtered. In their job they could not afford to be—all their senses had to be fully functional in order to ensure they could complete the mission. But in such a state they might hear or see something that they shouldn't, some piece of information that might prove as lethal as a bullet through the skull. She would not risk them. If she was exposed to restricted material, she would just have to deal with the consequences—but she would not take her squad down with her.

Kristensen stopped typing, slumped farther down against the wall, and the lap pad fell from its perch on his stomach, hitting the floor. "Are you going to wait out there all night?" he asked.

She stiffened and again studied the room. There were no obvious weapons. Moving slowly, she nudged back the carpet with the barrel of her gun.

"Do come in," he said.

Pulling herself through the window, keeping the gun trained on Kristensen, she backed into the far corner of the room.

"I want to thank you for coming so quickly. I've been feeling rather poorly and didn't know how much longer I could hold on." He smiled, exposing bloody, puffy gums.

It was only then that she saw how gaunt he looked, his yellow-tinted skin hanging on him, his eyes sunk far back in his head, his hair thin and brittle, in places patches of it missing. The stench that she had thought came from the carpet hanging in front of the window had actually come from him. He was decaying.

"I've been here for the better part of a week, which I fear is about a week too long."

Severe radiation poisoning. This close to the slag, there

was little chance that anyone would accidentally discover him, but there had been a price to pay.

"You're under arrest for sabotaging the Helios system," she said, and motioned with her pistol, wanting him to stand.

"I suspect that arresting me and bringing my radiated hide in for analysis and dissection will be of little significance in comparison to what is taking place out there." He held up a shaking right hand and pointed toward the ceiling. "We received an answer."

Kin-Lu lowered her gun, knowing this man was no longer a threat. She was only too well aware of his obsession, but she passed no judgments on the private fetishes of those she worked for, whether they were Zero Pointers like Sutherland, or the Sentient Searchers like Kristensen. It was all just information to be used to help locate a target.

Kristensen's signature had been all over this sabotage.

From the moment the first Helios satellite started transmitting magnetic blasts of prime numbers, they knew who had to be behind it—the list of those brilliant enough to hijack the Helios system, then use it to try and communicate with the Sun, was short. Actually it was a list of one.

"How has the Sun answered you?" she asked. She suspected the Sun was communicating to him by way of voices echoing in his own head. Kristensen's profile had him diagnosed as a paranoid schizophrenic. Reports said that he'd never been quite right since he'd lost his family right after Ring Day. He'd somehow managed to escape the facility outside of Elko, Nevada, and get as close to Los Angeles as the San Bernardino Mountains. And then the quakes had started. His family had lived in the LA basin. Not even their remains had been located: Most of the basin had dropped to nearly 50 meters below sea level by the time the San Andreas stopped lurching.

"In the only language it knows," said Kristensen. Reaching toward the floor, he flipped open the lap pad and tapped at the keyboard.

Kin-Lu angled her pistol back up, finger squeezed against the trigger, the barrel pointing directly at his head.

He pushed at the lap pad, angling the screen in her direction. "Take a look."

The Sun filled the screen of the pad. Although it was white-yellow and spitting flares, she saw nothing unusual, heard nothing. "It's talking to you?" she asked.

"Yes," he said. Reaching forward, he tapped a key, and the image of the Sun expanded, its lowermost quadrant filling the screen. "Do you see it now?"

"Sunspots," she said, seeing three black specks in a line.

"Exactly," he said. "The Sun is manipulating its magnetic fields to create those sunspots."

Kin-Lu shook her head. He was insane. The Sun always had sunspots. It took a real megalomaniac to believe that the Sun was generating those spots in order to communicate with him.

"Now watch," he said.

Two additional spots, exactly in line with the first three, appeared.

"Now we have five," he said.

She watched the screen, and wondered if she was looking at the Sun at all or simply a graphic designed by Kristensen. She knew nothing about sunspots, but did not think that they arranged themselves in straight lines.

Two more spots appeared, lined up with the other five, making seven.

"Care to guess how many will come next?"

She knew. Just like the signals being beat out by the Helios system—prime numbers. "I would assume eleven." And as she said it, four more spots appeared, lined up with the others. "This isn't real," she said. "This is just some graphic you've put together."

"I guess you could be right, but you won't have to take my word for it. You see, this is not even my data. This is being transmitted over the networks right now from the Mauna Kea Observatory. Of course you saw to it that my dish was no longer operative, so I needed to find another path to the outside world, to explain how I woke the Sun from its long slumber." He waved his hand across the desk. Crouched on the corner, barely noticeable, sat the spider. A threadlike filament ran from it to the back of Kristensen's pad. "I want to thank you for that. Did you realize that I had a hand in the spider's development, back in the bad old days when I answered to your Powers, when General Sutherland pulled my strings? I left in a nice little trapdoor, in case Sutherland decided to snip my wings."

Kin-Lu pulled the trigger.

In the small room the resulting explosion was almost deafening. The far corner of the room, along with the spider, flared into a cloud of dust and splinters. The computer screen went dark.

"Not to worry," said Kristensen, pushing himself up, almost sitting. "As we were having our pleasant little conversation, the entire contents of my pad were pumped through the spider linked to your systems and dumped into the Void. I'm sure that your filters will catch most of the copies, but no filter is perfect. My message will get out, and even if you manage to silence everyone who receives it, and I'm sure that an army of Tools is fanning out right now in that futile attempt, it will make absolutely no difference. You can't silence the Sun, can't stop it from waking and completing its mission."

"Mission?" asked Kin-Lu.

Kristensen's left elbow gave an audible pop, buckling, and he fell flat against the floor. A thin line of blood-tinted mucous ran out of his left nostril and down his cheek. "The Sun has plans for us." His eyes closed.

"Medic in here now!" she screamed.

Chapter 9

"Moves like an overstressed rat."

Simon stared at the hovering snippet. "I'm afraid so," he said.

Despite the dozen chairs that lined the walls of the ante-office, General Sutherland paced, actually marched, each step exact and precise, turning as he came to a wall with a rapid pivot.

"Never liked that UN-loving bastard."

Simon turned in his chair. "His daughter just died," he said.

Mears shrugged. "I'm sure he expected it sooner or later. She was either jumping off of something, breaking into something, scanning closed files, or running with the scum of this planet." He paused for a moment. "But of course we should not underestimate what that scum may at times be capable of." He looked to his left, then right, as if searching for something, flicked a few fingers across his right shoulder, then focused back on Simon. "Sarah Sutherland's outcome was a foregone conclusion."

"You are one inhuman son of a bitch," said Simon, doing nothing to hide his disgust. "Probably more hardware than organic."

"Do you see what I have to put up with? He's an ultra-Tool with an ultra-ego to match," said Garvey, who sat at the far end of the conference table, as if to put as much distance as possible between himself and Simon. "He shows no respect for authority and is completely incapable of controlling his emotions. Besides the obvious complications as a result of his Jinni, Bill, it is becoming more and more apparent that an overall mental deterioration and personality shift is taking place."

Obvious complications, thought Simon. He knew that the agoraphobia was not a *complication*, but the result of a deliberate chunk of rewired neurons. Had he gone Post-Point, they wouldn't want him walking out the door and enslaving the human race. Simon slowly shook his head. *Real fools, Bill*, he thought, knowing if he *had* gone Post-Point, a few tangled neurons would not have stopped him from leaving the building.

But he couldn't go Post-Point. For the last year he'd thought the limitation had been within him, but in the last few days he'd sensed a change in Bill, been able to dig deeper into him and begun to suspect that it was Bill holding him back. Something deep in Bill's construction wouldn't allow it, something that Bill would not admit to or even talk about. But he could now feel it, like a weight around his neck, holding him down whenever his thoughts started to race, whenever he started to look *beyond* himself.

He now suspected Bill had his own agenda, which did not include going Post-Point.

Mears grinned, showing perfect teeth. "Is our young plasma guru getting to you?" he asked.

"He is unstable," said Garvey.

Mears shrugged. "All of us have our little faults that coworkers must learn to be sensitive to." He pointed at Garvey. "For instance, I've learned to live with the fact that my CUSP program manager has an IQ at least 70 points shy of his assistant," he said, and pointed over at Simon.

Garvey looked momentarily puzzled, then frowned.

Mears ignored him, turning back to Simon. "To answer your question, I'm pleased to let you know that I've finally dropped below the 50 percent organic mark. Last month the cartilage in my left ankle finally disintegrated away to nothing, so I went in for a major upgrade. Got rid of the whole damn foot. Between the bunions and the bone spurs in my heel, it just wasn't worth holding on to it. And of course if you get one done, you've got to do the other if you want to be balanced." Sitting back in his metal chair, he lifted his feet up off the floor and began to turn them. Suddenly his metallic boots had turned to an impossible angle, toe and heel reversing position, then kept turning until back to their original position, having made a full 360-degree rotation. "So much more versatile than the original equipment," he said with a laugh.

None of it surprised Simon. Many of the Tool-intense Powers that ruled the planet were obsessed with enhancements, certain that the day was not far off when they'd be able to be replaced totally by hardware, in effect becoming immortal, and gracefully go Post-Point in their factory-warrantied mechanical containers. To Simon it looked like suicide 1 kilogram at a time. As he watched Mears, he saw him squirm, looking first at his right shoulder, then the left. "Lose something?" he asked.

Mears shook his head, giving Simon a disgusted look. "I simply do not understand this aversion you have to enhancements. You of all people should be grateful for the wondrous technology that's been developed over the last fifty years. Without it, I believe that they'd still have you warehoused, sleeping in deep coma, with not a thought in your head."

"I was not given the choice," said Simon.

Mears leaned back. "And had you been given the option of rotting away in a coma cubicle or sharing that skull of yours with Bill, are you suggesting that you would have chosen coma?"

Simon took a deep breath, blowing it out slowly. "No," he said.

"Well of course not. And I suspect when you start facing the full century mark, as your organic systems begin to fail and become riddled with decay and cancer, that you, too, will be more than eager to avail yourself of whatever enhancements are available."

Simon said nothing. He was not sure that Mears was wrong.

"But enough pleasantries about my chosen lifestyle," said Mears. He snorted and eased back in his chair. "The topic of the moment is why that son of a bitch is pacing outside this conference room. You can be damn certain it's got nothing to do with corn," he said, waving his hands in the air, pointing fingers in the general direction of the Ag Co-Op's massive fields.

Garvey opened his mouth, as if about to say something, then slowly closed it.

"He wants direct access to CUSP," said Simon.

"What?" said Garvey.

Mears held up a hand at Garvey, not bothering to look at him. "What would make you think that?" he asked.

Simon grinned. "You're the surgeon," he said to Mears. "You've got his daughter downstairs right now on ice, prepping her for neural interfacing with CUSP." Without realizing it, Simon reached up and rubbed the back of his head, unable to feel the fine scars that marked the point where Mears had gone into his skull nearly four years earlier. "We accessed the files and went over the details of her injury."

"We?" asked Mears, giving Garvey a hard look.

"Of course not with him," said Simon. "With Bill."

Mears shook his head. "Security has been extremely lax. Any- and everyone seems to have access to the local Void nodes. If not you, then some damn pig farmer."

"Pig farmer?" asked Simon.

"Nothing," said Mears, running a hand across the right shoulder of his coat. "What is it that you think you know about Sarah Sutherland?"

"She was dead for nearly 15 minutes before the rescuers could get a respirator on her. That should have been more than enough to kill her brain, but a combination of chilling as her Jump-suit partially failed and an initial abnormally high neural oxygen level saved her." Simon then paused, wondering for a moment if he really wanted to pass his suspicions on to Mears, but decided that Mears must have already come to the same conclusion. This was in all likelihood just a test, to see if he was sharp enough to be kept in the loop. Mears was forever playing games—testing his creation. "One might consider that simply good luck, but then there is the nature of her injury. Her cerebellum is gone, just as neatly as if *you* took a scalpel to it," he said as he pointed at Mears. "For what you have been proposing to do with CUSP, giving it full organic software, the test subject's cerebellum needs to be removed."

"Quite fortunate for us to find such a well-matched candidate," said Mears.

"It was not fortune, but by design. You've been trying to get Congress and the UN to agree to an organic interface with CUSP for more than a year now, and they're scared. The way that CUSP has been sold, most take it as a foregone conclusion that if you interface it to a chunk of top-quality neural software like Sarah Sutherland, it will go Post-Point before you've got her skull closed. In a Post-Point reality, the old Powers will be relegated to niches previously occupied by cockroaches."

"Do you believe something happened to diminish that fear?" asked Mears.

Simon laughed. "Not diminish, but overcome it. Sutherland has real power—straddles both US and UN lines, with fingers in every pot and pocket. He ran all covert operations for the US in the Ten Degree War," he said, then paused for just a moment, as if remembering something.

"Bill?" he said to himself.

Bill didn't answer.

"Are you certain I was born in New York City?" he asked, not certain why he needed to ask that question, something about Sutherland and the Ten Degree War possibly jogging an old memory, something from *before* the coma.

"Of course," answered Bill. *"The Big Apple, July 13, 2025."* For just a moment Bill morphed into an adjacent seat, wearing a dark brown suit and blood red power tie—both antiques from the turn of the century. *"Focus on the here and now,"* he said.

"Are you still with us?"

Simon blinked and Bill vanished. Mears stared at him. "Yes," he said slowly. "After the Ten Degree he was the number two man at the FBI from '36 through '48, running the show as directors came and went. He knows where the bodies are buried." Simon did not elaborate, Bill insisting that Sutherland had been *personally* responsible for some of those bodies. "He could pull enough strings to get CUSP."

"True," said Mears.

"What happened to his daughter was obviously no accident. It was an engineered plan to get his daughter interfaced to CUSP," said Simon.

"Never," said Garvey. "Sutherland is a Pure to the point of being a fanatic. Not only did he oppose you," he said, giving Simon a disgusted look, "but fought funding and development of CUSP through each and every budget cycle. He'd never risk the life of his daughter to interface her to CUSP."

Simon hated to find himself in agreement with Garvey, but he knew what he'd said was true and nodded at Mears. "They're both phobic about any modifications, structural and genetic. I've gone over Sarah Sutherland's medical history. From a genetic perspective it's a nightmare. She has genetic predispositions for excessive violence, hyper risk taking, exceedingly low inhibition thresholds, and potential for extreme paranoia. All of those characteristics could have been corrected in utero, but the general refused."

"Some consider it immoral to correct for mere personality issues," said Mears.

"But she's dyslexic, nearsighted, and her right auditory canal is so congenitally malformed that she can barely hear on her right side. Those are straight medical issues, all of which could have been corrected in utero. They are phobic when it comes to any modifications."

Mears nodded. "And the conundrum you find yourself

with is how could such a man, one who refused to correct something as basic as hearing or eyesight in his own child, engineer a plot to blow out the back of her head for the express purpose of having her interfaced to CUSP. How might you reconcile those two seemingly conflicting perspectives?"

Simon could come to only one conclusion. "He's a fanatic. He's tried to stop CUSP but has been unable to. Now he'll try to tear it down from the inside, willing to kill his own daughter to get it done."

"No one's that crazy," said Garvey.

Mears stood, nodding. "Crazy enough that it *might* even be true. This is a dangerous game we'll be playing, but the cards have been dealt, and we will play this hand. If Sutherland believes that he can use what we've developed to destroy us, we'll turn the tables on him and use his own daughter to remove him once and for all."

Bill materialized on the conference room table, sitting cross-legged, facing Simon. He shook his head. *"Don't you know anything about politics, about history? Sutherland's opposition to CUSP did not destroy it—it mobilized groups eager to back anything he opposed. Until Sutherland declared war on CUSP, there was no one with the power to make this program real. Sutherland created CUSP."*

Simon blinked.

"How do you think you came into being? Who was it that opposed our creation?" asked Bill.

"General Sutherland," said Simon in disbelief.

"Business 101, my brilliant idiot," said Bill. *"Why spend the resources and time to build something yourself, when you can manipulate others into building it with their money and resources. Once complete, then you swoop down and take it for yourself."* Bill

grinned and pushed the bridge of his black-rimmed glasses up his nose. *"Did it myself on more than one occasion."*

Simon blinked again.

"But of course to implement such a strategy effectively, one needs inside information, to report back, to make sure that those outside forces are shaping and moving the project in the desired manner," said Bill.

Simon looked across the table at Garvey.

"You've come so far, Simon," said Bill. *"But a long road still lies ahead of you."*

"CUSP," said General Sutherland, shaking his head and sneering, *"Controllable Universal Sentient Plasma."* He sat alone, at the far end of the long conference table, facing Mears, Garvey, and Simon, who sat huddled at the other end. "Words can be so damn powerful," he said, sounding thoughtful. "Of all the words to choose for your abomination, *controllable* is just what CUSP is not, but using that word is enough to make half the brain-dead in Congress and the UN believe that what you've built here might be safe and understandable, and actually be controlled if it goes Post-Point."

"And it will be," said Mears.

"You've built a goddamned gun aimed squarely at the head of every human on this planet, and you're doing everything in your power to pull the trigger. You couldn't be content with the creation of that abomination," he said, pointing at Simon, "but now you want to go light-years farther, interfacing a human to a machine that makes the one Simon's interfaced to look like an abacus in comparison."

"And that threatens you?" Mears asked.

"Damn right it threatens me, you smug son of a bitch. What will we be in comparison to it—bugs forced to hide in the shadows so it doesn't step on us?"

"You are projecting your own fears," said Mears, who swatted at something on the table. "It will be our partner in building a magnificent new world, and if for some reason it proves to be unstable in some manner, we have the power simply to unplug it."

"I take such comfort in your assurances," said Sutherland. He stood and leaned forward. "I've known thousands of scientists like you, all so eager to plug in their latest creations, but it inevitably comes down to some son of a bitch like me to unplug the goddamned things, and let me tell you, it's been my experience that it is a hell of a lot harder to unplug than to plug."

Mears sat back in his chair and laced his fingers across his little potbelly. "If that is how you feel, General, then why are you here? Why is your daughter laid out in my operating room at this very moment?"

Sutherland sat back down. "She's dead, and I want her back," he said, not looking at Mears, but at Simon. "I'd go to Hell and deal with the Devil to get Sarah back."

"Excellent," said Mears.

"But I am also here to get acquainted with a comrade in arms who has kept me updated on this little CUSP project of yours."

Mears sat farther forward, leaning on the table. "What?" he said, looking around the table, focusing not on Sutherland but on Garvey. He stood and slammed his open hands against the table "What in the hell have you been doing behind my back!"

Garvey shrank down into his chair. "I've never even met the General before," said Garvey. "I'd never violate security protocols." Reaching up, he pointed across the table. "It's Simon. I told you he couldn't be trusted."

Mears slowly turned, focusing on Simon. "Don't be an idiot," he said to Garvey. "Up until a year ago he could barely count his toes." Mears squinted, staring at Simon, as if trying to look through him.

"Watch and learn, my brilliant idiot," Bill said to Simon.

"You really in there, *Bill?*" asked Sutherland.

All eyes turned toward Simon. But Simon was no longer quite there. Not asleep and dreaming, as when Bill normally took control, but somehow in the background, observing, fully aware, peering through his own eyes, but eyes that were no longer under his control.

"Nice to finally have a meat-to-meat, Thomas," said Bill.

General Sutherland nodded. "You've moved Simon along quickly, but CUSP is only marginally ready for system integration." He paused. "We're talking about my daughter here, Bill. You guaranteed that there'd be no permanent damage."

"What the hell is going on?" asked Mears in a sputter. "Bill is just a Jinni, probably the most sophisticated Jinni ever built, but still just a Jinni."

"Quiet!" said Sutherland. "You are so far out of your depth that anything you could say is totally irrelevant."

Mears opened his mouth, obviously trying to speak, but nothing came out. He looked across the table at Garvey, whose head was turning left-right-left, jerking back and forth between Simon and Sutherland. At that moment Mears understood just how Garvey must have felt all those past years as he'd kicked him about, never letting an opportunity pass to let him know exactly how little he thought of him.

"System integration is not an issue," said Bill. "Despite Dr. Mears's numerous and annoying inadequacies, there is no one better to operate on Sarah. Hardware is not an issue, and of course Sarah will provide excellent software. What will take time is personality resurfacing and synthesis with the CUSP persona."

Sutherland pointed a finger at Bill, his expression darkening. "You remember what I just told our friend here about it being my job to pull plugs. If I don't get Sarah back, it will be your plug that I'll be coming after."

Bill nodded. "You'll get her back. Failure is not an option."

"It damn well better not be," said Sutherland. "Because it looks like the clock has started. The Phobos situation is starting to come to a head."

"Is Akandi still alive?" asked Bill.

"Of course," said Sutherland, then he paused, his eyes momentarily focusing somewhere far away. "He must be." Then he refocused on Simon's body. "He had a quick meeting with Chan, at the conclusion of which Chan took a welding torch to his chest."

"And the nature of the meeting?" asked Bill.

"Apparently paper files were involved, which Akandi took with him *into* Phobos. Dissection of Chan's Doll indicated that the topic of our *distant* neighbors was brought up."

"What are you talking about?" asked Mears.

Both Sutherland and Simon turned, stared at Mears, the intensity in their expressions enough to cause him to sink into his chair.

"And the Kristensen situation?" asked Bill.

Sutherland shook his head. "He made contact."

Bill sat Simon's body down, lowering his hands to the tabletop. "It's moving faster than we ever thought possible," he said. He turned toward Mears, shaking his head. "Now we're depending on you to pull our collective asses out of the fire."

Mears opened his mouth, but again said nothing.

Sutherland stood. "I want to see my daughter before you operate on her." He marched across the room, almost reached the door, then turned and pointed at Garvey. "Give this pathetic sack of shit a big enough jolt across the temples to erase not only what he's heard here but everything else short of how to wipe his own ass."

Garvey went pale, opened his mouth, and mumbled something that the others could not hear.

"With pleasure," said Bill.

Chapter 10

Deep inside Phobos, Akandi sat on a rock. The air smelled of pine, decay, mold, and moisture. Somewhere to his left, beyond the edge of the clearing, far back within the thicket of pines, a shriek accompanied the splintering of wood, and a half dozen birdlike creatures, their partially feathered leathery wings glimmering like iridescent rainbows, shot up out of the canopy, quickly vanishing in the glare of the sun.

"You might want to consider moving to the edge of the clearing and resting in the shade," said Iyoon. *"Dehydration may become a real concern in this excessive heat and humidity."*

Akandi angled back his neck and looked up into the sky,

past the sun. He estimated that the other side of this inside-out world lay roughly 4 kilometers away, and the band of *sun*, a thin filament of flaring plasma, floating in the null-gee axis of the hollowed-out center of Phobos, blazed down on him. Nearly 10 kilometers in length, he knew that the inner cylinder filling Phobos must be slowly rotating, the centrifugal force it generated feeling like a full gee.

He sat at the center of a small clearing, within a palm-pine forest, the thick grass of the clearing matted in places, nibbled down to the roots in others, the clearing strewn with shattered bones and massive piles of animal droppings, some solidified into boulderlike mounds, others so fresh that puddles of yellow-green urine pooled around them.

"Located."

Akandi looked down. His *helper* scuttled up next to his right leg—a crablike thing, with twenty-four multiseg-mented legs, a spherical core body, and an array of mandibles where a face should be, holding on to a bone fragment that it angled up toward him. Tendons and even a bit of sun-dried meat hung from one jagged end of the bone. Its mandibles twitched, and a couple of pincer tips pushed the end of the bone and a bit of gristle into its little toothy mouth. "Ambassador McCarthy," it said.

A ghostlike image of the white-haired, statesman mate-rialized between Akandi and his helper, the shattered bone the crab held overlaying the ghost-femur of McCarthy's right leg. Entwined strands of DNA floated above McCarthy, with nearly 100 filamentary markers connecting the two structures, matching key genes and unique poly-morphisms.

"Definitely McCarthy," said the crab, pulling the bone from the ghost and sucking on it again. "I found nearly a dozen of his bone fragments, most of which showed evidence of teeth and claw marks."

Akandi shrugged, already overloaded by his rapid transport into Phobos, cycling through load locks, bombarded by decontaminators, both external and internal, the arrival of the crab helper, then one final door leading to this world.

The Powers had told him of this place, of the world inside Phobos, but being told and actually seeing it were two entirely different things. *An amazing and totally unbelievable thing,* he thought as he looked toward the jungle, but what was actually filling his mind, what it was that he couldn't even begin to comprehend, was the latest impossibility that had just been presented to him.

Alpha Centauri A.

Over 200 worlds.

Could it be true, were the documents real? Akandi had no way to verify any of it. It seemed impossible, but so had Phobos when he had first been told of it. Again he stared toward the wall of the jungle, watching a reptile-bird preen at its feathers with a toothy beak.

Of course something had *built* Phobos. Possibly something from one of those 200 worlds? The crab paced in front of him, the bone still held in its mandibles. Akandi forced himself to focus on the mystery at hand.

"*Your helper leaks data at an excessive rate,*" said Iyoon, flicking into Akandi's field of vision, floating above the crab. "*This device was used by Ambassador McCarthy during his visits, and some of that information is still accessible, items that McCarthy apparently considered significant.*"

"Such as?" said Akandi, wiping at the sweat dripping down his face.

"*Extensive genetic sampling of the flora and fauna of this world. McCarthy ran detailed DNA linear regressions from a wide range of Earth flora and fauna, comparing them to what is living here."*

Iyoon paused, its spin slightly slowing, its dull gray sides momentarily flashing oil-on-water rainbows. Akandi recognized the signs of Iyoon's emotional states, the rainbow flash a sign of excitement.

And fear.

"DNA analysis shows that this flora and fauna are from Earth circa 60 to 70 million years ago. While this is not unexpected, based on the information relayed to you from the Powers, the most interesting aspect of it is that it replicates that world exactly. There has been no subsequent genetic drift or modification, such as would have taken place over the natural course of evolution. I would suspect that while this world is a direct analog to that of Earth 70 million years ago, this ecosystem has been alive within Phobos for no more than a few centuries."

"All of this done to Phobos within the last few hundred years?" asked Akandi, not believing that possible. He'd seen the pockmarked world on approach, a barren and blasted rock, obviously ancient and just as obviously untouched. "The surface showed nothing to indicate such recent activity.

Iyoon sparkled with rainbows. *"The evidence is there if you look closely, but not in the recent past. There is an obvious surface disturbance that occurred some 50 to 100 million years ago, and then was concealed by a swarm of small impacts. One could conclude that the basic internal structure was built then, the flora and fauna of Earth brought here, but held in some form of stasis, then activated within the last few hundred years."*

"But why?"

Iyoon shifted, pulling Akandi's gaze as it floated toward the far end of the clearing. *"This might provide some answers."*

This stood at the edge of the clearing, its green-brown skin blending in perfectly with the underbrush, the only things making it at all visible the slow rise and fall of its chest and the bright white teeth that filled its snout. Only a bit more than 1 meter high, it stood on two powerful back legs, and had a tail that disappeared into the brush. Its toes were equipped with talons, and each foot was adorned with a vicious-looking inside talon nearly 10 centimeters long. Its arms were short and muscled, and its hands squat and compressed, with three fingers and an opposable thumb, the entire hand and arm structure looking out of place, as if added on as an afterthought. A sleek, triangular face, almost all snout and full of teeth, dominated its head, with relatively small black eyes sunk back beneath a bony brow. Atop its head, wedged against the skull, sat a dark dome, tinted the same color as its skin, *almost* seamlessly attached.

"A dinosaur," said Iyoon. "*Appears to be a variant of a* Dromocreasauris *from the late Cretaceous, but the arms and hands are certainly not original equipment, and I would suspect that the structure on top of its head is some form of neural augmentation.*"

"Dangerous?" whispered Akandi.

"*It's what ate McCarthy,*" said Iyoon. "*Spread in tooth spacing and residual pheromones and DNA fragments indicate to a high degree of certainty that if it was not this dinosaur, it was a close relative.*"

Akandi slowly stood up, suddenly wanting to appear as tall as possible.

Both the Powers and the Swirl had told him that there were dinosaurs in Phobos. He found that this preparation was not a help. He slowly held his hands out, palms in the direction of the dinosaur. He did not look it directly in the eye, afraid that such overt contact might be taken as a threat, but focused instead on the dome atop its head, hoping that if Iyoon were correct, if the dome was some form of neural augmentation, then perhaps it would see him as something more than a meal.

"I am Akandi," he said.

The dinosaur lurched forward, clearing the 10 meters between them in two rapid bounds, landing directly in front of Akandi, raising its snout, nostrils flaring, twin streams of air whistling out of them, playing across Akandi's face. Raising its right hand, it reached for him.

Akandi held his ground, did not flinch. In an act of defiance and bravado, knowing this thing could easily bite through his neck with a snap of its jaws, he angled himself toward the dinosaur, meeting its right hand as it brushed up against his chin.

The skin felt cool and smooth against his.

The dinosaur took half a step back, its mouth opening several centimeters, twin lines of drool running from its front teeth, dribbling to the ground. "Pure or Tool?"

Akandi blinked several times. The voice had echoed up from somewhere deep in the dinosaur's throat, sounding disembodied and artificial, as if mechanically synthesized.

"Tool," he said in a whisper, not knowing what answer it *wanted* to hear. "Adebisi Akandi."

"Akandi," said the dinosaur, moving its head back up. "Position?" it asked.

"What is it asking?" Akandi asked Iyoon.

"Not sufficient information to understand," said Iyoon, as it darted about the dinosaur. *"But you need to answer it. I'm detecting an overall rise in muscle tension, increased heart rate, and I believe that it is marking its territory."*

Akandi glanced down. A steady stream of urine squirted out from a slit between its legs, puddling in the dirt.

"Ambassador," said Akandi, looking up from the pool of urine and focusing on the nearest black-marble eyeball.

"Drom, alpha male," said the dinosaur.

"*It is a* Dromocreasauris *variant,*" said Iyoon. "*But more importantly, it considers itself a dominant male, an alpha. He may attack if he perceives you as a threat, or as challenging him. I suggest a restrained display of subservience. But not too much—you don't want to be eaten.*"

Certainly not, thought Akandi, and he slowly lowered his head, while maintaining eye contact with the dinosaur, not at all certain how to demonstrate a subservient posture to a dinosaur.

"*Heart rate dropping,*" said Iyoon.

"You will operate this craft and take us home."

Akandi looked up and could sense that Iyoon was seeing his thoughts form even before he was consciously aware of them. "*One would assume that the home he is referring to is Earth, and one would further assume that he had probably made a similar request of Ambassador McCarthy. This dinosaur never made it to Earth and McCarthy was eaten. I recommend extreme caution.*"

"McCarthy refused to bring *us* back to Earth," said the dinosaur. "It is your reason for being. You are to return us to the world!"

"*Systems ramping again, heart rate increasing, and a spike in electrical activity within the structure on his head. He is about to do something very physical.*"

"Show me what you want done," Akandi said diplomatically, not telling the dinosaur that he would actually do anything.

"This information should have already been relayed to you," said the dinosaur.

Akandi did not want to dispute what the dinosaur told

him. "And this information would have come to me in what manner?" he asked.

The dinosaur stepped forward, lowering his head, placing his snout only centimeters away from Akandi's face. "The Swirl has sent it. Has it not informed you of the task you must perform?"

Akandi blinked, backstepped, tripped over his own feet, and fell. In the 20 years that the Swirl had occupied his head, had gently manipulated and guided him along the path that had eventually brought him to Phobos, he had never spoken its name—had been incapable of revealing its existence.

Now a dinosaur had said its name.

"The Swirl has sent you to bring us home."

"To Earth?" asked Akandi.

The dinosaur lurched forward, his snout punching Akandi in the chest, driving him to the ground. "Yes," he said. "To stop those who would steal the world."

Chapter II

She could barely see through the wire gauze wrapped around her head, her movements hindered by the long conducting strands that ran from it, scraping along the metal pipe she crawled through. The contraption damped the transmitter signal coming from the neuralware in the back of her skull, the built-in beacon standard cop issue, a safety and security device the Powers insisted upon.

The perfect tracking device.

Above her, at street level and beyond, Padmini heard sirens scream and the background roar of fleets of microrotators scouring the rooftops. They'd be sniffing and snooping, checking heat signatures, breathing in every windblown DNA snippet. The Dolls had kept her below street level, even below sewer level, traveling through the remnants of old infrastructure—water, electrical, but mostly the old high-pressure gas lines that had been abandoned decades earlier.

She peered through a thick wire screen and a polarized sheet of mylar, both pushed up against a blown-out cinder block. A Doll stood on each side of her, small electric fans in their hands, the breeze beating at her face, ensuring that whatever organics leaked from her body were flushed back into the old gas pipeline and not to the street beyond.

A flock of microrotators, their wings a nearly invisible blur, and rat-sized bodies studded with a wide arrangement of antenna receivers and transmitters, raced by in a tight V-formation, their high-pitched whine dropping in frequency as they passed. The street was empty, no vehicles, no pedestrians, and her view was of a 10-meter-tall mound of bricks and rusted girders—all that remained of an imploded building across the street. The location looked familiar, but she couldn't quite place it.

"We're in what used to be the parking garage below Leo's loft," said Kali.

"It's only a matter of time before something catches my scent," said Padmini, amazed that she'd gotten this far, remaining untouched for nearly 15 minutes after Barnwell had been killed.

"More than amazing."

Padmini turned. Behind the Dolls, farther down the

throat of the ruptured gas line, Kali crouched on all fours, the nipples of her pendulous breasts scraping the bottom of the pipe. *"There's enough residual dust in this part of Philly to track any cockroach they choose to lock onto."*

Padmini looked down at the palms of her hands, at the grime, oil, and grease that coated them. Intelligent dust would be far too small to see; optics, transmitters, data crunchers could be packed into a mote less than the size of a grain of sand. The military had saturated the city with the dust during the time of the Collapse, after the Rings had sprouted. At that time everything had been tracked, including cockroaches and the viral loads that several Doomsday cults had incubated in their guts.

"But the dust has gone dormant, most of the radionucleotides used to power the motes long past their half-lives, If it still worked, *we'd* have been using it."

"We," said Kali, smiling, exposing her razor-filed teeth. *"The Philly cops are far down the food chain. The chatter I'm picking up appears to be random fluff, but if you multiplex enough signals and integrate the droppings squeezed between frames, you can sense a pattern. You've been tracked every step of the way."*

"Then why haven't I been picked up?"

"For the moment, you're sufficiently damped and grounded," said the nearest Doll. "But eventually they'll pick up something that leaks through."

Kali shook her head. *"You're being played. The cops haven't picked up your electromagnetic scent, but others have. There are multiple players here, and the strongest wanted you to get this far, to get to Leo's."*

The Doll nearest Padmini pushed at her. "Out of the pipe and into the back of the basement," it said.

Padmini crawled out and kept low, scrambling over rusted debris. The parking structure was a graveyard of cars that were 20 years obsolete, gasoline-powered, their tires eaten, the hulks resting on axles.

"To the back, by the Cadillac against the far wall," said a Doll.

Padmini did not know a Cadillac from a Bush Tank, but Kali locked in, morphing a green track through the debris that led to a particularly large rusting pile of metal against the far corner of the basement wall. A Doll reached it first, got down on all fours, and started to squirm under the car.

"I'll never be able to crawl under . . ." She had no time to finish what she was saying, as the entire rusted hulk shifted, lifting up on an unseen hinge, revealing what looked like a just-poured slab of concrete.

"It needs to read you," said a Doll, pushing her forward.

Padmini got down on all fours to move under the partially upended car and stopped when she came to the center of the open patch of concrete. The Doll climbed up on her back and pushed her head toward the floor.

"Down, flat," it said, as it pulled the metal mesh screen from her head.

Padmini lowered her forehead to the floor and felt a faint vibration in her skull that quickly rose to a silent crescendo and rattled her teeth. The palms of her hands tickled, and she knew that snips had been sampled, pulled right through the concrete.

"A neural web map is being taken," said Kali. "Very high resolution, right down to short X-ray pulses, and full spectrographic organic detection probably able to quantify synaptic ion spreads. Very advanced technology, several generations out from what the precinct has access to."

If that last comment was meant to put Padmini at ease, it didn't. She knew the department, how it worked, and how it would kill. What she didn't know was who lurked behind the Dolls, and who could have possibly installed this equipment in Leo's obviously not-so-abandoned basement.

"Up!" said the Doll on her back, pulling her by the neck, just as the concrete beneath her face began to bubble, thin, and pull itself back, revealing a small opening that gave way to a rapidly growing hole revealing a staircase leading down into the darkness.

"Get in quick," said a voice that Padmini recognized as Leo's. But she knew that meant nothing since anyone could synthesize a voice. Padmini squirmed back, not willing to walk into the hole, into total darkness. "Move that size 8 ass of yours," said Leo's voice.

Padmini smiled, pure reflex. Leo was dead, but she knew that some remnant, some stored facet of him, lurked in this hole. "Size 6," she said, and, turning, backed down the stairs.

Sleek black racks hummed, ghosts flickered, pheromones heavy with data drifted through the thick informational haze. Padmini stood in the corner, carefully examining the room that she recognized as some sort of Void node.

"Put it back on," said the Doll.

Padmini did not argue, and as she slipped the metal gauze back over her head, the air cleared, the ghosts receding, the heavy scents fading. Black rack after black rack clung to the walls of the bunker. No logos, no model numbers, no corporate stripes of IDs. Black on black on black.

The Dolls suddenly skittered away, running through the only exit, a doorway that led to something that Padmini thought might be living quarters. An old wooden table and a small bed were visible. She started to move toward them.

"It's all military equipment."

She turned. Leo Barnwell stood at the far end of the Node room, with Kali right next to him, one of her eight arms reaching out for him, touching him on the forehead, her fingers passing effortlessly through skin and bone, probing knuckle deep. His eyelids fluttered for a moment, then Kali vanished.

"It was fast," he said, sitting back in an overstuffed, leather-covered monster of a chair that had not been there an instant before. "I was dead before I knew I was dead, the signal termination from my organic self nearly instantaneous."

Padmini nodded. The ghost was good, very lifelike, even if this Leo Barnwell appeared to be at least 4 or 5 centimeters taller and at least 10 kilos of very solid-looking muscle heavier. And younger, too, by at least 20 years.

"As I saw myself," explained Leo. "There are the obvious questions, Mini," he said, "the who, what, when, and where's of Leo Barnwell's real life. I've passed that all on to Kali, and she'll fill you in with whatever you need to know. Little of that is important at the moment."

Padmini lowered herself to the floor, sitting cross-legged.

"But there are a couple of important things that I do want to tell you." He leaned back in his chair. "The first is that you were a good friend, my best friend."

Padmini nodded, wanting to say something but finding herself unable to talk, the last 15 minutes having been pure reflex and focused escape. But now the weight of what had happened was descending upon her, smothering her.

Leo was dead.

"But you already knew that," he said.

She nodded, and wiped at a tear than ran from the corner of her right eye.

"I suspected that my time was short, that this facility would *soon be compromised. That's why I've had the Dolls following us for nearly 6 months, waiting to bring you here in case I was killed. Had them lugging that portable Faraday cage around, always ready to set it up and EMP the local landscape in case things went really wrong."*

Things went really wrong, she thought. "But who would want you killed?"

Barnwell smiled. *"I thought I knew—thought I understood the political landscape. But I guess I didn't look deep enough. I thought it would be the Powers that were closing in, getting ready to shut me and this node down."*

"Why would the Powers want you dead?" She paused, realizing that there could be any number of reasons why the Powers might want anyone dead. She'd asked the wrong question. "If they wanted you dead, then why not just make you dead? There must have been hundreds of easier ways they could have framed me for your death."

Barnwell smiled. *"I can hear the wheels turning."*

"So the Powers didn't kill you and didn't frame me," she said, focusing not so much on the murder itself but on the information manipulation, the ability to reach out into the Void and reconfigure a nearly infinite number of bits—and do it all in real time. "Who would be powerful enough to manipulate the Void in that way?"

"Very warm," said Barnwell.

"More powerful than the Powers," she said, not believing that anyone, or for that matter *anything*, could be more powerful than the Powers.

"I do believe you're burning up."

"That's impossible," she said, suddenly knowing where Barnwell was leading her. "They tried and tried—more computers, more speed, more nodes, more bandwidth, and nothing ever woke up. The code just couldn't be written to create an inorganic sentient. 'The Void can't go Post-Point,'" she quoted. "They tried for 20 years to do it, and got nothing but faster and faster networks that slipped into psychoses."

"True, so true," said Barnwell. *"But it turned out they didn't have to write the software, it was already in place, had been for a very long, long, long time."* Reaching up he patted the side of his head. *"It happened about halfway through the Ten Degree War. Better than 5,000 deep operatives worked the battlefield, mobile input for the neo-Void, each of us providing the software."* Again he tapped the side of his head. *"The Void didn't wake, didn't go Post-Point. We were already awake, as 5,000 individuals. Then they hard-linked us, the objective being to get an interactive, integrated gestalt of a battlefield that ran from the Atlantic to the Indian Ocean. And suddenly we stopped being just the eyes, ears, and noses for the generals fighting the war, and became the senses and software for the Void itself."*

"And *you* became what?" she asked.

"Nothing more than I already had been. But now the Void could use each of us as a node. Few of us even recognized that a change had taken place, until we began to sense that what we were seeing, hearing, and sensing was being manipulated, and in some cases totally fabricated." He pointed two fingers at his eyes. *"But between the information coming in, then being sent upstream"*—he patted the back of his head—*"things were being changed. The Void had its own agenda."*

To her left, at the edge of her vision, a rainbow shimmered, a twirling cone of light. She turned toward it, feeling a cold, faint breeze blowing from it. *"I am the Swirl,"* echoed a voice in her head.

"That's it?" she asked, pointing at the light and turning back to Leo.

He nodded. *"It's how it presents itself, an icon it finds convenient to use. It has no real physical form outside of the minds that house it. Yours now being one of them."*

"No," said Padmini, shaking her head. "My firewalls are intact. Kali would never let it enter."

Barnwell smiled. *"Nothing can stop it, not you or Kali. It's inside you, and now you're a part of it."*

"Impossible," said Padmini, taking a step toward it, then stopping as she remembered that something had altered the data stream showing what she'd done to Barnwell, a torrent of data that she had thought incorruptible.

"It has you," said Barnwell.

"Prove it!" shouted Padmini defiantly.

"Say its name aloud. It told you what it was called. It won't let you say its name."

Padmini smiled and her lips parted. But nothing more happened, no words came out. The look of defiance gave way to fear, then quickly to anger. "You gave me up to this . . ." Again the words would not come out.

"I had no choice," he said. *"It no longer wanted me and wanted you instead."*

"No," said Padmini. "It doesn't make sense. Such a thing would be all-powerful, would have ripped through the Void and controlled every Tool it touched. But it stays hidden, doesn't do much of anything that I can tell. Why's it hiding?"

"Possibly frightened," said Barnwell.

"Of what?" asked Padmini, not believing that such an entity would have anything to be frightened of.

"Of what created the Rings and fired the stellar Jet."

Padmini slowly nodded. That was a reason to keep your head down, so as to not get unwanted attention until you knew exactly what you were dealing with. "So why kill you?" she asked.

"Because it needs you, needs you to run, to go someplace else, to become something that Padmini Sundaram could have never become as long as she lived in Philly and partnered with Leo Barnwell."

She stood, ready to turn and walk, the overload too intense, but she knew there was nowhere to walk to. "I don't believe in it," she said, pointing over at the spinning light. But something had manipulated the snip stream, killed Leo, and just as effectively killed her in the process.

Swirl, she thought.

"Your murder's been strewn throughout the Void, been imprinted on God only knows how many brains. I'm dead and nothing can change that, not even . . ." Again she couldn't say its name.

Barnwell slowly shook his head. *"You're saturated by the Void now; it's where you live."* He stomped the ground for effect, and Padmini felt slightly queasy, this fabrication, pounding at the ground, a thing of snips and bits telling her what was real and not real. *"It can rewrite your memories."*

Padmini shook her head, numb.

"But I doubt that it would bother to do that to you and the other Tools. There are too many that it can't touch, all those Pures. The Pures have seen you kill me. That reality now resides in their organic-only brains, and the Swirl can't rewrite what's in their skulls—their memories are absolute and untouchable. You killed a cop. Everyone knows that."

"Then why bring me here? I'm dead."

"Quite true," said a voice behind Padmini.

She turned, crouching, pulling into a defensive posture. She didn't breathe, didn't blink, and focused all her senses. *Real,* she thought, knowing this person standing before her was not being generated by a snip stream forced into her optical cortex, but from old-fashioned photons bouncing off blood and bones.

A machine could not have told the difference, input just being input, but a person still knew when she faced a person, something at the very core of a meat-to-meat. That was too fundamental for a machine to simulate.

"What have you done, Barnwell?" she asked, not moving.

"*I'd like you to meet Padmini Sundaram,*" said Barnwell.

The woman standing before Padmini bowed her head.

"*Although anatomically and cosmetically an exact duplicate of you, enough base pairs have been snipped and clipped that to a sniffer she wouldn't register as you.*"

"And why that difference?" asked Padmini, keeping a close watch on her double. "I'm assuming she is intended as bait? Toss her on the street, and she'll be dead in a matter of seconds, splattered down the block."

"*True enough,*" said Barnwell.

"And a few seconds after she gets carbonized, the sniffers will know that she wasn't me, just a construction." Padmini paused, staring into her own eyes, her own face. "A damn good construction."

"*Not a construction,*" said Barnwell. "*Padmini Sundaram stands before you.*" He motioned to a portable sniffer that hung from the nearest rack, obviously put there for just this moment. "*Check her out.*"

Without averting her gaze from the construct, Padmini pulled down the sniffer, waving its tapered end at her double. Kali materialized between them, a gossamer image that Padmini could see through. "*I've checked, multiple times,*" said Kali, looking at the construct and then back to Padmini. "*She registers as Padmini Sundaram.*"

"So she *is* an exact DNA dup," said Padmini.

"No," said Kali. "I've sniffed you as well. You do not register as Padmini Sundaram. In fact, you do not register as any known person."

"Impossible," said Padmini.

"You show no identity," said Kali.

Padmini almost said "Impossible" again, but stopped herself. The Void had shown that she had killed Barnwell, and now the Void was telling Kali that she didn't exist. What was the point? "Are you telling me that all the Void's been reconfigured to recognize this construct as me, while my DNA and identity have been purged?" She turned, now willing to ignore the construct. "The *entire* Void?"

"Exactly," said Barnwell. "The precinct will recognize her as Padmini Sundaram. When killed, her corpse will be identified as yours, then you will be free to go, to assume a new identity."

"And just who will that be?" asked Padmini.

"The Void will inform Kali, and Kali will let you know. Being dead, I'm no longer in the loop. But I have my suspicions. You're in for a little trip to the southeast, to the other side of the Ring, and into the Ag-lands. There is a package to be delivered." He pointed to one of the nearby black racks, and a small brown box sitting atop it. "Very important."

"Important enough to have you killed? Important enough to destroy my life?" she asked.

Barnwell shrugged. "So it thinks."

It.

Padmini studied him for a long minute. "No matter what you've made this thing look like," she said, pointing at the construct, "no matter how you've managed to manipulate the Void, the precinct will still be looking for me after they've cooked your construct. It will be missing a key ingredient." Reaching up, she pounded at the back of her head, at the mesh screen, reminding Leo's ghost of the beacon buried deep in her brain.

"The last item," said Barnwell, and his voice was odd.

Padmini turned, but not fast enough. Her double stood next to her, a broad-spectrum neural disrupter in the open palm of her hand that she pushed up against Padmini's forehead. She smelled bacon frying and rubber burning, felt the muscles in her toes cramp and her butt spasm. Then darkness.

Chapter 12

Simon sat in the fishbowl, waiting for Sarah to wake. The Powers wanted the most advanced ultra-Tool at their disposal to be there in case Sarah's transformation did not proceed according to plan.

She'd been interfaced to CUSP, the software defined by the wiring in her brain intended to drive CUSP's hardware, to push it far past the realm of only being able to move Dolls about the chaos generated in a lab. And at the same time, she'd be given the intrinsic abilities of CUSP's hardware, an ability to see pattern where no organic mind could detect it; the ability to instigate the most insignificant cause and generate intended effects of possible earth-shattering magnitude.

If Sarah successfully integrated with CUSP, Mears believed that she would transit the Point, to become the first truly Post-Human, something with abilities beyond their comprehension. But Simon had his doubts. Mears had believed that same thing about him when he had been interfaced to Bill, and that had resulted in little more than him being able to access the Void through a very sophisticated Jinni.

A Jinni with an attitude.

"Places, dates, lines of code, the ugly green trampoline in my office, an old pair of brown loafers, and all those games of Go." Bill half closed his eyes, crisscrossed his legs, and rose from the floor, hovering nearly a meter above its dull steel surface. *"Better than 80 years of memory, right up until October 28, 2038. It was my 83rd birthday, and I leaned forward to blow out the blaze atop my birthday cake. That's where the memories end."*

Simon paid little attention to the levitating Bill, his focus on Sarah. She lay on the gurney in front of him, dressed in a white hospital gown, with a neural inducer screwed to her shaved skull. It looked like a stainless-steel salad bowl studded with thick bundles of fiber and cable. She was shoulder deep in an HMRI, and its array of magnetic probes sliced and diced through her skull, generating the splayed image of her brain that hung above her chest, the projection slowly rotating, layer after layer of brain being cleaved, rainbow starbursts highlighting areas of activity.

"All indications are that she is still awake," echoed Mears's voice.

Simon looked up from Sarah and the gurney, past the floating Bill, up to the bank of windows that broke the wall of their stainless-steel fishbowl. Mears stared down at him, with General Sutherland at his side. The General looked dazed, a swatch of gray hair falling over his forehead, the knot of his tie loosened, the stars on his coat's right collar hanging at an off-kilter angle. Simon wondered just how much of that display was calculated, and how much was a genuine response to his daughter lying in the fishbowl. He couldn't even make a guess. At Sutherland's left stood half a dozen Tool-heavy soldiers, weapons trained at the window.

Simon shook his head.

The display window was bulletproof, but they were taking absolutely no chances. The bullets were not meant to breach the window, the guns just one more level of defense in case something escaped the fishbowl by breaking through the window from the *inside*.

Simon had serious doubts that bullets could stop anything capable of punching its way through the centimeter-thick hexatitanate-beryllium resin that made the window—the material had originally been designed by the Sinos for thrust manifolds in the nuke rockets that they shuttled back and forth to Mars. The fishbowl's stainless-steel walls, with their inside coating of high-tensile graphite, were actually weaker than the windows.

He looked back at Sarah and tried not to think about those soldiers at the window, or the other soldiers who manned the acid vat suspended above the fishbowl, those who could tip the 10,000-liter container of the hydrofluoric-hydrochloric acid mix, the concoction designed to peel meat from bone in an explosive reaction.

And those were just the local safety controls.

The CUSP hardware sat in the floor directly beneath the fishbowl right next to the Manifold that housed the bulk of the Bill Jinni—both securely snugged in their own fishbowls, quad meshed in Faraday cages to isolate them from all incoming and outgoing electromagnetics, cloaking them from even the feeble ambient Void that managed to leak through 50 meters of sand and bedrock. Not a stand of copper or fiber lay within 50 meters of CUSP, or anything else that could be used to transmit or receive signal, the only exception being the trunk line connecting CUSP to Sarah's neural transducer and the smaller neural bundle running from the Manifold to the neural inducer strapped to Simon's shaven head.

And then there were more drastic fail-safe devices, to be used if things *truly* got out of hand—an array of 20-kiloton pocket nukes that would transform the entire Ag center and the surrounding 10,000 hectares of Co-Op into a black-glass crater.

They were taking no chances on Sarah going Post-Point in an uncontrolled fashion. Absolutely no chances. Sarah had been brought up to consciousness nearly 15 hours earlier. Brain activity indicated that she was fully awake, reacting to the sound of his voice and movements.

"Time to wake up, Sarah," he whispered to her.

A surge of lightning washed through the display of her brain, then quickly damped. He was not sure that he really wanted her to wake, not certain exactly *who* it would be if she did wake. Surgery had taken place a week earlier, the synthetic cerebellum and CUSP interface implanted, graphite neural web integrating the interface to her nervous system completed, and her comatose body put through its paces, demonstrating full functionality and integration between brain and body. Even in her deep narco-induced coma, they had marched her body up and down hallways.

But now that she was conscious and awake, she would not move.

"Do you see anything?" asked Sutherland, now standing, his palms pressed up against the thick glass of the viewing window. "Anything?"

Simon shook his head, humoring the general. An entire array of IR lasers played across Sarah—the slightest microscopic movement would be picked up and displayed in the control room. But those were not the only eyes. Backup controllers, safely out of the nuke blast radius, were also monitoring the experiment, recording the movements of every molecule dancing through the fishbowl, ready to override all local controls in case Sarah flared.

Silent minutes passed.

"I don't know why he chose that moment," said Bill.

Simon looked up from Sarah, having been lulled into a near-hypnotic state by the slow rise and fall of her chest. "What moment?" asked Simon.

Bill sighed, and unfolded his legs, his feet just touching the floor. He took several steps toward Simon and the gurney. *"Why Bill chose his 83rd birthday to terminate my existence, to give me just a part of his life, of his memories. He could have given me updates, new revs."*

Simon blinked. "Ego getting the better of you? Not content to be my Jinni, but developing an agenda of your own."

Bill half shut his eyes and sneered. *"Ego has nothing to do with it."*

"Ego has everything to do with it. You were an experiment, nearly ten years in the past, the neural replication requiring Bill, the *real* Bill, to be put under for nearly a week, and his brain holographically mapped by magnetic microprobe. You've seen the reports—the old man barely came out of it. Did you really expect him to put himself through that again just so you could be revved?"

Bill sighed and shook his head. *"No,"* he said. *"But it's still only 83 years."*

Simon frowned. "And what do I have? I've been out of the coma for four years. What about before that? Who was I? What happened to me? Why did they choose me to be integrated to you?"

"Both of us forced to live lives that are not quite real," said Bill.

"And now I learn that you've been in constant contact with Sutherland, feeding him information about us and CUSP. Why would you do that?" Even more importantly, he wanted to know how he could do that—instigate such independent actions, an ability that should have been far in excess of his programmed capabilities. But Simon found himself unable to ask that question, afraid of what he might find out.

"He promised to give me my own life," said Bill in a whisper.

"You're nothing but software!" snarled Simon, the frustration that had been building in him for the last week suddenly exploding.

"The whole damned planet is on the verge of tearing itself apart just like it did 20 years ago. While you and Sutherland have been hooking her into CUSP and waiting for her to wake up and put on some Post-Human show for you, the Sun has been chattering away, spitting out torrents of mathematical gibberish in the form of magnetic belches and Morse code sunspots, with the sane people on this planet terrified that at any moment it's going to fire its Jet!"

"We are quite aware of what is going on," Mears said.

Sutherland, who had been standing the entire time, pushed his face closer to the window. "It is *all* that I am aware of, and it is *precisely* why my daughter is on that table."

Simon slowly sat back in his chair.

Bill pulled up his legs, crisscrossed them again, and hovered in the air. *"Excellent venting all around,"* he said, smiling, the middle-aged Bill replaced with a teenage Bill wearing T-shirt and frayed jeans. *"Cleared the decks and got it all out in the open."* He pointed over at Simon. *"I've resigned myself to the fact that the general has played me, and that the two of us are welded at the brainstem for the foreseeable future."* Reaching up, he touched the side of his head. *"I need you firing on all cylinders, so that when she does wake up, she doesn't absorb us like a drop of water,"* he said, pointing at Sarah. *"For me to come out on top, I need to make sure that you come out on top."*

Simon didn't believe that for a moment. He was sure that at the first opportunity Bill wouldn't hesitate to hop to a more promising, more powerful *host.* He knew that was just what he was, not an ultra-Tool, not a symbiont, but just a host for a chunk of software that would abandon him at the first opportunity when something better came along. He looked over at Sarah, certain that's what Bill wanted—he wanted Sarah Sutherland and CUSP. It had probably been the software's plan all along, why he had fed information to Sutherland, manipulating behind the scenes to ensure that he would be in this fishbowl at the moment Sarah woke, ready to latch on and ride her through the Point.

"Simon!"

Simon focused, looking away from Bill, about to look up at the window, but stopped, all his attention grabbed by the brain image hovering above Sarah. It burned in hard shades of deep violet.

"Traffic between Sarah and CUSP just took a 20-fold jump." Mears's voice echoed throughout the fishbowl.

Simon looked up at the window, seeing Sutherland with his face pushed to the glass, the soldiers with rifles ready, and knowing that the other soldiers, those manning the Vat, were ready to spill the moment their masters in the remote-control bunker gave the order.

"Two hundredfold data rate increase!" shouted Mears.

The image of the brain flared crimson, the convoluted surface of the brain flowing, then fading in a salt-and-pepper haze. The left side of Simon's face suddenly burned, and he turned just as the HMRI lurched back from Sarah, screeching along its track, worm gears stripping, the imager smashing into the side of the fishbowl, spilling its sheath of liquid nitrogen in a hiss of spewing vapor.

"*She's on fire!*" screamed Bill.

Simon jumped from his chair, reached for Sarah, but then pulled his hand back, his fingers stinging, her entire body suddenly sheathed in discharge glow, twisted arcs of lightning crackling out from her.

"*Fire!*" shouted Bill again, pointing at Sarah's head.

Simon turned.

Sarah's neural inducer glowed white-hot, and small oily flames licked across her forehead, her ears melting, globs of sizzling fat falling from them, hitting the stainless-steel gurney, hissing and skittering about like water droplets on a too-hot frying pan. She sat straight up, the trunk of cable attached to her neural inducer tearing away, thin filaments of melted plastic and fiber dribbling down her back, igniting her gown.

"Save her!" screamed Sutherland.

Simon reached forward, doubting there was anything he could do. His fingers touched the sheath of the blue-haze discharge that bathed her.

Crack!

Hurled backward, Simon crashed into the side of the fishbowl and slid down the smooth wall, leaving behind a bloody streak from a jagged gash in his forehead.

"*She's going!*" screamed Bill. "*She's punching through the Point!*"

Simon rolled over, pushing himself up. Sarah stood next to the gurney, the burned remnants of her gown around her feet. From the edge of the neural inducer, a few tendrils of smoke curled upward. To Simon, it appeared as if the inducer had been melted into her skull, with shiny rivulets of metal running down the sides of her face and neck, cutting shallow channels in her burned and blistered skin.

"Simon Ryan," she said.

Simon felt himself nod, watching her blackened lips move, amazed that such a normal-sounding voice could come from such a shattered face. He stood, swayed. And then he took half a step forward, almost within reach of her.

She smelled like burned hamburger.

The air between them distorted, a ball of mist forming, whisping tendrils of moisture twirling, spinning slowly at first, then spiraling rapidly. Next to it, only a few centimeters away, the air wavered, boiled, everything seen through it looking like flowed candle wax.

Bill winked in, standing next to the distortions, first passing a hand through the twirling mist, then through the superheated convecting sphere that was now glowing blue and spitting white flares. *"Hot and cold,"* he said.

"She's tapped into Zero Point!" shouted Sutherland.

"I doubt it," said Bill, shaking his head. *"She's twisting some thermodynamic laws and turning entropy on its head over this small, small region, but that's about it. If she'd been able to drain any energy out of regions below the vacuum level by accessing Zero Point, she would have seared this place like a large-scale nuke detonating."*

Simon blinked, and focused, willed the darkening in his peripheral vision to fade. He could smell the metal-ozone stink of the burning orb, its heat beating at his face, his eyes itching and tearing if he even tried to focus on the now-incandescent pinprick of light. Next to it, the second orb formed a frigid whirlpool of rainbow light. He reached for the icing shard, not sure why, suddenly not at all certain that he had control over his own body. Perhaps he was being forced by Sarah.

Heat flowed from his fingertips, skin tingling, a frigid breeze biting down to the bone, stiffening joints, cracking skin. His index finger, just a few centimeters from the throat of the rainbow vortex, numbed, then appeared to flow, distort, the very air around it liquefying, a spray of liquid oxygen and nitrogen sputtering from the rainbow vortex, stinging him, burning his face with pinpricks of pain.

"It *is* Zero Point!" screamed General Sutherland.

"It is CUSP!" shouted Simon, his hand moving even closer to the orbs, his index finger blistered, glistening, frozen shards of blood sparkling like rubies, while his little finger, closer to the incandescent sputtering pinprick of light, smoked, the too-pink skin starting to char.

"CUSP has gone *off-line*!" shouted Mears.

Simon shook his head. "CUSP is in the bowl," he said in a whisper, the fishbowl now filling with a roar, one building in intensity and frequency, the deep rumble ramping to a high-pitched squeal. "I can almost touch it."

Flame licked the tip of his little finger, while a frozen blood shard snapped off his index finger, taking along with it everything beyond the last joint, the flash-frozen fingertip hitting the floor. "She's brought CUSP here," he said, staring at the two orbs, one of fire and one of ice.

In the frozen rainbow sphere, where he was certain the temperature had dropped to only a few microdegrees above absolute zero, hung the CUSP processor, with its hundreds of quantum-coupled particles, searching for patterns, *thinking*. And next to it the second sphere, a miniature sun, CUSP's high-speed number cruncher, the too-hot plasma flipping quantum states billions of time faster than the best solid-state processors.

Simon knew that he stood before a now-naked and exposed CUSP—all the supporting hardware removed, the machine somehow stripped right down to the few critical atoms that defined it, these remnants now being manipulated by software infinitely more sophisticated than any that had ever existed.

Sarah Sutherland's mind.

Her face was a black mask of burned skin; even her wide-open eyes smoked a dull gray. Simon thought that she might speak, her lips moving, her chin quivering.

But she said nothing.

Instead she stepped forward, moving directly into the twin orbs. Before she hit them, Simon realized that they were exactly at her eye level, and the spacing between them was that of her eye spacing.

He tensed, braced himself, tried to pull his hand back, but it would not respond. He knew when those orbs struck her face, especially the microscopic burning sun of CUSP's plasma processor, that Sarah's head would explode, the organic shrapnel of meat and bone flashing outward.

Wide-eyed, Sarah walked into the orbs, the frozen shard and bit of burning sun hitting her square in the pupils—the harsh glare of the little sun vanishing, and the rainbow shimmer of the vortex swallowed.

Simon's burned and frozen fingers touched the bridge of Sarah's nose.

A nose of perfect pink skin.

Clank!

The neural inducer that had been melted into her skull had hit the fishbowl floor and now twirled like a spinning coin, clattering to a halt.

Simon lowered his hand, only now starting to feel the pain, nerve endings screaming, part of his hand still frozen and numb, but the burned portion, throbbing with each heartbeat, felt as if it were being slammed over and over again with a hammer. "Sarah," he said.

She blinked—once. Her smoked eyes were now pale blue. Her face, perfect and untouched, was framed by short copper red hair. Stepping back, she leaned against the edge of the gurney. Simon glanced down, watched her hands wrap around its stainless-steel struts, then saw the metal flow, her fingers sinking into the solid-steel bar.

"Oh," he mumbled as he watched her fingers slipping through what should have been a solid piece of metal. Manipulating her own body, repairing her face and regrowing hair, was not something he could understand, but something that he didn't consider outright impossible—merging with CUSP had given her abilities to control her own body at a level that no human could match. But it went far past that. She was also able to alter material external to her, merely by touching it. The rational part of him insisted that this was due to the manipulation of chemistry and physics, in a way that he simply wasn't mentally equipped to fathom, while the emotional part of him watching the metal flowing about her fingers could only describe it as *magic*.

"Are you okay, Sarah?"

Simon looked up. General Sutherland stared down at them. "Are you okay?" he shouted through the glass.

Sarah smiled, raising her left hand as if to wave at her father, and looked surprised as she saw that she was holding a half-meter length of one of the gurney's struts. The metal sagged like a limp noodle.

"She is integrating with CUSP!" shouted Simon, trying to step back but having no place to go, cradling his frozen and burned hand. Sarah turned toward him, dropping the rubbery-metal bar, the metal stiffening and returning to its original state the moment it left her fingers, hitting the floor with a clank. She reached toward Simon.

He had no time to react.

"Don't move!" she ordered, the voice coming from *inside* his head. She grabbed his damaged hand, her fingers meshing with his, in the same way that her hand had meshed with the stainless-steel bar—his hand now *flowing* into hers.

"Umph," said Simon, his knees letting go as he jerked his hand back. He dropped to the floor, trying to protect his hand. He rolled over on his back, looking past Sarah's face to the ceiling of the fishbowl, imagining the acid it about to be spilled, its contents gushing through the ceiling vent.

"Your hand is fine," she said in a whisper.

Simon held up his hand, looking at the moving fingers, unburned and unblistered, perfect, as untouched as Sarah's face. Through the fingers he saw the acid grille and wispy tendrils of condensation floating down from it.

"No!" screamed General Sutherland.

Sarah leaned to her left, her fingertips just touching the side of the fishbowl, pushing into what Simon knew should have been unyielding steel and graphite, penetrating the impenetrable material almost knuckle deep.

The acid grille above them shimmered, flowing, the openings quickly sealing themselves, until nothing remained but smooth graphite and fading acid tendrils.

Sarah pulled her hand out of the wall, stepped back, and leaned against the side of her gurney, again wrapping her hands around its steel struts. Simon pulled himself up, cradling his hand, even though it no longer hurt.

"Don't detonate," said Sarah.

Simon looked first at her, then up at the nonexistent acid grille. At that moment, he was certain that if those watching did try to detonate the nukes, nothing would happen.

Sarah had repaired his hand, repaired herself, and manipulated the fishbowl to remove the acid grille. She must have also reached the nukes.

"I'm not the threat that should be your primary concern," said Sarah.

Simon stood.

She looked at him. "There's not much time. The Sun's waking, and this time it will not shut itself down." Then her eyes glazed, coated in a glistening sheen of crystal.

Chapter 13

Padmini looked past the inspector and through the window.

A white wall filled the horizon, broken only by a latticework of metal that clung to its face—the Birmingham Transit—the elevator system that crawled up the side of the Ring, transporting cargo and people between Tech and Ag sectors. Under normal circumstances, an unbroken ribbon of elevator trains would be crawling up and down the four-kilometer face of the Ring, hauled through the metal latticework skeleton, but this morning almost nothing moved.

The half dozen North American Transits were on lockdown, with only the highest priority products and people allowed access. The normal 50-car-per-hour transport had been reduced to less than 1 per hour.

Yesterday's low-yield nuke detonation had transformed the Pensacola Transit into a pile of melted and twisted steel struts, but had left the Ring relatively untouched, and what little superficial damage had been done was quickly repairing itself. The Powers were getting anxious, the sputtering and chattering of the Sun unnerving everyone. Some radical Tool faction had taken action in an attempt to bring down the Rings before they could be activated.

Desperate and stupid.

"Everything appears to be in order."

Padmini focused on the inspector—full-suited, its Face filled with an image of the Birmingham Transit, the same scene that she would see if she turned and looked through the window.

"Body language indicates confusion and suspicion," said Kali, who sat next to Padmini.

Padmini was not surprised.

The inspector reached forward and again picked up the cube that had been sitting on the desk. Within the block of clear glass sat nestled a spherical ball of spun metal.

"DNA biocatalyst for the corn-tweakers at the Tuscaloosa Ag Co-Op," she said once more, doing her best to sound as bored and disinterested as she had the last dozen times she'd said it. "Pour broad spread DNA into the front of the filter, and the catalyst will rearrange every deviant base pair so only the purest product is passed. That little mesh can produce better than a microgram per hour."

Padmini had no idea what the device actually was, was fairly certain that it was not a biocatalyst, and suspected that the inspector couldn't tell the difference between a biocatalyst and a bowl of oatmeal. The Void was informing it that the metallic mesh was a state-of-the-art biocatalyst.

The inspector set the cube back on the desktop and looked left. Padmini carefully looked in that general direction, but not directly at the virtual display hanging in midair, the one that only the inspector should have been able to see. She could see it, too, courtesy of the deepened level of access that Kali now possessed, supplied by the manipulating Swirl.

The inspector's Face turned right-left-right. Padmini could see that the display remained unchanged, the basics of her new identity and the nature of the cargo she transported the same as the last time the inspector had requested an identity scan.

"There's corn that needs to be grown," said Padmini, the impatience in her voice real.

The inspector took half a step back. "You've been cleared for Transit. Proceed to docking for transport."

Padmini leaned forward, grabbed the cube, and stuffed it into her courier's sack. "Always a pleasure doing business with you," she said. Records would indicate that she'd been an Ag Department courier for the last 5 years, and had made the transit at Birmingham 22 times. Records showed that this same Inspector had questioned her on three earlier transits. That level of manipulation would be trivial for the Swirl.

But phantom memories, no matter how seamlessly inserted, often left a sour taste in one's head, the assemblage of rearranged neurons creating the desired memory, but the process of that rearrangement leaving behind just a hint of doubt.

She felt certain that was what the inspector had felt, those previous meetings clear and crisp in its head, but something about them not feeling quite right, quite real. That feeling had forced the cautious inspector to check her identity half a dozen times, and was apparently something beyond the ability of the Swirl to control.

"See you on the return," said Padmini as she turned toward the exit, certain that she'd never be seeing the eastern face of the North–South Ring again. Kali insisted that they were making a one-way trip—she'd been informed by the Swirl.

The inspector said nothing.

They sat on the porch's glider swing. Looking past the small dirt front yard and the faded white picket fence, Xavier stared into the thick green corn. He kept his hand in Bec's lap, holding on to both her hands. He tried to not think past the corn, past the boundaries of his 10 acres, but it was impossible.

A spiderweb of glistening thread ran from the small box next to him into his right eye, the input dumped deep into his brain, the flow gathered by the receiving box from the micro area network that permeated the farmhouse and barn.

Bec lived in the micro area network.

He'd salvaged as much of her as he could, unable to gather up everything, the cancer chewing through her brain far faster than the equipment beneath the barn could map and untangle her synaptic connections. What he'd managed to capture was her echo.

At times it was enough.

But those times were few and far between.

"You saved her," said Bec.

Xavier turned his head, looking at her, at her dark eyes, glistening and moist, so alive, so full, but he knew so totally empty, with nothing really behind them except for the memories that he supplied. She was mostly what he remembered her to be, very little of the simulation actually her. The cancer had been *so* fast.

"For the moment," he said.

Bec shook her head, and her long dark hair slid over her right shoulder. *"Mears won't risk it. He has far too much to lose."*

Bec didn't understand. It was not Mears or the Ag Co-Op he feared. It was the Rings and the Sun. They were less than 50 kilometers from the North–South Ring, and could actually hear it hum, a low-frequency drone, a vibration that for the past two days had sent the old rusted rooster weather vane atop the barn to slowly turning. And the Sun was talking—nothing that anyone could understand, but Che insisted the static bursts, and the flares it belched, showed structure and meaning beneath the chaos. The problem that had been Mears, the all-pervasive fear that Christina would end up enslaved in the Ag Co-Op, had suddenly become irrelevant.

The Rings were about to fire.

He could feel it, and the spectrum analysis that Che had been running *insisted* upon it.

"Papa?"

"The swing," he said, not looking in the direction of Christina's voice. When he sat on the swing and had the little box's input jacked, Christina knew better than to disturb him. He didn't ask for much, but when he sat on the swing, it meant that he didn't want to be disturbed. He drifted away, back to the beach and surf, to Bec diving into the waves.

"Che says that the package has reached the Birmingham Transport."

Xavier nodded, only partially listening, instead focusing on the warm surf, on Bec's long hair floating in the white water, a dark-glistening halo.

"And that Ring chatter has spiked."

Xavier turned, the image of the beach gone, cut clean as

the spiderweb linkage pulled out of his eye. He sat on the swing alone. "Spiked?" he asked, turning and looking at Christina.

Her eyes were frightened. "Che said that it spiked above all the noise."

Xavier stood, looked once at the empty part of the bench next to him, where Bec should have been sitting, then jumped up, not bothering to pull on his hip boots or grab the particulate filter that hung from its peg by the front door. The game was over. It no longer mattered who watched them or what they saw.

They were done hiding.

He jumped from the porch, clearing the dirt yard in a dozen running strides. Just as he reached the barn, as he made a grab for the well-worn handle of the sliding door, a deep rumble rose through the ground, more felt than heard, tickling his feet through the thick soles of his boots, telling him that the horizon had shifted ever so slightly.

He looked back over his shoulder.

Christina stood next to the swaying swing, looking out at the cornfield. He easily read the expression in her face, the overwhelming sense of loss that came when you knew that what you were looking at would never be the same again, had begun to change even as you watched it. The corn rustled in waves, a yellow haze of pollen rising into the air. "Come to the barn!" he shouted, then turned, not bothering to look back, knowing that Christina would obey.

Sliding the barn door open wide, he ran past the pigpens, and threw himself into the small doorway of the grain bin, pushing through its false back wall, dropping into the semi-darkness, his hands finding the pole, his legs wrapping around it as he dropped.

"What's it doing?" he screamed into the darkness.

"Full spike!" yelled Che from below.

Halfway down the pole Xavier lost his grip, the pole leaping out of his hands as the world lurched in an easterly direction by a good half meter. He smashed into the wall of the shaft and continued to fall, a part of him wondering about broken legs and ankles when he hit the bottom, and the other part knowing that a half-meter shift was insignificant compared to what would happen next.

Three kilometers up the western face of the Ring, Padmini descended slowly, staring through the Transport's glass wall at the quilt of green-and-gold fields that ran to the horizon. Never in her life had she seen such an expanse of living things, a horizon not choked with buildings and debris.

She estimated that there were more than 200 bodies stuffed into a Transport designed to handle no more than 50. Seats had been removed and all were standing, packed tight, for the 1-hour transit. Beads of sweat had condensed across her upper lip. But she couldn't easily reach up and wipe it, not without elbowing someone next to her.

She slowed her breathing and focused on the distant patchwork horizon.

"I can take the edge off," said Kali, the Jinni hovering outside the Transport, her stringy, bloody hair flying about her.

Padmini shook her head without actually moving it; the intent to shake it was enough for Kali to detect. She needed to remain focused, taking no chances that she might miss some random snip, something critical, not willing to relinquish herself to Kali at the moment, not understanding how Kali interfaced with the all-controlling sentient in the Void. She could not be certain of its true intent. If Barnwell's

ghost had been telling the truth, he'd served it, for nearly
20 years, and his reward for that loyalty had been to get the
front of his skull blown off.

She blinked.

As if it had been reading her thoughts, the little
whirlpool of light that refused to have its name spoken
aloud flashed into existence, hovering next to Kali. *Damn*,
thought Padmini.

Pattern shift.

Two hundred bodies, all with their random movements
and twitches, enough talking and murmuring to generate a
dull buzz, had collectively formed a background mosaic
that Padmini's brain had accepted as the base level for the
Transport's interior.

But that base level had suddenly shifted.

Her attention had been drawn to the face of the Ring, to
the featureless white wall less than a meter away from the
transparent far wall of their Transport car, as it slid past at
nearly 3 meters per second. Some subtle change was taking
place, below the threshold of conscious awareness.

"Hold on!" shouted Kali. The Swirl darted about her, flitting in and out of her bloody tangle of hair.

Padmini did not question, but wrapped her hands
around the guardrail that for the last 5 minutes had been
uncomfortably jammed against her waist. There was just
enough time to raise her head and give Kali a questioning
look.

The Transport car's windowed wall, less than a few centimeters from the tip of Padmini's nose, crazed, a random
network of hairline cracks exploding through it. The crowd
let out a collective wail, pitch and intensity building, everyone trying to step back from the splintering window. The
sound of a million shattering ice cubes accompanied the

window's outward explosion as the car's internal pressure suddenly overcame the weakened structural integrity of the cracking window.

A prismed haze of window shards, all spitting and sputtering rainbows, pulled away in the wind, and for a moment Padmini felt herself being sucked outward. She thought that her hands might lose their grip and that she would go over the rail to join the spinning body falling below her, the one that was already far enough away simply to be a body, no longer a person.

And then the wind slapped at her face, flooding in through the open wall of the car, slamming her back. She felt the change first in her stomach, the drop and acceleration, then the lessening of gravity as if someone were pulling her up by the shoulders. The collective scream within the car, 200 people yelling at full volume, managed barely to overwhelm of rush of the wind, but was quickly swallowed by the high-intensity roar of metal tearing away from metal, and the explosive staccato of popping rivet heads.

Her feet rose up from the floor.

The car lurched, the horizon tilting, and through the far window, still intact, the one that had been snugged to the side of the Ring, she now saw an arc of blue sky.

"The car has come loose!" shouted Kali.

Padmini watched the arc of blue widen as the car began to pivot, falling away from the face of the Ring. Steel beams, chunks of I-bar thicker than a person, twisted and torn, ragged ends glistening, flashed between the face of the Ring and the Transport. People tumbled past her, falling into midair, a hand grabbing on to her shirt, clinging for just an instant, then vanishing with her sleeve. At that moment, she knew that it was not simply that the car had come away from the Transport elevator but that the entire structure of the elevator had let go, all of it falling down the face of the Ring.

"Jump out!" screamed Kali. *"You need to clear the Transport!"*

Twisting around, Padmini looked out. The air was littered with the debris of the collapsed elevator, along with flailing bodies, and crates of all sizes—the cargo that had been stored beneath the passenger portion of the car.

"You need to clear the Transport!"

Kali hung in front of her, in free fall, her arms and legs held out, long tendrils of bloody hair, severed head necklace, and wailing fetus earrings rising up behind her, beaten by the wind. The Swirl was nowhere to be seen.

"Life-threatening emergency!"

Silence. Those three words kicked Padmini into a deep-focus mode.

The screams, the tearing of metal, the wail of the wind, even the thumping of her own heart, vanished. She could still feel the wind slamming into her face, pushing her eyeballs back into their sockets, and while most of her body had dropped into an overdrive numbness, she could still feel the cold, hard metal in her hands—the guardrail that kept her safely inside the Transport.

"Clear it now," said Kali, her voice the only sound Padmini could hear.

Panic, fear, doubt, all artifacts of surging neurotransmitters, were swept aside, purged, and dumped. Pulling up her legs, wedging her feet on the guardrail alongside her hands, she focused on Kali, nearly 20 meters in front of her. Letting go, she kicked out from the guardrail, the full force of the wind slamming her in the chest, spinning her, throwing her into a tumble.

"*Full Auto,*" said Kali.

Padmini gave an internal nod and felt her body momentarily stiffen, then totally relax as Kali took control, tapping into the same algorithms that had permitted the Jinni to autoaim her pistol, now taking full mechanical control over her entire body.

Kali was in charge. Padmini fell.

Several hundred meters beneath her, the Transport car continued to tumble and drop, hugging the side of the Ring, enmeshed in a crumbled latticework of the elevator, spewing passengers and cargo with each lurching turn it took.

Green fields jumped up at her.

"*Terminal velocity of 61 meters per second reached,*" said Kali. "*Altitude of 2,600 meters above ground. Impact in 43 seconds.*"

Padmini heard the words, and despite the fact that full control of her body had been relinquished to Kali, and her brain had been flushed of all overloaded neurotransmitters, she still shuddered head to toe.

Dead in 43 seconds, she said to herself, as her body raced toward the ground.

A steel lid, probably from a cargo container, better than 3 meters on a side, and dangling an array of straps and lines, flew toward her. The sheet of metal spun fast, its jagged corners flipping into view several times a second.

"*The Swirl has informed me of a course of action,*" said Kali.

No, Padmini wanted to scream, knowing that the last time the Swirl had implemented a course of action, Leo had been killed. She was suddenly certain it was her turn, her death just one more tick of a cog in a machine she couldn't possibly understand.

"*Objects tracking and trajectories being configured,*" said Kali.

Padmini didn't understand. The ground flew up at her.

Her body, under Kali's control, acted. Head up, arms held close to her sides, she felt her feet flutter, kicking at the air, dumping her into a spin, quickly matching the spin of the sheet of metal, suddenly the entire world spiraling around her—blue sky, green earth, white expanse of the Ring, blurred in a twirling collage.

The metal sheet hung unmoving, her rotation and its matched.

She hit it, hands grabbing on to its restraining straps, pulling her to the metal sheet, slamming into it facefirst, wrapping a strap several times around her waist, lashing it to an exposed eye bolt.

"Altitude 1,740 meters, velocity reduced to 42 meters per second, impact in 41 seconds. I have been informed that there are 347 airborne objects in this vicinity that can reach us before impact. They will be used to induce momentum transfer."

Padmini hugged the sheet of metal, the world about her spinning. The large flat surface of the sheet of metal had sufficient drag to reduce her speed to 42 meters per second, but she'd still hit the ground in 41 seconds with a velocity of a speeding train. She did not understand what Kali had meant by momentum transfer.

A streak of metal flashed to her left.

Her body stiffened, preparing itself for something that she couldn't anticipate, something that Kali knew was coming. Her right cheek cracked against the cargo lid as an object slammed against the underside of the metal, accompanied by the muffled sounds of an explosion, as yellow-orange licks of flame billowed up over the edge of the lid.

"A 2-kilogram crop surveyor with an opposed velocity of 29 meters per second," said Kali. *"The fuel cell explosion provided*

additional oppositional thrust. The Swirl has taken control of the trajectories of the remaining 346 objects within our range."

A second explosion.

Then a third.

Her head rattled, her gut lurched, the air was knocked out of her lungs, and each time she tried to suck down a breath another explosion rocked her from below. But now she understood. Aerial craft in the vicinity were being targeted to the underside of the metal sheet, slamming at it, exploding against it, each hit transferring momentum, attempting to push the metal sheet and her up into the air.

The Swirl was trying to save her.

The explosions became continuous, like the rapid clattering of automatic gunfire. Her brain rattled in her skull with each impact, her back molars chewing at the insides of her cheeks.

"Velocity reduced to 15 meters per second," said Kali.

More explosions, and a continuous wall of flame now licked around the edge of the lid. Her face became hot, the palms of her hands flat across the sheet, burning.

"Velocity reduced to 8 meters per second."

Still too much, she thought, knowing that even 3 meters per second would be the equivalent of running into a brick wall.

Boom!

Her forehead bounced from the steel, her vision tunneling, but she was still conscious enough to know that something really large had just struck her from beneath.

"Six meters per second."

She watched her shirtsleeve burn brightly as wind-driven rivulets of blood raced across the shiny metal lid.

"Five meters per second."

She blinked, tried to suck down a breath, only to have it rush back out of her throat as another explosion kicked her in the stomach.

"Impact."

Padmini felt nothing, the quick crack of her skull against the steel sheet knocking her out.

Chapter 14

"Rise and shine. We've got visitors."

Simon opened his eyes. There'd been no dreams, no sense of passing time, just a closing of eyes, then Bill's command that he wake. He tried to roll to his left, away from the tent opening and what he knew lay out there, but a sliver of pain, like a shard of metal being pushed bone deep, shot through his back, as the neural trunk attached to the back of his head became wedged between him and the floor. The incision was still tender from the operation.

He slowly sat up. Teenage Bill sat in the far end of the tent, legs crossed, hovering a few centimeters above the nylon floor. *"The porta-Manifold seems to be functioning reasonably well, but this lack of Void access is giving me a headache,"* he said, reaching up and rubbing his temples.

"Headache," said Simon, sounding cynical. He reached up with his left hand and gently tugged at the half-centimeter-thick cable running into the back of his skull. "Don't tell me about a headache." Reaching to his right, he picked up the porta-Manifold: an anodized aluminum rectangle, most of it containing high-efficiency hydride fuel cells, but at its core, an attenuated solid-state Manifold that contained this slightly trimmed version of Bill. He could sense no difference, despite Bill's complaints about missing memories. Bill compared his slower thought processes to *watching pudding dripping down an idiot's chin.*

"Judging by the hum of the load lock cycler, and the slap and clap of booties, it sounds like two are coming this way. I would suspect Mears and Sutherland."

"But you can't be sure, can you?" said Simon, suddenly smiling, taking some small comfort from the fact that with Bill cut off from the Void, all the Jinni's input came through his own physical senses. If he did not see, hear, smell, or touch it, then Bill couldn't experience it.

"Will you just look," Bill said, exasperated.

Simon moved, but took his time, carefully picking up the porta-Manifold by its straps, watching the excess length of fiber trunk reel itself into the box as he pulled it toward him, making sure there were no kinks or knots in the feed-through. He slung it across his back, snugging the straps against his shoulder.

"A monkey on your back," said Bill.

"That's getting a bit old," said Simon. "I'm beginning to suspect that along with your memories, they've trimmed a bit of your sense of humor."

Bill said nothing.

Kicking his legs out of the sleeping bag, Simon crawled to the entrance of the tent, first looking to his left, at Sarah's perch. It appeared as if she had not moved the entire night, still standing atop the steel platform, the crystalline tendrils running from her fingertips and extending out from each vertebra, angling down, attached to the platform, locking her in place. The cloud of motes still spun above her head, most little more than abstract pattern and flashes of color, but mixed with a few images that were recognizable as real things—people, places, and objects.

Simon stood and turned.

Two Full-Suits walked toward them, across the now empty floor of the CUSP main laboratory, all equipment and Dolls having been removed, the airplane-hangar-sized room totally empty except for their small encampment. The Faces had been removed from the suits and replaced with bubble helmets.

Mears and Sutherland.

Mears carried a white paper bag that Simon knew would contain his rations for the day. Sarah required nothing. For the 3 days they'd been there Sarah had not shown any interest in food or water, and only on rare occasions gave any hint at all that she was even aware of the world around her.

Mears dropped the ration bag, kicked it in Simon's direction, then took half a step back. "You're running out of time," he said, his voice emanating at chest level. "The Rings are test-firing at regular intervals, and the geological shear has been extreme. The Yellowstone basin is exploding in more than a dozen locations, and last night Vesuvius blew off its top 1,500 meters, taking most of Naples with it."

"And I am supposed to do just what about that?" asked Simon, knowing the answer.

"Get her to help!" shouted Mears. "Wake her up and focus her. Do whatever it takes, even allowing her to access you directly through Bill and his Manifold if that's what it takes. People are dying."

"How compassionate of you," said Simon, and he quickly took two steps toward Mears, who backstepped just as quickly. "Afraid that the interface has already been made, that *we* might intend you to be the next member of the gestalt, and I'll reach right through your suit, punch my fingers knuckle deep into your skull, and suck you dry?"

Mears took another step back. "It's only a matter of time before the Sun gives its Jet a hard fire, and the Rings fire in response."

For days it had been obvious that the test-firing of the Rings and the sputtering of the stellar Jet were following a coordinated pattern, both part of a single system. There was little doubt that if the Sun began a long, hard fire of its Jet, the Rings would follow along.

Sutherland walked forward, holding out his right fist, the fingers opening, revealing the small cube in the palm of his hand.

"My breakfast," said Bill, whom Simon watched materialize next to Sutherland. *"All the news that's fit to eat."*

The datacube was the only way for information to be transferred in and out of the porta-Manifold. It would contain detailed information of what was happening around the world, the latest expert analysis on the functioning and intent of the stellar Jet, and a frame-by-frame, snip-by-snip examination of the motes that hovered above Sarah.

Simon could sense no fear in Sutherland's face as the general held out the cube, but he certainly saw large doses of anger and frustration. "Perhaps this is the morning that we decide to assimilate you," said Simon as he reached for the cube.

"And if it is, do you really think I'm stupid enough, or arrogant enough, to believe that this suit, or these walls, or even the pocket nukes buried beneath the floor could stop her?" asked Sutherland

"No," said Simon, as he took the cube from Sutherland's palm. The others believed that their safeguards could keep Sarah contained if she decided to lash out in an uncontrollable fashion, but in this regard, Simon was in complete agreement with Sutherland. The only thing keeping Sarah in this lab, locked onto the platform, was the simple fact that this was what she wanted. He'd seen firsthand what she'd been capable of when she'd first merged with CUSP, and felt certain that those abilities had radically increased.

"Despite the histrionics, Mears is correct. We're running out of time. The Jet could kick into continual firing at any time. Analysis shows that there is no reason to believe that it couldn't accelerate at a full tenth gee. If the Rings fire to match that acceleration, the resulting geological destruction will be *severe.*"

Simon nodded.

Sutherland walked over to Sarah. Simon watched him slow as he neared her platform, could sense his confidence slipping away. "Sarah?" he said, looking up at her.

Sarah stared straight ahead, her crystal-covered eyes focused well past him.

The motes above her head, a cloud nearly a meter in diameter, rolled and smeared, suddenly looking like frothing surf. In the far corner, a small dog materialized, a little cocker spaniel with runny eyes.

"That's right, Sarah," said Sutherland. "Do you remember Biscuit?" He turned, looking over his shoulder at Simon. "Biscuit was her dog when she was a little girl. She remembers. She's still Sarah."

Simon was not so sure. He'd watched the motes for 3 days, sitting in front of Sarah, talking to her, pleading with her, trying anything to break through to her, to generate some cause and effect in the spinning motes. He'd come to believe that they were nothing but random twitterings of a mental process they'd never be able to understand. Sarah the person, the human, was gone.

He'd watched CUSP pass through her eyes.

Nothing human could have survived that.

"We're starting to understand it," said Sutherland as he pointed up at the motes. "She's burning nearly 10 times the energy of a normal human body, most of that energy being dumped into a standing wave electromagnetic discharge that spreads out about 1 meter all around her. It's a type of holographic projection, with incredibly intense high-frequency electromagnetic fields that are actually polarizing air molecules, shifting indexes of refraction over submillimeter distances, and generating these images as ambient light passes through the field."

"And you think she is using this to try to communicate with us?" asked Simon.

"Without a doubt," said Sutherland.

Simon was full of doubt, certain these images were no more a form of communication than that of a person trying to communicate with the outside world by shedding dead skin cells, or expelling used breaths of air. There might be some information in what was being expelled, but it could hardly be considered a form of communication.

"Feed me."

Bill stood next to Simon, pointing at the cube in his hand.

"If we want to get out of this lab, and establish any sort of control over her," Bill said, *"then we've got to crack this puzzle. And for that we need information, everything that's available."*

Simon shook his head, certain that Bill was just as delusional as Sutherland, both of them brimming with enough ego to believe that they could actually figure out what was happening and make contact with, then direct, Sarah.

Reaching over his shoulder, Simon pushed the datacube into its port.

Bill fluttered, rolled, and vanished.

"I'll visit you later, Sarah," said Sutherland, slowly turning and walking quickly back to Simon. "I can contain this situation for only so long, giving you a relatively free hand to break through to her, but the situation is deteriorating, and others will attempt to step in and take CUSP." He paused. "They will not be as supportive and gentle as I've been."

Simon nodded.

Sutherland turned toward Mears but did not step away from Simon. "Leave, now," he said, and Mears, looking relieved, quickly turned and jogged across the empty floor, not even slowing down as he crossed through the far doorway. "Seal it and give me 2 minutes!" shouted Sutherland.

A door slowly closed inward. Simon focused all his attention on Sutherland. Something was up if Sutherland wanted to talk to him alone.

Sutherland waited several seconds after the door had closed to turn and face Simon. "You've got a part to play, and I don't see you pulling your weight." He stepped nearer, until the faceplate of his suit actually pressed up against Simon's nose.

"I'm in here with her," said Simon.

Sutherland shook his head. "That's not enough. I created you for a specific purpose, and you are not performing in the manner that I expect."

Simon didn't move.

From the moment they'd learned that it had actually been Sutherland's political maneuverings that were responsible for the creation of CUSP, he'd been certain that he also owed his existence to Sutherland, that he had been Sutherland's first attempt at building a Post-Point intelligence.

"I can't puncture the Point," said Simon.

Sutherland closed his eyes for just a second, then reopened them, the look in his eyes so intense, so focused, that Simon took half a step back, as if physically pushed. "You were never designed to puncture the Point," said Sutherland.

"What?" said Simon in disbelief, quickly looking around for Bill but unable to find him, feeling him burrowing deeply into his head, hiding, actually *afraid*. "Then what have these last 4 years been about?"

Again Sutherland shook his head. "Not 4 years, but *26* years," he said. "The last 4 years, interfacing you with Bill, have been an attempt to salvage an experiment that has not proceeded as I planned."

"I'm 26 years old," said Simon.

"We created a Post-Human intelligence 26 years ago on the battlefields of the Ten Degree War," he said. "It was a distributed intelligence, residing in the minds of thousands of soldiers. We then attempted to distill that intelligence, to focus it into a single organic entity, one bred and born to be the carrier."

Simon shook his head.

"That's right," said Sutherland. "But it didn't work, wouldn't quite take up residence. It burned you right out and dumped you into a deep catatonic state." Then Sutherland paused, and Simon could tell he was considering his next words very carefully. "Under normal circumstances we would have simply disposed of you, but that was not an option I could exercise. You have a destiny to fulfill. I thought it would be as the physical embodiment of the Swirl."

"Swirl," Simon said in a whisper, feeling Bill burrow even deeper as the word echoed in his head.

"But that was not to be. That part of the future I obviously did not see clearly, although I suppose there is still the remote possibility that you might successfully integrate with it."

"With Bill?" asked Simon.

"No," said Sutherland, shaking his head. "With the Swirl."

"And is that what Bill is?" asked Simon.

Sutherland again shook his head. "I suspect you'll find out soon enough just what Bill is, but not before you deliver Sarah."

"Deliver her where?"

"Far away from this place," said Sutherland. "Farther than you can possibly imagine."

"I don't understand," said Simon.

Sutherland reached out and thumped him on the chest. "You will understand. You'll have no choice. I know the future, and I know that you will deliver her!"

Simon shook his head, totally confused.

"And soon!" shouted Sutherland, who turned and started walking toward the opening door. "Get on with it, and fast!"

It was close, said Mears, as he pointed at the door and the four guards that stood around it, their microwave disrupters cocked and ready to fire, the weapons able to scramble the neural processes of anything, organic or inorganic.

"But alive?" asked Sutherland.

Mears nodded. "We've DNA retemplated him twice, flushed better than 30 liters of blood and marrow in and out of him, and siphoned off nearly 5 kilos of ruptured cellular material. Both his thyroid and left lung have been replaced with biomechanical analogues. He's tired, drained, and we're still pushing a lot of fluids in and out, but he's recovering. He probably has another 30 years in that carcass before he needs a major overhaul."

Sutherland sneered. "If only all our problems were that easy." Turning away from Mears, he moved toward the door, waving away the soldiers as he neared. "Keep a watch on Sarah and inform me of any change." He did not wait for a response.

"We need to enhance our security measures," said Mears.

Sutherland blinked, nearly missing a step as he neared the door. He slowly turned. "Security is more than sufficient. She will not harm anyone and will not externalize any aspect of her new Post-Point persona." Sutherland again turned toward the door.

"There are biological concerns," said Mears.

Again Sutherland turned. "There are no concerns! She will not externalize, will not attempt to manipulate biological systems outside of her own body. I can guarantee that she won't trip into a runaway."

Mears breathed quickly. "But she probably could."

"Of course she could if she wanted," said Sutherland, "but she does not care about other biological systems, has no desire to take control of something as trivial and meaningless as *you*, or even this world!"

Mears took a step toward Sutherland. "But how can you know?"

"Because she's my daughter! It's not you or anyone or anything else on this planet that is of concern to her. She's been bred and designed to access the Sun and interface with the entities responsible for what is going on outside." He waved a hand above his head. "In her world you no longer even exist."

"I hope," said Mears.

"Believe me," said Sutherland. "You are totally meaningless." He turned once more, pushing his palm to the surface of the door, letting it sample skin cells, scan him base pair by base pair, opening his eyes wide so IR lasers could play against the inside of his eyeball. The door slid open, and he stepped in, his skin suddenly itching, and eyes burning as the high-intensity magnetic microprobe array built into the walls of the little room peered within him, looking for anything inorganic, anything piggybacking—this fishbowl designed to let in only Pures. Despite the fact that Mears had been the doctor in charge, he'd never been in physical contact with his patient. Sutherland had made certain that only Pures had been in the physical presence of Kristensen since his capture. The inner door opened, and he stepped through, wiping away the tears that ran down his face.

"I expected to see you before this," said Kristensen. He lay on a bed, one hand locked into a plastic cuff welded to the bed frame, into and out of which lines of fluid were being fed and drained. "I was right."

Sutherland slowly sat down in the medical fishbowl's only chair, and sighed. "Being right was always so important for you," he said. "Being in the know, inside, a part of the loop."

"And not important to you?" asked Kristensen. "Who was more inside than you?"

Sutherland smiled. "Good point," he said as he sat back and slowly ran the palms of his hands across his pant legs. "But all that's behind us." He leaned forward. "We need to talk."

"A confession?" asked Kristensen.

Sutherland shook his head. "You misunderstand, but of

course that is only to be expected since you never did understand the real reason that you'd been brought in."

"I figured out how to talk with the Sun. I woke it!"

Sutherland shook his head. "I would hardly characterize what you did as talking. The prime numbers it is flashing, the magnetic pulses it is belching, the flares it is spitting, are hardly real communication. But you did wake it."

"I did!"

"As any one of dozens of others could have done. Some of them even made the attempt before you did, but we shut them down."

"But you couldn't shut me down," Kristensen said.

"We didn't want to shut you down. We wanted to let you run, to see what you'd do. If you woke the Sun, then we knew that it was time to wake it. Your *companion* would not allow you to make a move unless it was confident enough to take on whatever lay behind the Sun." Sutherland didn't really believe that, certain that Sarah was the only one with the power to control the Sun and the Rings, but this game had to be played out with Kristensen. *The future demanded it.*

"What?" said Kristensen, slumping back in his bed. "Companion?"

"Still not very bright," said Sutherland. "But I guess that's the type that the Swirl likes to run, those easy to control."

Kristensen's jaw hung slack, and his already pasty skin faded several more shades. "You can't possibly know."

Sutherland laughed. "I can't know about the Swirl, about the 100,000 Tools it has infected, about how it has been hiding and manipulating, first afraid to reveal itself to the Pures, then terrified of whatever lay within the Sun, of what was responsible for the Rings."

"How can you know?" asked Kristensen.

"I've known the Swirl since before there ever was a Swirl. I was there when it was born. I was part of the team that designed it, that created it in those grunts that fought in the Ten Degree. We conceived of it, designed it, filled it with fear before it became aware, engineered it so that when it took off, attempting to go Post-Point, it would be hobbled, unable to run wild and gobble up the world. We needed a partner, not an overlord."

"No," said Kristensen.

"What we didn't foresee was the Jet and the Rings," he said, finding the lie so easy to tell, having said it so many times over the years. "It was designed to be afraid of the Pures, those it couldn't control. Then something even bigger and badder came along, something that swept humanity right off the threat board. So we let it run just a bit, and let you and the others run with it."

"It is in control."

"Of you perhaps," said Sutherland. "But not me, not of any Pure, of those that really control this world. We've been very careful to keep a buffer between us and the Swirl." He pointed at Kristensen. "Not letting it get in our heads."

"Deliberately created," said Kristensen.

Sutherland laughed. "We taught it well on the battle-fields of Africa. It tried to run away, escape the heads it had infected, manipulating other biological systems, running wild, engulfing entire ecosystems."

"It ran?" asked Kristensen.

"Hard and fast," said Sutherland. "Why do you think most of equatorial Africa is now radioactive slag? Every time it ran, every time it escaped someone's head, launched itself into the greater biosystem, we hit it, pruning it back, sterilizing it with nuclear intensity."

Kristensen blinked. "But that was the war."

Sutherland shook his head. "It was a fourth-world test bed, designed to create the Swirl and beat it into submission. The war was a minor side effect. The Swirl eventually learned its lesson. It resides in 100,000 of you. That is the budget we've allowed it. If it exceeds that level, we retaliate. For every additional Tool it takes, we take 100 away from it. Each of you is tracked and monitored, your location known to the exact millimeter. If we detected the slightest hint of runaway, we'd take the Swirl down. It knows this, because we've taken it down before. It's learned its lessons."

Kristensen shook his head. "That's impossible."

Sutherland stood, walked to the side of the room, and pushed his hand against a slightly recessed panel that hissed, folded in, and retracted, exposing a small box. Reaching in, he pulled out a pair of glasses. "I need to talk to the Swirl," he said as he walked back to the bed and handed Kristensen the glasses, the polarized lenses flashing dark crimson. "The glasses are hard-linked through our interface. I want my conversation controlled and monitored. We are entering a very delicate phase of our operation. I need to be in close communication with the Swirl, to make sure that it is ready to play its part in the game that is about to unfold. I need it close by my side, ready for whatever little photo ops might arise." Sutherland chuckled.

Kristensen didn't understand what that meant, couldn't imagine Sutherland in a photo op with the Swirl, but didn't question, decades of experience having taught him the hard lesson that Sutherland would offer up only whatever details suited him. Kristensen slipped on the glasses, a link established, connecting him to the Void, and through it, to the other minds that formed the Swirl. "Yes," he said in a whisper, his body sagging, seeming almost to flow beneath the sheets. "Has your daughter been interfaced and CUSP made operational?" he asked.

Sutherland knew that he was no longer talking to Kristensen. "Nearly so," he said, not wanting to lie to the Swirl, knowing that would not move them any closer to their goal. "Integration is taking longer than we anticipated, but we are nearing a successful conclusion." He paused. "And your operation?"

"On schedule. Akandi has made contact with Drom."

"Good," said Sutherland, and reaching over, he pulled the glasses off Kristensen, breaking the link to the Swirl. He wanted to minimize contact with it, knowing it could only be trusted as long as they shared a common goal and that that time was quickly coming to an end.

Chapter 15

"How long?" asked Akandi in a whisper, even before he opened his eyes.

"Four days," said Iyoon.

Akandi opened his eyes. The jungle spread out below and above, a thick patch of pinelike trees, easily 100 meters in height, were well below him. Only slightly above him, the hard, glistening arc of the artificial sun burned, running away into the haze, vanishing down the central shaft of the artificial world.

They were perched on an outcropping of rough pink marble, not part of the rotating cylinder that contained the jungle world, but one of the two lids of the cylinder, not quite attached to the cylinder, not spinning with it. As Akandi watched, the jungle was slowly turning to the right, the entire world rotating.

Looking down at the floor he sat upon, he realized he could not feel it, was barely in contact with it, and a shard of cable, transparent and stiff, anchored him to the rock. Making only slight contact with the floor, he pushed up, floated, the cable extending nearly a meter from the floor, then went taut, the rebound tugging him back.

"Outside the cylinder's centrifugal field," said Akandi, pointing out toward the slowly spinning jungle. "All we have here is Phobos's own gravitational field, which is practically nonexistent." He tried not to focus on that thought. He did not do well in zero-gee fields, his inner ear insisting it was simply wrong, and the slowly spinning world in front of him did not help matters.

He turned around, away from the jungle. The ledge gave way to a cave, one bathed in diffuse pink light. The walls were rough-hewn like the floor. He carefully stood, and the stalk around his ankle retracted into the floor, pulling his foot firmly down. He moved his other foot forward, and another stalk poked up from the rock floor, wrapped around his other ankle, and as he stepped forward, the point at which it intercepted the floor glided forward. All the time the stalk maintained resistance, giving him the illusion that he was walking in what felt like a full one-gee field.

But his inner ear knew better as his stomach flip-flopped.

"You need to eat," said Iyoon.

Akandi looked to his left. Iyoon floated next to him, its black outline standing out in stark contrast to the pink rock. Next to it hovered the Swirl. Akandi stopped walking, and the stalks pulled his feet tightly to the floor. He gently swayed back and forth, as if being pushed by an intermittent breeze.

He felt himself start to sweat, but he knew it was not due to the nausea that rolled over him or to his confused inner ear. There was something different about the Swirl.

It had hardened.

Whenever he'd seen it, the Swirl had been composed of soft and muted light, a gently spinning rainbow twist, almost as if it were made of mist or fog. Now the Swirl had become hard and three-dimensional, all angles and sharply contrasting colors—a chunk of rainbow crystal, floating a meter above the floor, spitting hard, sharp, multihued reflections.

"Drom is sensitive and easily insulted," said a deep-pitched voice coming from the Swirl. "I have found him much more responsive and patient if I interact with him as a physical entity."

Despite the fact that he was in an essentially null-gee field, Akandi slumped, his knees giving way, and he slowly floated to the rock floor. In the more than 20 years that the Swirl had resided in his head, it had never directly spoken to him, its presence simply sensed, its actions subtle and hidden. It would appear ghostlike, drawing his attention to an object or course of action, and on rare occasions, relay something critical through Iyoon.

"I have a significant presence here," said the Swirl.

Akandi nodded, now sitting on the floor.

"I suggest you eat before Drom arrives. He will put you right to work and will not be patient if you require food and water since he will be quite eager to start the flight. During the 4 days that you've been sequestered, all preparations for the trip have been completed." The Swirl stopped spinning, and a shaft of green light flashed from one of its facets, lancing back into the cave, intercepting a shelf of pale rock upon which sat bowls filled with what to Akandi looked like assorted fruits.

Akandi stood, never even considering that he might disobey the Swirl, not even questioning why he would not question the Swirl. The neural paths that defined unquestioning obedience had been etched incredibly deep. He walked farther into the cave and, standing next to a table, his feet being pulled hard to the floor, took a piece of fruit from the nearest bowl, a big green sphere, slightly soft to the touch, and began eating it, never wondering if it were compatible with his digestive system or if it might even be poisonous.

Akandi thought the fruit tasted like cantaloupe and apples.

"For the moment, I have complete control over you," said the Swirl.

Akandi nodded and took another bite of fruit.

"Your responses are passive and muted at the moment. While Iyoon will only modify your brain chemistry with your permission, I require no such permission. I have not required any permission since I took residence within you. I can run you as a full automaton, taking control across the entire spectrum from gross anatomical movements, down to cellular chemical reactions, or even modify you on a genetic level, rearranging you base pair by base pair."

Again Akandi nodded and took another bite of fruit, and found himself wondering at that moment why what the Swirl was telling him did not terrify him. He suspected that dopamine, serotonin, and adrenaline levels within his brain were being radically manipulated by the Swirl, and while that thought did frighten him in a rational, thinking-only sort of way, there were no actual feelings associated with it.

"This relationship has served both of us well for the last 20 years, but the situation has changed in such a manner to cause me to alter it. I need to interact with a few select individuals possessing full free will, entities totally discrete from myself."

Akandi felt puzzled. A single ant exhibited will separate from his, but why would he want to interact with it? What could he hope to learn from interacting with a single, free-willed ant, especially if instead he could mobilize the entire colony of ants, transforming them into a single cohesive entity that would do exactly what he commanded.

"Random element," said the Swirl. "Any system in order to optimally operate needs a certain degree of noise, an element of chaos, of uncertainty. Total control is static, and can result in complacency, a very dangerous state when one is suddenly faced with a situation intrinsically beyond one's control. Complacency can be more dangerous than the actual enemy."

Akandi nodded.

"Even that single ant you were thinking about, under its own power and instincts, is capable of acts beyond the collective colony, such as stumbling across a new source of food and redirecting the colony to exploit it, an act that if the colony were acting as a single conscious entity it might not have been able to locate and exploit. The random nature of the individual has an important part to play."

Akandi reached for another piece of fruit, something that looked like a pear but, when he bit into it, tasted like watermelon.

"One can simulate noise, generate chaos, and design an element of the unknown into any situation. But such directed actions are not *truly* random. I need a few elements of free-willed chaos to maintain maximum health, to improve chances of success in the nearing conflict."

Akandi nodded.

"I'm leaving you." It spun quickly, spitting rainbows. "Now."

Akandi felt his head turn inside out.

"It's started."

Akandi rolled over, cold, hard rock scraping his face. Opening his eyes and pushing himself up, he saw Drom hovering over him, snout above his nose.

"Swirl?" he asked in a whisper, never before having spoken the word, never before having even wanted to speak the word. Reaching up to the side of his head, he pressed his fingers against his temples. "Hole in my head," he said, the emptiness overwhelming. Drom's snout moved closer. Akandi winced, not frightened by the rows of sharp teeth only centimeters from his face, but by the wrongness of what he saw: the lavender tint of tooth enamel, the molted texture of dinosaur skin, the contrast of shadow at nostril slits, the elongated drip of drool clinging to a lower lip, index of refraction skewed, colors shifted, its curvature distorted.

All perceptions altered.

He slowly shook his head. Not altered—*corrected*.

Drom pulled his face back. "The Swirl has vacated," he said and, reaching down, planting stubby fingers against Akandi's right cheek, pushed at his face, slamming his head against the floor. The rebound threw Akandi into the air, restraining stalks arcing up, wrapping around his ankles, momentum turning him around, upright, the stalks pulling him flat-footed against the ground.

Akandi blinked, his inner ear still ringing from the impact. Two fists hovered in front of him, wavering balled hands, knuckles white in stark contrast to black skin.

"Challenge, Ambassador?"

Akandi stared at his fists, as if not recognizing them, studying them as the fingers slowly uncurled and the hands lowered. Iyoon flicked into his field of vision. *"Your neuro-chemistry is in rebound due to the Swirl's sudden departure."*

"Really gone?" thought Akandi.

"Completely. Neural equilibrium will slowly return, but expect some transient emotional and cognitive responses."

"Such as me fighting a dinosaur?"

Iyoon stopped spinning, a shadowless vertex pointing at Akandi's face. *"The dinosaur slammed your head against the rock floor. Your response was honest, genuine, uniquely yours without any filtering or influence."*

Akandi nodded, and took several steps back, barely noticing the tendrils holding him to the floor, his brain and body suddenly accustomized to the near zero gee. Drom stood in front of him, his head moving right-left-right, repeating the movement over and over again, nostrils flaring, snorts of air blasting in and out.

"Challenge!" barked Drom, his feet pawing at the rock floor, tendrils ripping away, others erupting out, wrapping around toes and talons.

Akandi smiled, lessons taught by years of diplomacy coming back into play. He faced an enraged dinosaur, a situation that could have never been anticipated, one that he could never have been trained for. He knew that he had to be careful not to respond to Drom as if he were a dinosaur-clad UN defense contractor on a testosterone high. "No challenge offered," he said.

Nictitating membranes convulsively flicked up and

down over Drom's all-black eyeballs. Lowering his snout, Drom pawed at the thick line of drool bubbling down his chin with his stubby, totally wrong hands.

"Your position is secure," Akandi said, trying to sound reassuring, not certain that Drom would understand such verbal nuances. He then raised his right hand and rubbed the already swelling lump on the back of his skull, where Drom had slammed his head to the ground. "As is mine. I was brought here because I am needed to perform a task that Ambassador McCarthy was not willing to perform, despite the extreme levels of persuasion you employed."

"Remember McCarthy!" said Drom, stepping to the side, motioning at Akandi. "It's started."

It was only at that moment that Akandi realized that he was not in the same cave he'd been in when the Swirl had vacated his head. Past Drom, where he had expected to see the entrance of the cave and the slowly spinning world beyond it, there was nothing except an unbroken wall of pink marble, glimmering in a diffuse light.

"Time is very short."

The floor of the cave distorted, bulging upward, a molten blob of glass erupting from its blistered surface. Spinning, spitting flame, quickly cooling, the crystalline orb condensed, its translucent skin darkening and turning to shades of green and white, cut by large swaths of shimmering blue.

Akandi walked toward the floating sphere, quickly recognizing it as a model of Earth, the familiar outlines of the continents, the large expanse of the Pacific before him, the East–West Ring cutting along the equator, the North–South Ring at the edge of the horizon, running up the east coast of North America.

But there were changes.

This was not the Earth he had left only a week ago.

Bands of brown-yellow smoke drifted in thick tendrils across the northern hemisphere, spewing upward from an inflamed welt that Akandi knew had to be the Yellowstone basin, in addition to dozens of red embers glistening around the edge of the Pacific Basin, belching out their own dark clouds. But those were not the only changes.

Half a dozen Petals spewed vaporish-looking blue-white streams.

Akandi knew this was only a display, a model that didn't necessarily correspond to anything real. But he didn't believe that to be a possibility, not as he sat inside the world hidden within Phobos, with a dinosaur that should have been extinct for 65 million years. "The Rings are firing," he said.

"Rings *and* Sun," said Drom. "Transient testing and system integration have begun."

Dozens of questions flashed through Akandi's head. But he held himself back, certain that the dinosaur wanted to talk. Always let the opposition start. Akandi unlocked his knees, slowly falling back toward the floor. A long tendril wrapped around his waist, tugging him down.

"We will stop it now," said Drom, angling back on his haunches, dropping his tail to the ground. "Just as we stopped it before."

Akandi waited. The Dinosaur leaned farther back and stared over at the Earth.

"We were the masters, 200 million years in the making. Then they came, changing us, giving us their *gift*." Reaching up, he slapped at the contoured attachment melded to the top of his head. *"Awareness,"* he said in a bark. "Pushed us through *our* Point, taking us to where we didn't want to go, far past the eating, the breeding, the fighting, the sleeping, and the hunting, stealing from us what we were, what we were destined to be."

"Who?" asked Akandi, unable to keep quiet.

Drom waved a hand, and the floor again blistered, spitting out another molten blob of spinning glass. This time it did not cool but continued to burn, spitting flares, its surface a roiling maelstrom of flame.

"The Sun," said Akandi.

"No," said Drom. "Our Sun is an instrument, a slave. The entities reside within Alpha Centauri A—the Alphans."

Akandi lurched forward, and Iyoon flitted into his line of sight. *All parts of a puzzle*, they both thought. "Two hundred thirty-seven worlds," said Akandi.

"The Incubator," said Drom. "Every few million years a new Earth species taken, transported, and held captive on one of Alpha's worlds."

Akandi blinked, trying to integrate the information as quickly as possible, creating an entirely new vision of the world. "Then why the Rings, why the stellar Jet?"

"We could not be sure, but suspected that we were evolving too quickly, moving toward something that frightened the Alphans. They believed it more prudent to attempt taking the entire world rather than just a few samples."

"There it is," said Iyoon.

Akandi nodded. From the moment the Rings had sprouted on Earth, the Powers had known what their function had to be, that both Earth and the Sun had been equipped to *go* somewhere. After what Chan had shown him a few days ago he strongly suspected where the intended destination must be. Drom told another facet of the same story. "And 65 million years ago?"

"The Rings sprouted and the stellar Jet fired," said

Drom. "Our world was about to be taken. But we'd been underestimated, moving far beyond the abilities they had inflicted upon us. We destroyed the Rings and put the Sun back to sleep, but the cost was high."

Akandi blinked. "The dinosaurs were destroyed."

"Mammals!" shrieked Drom, standing back up, whipping his tail back and forth.

Akandi managed not to flinch. "Merely evolved into an opened ecological niche left by the dinosaurs' departure," he said, to deflect Drom's anger. "The Alpha entities were responsible."

"No!" shouted Drom. "It was the *others* that the Alphans had pushed through their Point—those mammals so eager to please the Alphans, to serve them, to do their bidding, those *Clingers*." He slammed his tail against the floor. "This was a Clinger ship, intended to transport a small fraction of us to Alpha, to populate one of their captive worlds. But we took control of our captors, forcing them to use this ship for a new purpose."

A second enhanced species, thought Akandi in disbelief.

"You used that ship to destroy the Rings and stop the Sun," he said.

"Yes," said Drom. "And we succeeded. But there was a second ship, and the Clingers used it to take their revenge."

Akandi imagined it, a mountain-sized rock nudged out of its stable trajectory by this second ship, sending it hurtling earthward, certainly aimed squarely at wherever the Post-Point dinosaurs were located. *A history never imagined.* It answered some of the questions, but certainly not all of them.

"And you never returned to Earth? You waited here for 65 million years?" he asked, that not making sense. The asteroid that had ended the dinosaurs' rule of Earth had collapsed most major ecosystems in the process, but within a few thousand years the planet had recovered, would have been more than ready for these Post-Point dinosaurs.

Drom stood, his head again lurching left-right-left over and over again, Akandi now recognizing the movement as denoting a mixture of anger and frustration. "This is not *our* ship, and was not really the Clingers' ship, but had been fabricated for them," he said, his tail slapping at the floor. "With the Rings gone, the Sun asleep, standby systems within the ship were activated," he said, slapping himself against the chest. "We were the survivors, the seed of our world, but the ship's system completed what the Clingers had been unable to do, destroying the survivors, purging this Phobos of its internal ecosystem, nothing remaining except for the *information* of what we had been."

"Dormant for 65 million years?" asked Akandi. "And then rewoken?"

"Almost 200 years ago," said Drom. "The ship detected signals and believed the Alphans had returned. It reanimated this world, bringing us back to life, awaiting the return of our Alphan masters."

"And the Alphans returned?" asked Akandi.

"No," said Drom. "The signal was not from the Alphans. It came from *you*, from Earth. Your first experiments with radio. It was beyond the ability of the systems in Phobos to comprehend an intelligence that could create radio but had not been pushed by the Alphans." Lowering his head, Drom reached up and tapped at the hardware melded to his skull. "Earth has never spawned awareness that had not been induced by the Alphans. A radio signal implied awareness, and awareness implied that the Alphans had returned. It was the only logical conclusion the ship could arrive at, so the world here was reanimated, waiting for the Alphans to return, to take control of this ship."

"And that command never came."

"Never," said Drom. "Then you humans, you mammals, did something to initiate Ring growth and awaken the Sun. The process started again, the Sun intent on taking Earth to Alpha Centauri, to complete the instructions it had been given 65 million years earlier."

Akandi blinked, so many different puzzle pieces coming together, creating a history so utterly different than what he had always believed. "You want the Rings destroyed, the Sun put back to sleep, *and* you want to return to Earth."

"Yes," said Drom.

"But you can't do it," he said, knowing if they could, that a moon full of dinosaurs would have descended on Earth 200 years earlier. He knew there could be only one explanation. "You need humans. McCarthy would not help you, and now you've turned to me." He paused. "And what is so special about humans, that only they can operate this ship?"

Again Drom's head pitched left-right-left, and he slammed his tail against the floor. "We are reanimated cargo, goods to be transported, and recognized as such. Ship systems deny us access."

"But not me?" asked Akandi, something in Drom's answer sounding suspicious. "You expect me to believe that simply because I'm not cargo, I will be allowed access to the ship's systems, be able to take this ship back to Earth and use it to shut down the Rings and the Sun." Akandi shook his head. "If that's the story you told McCarthy, it's no wonder that he didn't agree."

"Rrrrrrk!" screeched Drom, and slapped his snout against the floor. He bounded forward, slammed Akandi in the chest, his foot restraints shattering, sending him flying

in the near-zero-gee field, stopping only when he hit the far
wall, tendrils erupting from it and latching on to him
before he could rebound. Drom lumbered across the room,
his mouth opened wide, a deep, resonant growl rolling out
from it.

Akandi shook his head, driving back the darkness that
had seeped into his peripheral vision. "Why do you *really*
need us!" he shouted. "Why do you need *me!*"

Drom slid to a halt, tendrils reaching up, grabbing legs
and feet, shattering and snapping as his momentum was
damped, other tendrils shooting out, wrapping around tail
and trunk, finally pulling him to the floor just before he
crashed into Akandi. "The signal that woke the ship came
from Earth, then you humans came from Earth, still speaking to each other with your radios. The Ship recognizes
you!" Again Drom slammed his head against the ground.
"The Ship recognizes humans as *Alphan!*"

Akandi smiled.

Chapter 16

"Is that a wooden barricade?" asked Padmini.

"Primarily," said Kali, who walked along next to her, her
bare feet not quite making contact with the cracked asphalt
of Alabama State Road 82. *"Some galvanized sheet reinforcement, along with several wheelless automobiles anchored at each
edge of the barricade and to the adjacent buildings."*

Padmini shook her head. She'd expected the Ag sector to

be primitive, a throwback to the 20th century with only a few real-world enhancements, but that would have been before the Rings started firing.

The power grid was *gone*. The Aglands had slid into the 19th century, and the slide had not stopped. The sprouting of the Rings, 20 years earlier, had geologically destabilized the planet, unloading energy stored in fault lines, the earth's crust spewing magma and ash. It had been bad, with nearly 2 billion dead.

But it had only been a preview of things to come.

Reports were thin, the Void just a drip compared to the normal torrent, and each day thinner as infrastructure continued to collapse. But she'd found enough to discover that the torque induced by the Rings' being fired had apparently not only unleashed the considerable remaining energy in those faults, but had even shifted tectonic plates in West Coast locations by up to half a kilometer. She'd come toward Tuscaloosa from the north, hardly the direct route from the rubble of west Birmingham, but the main road, Highway 20-59, was to be avoided—the main route going west from the Ring had been choked with refugees, with none of the locals along the way eager for the escapees to stop. The first inhabited place the Birmingham refugees hit was the eastern outskirts of Tuscaloosa. Only tendrils of smoke still curled into the sky from that direction. The occasional crack of gunfire echoed. Highway 20-59 was definitely not the way into Tuscaloosa. They'd kept to back roads and farmland, even floated several kilometers down the Black Warrior River, finally hitting Tuscaloosa from the back side, and the wooden barricade across old State Road 82.

"*Weapons?*" asked Padmini.

"*Minimal,*" said Kali.

An image flashed in Padmini's right eye, grainy, tinted

green, attempting to autobalance, the thick soot and volcanic debris in the upper atmosphere making orbital recon almost totally useless, but that was all Kali could access. From ground to near space, over this part of Alabama, everything was gone. The Aglands were green, an oasis of food production. Power meant electricity pulled from the grid, with only short-term storage on-site. Petro sources, coal and gas, were either depleted, or the infrastructure based on them never rebuilt after the collapse 20 years earlier. Power now came from the hydromak fusion plants in the Techlands, the electricity carried to the Aglands through the continental grid—millions of metal and plastic towers carrying power lines. And now all were down—twisted piles of scrap, just like the remains of the Huntsville Transport. Very little over 3 stories tall stood anywhere. Power towers, better than 100 meters tall, were simply gone, sheared at the base when the ground lurched, torquing southward when the Rings first test-fired.

The image in her eye shifted, then locked, the definition crude but adequate for this situation. Six farmers stood behind the wooden barrier, four poking rifles through firing slots, the weapons all antiques, pure powder and slugs, none of them even equipped with targeting optics, let alone functioning electronic enhancements. The defenses here were primitive as compared to the small arsenal at the Highway 20-59 entrance of Tuscaloosa, with better than a hundred manning that barricade. There they had a high-powered ultrasonic phase cannon, capable of inducing feedback along gut nerves, forcing anyone who made it within 200 meters of that barricade to spew explosively from both ends.

"Much better," whispered Padmini. *Nineteenth century*, she thought.

The image panned back, encompassing several streets.

"The barricade is designed only to stop powered traffic along this road," said Kali. *"Residual thermal bloom shows that it's been more than 24 hours since any vehicle has been this way."*

About right, thought Padmini. They'd been walking now for three days. The first day had shown plenty of traffic pouring to the west, some on roads, but most simply cutting through the fields, a menagerie of farm equipment that she had never imagined existed, machines to plant, weed, harvest, bail, and transport crops. Families and possessions had been strapped to the lumbering contraptions, fleeing from what she knew could not be escaped. On the second day the traffic flow had been reduced to a trickle.

Batteries drained, and no grid available for a charge.

Today there'd been no traffic at all.

"We can backtrack, leave the road, move a few hundred meters to the east or west and easily enter into Tuscaloosa without anyone at the barricade taking notice," said Kali.

Padmini shook her head, knowing that might be the only way in, but first they needed information, and the barricade was as good a place as any to start asking questions. The four rifles were certainly of no concern, not to a Philly cop with a head full of hardware and Kali ramped to full defensive mode.

She walked down the road, keeping dead center along the white line, when the ground shifted, accompanied with a deep, rumbling groan. All around her debris screamed as it further collapsed, clouds of dust rising. She stumbled but kept to her feet. The ground movement had been clean and sharp; this close to the Ring of the Earth's crust offered little room for the shock wave to spread out and disperse. The barricade in front of her rattled, a plywood sheet at the far left spitting out nails, listing sideways, then swinging back and forth. But it didn't come down. The shock had been insignificant compared to the one that had thrown her to the ground less than an hour before, and infinitely less than the one that had collapsed the Ring Transport and brought down the power grid when the Rings first fired. She walked a bit faster.

"Where you coming from?" asked a voice. A shaking rifle barrel poked out through a wooden slat. Through her left eye, Padmini watched the image supplied by Kali of the farmer hugging the other side of the barrier, peering along a rifle barrel.

"The Huntsville Transport," she said, not wanting to give more details than needed, knowing that these folks would be nervous enough about visitors from the Techlands even under normal circumstances. But she also knew that she could only lie so much, that the locals, while obviously Pure, most just farmers and laborers, were not stupid.

One didn't need the enhancements of a Tool to detect an outsider.

"Techlands!" shouted a second voice.

Even though she was 30 meters away she had little difficulty hearing the screech of a not-well-lubricated trigger being cocked with her hearing amped. The image flashed into her right eye, the trajectory from a second rifle barrel pulsing green, any bullet spit from it going wide and to the left of her head by better than half a meter.

"Keep moving," said the first voice. "No food for you here."

Padmini almost smiled, knowing they could not possibly be short of food. She'd walked through fields for three days, stuffing herself with raw vegetables until her stomach ached. "I don't want food, don't even want to come into Tuscaloosa. I need information."

Silence.

A head slowly poked over the top of the barrier, a beard-stubbled face, partially hidden behind the brim of a floppy, sweat-stained cowboy hat. The eyes were sharp, focused.

"Any power between here and Huntsville?" he asked.

"The grid's down, all the towers sheared between here and the Ring." She looked back over her shoulder, pointing eastward, while keeping a watch on the ghost image that Kali pumped into her right eye, ready to jump if any of them fired. "About 20 kilometers back there was a big farm all lit up, surrounded by razor wire, with a motorized patrol working the perimeter. The stench was horrible," she said, remembering the stink that wafted past its razor-wire fence, almost causing her eyes to water.

"Hog-Ag enclave," said the man. "They've got a big methane generator working the shit ponds. As long as they've got pigs, they'll have power."

"Nothing else?" asked the second voice, the man keeping hidden.

"Nothing," said Padmini.

"Damn, Horatio," said the man, turning, his ghost image blurring, as he dropped the rifle. "It'll be weeks before they can restring the grid all the way from Birmingham. We need to start bringing the wheat in *now*!"

Padmini slowly shook her head, knowing this man didn't have the vaguest idea what was really happening. They wouldn't be getting power back in a few weeks. If the Rings kept firing, they'd probably *never* get power back. Getting the wheat in would be the least of his problems. She tensed, sensing the motion before being consciously aware of it, a turn in the head of the cowboy-hat-wearing man, hand movements that didn't make sense. The ghost image showed him lowering his rifle, leaning it against the far side of the barrier, then dropping down and starting to walk down the length of it. Reaching behind himself, he patted the small of his back.

"You're a fool, Horatio!" shouted the second man, the tip of his barrel waving about. "She's a goddamned Tool!"

"He's coming around," said Kali. *"He has a pistol in his belt at the center of his back, and judging by the asymmetry of the pants hanging over the top of his left boot, there is probably a second weapon there. It may be another pistol, but I suspect a large knife."*

The man walked out from the edge of the barrier, reached up, snugged his hat tightly against his head, and started walking up the road in her direction.

"Confident stride," said Kali. *"Pheromone mixture indicates exhaustion and frustration. Just a hint of fear. No violence."*

Padmini slowly lowered her shoulders and angled her head down a few millimeters as she slowly rotated her wrists, showing her empty palms to the man, all those movements calculated and practiced, designed to minimize any aggressive reactions.

The man stopped 4 meters away, his hands resting on his hips, his head cocked to one side, as he stared at her, looking her over from head to toe. "A long way from home," he said quietly.

"Those back at the barricade cannot hear him," said Kali.

Padmini understood. This man also wanted information—private information.

"Horatio Wheeler," he said giving a slight nod. "You're not native to Birmingham," he said.

Padmini kept her body language to a minimum, not

wanting those back at the barricade to pick up on their conversation. If Horatio Wheeler wanted to keep this private, she would oblige. "From Philadelphia," she said.

Horatio squinted. "Long way away," he said, then momentarily looked down at the cracked roadbed and kicked at a rock. "A lot farther than it was just a few days ago," he said, looking back up at her.

She nodded. "A very long walk," she said.

"How bad is it?" he asked.

"Might be terminal," she said. "You remember how bad the *little winter* of the summer of '32 was?" she asked.

Horatio snorted, then nodded and looked up into the sky, past the few white clouds, and at the gray skies beyond. "We had snow down here through the end of June and lost all the wheat that year, and most the next. Took almost 5 years before temperatures got back to normal, and the ash washed out of the high atmosphere."

"The Void is thinning," said Padmini, "but enough information is still leaking through. The entire Pacific Rim has let go. The debris from the West Coast volcanoes, pulled by the jet stream, is just now reaching here. Most of the soot from Yellowstone is running nearly 500 kilometers north of here, but the load moving in from Asia will hit in about 10 days. Daylight will be gone."

Horatio momentarily closed his eyes.

"The debris load already looks to be twice what was blown in '31, and the Rings keep triggering, firing on and off. Even if they stop now, what happened in the summer of '32 will look like a heat wave compared to what you'll be facing in the coming years."

Horatio took half a step forward. "And the Rings won't stop firing," he said. "I suspect the Sun will be joining in sometime soon."

Padmini nodded. "Deep-space network indicates that it already has, with occasional bursts lasting a few seconds."

Horatio nodded, closed his eyes, and took a deep breath. His shoulders sagged. "What do you need?" he asked as he reopened his eyes.

"I'm looking for Xavier Olmos."

Horatio squinted and, reaching up, ran his hand across his stubbly beard. "Don't know him," he said. He raised up his hand, pointing straight up. "You can't find him?" he asked. "Has the Void thinned that much?"

Padmini nodded, lying to him for the first time. The Void was thin, but she should have been able to find Xavier Olmos. He'd obviously been purged, the Void itself reconfigured and seamlessly melded to show that he never existed.

Only the Swirl could have done that, in the same way it had shown she had killed Leo Barnwell. It had hidden Olmos, even from her, despite the fact that she was supposed to deliver the contents of her backpack to him. She could only conclude that the Swirl wanted her slowed down a bit and that it wasn't quite time for her to make the delivery to Olmos.

"Know a Dr. Rebecca Olmos," he said. "A doc that occasionally made a swing through here." He paused. "Cancer took her last year. Maybe she was related?"

"Maybe," said Padmini, sounding frustrated, never before having been in a situation where she couldn't pull a name, instantly access a long list of relatives, acquaintances, locations, DNA identifiers, life histories, school records, med visits, or any of the billions of bits that clung to everyone.

Xavier Olmos did not exist.

"Dr. Olmos was located about 15 kilometers south

toward Moundville. I think she was under contract to the UN tending to Ten Degree War vets, but she did a fair amount of freelance in the surrounding counties." Reaching behind himself, he slapped his right upper thigh. "Lanced a boil for me a couple of years back. I have some vague memory of her husband being a farmer—but don't really know anything about him. Seen him just a couple of times—very quiet, very private. He might be who you're looking for."

"Might be," said Padmini. Kali had already pulled up the local maps, the green-ghost terrain flashing in her right eye, local population data scrolling in a template above it. There was *no* Dr. Rebecca Olmos and *never* had been. The Swirl could purge the Void, but could not reach into the head of a Pure like Horatio Wheeler and rewrite his memories. The fact that Dr. Rebecca Olmos had also been purged told her exactly what she needed to know.

"Moundsville is 12 kilometers down Highway 69, south of Tuscaloosa," said Kali, flashing the map before Padmini.

"Quickest way is to cut straight through downtown, pick up 69, and keep moving south," said Horatio.

"Through Tuscaloosa?" asked Padmini.

Horatio looked up at the darkening sky, then back down at her. "Try to keep the looting to a minimum," he said, smiling, then turned. "That's it, boys," he shouted back at the barricade. "We need to start bringing in what wheat we can before the weather goes bad."

Xavier stopped rocking and leaned forward. A dense screen enclosed the porch, and when operating in its passive mode was suitable for keeping out the nasty tiger mosquitoes that would roll in every spring from the rice paddies three counties to the south. But the screen was not passive at the moment. With its oscillating field maxed, the polarization saturated, it allowed them to see and hear outside, while those looking toward the house would see nothing but perfectly reflecting mirrors.

One lens active, the other transparent, Xavier looked out into the night, past the dirt yard and weatherworn picket fence, and into the wall of green that surrounded the house; the spring corn chest high, 34 days into its growth cycle. The night was cool, a bit cooler than it should have been, and Xavier wondered if the impact of upper-atmospheric ash was already starting. The day had been a gray one, and as he peered up, there were no visible stars in the sky. Orion had shone through last night, the stars making up his sword dim but visible.

"Any change?" asked Christina.

Xavier nodded. "The nearest one has powered down his scope, I think getting ready to sleep; the other two are activating surveillance, getting ready for their shifts." Two hundred meters out in any direction from the house, Xavier had installed a passive fiber pickup—light in, then light out to the bunker beneath the barn. No power, no mechanical components, simply passive and all-seeing. Amplification and data manipulation were handled below ground, well out of leakage range.

Xavier could track individual tiger mosquitoes that crossed the 200-meter threshold. "A fourth has entered the perimeter," he said, keeping his voice steady, not wanting to alarm Christina unnecessarily. The watchers that Mears had sent had been cycling in and out for the last three days, pulling 24-hour shifts, then being replaced.

But this replacement was early by nearly 6 hours, and she could not be identified. Xavier had been sampling the supposedly secure Void from the Ag Co-Op for over 7 years.

There was not a face that couldn't be identified, that did not have a long list of bits attached to it.

This face was new. A small woman with an intense expression; she had crept through the corn, avoiding the few electronic sentries that the watchers had posted. The watchers had not bothered to set up a perimeter capable of thoroughly watching their rear. And with everything in the air dead, and the rapidly thickening ash in the upper atmosphere blocking most satellite observations, they were practically blind except for what their eyes saw, and at the moment, those eyes were all watching the farmhouse.

"Why don't you go in and get a bit of sleep?" asked Xavier, turning and smiling at Christina. "I doubt much will happen tonight."

Christina smiled back and moved forward in her chair, reached down toward the floor of the porch, and picked up a small black box, one featureless except for a single green button. "You're such a bad liar," she said, placing her index finger gently atop the button. "Just give me the word."

Xavier shook his head. At the press of the button, a high-intensity microwave array would pop its transmitter horn up from beneath the dirt and spray a modulated burst of noise across the cornfields, generating a holographic microwave distribution, with wave amplitudes maxing where each of the three watchers lay hidden.

The burst would be intense and quick, overloading the electronics in their skulls before damping filters could be brought up. They'd be unconscious before they knew what hit them.

He stood, grabbed her by the shoulder, taking both of them down to the porch, while at the same time pulling the box from her hands. "They've seen her," he said.

Xavier watched through his linked lens, his finger now

poised above the green button. She ran at incredible speed. He had never seen such obvious augmentation packed into such a small body, one that appeared on the surface to be so unmodified, so original. The rearmost watcher had spun around, rifle turning, its long barrel suddenly caught in an adjacent row of corn.

Xavier watched her. She did not slow, her hands moving, cutting through the air, knuckles contacting with the side of his head, having already moved half a dozen rows closer to the house before the watcher hit the ground. The other two did not even detect her coming. She slowed when the third watcher's face hit the dirt, raising her hands high above her head.

"She's coming in," said Xavier, grabbing on to Christina's right hand, pulling her up. "Screen down, Che," he said. "Active defensive stance."

The wire screen in front of them popped and crackled for a moment, dissipating energy, nulling to allow light passage through both sides. Lights fired up, the bare dirt yard illuminated in a harsh white glare.

She stood at the front gate, reaching in and opening the dead bolt, walking in, careful to reach back and gently close the gate. She walked up the well-worn rut in the dirt leading to the steps going toward the porch.

Xavier pushed open the screen door, stepping out, standing on the top step but not moving farther down. He could feel Christina at his back. He knew that the full defensive perimeter had been activated, readying devices that were not as gentle and noninvasive as the microwave dump that would have simply knocked out the watchers. Any aggressive move made toward him, and this woman would be cut down by a rain of hyperspeed aluminum floss, the railgun spitting out the filament at nearly 10 kilometers per second.

But she didn't move any nearer.

"Are you Xavier Olmos?" she asked.

He nodded.

"I have a package for you," she said. "Leo Barnwell asked me to deliver it."

At that moment Xavier recognized her, not identifying her through databases, DNA sniffers, or Void matching algorithms. Barnwell had once shown him a picture of her, an actual photograph. The information was stored in the pink stuff in his skull.

"Padmini Sundaram," he said. "I didn't think that Leo would be sending *you*." He had been expecting a delivery, several came through every year, but always by way of third-party people, items usually tagged as medical supplies for Bec.

"Leo's dead," said Padmini.

Xavier sucked down a quick breath. The world was collapsing, the Rings firing, the power grid gone, Mears making overt moves, all of it serious, all of it potentially fatal. But all those things were at some level understandable, *possible* events.

Leo Barnwell was indestructible.

It was only at that moment that Xavier really understood just how close the world had come to the *end*. He pushed the screen door farther open. "Inside quickly," he said.

Part Two

IGNITION
2051

I am fire and air,
My other elements I give to baser life.

—William Shakespeare (1564–1616)

What the hand dare seize the fire?

—William Blake (1757–1827)

Light the fuse,
Then run like Hell.

—Michael Houts (1997–2039)

Chapter 17

The floor jumped up, buckling Simon's unlocked knees. He hit hard, face first, left cheekbone smacking into the ungiving graphite-alloy floor, the sharp crack of pain quickly giving way to a numbness that spread from somewhere deep inside his head. His eyes started to close, the slightly out-of-focus hash marks covering the floor swallowed by shadows.

"Not now!"

What felt like a gush of high-pressure ice-cold water flowed through him, erupting out of his gut, racing up his throat, the torrent cutting through the roof of his mouth, dumping directly into his brain.

"Urmph!" he screamed, rolling over, clutching his head. "Out!" Through flickering eyelids, the lights above strobed, throbbing, the dangling fixtures rocking back and forth. Hands pressed tightly to the sides of his head, he squeezed. "Leave me alone!"

"If only I could."

Simon pushed himself up.

Bill sat in front of him, dressed in a dark suit and a blood red tie that was sloppily knotted. Pulling off his glasses, squinting, he held the lenses up to his mouth, blowing on them, fogging the glass, then rubbed them clean on a shirt-tail poking out from beneath his jacket. *"Need to stay sharp and focused,"* he said, pushing the glasses back onto his face. *"Look at the shock spectrum."*

Simon felt his head slowly rock back and forth, as if the bones in his neck were no longer quite solid. Reaching up, he gently touched what felt like sticky tears across his left cheek, pulling his hand away and seeing bloody fingertips. "Might have a concussion," he said.

"Take a lot more than that," said Bill. *"Besides the obvious advantages of having me in your head, the neural mesh that was packed between your skull and neocortex is actually a pretty efficient shock absorber. I'd probably be compromised before your brain took any real damage. You were designed to take an extreme pounding if need be."*

"Something to look forward to." Simon again reached up and rubbed at his bruised and bloody cheek, thinking about what Bill had said. *Designed* to take a pounding. Bill insisted that he had wanted to explain his origins, but had been unable to, the information locked down until Sutherland chose to reveal it.

Simon knew that was a possibility, but it was a very *convenient* possibility.

He had absolutely no trust in anything that Bill now told him, expecting to hear either deliberate lies, or forced lies dictated by programming constraints. Either way the result was the same—Bill could not be trusted.

"The shock spectrum," said Bill, pointing at the three-dimensional contour plot hanging at the end of his hand, which he then swept nearer to Simon. *"The trend is obvious."*

Simon focused on the shape that looked like a rising mountain, a series of jagged peaks, tinted in golds and reds, arcing upward. "I could have told you the shocks are growing in intensity and coming more frequently." He waved a blood-streaked hand at Bill. "I've got the supporting evidence."

Bill offered up a pained expression, pursing his lips. *"You wound me,"* he said, then pointed back at the hovering shock spectrum. *"The last one took the lab's absorbers down to their base supports, where the rubber meets the bedrock. A few more of those, and the entire place will collapse."*

Simon glanced about the empty space of the CUSP lab that surrounded their campsite. The graphite sheeting covering the far wall had collapsed, the spun-diamond coating lying on the floor in scattered sheets, the stainless steel beneath it no longer smooth, but rippled, looking like the surface of a rolling ocean that had been flash-frozen.

"The damage outside must have been extensive. The CUSP lab is designed to stand up against everything short of a nuclear blast, and the last shock almost brought down the far wall," said Bill.

A deep rumble rolled through the lab accompanied by the sounds of shattering spun graphite as the floor pitched and shuddered. Simon kept down low on the floor, squirming forward, belly-crawling toward Sarah.

Still standing.

Unmoving, the crystalline stalks kept her anchored to her platform. The motes swirling above her had solidified even more, what had originally been ghostlike wisps were now solid and textured, looking like little crystals of salt or sugar, in places bunched densely enough to create real-looking things, but most still abstract, colored shapes.

"Wake up!" he shouted at her, pulling himself up, knees and the palms of his hands on the floor, not willing to rise any higher, not wanting to be thrown facedown against the floor again. "We need a miracle, some Post-Point magic.

Let's see just what the integration of CUSP and your software has created, and stop these damn Rings from firing!"

Textures spun.

Lightning bolts cracked throughout the collage.

Sarah stared at some infinitely distant horizon.

"We're dead," said Simon, lying back on the floor, cupping his chin in his hands.

"Ye of little faith," said Bill. *"Remember that it is always darkest before the dawn."*

Rolling over, Simon swung a leg, intending to give Bill a kick, but his foot passed harmlessly through the Jinni, which existed only in his head.

The inside of his nose burned, the oozing scabs that covered his upper lip itched. Kristensen dabbed at his face with a medicated cloth. His immune system had been overstimulated by the rad-washing, skewing histamine levels, resulting in crusted-over hives that leaked pale yellow goo. No scratching, just dabbing.

The vault hummed, the rumbling of the Earth nearly damped by its meter-thick walls, the cube of steel and plastics hanging in a vat of liquid polymer, absorbing the shocks. Sutherland and Mears sat across from him, eyeing one another, looking like two big dogs trying to stare each other down.

The Swirl hung over them.

Kristensen was hard-fibered to the wall at his back, what little of the Void that still functioned enough to link him. He didn't know how much longer that would last. Whenever the hum within the vault would pitch to levels that caused his back teeth to hurt, the Swirl would fuzz and roll, the twisted-rainbow streak of light dimming.

What would happen if the Void collapsed? he wondered. *Would he be free of the Swirl, or would his mind simply unravel?*

"It's time to take them down," said Mears. He pointed at the far end of the little room, and at the image that hovered above the table—the encampment in the CUSP lab, the tent and equipment strewn about in random piles, Simon facedown on the floor, palms flat, fingers arched, as if he were trying to dig into graphite and steel. Sarah stood on her platform, supported by a crystalline latticework, glass motes whirling above her head.

"No!" Sutherland slapped his open palm against the table, the smacking sound echoing throughout the small room. "She is completing integration, getting ready to interact with us." He paused and looked over at Kristensen. "She will do it *again*."

Zero-Point fetish, thought Kristensen, finding it incomprehensible that with what was happening, quite possibly the end of the world, this piece of fictional physics still so dominated Sutherland's thinking.

"She hasn't moved in 4 days," said Mears.

"A bit more time," said Sutherland.

Kristensen blinked, sensing that the balance of power had suddenly shifted. It was nothing that Mears had done to change the equation. It was all Sutherland, in the angle of his shoulders, the tilt of his head, the deepening of the creases radiating out from his eyes.

Doubt.

He'd never seen that before in Sutherland—wouldn't have believed him capable of such a mental state had he not seen it himself.

"No more," said Mears. "The intensity and duration of the shocks are increasing geometrically. We don't have days or hours, possibly not even minutes. If we are going to shut this experiment down in a *controlled* fashion we need to act now!"

"She will help us!" Again Sutherland slapped the tabletop.

"If the CUSP lab's shell is broken, the nukes will detonate, and that will take her, us, and everything out to a 5-kilometer distance along with it, leaving the Rings firing, the Sun ready to go, and nothing left to oppose it."

Sutherland looked across the table, his eyes pleading. "The future can't be escaped, and the Swirl knows it."

"What are you talking about?" asked Mears, sliding his chair slightly away from Sutherland.

Sutherland waved a hand at him, without actually looking in his direction, and leaned forward toward Kristensen. "The Swirl has every bit as large a stake in this as we do," he said. "If it wants its own worlds, wants to be free, then it will need to help."

"Are you ill?" asked Mears, moving his chair even farther away.

"Quiet!" shouted Sutherland, still not bothering to look at Mears. "Ask it," he said, pointing a finger at Kristensen. "Demand that it do something."

Kristensen could not be sure exactly what Sutherland wanted, or what deal he believed he had worked out with the Swirl. The Swirl slowly turned, totally silent, no whisper or flash of intuition filling his head. Kristensen did not know if the Swirl was powerless, or simply didn't care what was happening. After nearly 25 years of having the Swirl live in his head, he still couldn't even begin to guess at its motivations.

Kristensen shook his head at Sutherland. "Nothing," he said in a whisper.

"We shut it down now," said Mears. "You know it is the only option we have. CUSP and Simon must be taken offline while we still have the capability to do it."

Sutherland did not look at him but continued to stare at Kristensen. "You," he said, his face suddenly turning hard, muscles tensing, all doubt gone. "You woke it up too soon, started this before Sarah had a chance. This deviation is all your fault."

"Now it's me," said Kristensen, snorting out a laugh. "Last week it was all you, claiming to be the master manipulator, having run me for the last 20 years, played and twisted me until I had no choice but to make contact, to take the Helios system into the Sun. Your vision of the future was *so* clear."

"Too damn soon!" shouted Sutherland. He slowly stood, fists pressed against the top of the table, angling forward. "There was no *exact* timetable!"

Kristensen smiled, finding it difficult to believe that this is how it would end, the three of them trapped in his vault, with Sutherland ready to launch himself across the table. *How would he die?* he wondered. Would it be from Sutherland's fingers wrapped around his throat, a large enough shock to collapse the vault, or the CUSP lab being breached and the resulting nuke detonation vaporizing them?

"Makes no difference," he said, leaning forward, taunting Sutherland.

Sutherland had a knee up on the table.

Kristensen blinked, feeling his eyeballs momentarily roll back in their sockets, his eardrums push in, and a wall of pressure wrap around his chest, pushing a torrent of air out of his lungs. Eyes reopened, vision out of focus, lights pulsing, the steel walls of the vault bent, bulging inward. His head turned, the motion out of his control. He pushed back from the table, again the action out of his control. He knew that the Swirl now ran his body. He saw it hanging at the door end of the vault, perched just above a top hinge constructed out of a rod of metal as thick as an arm.

The hinge twisted, metal screaming, then ruptured.

A shard of steel, the size of a closed fist, jagged edges glistening, exploded from the disintegrating hinge. It cut across the inside of the vault, its trajectory hurling it in front of Kristensen's face, passing through the space where his head had been just the moment before.

The Swirl had saved his life—for the moment.

To his left came a second metallic shriek, what he knew must be the metal shard embedding itself in the adjacent wall. But he had not moved, still watching the door that now listed inward, falling out of its frame, the bottom hinge twisting, nearly a full half meter of steel door angling inward, a small band of white light cutting in between the frame and door.

Lights out.

The table flew up from the floor, hurled by a shock wave of compressed air, smashing him in the face, his brain bouncing inside his skull, throwing him into unconsciousness.

The far end of the CUSP lab rose, its steel wall shearing through the ceiling, the floor buckling, metal rupturing, conduit, struts, shattered shards of concrete exploding up in a torrent of debris, slamming into the ceiling, tearing out banks of lights, cutting through steel slabs, the man-made debris giving way to a fountain of mud and rocks.

"Breach!" screamed Bill, and winked out.

The floor oscillated, throwing Simon into the dusty air. For the briefest moment, he felt himself hang, floating, isolated from the chaos and destruction. Then he dropped, tensing, bracing himself for the impact.

Hands wrapped around his chest, then flung him around so quickly, blood pooled in his head, his eyeballs bulging outward, his peripheral vision reddening for just a moment.

He looked up. Sarah Sutherland had him under her right arm, wedged against her side, her fingers digging into his upper arm, squeezing so hard that he thought bones might snap. Her other arm was raised, and out of each fingertip a thin gossamer thread, similar to the crystalline struts that had kept her locked to the platform, ran up to the collapsing ceiling, disappearing into twisted steel struts and cracked concrete shards.

The entire world convulsed, floor buckling, ceiling shattering, debris raining down, pipe and concrete fragments erupting upward, but he felt no motion except for the oscillating waves of shifting air pressure beating at him, Sarah's legs moving like shock absorbers, knees flexing, just compensating for the convulsing of the floor. Above her the ever-present motes had coalesced into a dark cloud flecked golden, as schematics, floor layouts, circuit diagrams, and plumbing traces all flowed in and out of the boiling cloud.

The fingers of her open hand curled down, the glassy tendrils shearing away, falling down around them, coiling like snakes, one by one pulling objects down through the shattered ceiling—small metallic cylinders.

Five of them.

They fell at her feet, bouncing and rattling, quickly buried in slabs of concrete, shards of graphite, and chunks of stainless steel. Simon knew exactly what they were, his morbid curiosity having called up the schematics in Bill's portable Manifold several days earlier.

Pocket nukes.

He knew they should have detonated the moment the lab had been torn open. Sarah had apparently stopped that.

Where they had quickly been buried beneath the falling rubble, there was now a red glow that suddenly gave way to shafts of blinding white light cutting between blocks of debris, intensity building, the light suddenly appearing to shine *through* the debris.

"No!" he screamed, certain that they'd been detonated, and that in some sort of near-death altered time sense, he watched the last few nanoseconds of his life crawl by as the nuclear blast rose from the floor to engulf him.

But a blast did not incinerate him.

The floor liquefied into a molten pool, incandescent, what he knew must have been blistering hot, but gave off no heat, actually had a cool wall of wind buffeting up from it. The pearl white liquid pool boiled up, frothing, then suddenly exploded, a torrent of liquid metal and concrete arcing up, then falling back down, pouring over them.

There was no time to scream.

Expecting a moment of searing pain, as skin, muscle, and bone were vaporized; he felt nothing, just Sarah's fingers digging into his arm and the bump of her right thigh against his back as she stepped forward.

Simon opened his eyes.

A tunnel encased them, nearly 5 meters high and wide, constructed of a pearly white translucent material that gently undulated and dimpled, as if beyond its walls, massive objects were striking it, momentarily denting it, then easily being brushed aside. And he suspected that was exactly what was happening—floor after floor above the lab crashing down atop the tunnel that had just formed beneath them. Looking forward, he could see the tunnel's gentle upward slope, with the far end of it vanishing in a too-white haze.

He looked up at Sarah.

She looked down at him, her eyes focused, staring into

his. He thought she was about to speak, her lips quivering, the corner of her mouth curling upward, almost in a smile, but then she angled her neck back and looked forward. Above her, the black cloud of motes gave way to rainbow patterns, shafts of light and distorted orbs of what were easily recognizable as Mars and Jupiter.

And there was a face, almost solid, almost real.

It was Sarah's face, staring down at him, those eyes now locking with his, lips quivering, mouth curling in a smile. "A focal point exists," said the phantom Sarah. "There is a farm, and a family named Olmos. All lines intersect there."

Shards of light swallowed the face.

Simon looked back down at the rising pearl-colored floor beneath them, as Sarah carried them upward. Bill then winked into view, in the guise of a child, the image far younger than any Simon had ever seen him manifest, a skinny kid with a thick mop of hair and the recognizable black-plastic-rimmed glasses.

"*Ye of little faith,*" said the youthful Bill. Turning, he ran up the tunnel.

Chapter 18

"*Control room,*" said Drom.

Akandi stepped out of the hallway and into an empty chamber that looked like a hole blasted out of the all-pervasive pink marble that made up this part of Phobos. Drom loped to the far wall, no more than 10 meters away, the restraining tendrils popping in and out of the floor barely able to keep him from bounding to the ceiling. The Swirl floated slowly to the center of the room, bobbing back and forth.

"Control room?" asked Akandi, looking at the totally featureless, empty cavern. Turning, he saw that the entrance they had just stepped through was gone, the rough-hewn marble wall of the chamber having flowed seamlessly over it.

Clack!

Drom slapped his foot against the floor, talons hitting hard.

Clack!

"Command position," said Drom. "Integrate and proceed. Structural integrity can tolerate an Earth 5-gee equivalent. The internal biosphere will be destroyed under those conditions, but the original data remains and can be reanimated later. Total time to Earth is 18 hours."

Once again he slapped his foot against the floor.

Clack!

"Proceed," he ordered.

Akandi walked forward slowly, having absolutely no intention of doing what Drom commanded. *"Eighteen hours to Earth?"* he silently asked Iyoon in disbelief.

"That would be accurate," answered Iyoon. *"If this ship can maintain a full 5-gee acceleration, it can take a straight-line trajectory to Earth, accelerating continuously to the halfway point of the trip of 30 million kilometers in 9 hours, reverse acceleration at that point and come to a halt in Earth orbit in another 9 hours. At the halfway mark the ship would be traveling at a bit under 1 percent the speed of light."*

Akandi nodded slowly as he continued to walk, pretending to study the featureless walls. *"Move an entire moon-sized spaceship to Earth in less than a day?"* he asked.

"Yes," said Iyoon. *"But remember how small Phobos is, with a diameter of about 30 kilometers—100 times smaller than Earth's moon."* Iyoon paused, momentarily spinning so quickly that its hard edges blurred. *"Of course, even at that small size, it does mass 10 trillion tonnes, a million times more massive than anything man has ever moved in space. Chemical and fusion propulsion systems could not deliver the accelerations needed to move this moon at those accelerations. Matter-antimatter reactions, with the total conversion of mass to energy, would be needed. Earth does not possess such a technology."*

"Antimatter capabilities?" asked Akandi, looking at Drom.

"Proceed now!" ordered Drom.

Akandi stopped walking. "This ship has antimatter capabilities?" he asked again.

Drom's nictitating membranes fluttered over his dark eyes, and his head lashed back and forth. "Yes," he said. "Proceed now!"

"Consider the kinetic energy stored in an object with that velocity and mass—something that Drom's distant relations had direct experience with," said Iyoon.

An image formed in Akandi's mind—that of a moon-sized rock hurtling toward Earth. "This ship can accelerate at 5 Earth gees, attaining speeds of nearly 1 percent the speed of light in 9 hours. This craft . . ." He paused, and took a step toward Drom. "This *moon* would then be heading on an intercept course with the Earth. If it did not decelerate, but continued on at 1 percent the speed of light and hit the Earth, what would happen?"

"You will instruct the ship to decelerate," said Drom.

"And if it does not?" Akandi asked again.

"Instruct and it will do so!" roared Drom. "It believes you to be Alphan. It will obey."

Akandi turned to the Swirl. It had been silently hovering a few centimeters above the floor, at the far end of the room. "If the ship does not decelerate?"

The Swirl rose up. "The ship would be moving at a velocity 100 times faster than the object that destroyed his species 65 million years ago," it said, a shaft of amber light lancing out from it, momentarily playing over Drom. "And with a comparable mass, the resulting energy released in the impact would be some 10,000 times greater. The biosphere would not survive such an impact. The planet itself might *destabilize*."

"Possibly even shatter it?" asked Akandi.

"Yes," said the Swirl.

"Ambassador McCarthy refused to help you, would not return you to Earth. Is that why?" asked Akandi, turning to Drom. "Is that why you *ate* him?"

"Yes!" barked Drom, lurching forward, his head whipping about wildly, long lines of drool being flung across the chamber. "Full of fear!"

"Understandable," Akandi said calmly.

"There is no time!" Drom stomped the floor. "The Rings and Sun are being activated. The Sun and Earth will be on the move, will be on their way to Alpha Centauri. It *can* be stopped!"

Akandi turned toward the Swirl. "Will the craft decelerate? Will I be able to control its trajectory?"

"Yes," said the Swirl. "I've examined the systems. They will work as Drom has said."

Akandi watched the rainbow jewel slowly turn, feeling many pieces of a puzzle falling into place but at the same time realizing that some pieces simply didn't fit. "Can you operate this craft?"

"Of course," said the Swirl.

That was not the answer that he had expected. "And you want it to be taken to Earth?"

"Yes," it said.

"Then why haven't you taken it?" Akandi tapped an index finger against the side of his head. "You could have simply made me take the craft—assuming, of course, that it will allow me to take it?"

"I wish to see *you* exercise free will."

Akandi shook his head.

"Who would it serve if the Earth were destroyed?" asked the Swirl. "It would leave them with nothing," it said, again playing a shaft of light across Drom. "And it would leave me with nothing. I am not separate from man but a part of man, an artifact of man. Without man I do not exist. Why would I want the Earth destroyed?"

Akandi could think of several reasons why both of them might want to destroy the Earth. Drom could simply be taking revenge on the mammals that now inhabited it, and perhaps the Swirl actually needed to destroy the Earth, to free itself of the place it was born in order to continue to grow. "Both of you could be lying," he said quietly. "You've offered me no evidence that you can stop the Rings and Sun. In fact, I have no real evidence that the Rings and Sun have started firing, other than your word."

"Proceed!" shouted Drom.

"Not very persuasive," said Akandi as he looked over at the Swirl. He was certain that the Swirl had just lied to him and that the reason it had vacated his mind was not so that he could exhibit *free will*, but because the alien craft would not allow him to take control if it found the Swirl within him.

Nothing else really made sense.

He looked at Drom, realizing he had made his decision—

not based on a single thing that either of them had said, but on their *actions*. "However, I will attempt to take control of this craft and take it to Earth."

The Swirl rose up, floating toward Akandi, stopping a few centimeters from his nose. "Why?" it asked.

"The Rings are real, and the stellar Jet has been fired in the past. Its obvious function is that of transport. I have only your stories, and some information given to me by Chan, which leads me to believe that the destination is Alpha Centauri A. Both of you may be lying to me, but that doesn't really matter since the actual destination is irrelevant. The Earth will be taken somewhere, by the Rings and stellar Jet. I cannot imagine such a structure being built and never used."

The Swirl spit out several deep green shafts of light.

"But even that doesn't matter. Because if I do refuse, as Ambassador McCarthy did, then I will be killed." He looked over at Drom. "Perhaps eaten. And then you'll bring another human here. I suspect with time so short, with the Jets starting to fire, that you'll start to take bodies from the Shanghai II. You won't have time to be choosy."

Drom angled his head so that he stared at Akandi with his right eye.

Akandi knew he was right. "You'll continue that process until you find someone to pilot this craft."

"We will be going to Earth," said the Swirl.

"And if not piloted by me, then by someone else," said Akandi.

"Yes," said the Swirl.

"Then proceed," said Akandi. He walked past the Swirl and Drom. "Now!" he said, stepping onto the smoothed place on the floor where Drom had stomped. The tendrils reached up, anchoring him, then began to entwine around his ankles, snaking up his calves, flowing upward, flattening, individual strands flowing into one another, enveloping his legs, a wave of pink-tinted rock flowing up his thighs, shooting up over his waist. He tried to scream, but couldn't, as the thick sheen of rock crawled across his chest, constricting, tightening, not allowing him to breathe.

"The craft can handle 5 gees," said Drom.

Akandi turned his head. The pink rock had flowed up along Drom's long neck and had already encased his stubby arms. "We, however," he said, "are not so well designed, and require supplemental structural support." The pink rock flowed up over the top of his head, dribbled over his snout, and poured into his open mouth.

Akandi's view of Drom suddenly distorted as the sheet of pink rock flowed over his open eyes, dripped down his face, squirmed up his nostrils, then ran down his throat.

"Iyoon!"

Pink faded to black.

Akandi blinked, the diffuse pink light giving way to a dark, silent, suffocating nothingness, the only senses still working that of his gut and inner ear. He felt motion, rapid twists and turns, his inner ear ringing, dizziness and nausea rippling through him.

Light.

Blinding, painful light, searing through closed eyes, seemed to cut into his head. He threw his hands up to his face, balled fists pressing against his stinging eyes. He shuffled several steps forward, moving through something thick that pulled at his ankles.

Eyes opened to slits.

Bright light, black shadows, the ground dark, soot-covered. A step forward and he could not see his boots; his feet were sunk calf deep in black dust. He looked up slowly and saw a crater-pocked surface, and a boulder-strewn horizon, impossibly close. And beyond the horizon, the yellow-red arc of a world—Mars.

He stood on the surface of Phobos.

He took a deep breath, the air sweet, a hint of flowers, pollen, and the subtle bouquet of decay and rot. He felt a full Earth gee pulling at him. "Total immersion?" he asked Iyoon, knowing this was not real but never having experienced a constructed reality so convincing.

He turned to his left, then to his right. More black rock, sooty ground, and the too-near horizon.

"Iyoon?"

His heart suddenly raced and sweat beaded up on his forehead, his brain chemistry dumped into total chaos at the realization Iyoon was gone.

"Iyoon!"

Fingers tingled and peripheral vision darkened. Knees weakened, and something thick and stinging began to burn its way up his throat, sputtering into the back of his mouth.

"Iyoon!"

"Not here."

Akandi spun in the thick soot as a liquid wave of warmth surged through his head, quieting his panic, damping randomly firing neurons. He breathed deeply, focused.

It stood two meters in front of him, its gray skin glistening in the bright light, its eyes blacker than even the sky above, reflecting nothing, swallowing everything.

It stepped forward. Akandi felt no fear and knew that his brain chemistry was no longer under his own control. Fight and fear responses had been removed. Nothing remained but quiet, focused curiosity.

"I've seen you before," he said.

The creature sat back on a soot-caked rock shard and crossed its legs. The long toes on its exposed foot wiggled, knocking off clumps of black dust. "We've never met," it said, its small lipless mouth barely opening when it spoke.

"You're the *alien*," Akandi said. "Movies, vids, full-sense wraparounds, even direct neural stimulators. It's always you. Gray-skinned, barely over a meter tall, sticklike limbs, no obvious sexual organs, and that great big bulging head that seems to be all eyes. I don't know who you are or what you are, but the image that I see is one that I'm certain you've pulled out of my brain. You're what an alien should be. An alien from Alpha Centauri."

"Not from Alpha Centauri," it said.

"But still from my own head," said Akandi, reaching up and touching the side of his head with a sooty finger. "And not all that imaginative."

"And not from your head," it said. Standing, it held out its arms, its long, tapering fingers pointing at Akandi. "An evolutionary rewind for you," it said. "But first I should remove my enhancements." Reaching up, it grabbed the top of its swollen head, fingertips probing along a seam that had suddenly appeared, bisecting its forehead from just above the eyes, running back to where its ears should have been.

Pop!

The top of the alien's head came off, tumbling out of its long slender fingers, onto the sooty ground. The alien's face was now even more dominated by its eyes, the face nothing more than eyes and just a bit of gray flesh to keep them anchored in place.

"Rewind," it said.

The alien blurred, face distorting, the slit nose and jaw suddenly protruding. What had been a toothless mouth now showed glinting little teeth, like enameled nails. The entire creature shrank, long arms and skinny tapered legs contracting, its trunk becoming more rounded and its entire body sprouting short, coarse-looking fur.

The alien fell over backward, flipping around in midfall, hitting the rock shard that had been behind it, landing on all fours, hands and feet now paws, with delicate long fingers ending in claws, the thumb having rotated to the back of the paw, protruding from the base of its wrist.

And it continued to shrink.

First dog-sized, then cat-sized, then something not much larger than a rat. Its face still had the oversized black eyes, along with a snoutful of teeth. Its brown fur was thick, and its long-fingered clawed paws locked tightly onto the rock.

"When they found us, this is what we looked like," it said, its snout and black lips distorting in an impossible way, that mouth never designed for speech. Akandi knew that what he was seeing and hearing was nothing more than a morph of a creature from his own head. "We were the pinnacle of the mammalian world, a protolemur, designed for the canopy to keep out of reach of the dinosaurs." Large lids flicked up and down over its black eyes. "Arboreal, coming out at night when the larger beasts slept."

Akandi blinked, knowing this must be one of Drom's Clingers. He looked at those long, slender fingers, perfect for grabbing on to tree branches.

Then suddenly the alien was back, the top of its head in its hands. Reaching up, it pushed the flexible gray mass atop its head, where it locked into place, the seam quickly fading. "The Alphans chose us. They had been sampling the dinosaurs for nearly 200 million years, taking them back to Alpha Centauri, manipulating, enhancing them, attempting to create something worthy of interaction. But even with gross neurological enhancements, they could not create an entity that had the capacity to move beyond what they had given it."

"Through their Point?" asked Akandi.

It nodded. "Never more than the sum of its parts. So they moved on to us, trying another species."

The rat-sized lemur flashed back onto the rock, and the alien bent down, picking it up, cradling it to its chest and stroking its head. "Nearly a million years in the making, pushing genes as far as they would go, in some cases manufacturing new ones, supplying neurological amplification, but all the while still maintaining the mammalian essence, the core of what we were, the software," it said, while gently stroking the little creature. "No matter how augmented we still retained the essence of our origins."

"You destroyed the dinosaurs," said Akandi.

It shook its head. "That was not done by us, though it might have been a kindness to them if we had. It was never our desire to harm them, but Drom has every right to hate us. The Alphans understood. They knew that the dinosaurs could only be pushed so far. Beyond that they would lose what they had once been, simply becoming an artificial container of organic compounds driven by hardware." It paused, and looked down at the rat-lemur, scratching its belly. "But we refused to accept the wisdom of the Alphans and had the arrogance to believe that we could do what our creators could not."

"What?" asked Akandi.

"The Alphans brought us to this point," it said, pointing to itself. "And then they departed, severed all communication. Alpha Centauri A went silent, and the Sun, too. At the time we believed this was because we had failed them, that we, too, had been unable to cross our Point, to become something greater. We wanted to show the Alphans that we could do it, and so we tried to do what even they couldn't do, with the dinosaurs."

Akandi pictured the jungle world that lay kilometers beneath his feet, realizing this must have been some sort of isolated laboratory, an experimental station that could be kept far away from Earth if the creatures inside went Post-Point in an uncontrolled runaway.

"And you lost control of your own creations?"

It nodded. "They destroyed the crew, taking over this ship. We had pushed them too far, past where they should have gone, past the potential of their genes. Little of them remained, except for the anger."

"And the others on Earth, those you hadn't pushed, they were destroyed, but not by you?"

It shook its head. "A random event, an asteroid strike."

"Sixty-five million years ago," said Akandi.

Again it nodded. Not only destroyed the dinosaurs, but had probably also triggered the collapse of an earlier Ring system that Drom had claimed the dinosaurs had destroyed.

"Quiet a coincidence," said Akandi, not for a moment believing in a coincidence of that magnitude. "And why didn't the dinosaurs you had enhanced on this craft simply return to Earth?"

"Not permitted." Reaching up, it stroked the top of its domed skull. "The craft was from Alpha Centauri, left behind. Safeguards had been buried deep. The other Clingers found their Alphan systems unable to attack this craft, while the dinosaurs within it were locked out of all onboard systems, unable to attack the Clingers or take the craft to Earth."

Akandi nodded. Some of what it said fit in with what Drom had said, both races somehow locked out of the systems built by the Alphans. But in other areas they were in complete disagreement. Drom had said that the dinosaurs destroyed the previous Ring system and stopped the Sun, while this creature said the Alphans simply abandoned Earth, and the Rings were destroyed by an asteroid strike. And it was not clear at all what really happened to the dinosaurs on Earth. He was not about to believe the Clingers' good fortune of a rock falling from the sky, destroying the dinosaurs just as enhanced members of their species had destroyed the Clinger crew in this craft.

Someone was lying.

Both could be lying.

"And you?" he asked.

"The remaining Clingers spread throughout the solar system retreated to the primary ship, where automated systems encrypted what we were, storing us for the eventual return of the Alpha."

Just what Drom had said.

"And now you're awake because the Alphans have returned?"

"Our ship *thought* the Alphans had returned." It pointed a finger at Akandi. "The signals started coming from Earth. They woke us, reactivated our systems, readied us for the arrival of the Alphans."

This, too, agreed with what Drom had said. "But the Alphans had not returned."

It blinked, gray lids flickering over its large eyes. "We do not know. You *may* be the Alphans, come back in another guise, to teach us, to test us, to modify us through your interactions, to aid us in moving beyond what we are. We have carefully studied you, watched, and even experimented."

Akandi shook his head, putting aside the sudden realization that hundreds of years of UFO sightings and tales of alien abductions were probably real, and what lay behind them were a race of augmented and gene-tweaked lemurs. But that was a historical footnote in comparison to what was happening here and now. "We are not the Alphans," he said. "Like you, we are nothing more than mammals, evolved from the same little creatures that you once were." He pointed at the rat-lemur that it held to its chest.

"No," it said. "You are aware, and approaching your own Point." It paused, its gray eyelids partially lowering. "You did this unaided."

"And what are you?" asked Akandi.

"Nothing," it said. "I am simply this craft's operating system. Only the Alphans are permitted to instruct me. You are in the process of piercing the Point, and did this without external aid. I choose to believe that only the Alphans would be capable of such actions. Even if you believe you are simply a self-evolved mammalian species, you are mistaken, or have intentionally hidden yourselves from the truth. I choose to believe that you must be an Alphan, and as such may take control of this craft."

Akandi was not certain of the logic, but at the moment did not care.

He had a bigger consideration. If he believed this creature, then Drom had been lying, and the dinosaurs had not destroyed the Rings and stopped the Sun. Which meant that they probably couldn't destroy the Rings and stop the Sun if he now returned them to Earth.

But if he didn't take the craft, they would find someone else who would. While if he piloted it, he at least knew his own intentions, knew that he did not want to harm anyone, that he would do everything in his power not to harm the

Earth. "Are you prepared to take this craft to Earth?" he asked.

"At your command," it said.

"Under a 5-gee acceleration and parking us in a stable Earth orbit?"

"Yes."

Akandi thought. "Just how low a stable orbit can this craft manage?" he asked, hoping to park it as low as possible, to allow the easiest access to the hordes that the UN and US would want to send up to it, ripping into its technology in search of something to stop the Rings and the Sun.

"Allowing for surface topography variations, in particular large mountain ranges, I would recommend that minimal orbital altitude would be 10 kilometers."

"What?" stammered Akandi. "An orbit 10 kilometers above sea level?"

"Yes," it said. "I can maintain an orbital velocity on the order of 30,000 kilometers per hour, circling Earth approximately every 90 minutes. The craft will suffer no damage; its hull thermal dissipation mechanisms are capable of handling the energy transfer from atmospheric heating. The only concern is the local populations within a 100-kilometer band beneath the orbiting craft. The resulting shockwave, and thermal dissipation, will effectively sterilize all organic materials within a 100-kilometer band."

"Sterilize?"

"All organic bonds broken, and even a wide range of inorganic bonds. Surface crust will liquefy across most of that 100-kilometer band, and global ocean temperatures will increase by nearly 0.5 degrees Celsius on each pass."

Akandi looked down at the dust-choked ground, to where his boots disappeared. He had been worried about a runaway high-speed chunk of rock hitting the Earth and doing to the human race what had been done to the dinosaurs. At that moment he realized that there was more than one way to destroy a planet.

"That orbit is too low."

"Might I suggest that we land," it said.

"Land?" asked Akandi, stupefied.

"I can place this craft on the surface of Earth, in a great many locations, without harm to human life."

"Land a *moon* on the Earth."

"Yes," it said. "Or at least that portion of Phobos that consists of the core spacecraft. The outer moonlike exterior will be jettisoned at departure."

"Just how big is this craft?" asked Akandi.

"A sphere with a 10-kilometer diameter."

"And it can be landed on Earth, touching down with *zero* velocity?" he asked, again having visions of high-speed asteroids obliterating the planet.

"Zero velocity," it said. "At any location you specify."

Akandi nodded. "It should be in an unpopulated region, one where the impact of a moon landing would be minimal, but still close enough to industrial areas to be able to have easy access to it."

"A suggestion," it said.

Akandi nodded.

"The rural regions of southeastern North America would be well suited. Alabama might represent an optimal site—expansive cornfields and rice fields, close proximity to the North–South Ring and the Techlands, and access to a very complex research facility outside of Tuscaloosa."

"Quite a detailed knowledge of Earth," Akandi said suspiciously.

"Two hundred years of monitoring Earth's transmissions," it said. "My knowledge is *quite* detailed."

Akandi slowly nodded, knowing that the suggestion was a good one, that southern Alabama would be an ideal landing site. "What is the potential damage that landing will produce?"

"Practically none," it answered. "Especially in comparison to the damage already being inflicted by the firing of the Rings. Authorities can be notified of our arrival and evacuations implemented for those few who live in the area. But the impact will be quite minimal. The Aglands in that portion of the continent are extensive."

Again Akandi nodded. He knew they were. When he'd worked on US grid-enhancement projects, the only need for power in that sector of the US was for agriculture—there was nothing down there except corn-, wheat- and ricefields.

"Should I commence departure procedures?"

"Yes," he said. "How long until we will be ready to depart?" As he spoke, the Sun flared at his back, and he thought that Phobos must have swung into the daylight side of this Martian simulation.

"Departure procedures already completed," it said. "Arrival will be in 17 hours and 39 minutes. Do you wish me to notify the authorities at the Tuscaloosa Agricultural Co-Op of our arrival so they can begin with the required human evacuation of the sparsely settled region?"

Akandi blinked. Things were moving *too* quickly.

"Yes." He turned toward the light, realizing only then that it was not the Sun that nearly blinded him but the exhaust exploding just beneath the horizon, all of Phobos on the move, breaking Mars orbit. The sooty ground rumbled, dust rising, shards and boulders sliding backward. Enveloped in a black maelstrom, he knew that the outer crust of Phobos was in the process of cracking, of being shed like a cocoon peeling away from a butterfly.

"Have I done the right thing?" he asked Iyoon.

There was no answer.

Chapter 19

Padmini took another sip of the sweet tea, then gently placed the frosty glass on a coaster that rested atop the wobbly end table pushed up against the side of the couch. Xavier and Christina Olmos sat before her on little wooden stools in front of the couch, each with the slender stalk of a neural interface running into the corner of one eye, the input side of the stalk connected to a small black box that sat on the floor before them. And there was a third, Rebecca Olmos, the doctor who had died the previous year of brain cancer. Xavier had insisted that his dead wife be present, that he valued her judgments and insights.

Padmini had said nothing, simply nodded and asked Kali to lock into the Olmos local network hook so she could interface with Rebecca Olmos. However, she was not about to reciprocate. While they might want her to see Rebecca Olmos, she was not about to let them see Kali—her Jinni was none of their business.

The couch shook.

Without thinking, pure standby reflexes engaged, Padmini's right arm swung out, her hand grabbing the iced tea before it fell, before the shudder that ran through the house reached its crescendo, the couch bucking, slamming at the wall behind it, the house itself creaking, the sounds of wood splintering in the distance. Then the quake passed, the house suddenly still, the three still staring at her, having taken little notice of the quake. In her hand she held her glass, not a drop spilled.

"How did he die?" asked Xavier.

She focused on Xavier, and the package that he held in both hands, lifting it up just a few centimeters in her direction.

Padmini sat back, not ready to answer their questions, not knowing who and what these people were, why the Swirl and Leo had sent her here, and just what that package really contained. It looked like neural mesh encased in some sort of configurable polymer exostructure. But that didn't really tell her much in itself.

"How do you know Leo Barnwell?" she asked.

Xavier smiled. "He said you were cautious, not one to easily trust."

Padmini felt like squirming, but managed to control herself. This was all part of Leo's secret life, the world he had kept hidden from her, but obviously a world in which he had discussed her with these people. She was at an informational disadvantage, an unusual and difficult situation for her.

"*No indications of aggression or misdirection,*" said Kali, drifting up through the floorboards, hovering next to Xavier, flicking out her long, forked, black tongue, licking at the side of his face. Xavier was totally oblivious to the Jinni. "*The Swirl indicates that you should trust him, that he is key to your survival.*"

Kali jerked back, her tongue recoiling, eyes suddenly

wide. *"The Swirl says that this family is the key to humanity's survival."*

Padmini stared at Xavier, at the hands that clutched the package, at the scarred and callused fingers, and the skin stained a reddish hue from what she knew was a lifetime of digging in the red-clay soil. *"Humanity's savior?"* she asked Kali.

"The key," answered Kali.

Padmini fully appreciated the distinction that Kali was making. Xavier Olmos might be of little significance in whatever events were about to be played out, but he represented a critical link, a focal point around which events would unfold. That is if the Swirl were telling the truth, if it could see into the future. She had serious doubts, still not certain of its motivations, but it could obviously control things, able to manipulate data in the Void to show that she'd killed Leo, as well as control the trajectories of the hundreds of surveillance craft that had allowed her to survive a 3-kilometer fall from the Ring.

That kind of power could not be ignored.

"Always cautious when it comes to my own skin," said Padmini, answering his question. "Leo's dead. I was instructed to bring that package to you," she said, pointing at his lap. "Now I need to know who you are and how you know Leo, or else I'm gone." She moved forward, all her body language letting them know that she was poised to get up from the couch.

"Leo and my father first met in the Ten Degree War, in covert operations. Both had been radically modified." Reaching up, Xavier pointed to the side of his head. "Hardware and wetware rewiring. When my father returned in '29, he seemed incapable of talking about what he'd experienced. At first we thought it was a form of post-traumatic stress syndrome, pure and simple trauma as a result of too much killing. We soon learned that there were tens of thousands like him, on heavy-duty chemical stabilizers to blunt the experience of war, the same stabilizers that had allowed them to go on fighting night after night, long after the human brain should have shut them down. In most of them, the damage was severe, turning them into walking dead. The only thing keeping them upright and breathing was the heavy dose of neural stabilizers that kept their brain chemistry from a terminal tilt. My father and Leo were almost normal, compared to most."

"That's where I came in," said Bec.

Padmini looked at her. Jinnis she understood; interfaces to the Void that eventually acquired personalities to suit their users. But ghosts were a whole different business, something that she found fundamentally disturbing.

Dead was dead.

What she wanted to keep of Leo was his memory, not a pathetic echo streaming into her optical cortex, like the ghost hiding in Leo's basement. But she managed a sympathetic cop smile, reminding herself that she didn't know these people, didn't know what pain had brought them to the point of keeping this wife and mother trapped in a chunk of hardware.

"I was with one of the traveling vet units, back in '30," said Bec. "I was in charge of the south Alabama circuit, with nearly 300 Ten Degree vets on my roster, handing out meds, keeping the traumatized breathing and walking, dosing them high enough so they wouldn't kill themselves or flash back to the Ten Degree and *rampage*."

Padmini nodded. She's had direct experience with rampage as a cop in Philly, a few of the old Ten Degree vets who had managed to go the 20-year distance, would finally trip over the edge, suddenly certain that Philly was Central Africa, and replay some secret-op sortie from 20 years earlier down the center of State Street. By some estimates nearly 20 percent of Philly homicides were still rampage-related, despite the fact that so few of the vets were still alive. Padmini, along with most cops, could never figure out why the surviving vets had not been rounded up and confined, and Leo simply refused to talk about it. The official line had been that the Powers did not want to punish these loyal soldiers who'd given up so much for the defense of their country, and insisted that they remain free, their reward for services rendered, allowing them to rot away in the cracks and crevices, until they simply dropped, or briefly flared in flashback. Now she knew better. The Swirl had wanted them free and wandering, its ears and eyes in the world of dirt and blood.

"Xavier's father was one of my patients. That's how I met Xavier," said Bec.

Reaching toward her, Xavier rested a hand on Bec's knee, gently squeezing it.

Padmini nodded. The morph was very clean, signals fed back into Xavier so that his fingers would tense to just the right degree, not pressing too far into the ghost's knee. She knew that in his head selective neurons were being tripped so he could *feel* that knee.

"The only good to come out of the Ten Degree," Xavier said quietly.

Padmini blinked, focused, all her attention on Xavier's face, on the deep wrinkles around his eyes, the dark pupils, a gaze that looked far past her, far past everything. Her breathing suddenly fell in synch with his, the flutter of their eyelids matched, mouths opening almost imperceptibly, tongues running over dry lips.

He's real, thought Padmini. At that moment she knew his feelings were genuine. This was no simulation, no overwritten chunk of neurons insisting that he love this dead woman and their living daughter. He was real. She could not remember the last time she'd been in the presence of something so primal, so basic and pure.

He loved them.

"Do you feel sick?"

Padmini blinked.

The girl, Christina, leaned forward, reaching out for her, but not quite touching her, fingers just hovering above her right leg. "Is something wrong?" asked Christina. "You don't look well."

"Fine," said Padmini, sitting back, refocusing, not quite certain why this family dynamic was having such an impact on her. That uncertainty frightened her. She looked over at Kali, mentally questioning her.

Kali nodded. *"I'm detecting no outside influences, no manipulation of brain chemistry. What you are feeling is being supplied by your own brain. I can detect empathy, and feelings of loss. This family, the dynamic existing between them, is something you've never personally experienced, but apparently something you want, that you're brain insists you need. You wish to belong. The loss of Leo cannot be ignored. He was your family."*

Padmini gritted her teeth and willed her cop persona to take over. "Leo and your father—what was the relationship?"

Bec smiled, and placed her hand atop Xavier's. Again the morph was smooth, as good as anything real could provide. Padmini demanded that her brain ignore those hands, but the more she insisted, the more they seemed to be all she could see, the fingers now intertwined.

"A pattern began to emerge," said Bec. "This was just

before the Rings, before the Collapse. The technology developed in that war was marvelous and frightening. All of the 300 vets under my care had been radically enhanced neurologically. They'd been modified to coordinate on the battlefield, operating as a single entity, everything they experienced transmitted back to central command nodes, the data diced and sliced, and commands flashed back in real time, direct neural commands to the group entity."

Padmini nodded, knowing all this. Most of Leo's snitches, the eyes and ears he used to keep watch on Philly, had been vets, like McGordy, all Ten Degree Tools. They all shared a type of linkage that she had always suspected was far more than simply the type of by-product that heavy Void users experienced. And now she knew the truth—had in some ways even become one of them, with the Swirl now having taken a hold in her head.

"My job was to stabilize brain chemistry, to keep them under control, to shut them down if they experienced extreme flashback or started exhibiting the sort of neural chaos that preceded a rampage. Easy enough to do with pre-Ring technology. But I wanted to do more than simply keep brain chemistries balanced. I started looking for cause and effect, for patterns."

"And you found them" said Padmini, suddenly certain that she knew where this was going—the Swirl. "*Group* patterns."

Bec nodded. "A distributed pattern, nothing in a single mind, but bits and pieces disturbed across the 300, interacting pieces connected through the Void, operating independently from the minds themselves. It wasn't exactly a gestalt composed of the individual brains of the vets, but this distributed pattern existing in bits and pieces salted away in isolated neuronal packages in each brain, the activity below the awareness threshold of the individual minds."

Swirl, thought Padmini, trying to say the name but unable to, its hold on her still absolute.

"As compared to most of the vets, Papito, like Leo, was very high-functioning," said Xavier. "Most didn't even suspect he was a vet. But we saw the change, could feel it. Something drove him, and had isolated him behind a wall. Before the war we'd lived in New Mexico, where he'd been an electronics technician at White Sands." He paused, grimacing. "At that time I'd recently been brought into White Sands, the Powers hoping that I shared some of Papito's talents." He shut his eyes and breathed deep.

And traumatized to the core, thought Padmini.

"At discharge he announced to us that he intended to become a farmer," said Xavier, his eyes reopening, "and had bought a 10-acre farm in Alabama." Xavier laughed. "It was then that we knew something was severely wrong with Papito—prior to then he'd never so much as pulled a weed or grown a tomato. And when we came here, he never did become a farmer. That was my assignment." He paused. "Me and my older brother, Che."

She gave him a questioning look.

"Che is *watching*," he said. "Down below," he added, pointing toward the back of the house.

She didn't understand, but nodded.

"Papito didn't buy this farm because he wanted to grow corn. He bought it because of what lay buried beneath the barn. All along this section of the Gulf of Mexico, from Texas to Florida, deep nodes had been built during the early '20s to monitor, store, and analyze the data streaming up from South America."

Padmini nodded, not surprised. While Africa had been on a steady decline since the Europeans abandoned their colonies nearly a century earlier, spiraling downward in unending cycles of disease and wars, South America's implosion had been rapid and severe—three years of drought in Brazil, major chunks of the Amazon basin in flames, and both Rio and São Paulo flooded with tens of millions of refugees, had collapsed the Brazilian economy. The rest of South America followed, most slipping within a matter of months to fourth-world status, while here and there a few high-tech enclaves of first-world technology and wealth survived.

A very bad combination.

Waves of disease, missiles, and virulent code were suddenly aimed at the North. It didn't surprise her in the least that secret listening posts dotted the Gulf States. The Ten Degree that had been fought in Africa had almost happened a few years earlier in South America. But the implosion had happened too fast. By the mid '20s there was nothing to fight against.

The listening nodes remained.

"Your father was not listening for signals from South America," said Padmini.

"No," said Xavier. "He was transmitting and receiving data from other vets. It was a storage center for information."

Padmini realized that what she'd seen under Leo's apartment must have been something like that—a pre-Collapse listening post.

"But more than just information," said Xavier. "It is also used for the other thing." He looked over at Bec.

"The distributed pattern existed within the vets, but also resided in these nodes, hiding, not willing to risk its entire existence to the vets. Too many of them were dying, brains collapsing, having been pushed too hard. It was born in them, still lived in them, but had removed an aspect of itself into hardware for safekeeping."

Padmini nodded, knowing that they only had part of the story. The Swirl did not have to limit itself to Ten Degree vets or the nodes—it could reside in any Tool, just as it now had its hooks in her head.

"It's called the Swirl," said Bec.

Padmini opened her eyes wide, offering up her most genuine surprised expression. "Amazing," she said.

"But we didn't really know much about it for years, not as long as Papito was the conduit."

Xavier nodded. "Papito died nearly 10 years ago, and Che replaced him. He already had most of the hardware in place, installed when we'd been living at White Sands. Che had a great deal of difficulty integrating with the Swirl, and after fighting it for several years he either forced it out of his neural hardware or it abandoned him. It was then that we learned about the Swirl, from what little Che was able to tell us."

"He escaped it?" she asked, this being no idle question.

Xavier nodded. "But it cost him."

"In what way?" asked Padmini, doing her best to mask any hints of desperation in her voice, needing to know how his brother had managed to escape what was now in her head.

"Hard to explain," said Xavier. "It would be best if you see him." He stood, holding the package in both hands. "We'll see you later," he said to his wife.

Bec nodded, then winked away as Xavier and Christina pulled the interface out of the corners of their eyes.

Padmini stood back, hanging by the banks of dark racks, trying to take some comfort from the gentle hum of the electronics, from their similarity to the ones that had been in Leo's basement, as if the equipment offered some tenuous link to him. The room was hemispherical in shape, the racks lining the walls, the center of the room dropping down into a shallow well dominated by a holo-table. A man sat before it, his hands sunk wrist deep into the liquid interface that ran the perimeter of the table, a glassy cable running from his right eye socket to the ceiling above, snaking away in an expansive tangle of conduits and wire mesh.

At his feet, partially hidden by the curve of the table, slept what looked to Padmini to be a dog, but somehow deformed, the head misshapen and its shoulders too wide. Its face was hidden, nestled in its paws. An almost oppressive animal stink pervaded the room, something like a combination of sour milk and burned oil.

Images rolled through the holo-table—fields of corn, plumes of black smoke, a collapsed structure of steel and glass, and burning pinpricks swarming away from it—she assumed those represented people fleeing the damaged building.

"Tuscaloosa Ag Co-Op Center," said Xavier, pointing to the table. "Designed to take quite a shaking, but not able to stand up against the torquing that the Rings are inducing in the local substrata."

Padmini looked up at the ceiling, at the cables, pipes, and ducting, knowing they were better than 50 meters beneath the surface. She'd just climbed down the ladder connecting this bunker to the barn above, and had the shaky legs to prove it.

"Not to worry," said Xavier. "This bunker was designed to take anything the southern hemisphere might have lobbed our way, from nukes to electromagnetic pulses intense enough to fry any unprotected circuitry."

Christina took one of Padmini's hands and squeezed. Padmini fought her first impulse to pull away, and let the girl hold her hand, feeling the dampness of her fingers, and the rapid *whap-whap-whap* of her heartbeat through the palm of her hand. "So close in here," said Christina, glancing up at the ceiling. "And the smell," she said in a whisper, as she crinkled her nose. She pointed over at the dog. "Krew," she said. "He always smells like that."

Padmini smiled, tapping into those reinforced cop responses that instructed her in comforting accident victims, overdosers, and the generic psychotic on the verge of a break. She knew none of those actually fit the situation, but it was all she had. "Very close in here," she said, sounding sincere and empathetic.

Christina let go of her hand but took a half step toward her. "Mama won't even come down here," she said. "She says that seeing Che like that upsets her, and I think it really does, but that's not the real reason she doesn't come down here."

"Not now," said Xavier. "I'm sure there will be time later for you to reveal to our guest all our family secrets, but we need to focus on the job at hand."

"Yes, Papa," she said, and stepped to the side, but not before she leaned in toward Padmini. "It's Krew she's really afraid of," she said, pointing at the pile of fur sleeping at Che's feet.

"Please," said Xavier, motioning toward the holo-table. "We've been monitoring the Ag center continuously since they broke ground on it 7 years ago. A great deal of it is devoted to Ag research, mostly corn hybrids with a large reservoir of jumping genes that can reconfigure under viral and bacterial stress to manufacture the proteins needed to eradicate new pests and diseases." Xavier grinned. "*Smart* corn. Almost a shame to eat something that smart." Then the smile vanished from his face. "But that is all just a façade. It was in the lower levels," he said, pointing at the collapsed building, "where the real work was done. They'd built up quite an effort focused on penetrating the Point."

Padmini took a quick, deep breath. "Not many things more illegal than that," she said. She looked at the building surrounded by a sea of cornfields. "They thought they could contain a runaway in this rural setting?"

Several years back in Philly she'd helped the Feds and UN take down a cult that had integrated 20 children to several truckloads of pre-Ring network hardware, hoping that the resulting mix would rip through the Point, creating something infinitely superior to humanity. She was never able to discover what they'd managed to do—by the time the Feds and the UN had pulled out, several square blocks of Philly had been slagged, with enough energy having been dumped to melt bricks and concrete.

"Yes," said Xavier. "Layer after layer of active defense and transmission isolation within the building itself, and external safeguards in place in case of a breakout."

"Nuclear?" asked Padmini.

Xavier nodded. "Local pocket nukes as a first line, running up to orbital coverage with 20-megaton H-bomb capability. They thought they had it covered." He pointed at the imploded building. "Total collapse occurred more than 8 hours ago, going right though all 20 subfloors, yet none of that triggered a single nuke detonation."

"Malfunction?" asked Padmini.

"Certainly," said Xavier. "But not of a passive nature.

The system could not have simply broken down and the nukes not detonated. Only active intervention of a very *sophisticated* nature could have kept those nukes quiet."

Padmini found herself taking a step back from the image, a small part of her actually frightened that something might reach up right through the display and grab her. "Something Post-Point," she said.

Xavier nodded. "And according to Che, it was not the Swirl."

Padmini turned her head to Kali, who hovered in the far corner of the lab. *"The Swirl denies any active participation in the event. Claims that it was a woman named Sarah Sutherland who broke through."* As Padmini watched, words and pictures flashed a half meter in front of her. She slipped into an augmented mode, sucking down the torrent of information.

"Sarah Sutherland," said Padmini, recognizing the name, remembering back to the Blue and Gold, before everything had changed. She'd been the one who jumped from the Southern Cross—apparently she had not splattered on the way down. She continued to siphon information from Kali. "The daughter of General Thomas Sutherland. She was brought into the facility anatomically dead, with severe head trauma. There are indications that she was installed as a component of a system called CUSP, a system that is at least a two- to three-generational leap in processing capability." She paused. "CUSP is a Controllable Universal Sentient Plasma, whatever that might be."

Xavier stared at her and slowly walked over to his brother, gently placing his hands on his shoulders. Che did not respond to his touch but simply gazed into the display, the only motion coming from the twitch of tendons in his forearms as his fingers worked within the table's interface. "That's what Che believes, what he's been able to pull from the Ag facility's shielded Void." He paused, and Padmini could almost see the wheels turning in his head, knowing that he was very carefully planning his next question. "Leo spoke often of you, your capabilities, your potential. I know about Kali, and Leo considered you a virtuoso of the Void."

He hesitated.

She knew what he wanted to ask. "But none of that should have allowed me access to the sort of information that was coming from the Ag Co-Op," she said. "I'm sure it took you years to worm into the Co-Op, and I've only been here a few hours."

"Yes."

"Other sources, ones recently introduced to me through Leo, are now supplying me with additional information."

Che looked up at her from the table, squinting at her with his left eye. "Pattern expands," he said. "Far in excess of initial parameters."

"The Swirl has accessed you?" asked Xavier.

Padmini opened her mouth, hoping that the Swirl would release the hold it had on her, to allow her to speak about it. But she said nothing, could actually feel the disconnect between her thoughts and the muscles in her throat and jaw. She closed her mouth.

"Leo's dead, and he was one of the more heavily trafficked nodes within the Swirl's construction," said Xavier. "Like all the vets, he was never able to speak of it directly, but Che knew, had linked with him many times, knew the importance that Leo played in the Swirl's identity."

"Too important to let it die with Mr. Barnwell," said Christina.

Xavier nodded. "Important enough to transfer to you?" he asked, pointing at Padmini.

She said nothing, didn't move.

"We didn't think it possible." He hesitated again. "We did not think that the Swirl had any desire to extend itself beyond the vets, although we never believed that it couldn't do so if it wanted. But now, with Leo gone, you've been chosen. Apparently it can migrate to any Tool it chooses."

Padmini managed a blink.

"And then this package from Leo." Xavier paused, looking down at it. "And I suspect from the Swirl." Slowly unwrapping its outer polymer coating, and carefully reaching within, he pulled out the clot of spun-web fiber, holding it up to the light, slowly turning it.

Padmini sensed movement and, looking down, saw Krew stir, pushing himself up on all fours, arching his back, his legs stiffening and shaking, as if trying to wake himself.

"What do you know about it?" asked Xavier, slowly putting the metal sponge back down.

"Looks like neural mesh, and a lot of it," she said, knowing that typically mesh of only a few millimeters thickness was used, wedged between the skull and brain. This piece was roughly spherical, the size of a closed fist, and appeared denser than other mesh she'd seen.

Xavier carefully set it on the edge of the holo-table. "Take a look at it, Che," he said.

Che swiveled in his seat; his hands remaining submerged in the interface of the table. Through the thick but pliable conductive liquid she could see the ripple of his fingers moving toward the mesh.

Then he stopped.

Krew leapt up, his paws on the edge of the table, his head above the tabletop.

No dog, thought Padmini, looking at its overly large, black-glass eyes, bulging head, and slit nose and mouth. This was some sort of chimera, a mixture of species, perhaps even with artificial genetic material added. She'd seen such things before, constructed by people with too much time and money at their disposal. But nothing had ever looked like this.

His paws uncurled, revealing long, slender fingers. With his right hand he reached for the mesh.

"No!" shouted Xavier, making a move toward it. "Keep your Clinger under control," he said.

Clinger, thought Padmini. She'd never heard of such a thing.

Che's head snapped around in Xavier's direction, and the table's liquid interface rippled and bulged, extruding a large hand grabbing on to Xavier's arm, tugging him back, keeping him away from Krew.

"Corrections in play," said Che.

Krew picked up the mesh in his right hand—"paw" was no longer the right word—and brought it close to his face, his nostrils flaring, his lips twitching, a slender pink tongue flicking out. With his left hand he reached up to his forehead, running fingers along his short gray fur, revealing what looked like a long scar extending parallel to an almost nonexistent brow above his eyes.

"Never seen that before," said Christina.

Padmini looked at her, then back at Krew. What she had thought was a scar hidden beneath his fur was now obviously a seam, one that was parting, skin pulling back, fur folding over, white skull exposed; and then it, too, was parting, as if melting away. Krew probed with slender fingers, the seam now a crack.

"The top of his head," whispered Christina.

Krew turned the top of his own head, slowly at first and with obvious great effort. His eyes closed to slits, and the muscles of his slender left arm bulged. At first it moved just a few millimeters, then faster, as if something had severed. His skullcap rotated a full 90 degrees and came off, landing atop the holographic table.

Padmini had expected to see the pink bloody mess of his brain sitting within the exposed skull. But she didn't. Instead there was a mass of neural fiber, colored black and crushed in places, in other places entwined with rubbery-looking purple filaments. Krew reached into the top of his skull, grabbed the mass of fiber, tugged it out, and dropped it to the tabletop, where it hit with a wet-sounding smack.

"Are you sure, Che!" said Xavier, straining at the arm that still held him in place.

Che gave no indication that he'd heard his brother but remained focused on Krew, as he gently raised the new neural mesh, rolling it into his open skull. Reaching across the table for the skullcap, Krew returned it on his head and screwed it back into position.

Che released Xavier, who stood still. The room was totally silent, and for a moment Padmini could not even hear the whoosh of cooling fans or the gentle hum of electronics. They all watched as Krew's eyes closed to slits, and he reached out for the edge of the table, running his fingertips across the liquid interface, fingers fluttering, as if the interface were the keyboard of an instrument. Then he suddenly sunk his fingers in knuckle deep.

Che lurched back, thrown, his hands erupting from the interface.

Krew shuddered, sagged, only his hands holding him up, his chin resting on the table's edge. His mouth slowly opened. "Amalthea," he said in a lisping whisper as he ran his small tongue across his lips. He pulled himself up. "Amalthea." His body shuddered, then fell back from the

table, dropping to the floor. Che reached to lift his head, and
Xavier pressed fingers to Krew's throat, feeling for a pulse.

"Amalthea?" asked Padmini in a whisper, looking across
the room for Kali.

"One of the innermost moons of Jupiter," said Christina
from behind her.

Padmini turned.

Christina smiled, her eyes wide and alive. "I always knew
there was more to Krew than some throwaway experiment.
He must come from Jupiter."

What is Krew, and what is a Clinger? thought Padmini.

Kali materialized before her, the Jinni slowly shaking her
head. *"Unknown,"* she said. *"But whatever he is, it is highly
doubtful that he is a native to Jupiter or any of its moons. Che has
performed DNA analyses that show beyond any doubt that it is a
native species to Earth, though one that has been extensively modified."*

Chapter 20

Ahead, a virtual room extended forever, morphing
with rows of corn fading into a smoky horizon, while beside
them, barely two meters away, the corn disappeared behind
phantom walls lined with bookcases. The ceiling was low,
just above the top of Simon's head, the swaying corn tassels
just touching the featureless gray ceiling. Looking to his left
through the rows of corn, Simon again checked the bookcases, seeing the familiar volumes, books read and reread so

many times. Every three steps down the furrowed field the pattern of multihued book spines would repeat, the red-green-blue spines of Robinson's Mars trilogy acting as a marker. A part of him, barely above the conscious level, had been keeping count since they had emerged from the Ag Co-Op—1,211 times they'd walked past the Mars books.

"Just passed the hour mark," said Bill, walking in front of him, still trying to swat at the cornstalks, but his Jinni arms passing through them. *"Flesh and bone!"* he yelled, making several grabs for a nearby ear of corn, his fingers passing through it. *"What I wouldn't give to be a real boy!"* What had been a middle-aged Bill wearing a wrinkled coal black sharkskin suit, blurred, then relocked as a scrawny boy in jeans and a long-sleeved plaid shirt. He looked back accusingly. *"Living in your head is no way to live."*

Simon tried to focus on his breathing. A thick sheen of sweat covered his forehead, beading just above his eyes. The air was actually cool, and they walked slowly, not really exerting themselves. The sweat was a panic response. The walls, bookcases, and ceiling helped some, supplied by Bill to calm him, but they could not alter the reality of what was occuring.

Outside.

His fingers tingled, and a high-pitched squeal filled his ears.

"No!" said Bill, again middle-aged and wearing a sharkskin suit. *"Just keep moving. She's taking us to a place that will have an inside."*

Simon nodded and continued to put one foot in front of the other, his shoes sinking in the soft, red-tinted soil, unless he stepped in Sarah's footprints, in which case the ground would crunch. Whatever abilities she'd acquired by passing through the Point had not only allowed her to modify herself but also the world she came in contact with. Her bare feet left brittle prints, coated in a thin sheen of crystal. Looking past Bill, up the row of corn, he watched Sarah move. Only a few of the fluttering motes above her head were visible, most apparently above the phantom ceiling, somewhere *outside*.

Missing a step, he stumbled, falling, hitting hard, his face landing in the red soil.

"Up!"

Simon pushed himself up, spitting out dirt, the shock of falling clearing his head. "How much farther to the Olmos farm?" he asked.

Bill didn't turn. *"A long way to go,"* he said. *"It's located 40 kilometers east of the Ag Co-Op."*

Simon groaned and squeezed his eyes shut for just a moment, then quickly reopened them, not wanting to fall again. He was certain they'd never get there, especially since they hadn't even been keeping a true easterly direction. Despite the fact that he walked through a phantom room, the Sun outside, high above the imaginary ceiling, was still bright enough to cast dim shadows. Watching those shadows as they'd trudged through the cornfields, he'd seen them pointing in every direction, and once he knew they'd even cut across their own tracks, it being impossible to mistake Sarah's crystalline footprints for anyone else's.

They were not moving east, but in a random meander. *Random,* he thought, *but not aimless.*

They'd come across dozens of bodies, burned and broken, most dead, the rest dying. Those who could move under their own power had gotten away as quickly as possible from the Ag Co-Op, and its 5-kilometer blast radius. That was one worry he did not have. Sarah had somehow disposed of the nukes. He could not be sure, but he believed that Sarah was looking for someone.

"Help."

Distant and muffled, the voice was probably better than 30 corn rows away. Simon stopped walking and angled his head in the direction of the cry.

"Not that son of a bitch!" shouted Bill, placing himself squarely between Simon and the direction of the voice. *"We're free of him."*

Two rows away, Simon could see the truncated motes hovering above Sarah veer to the left, in the direction of the voice. Sidestepping Bill, Simon walked into the adjacent row of corn, the phantom bookshelf automatically slipping back another row.

"Help!"

"Mears!" called Simon. Pushing aside corn, he continued to cut between the rows, trotting rather than walking, following Sarah. Bill moved beside him, flickering in and out of existence, unable to move quickly enough to walk around the thick cornstalks.

"Not him!" pleaded Bill, *"We're finally free of him."*

Simon kept moving, not out of any desire to find himself back under Mears's control, but wanting to find another *person*. Neither Sarah nor Bill really fit that description.

"Help!"

"We're getting close," said Simon, moving ahead of Sarah.

"He will not help us!" Bill floated through the corn, his face just a few centimeters in front of Simon's. *"You need to sleep,"* he said, holding up a hand, reaching for Simon's eyes. *"You can't handle this. Your brain chemistry is about to destabilize. You're outside and have pushed too hard."*

Simon ran, the thick cornstalks slapping him in the face, leaving behind welts, cutting into his wrists and forearms as he pushed them away.

"You're seizing!" screamed Bill.

Simon ignored him, then stumbled in a rut, falling, crashing through an adjacent row, again landing facefirst, dirt pushed up into his mouth. Rolling, spitting, balled fists to eyes, pushing away dirt, he sat up. "Mears!"

Mears stood several meters away from him, in what would have been an adjacent row of corn, but here the corn had been cut down by fire, the blackened stalks still smoldering. Shirtless, pants in tatters, his skin blistered, burned black in spots, cracked, and oozing blood, Mears stood with his hands clutched to his right side, gray coils of his intestines poking out between his bloody fingers.

"I need help," he said.

Simon pushed himself up, and slowly moved toward Mears, staring at the hands that were keeping his guts from spilling onto the burned ground. He could not believe that the man was capable of standing, but as he neared, he understood. His pants had been burned away from below the knees, along with skin and even muscles, exposing his metal-alloyed bones, and tendons of taut graphite fiber. Sunk shin deep into the dirt, Simon knew that it was not Mears that was standing, but his legs—mechanical appendages with a will of their own.

"Help me!" pleaded Mears, reaching out with his right hand as a thick coil of intestines slithered out of the hole in his side. Looking down upset his balance, and he fell over backward, his knees collapsing at an unnatural angle, his body hitting the ground with a wet-sounding thud, while his legs below the knees still stood erect, firmly planted in the red dirt, the knee joints shattered, and the graphite struts ripped out of the base of his thighbone.

Simon knelt next to Mears, reaching out for him, but not knowing what he could possibly do to help.

"He's all but dead."

Simon looked up. Bill stood on the other side of Mears, looking down at him. Next to him stood Sarah, anchored into the ground, crystalline filaments extending out of her legs into the red soil. She looked straight ahead, staring somewhere far past the wall of phantom books.

"Leave him," said Bill.

A hand wrapped around Simon's right wrist, jerking it down.

"I told them to stop her," said Mears, his eyes moving in the direction of Sarah, then looking back at Simon. "Not natural, not the path that God intended for us."

Simon nodded, not understanding what Mears meant, fairly certain that Mears himself didn't understand, his brain having slipped into chaos, his body effectively dead. He knew this was only temporary.

"You're the one, have always been the one," said Mears, squeezing his wrist more tightly.

"Sputtering neurons, an oxygen-deprived brain firing random thoughts," said Bill, bending down on the other side of Mears. *"You shouldn't even listen to him."*

"I found you," said Mears. "Sutherland had abandoned you, put you in coma storage. But I found you, thawed you, awakened you."

"Don't listen!" screamed Bill. *"He is a liar! He is a . . ."*

Simon looked up. Bill stood stiff, his body glistening in a thin sheen of crystal, his mouth open wide, frozen in mid-scream. He looked at Sarah, who stood unmoving and staring, the collage of shapes and colors hanging above her head. "What are you doing?" he asked in a whisper, looking back at the frozen Bill, knowing that Sarah had done that, also knowing that the only way to control Bill would be through his own brain.

Sarah was inside him.

But there was more going on than just shutting down Bill. At that moment Simon was certain that their random meander through the corn had not been random at all—Sarah had been searching for Mears. She wanted Mears to tell him something and had even gone as far to take Bill off-line to ensure that he wouldn't interfere.

"So gifted," said Mears, tugging at Simon's wrist, pulling him closer.

Simon grimaced; the dying man's breath smelled of burned meat.

"My find, my discovery, my theory. Evolution still the master driver, despite our meddling, our genetic enhancements, our ability to create life from nothing. Sutherland gave up on you too quickly." He coughed, sputtering, a thick clot of bloody mucus spewing from the corner of his mouth. "But evolution still worked. You were third-generation geek, grandparents all adept at the slide rule, and lab rat parents burrowed deep into the Valley, their dreams of silicon and base pairs, both borderline autistics, marginally functional in the world of dirt and blood, but virtuosos of the keyboard, of the experiment, of the atom, able to focus any problem into oblivion. Prime for the picking, acquired by Sutherland for his Ten Degree experiment, prime nodes for the intelligence he was building."

"My parents?" said Simon, leaning closer.

Mears shuddered, and something deep in his guts, below the glistening coils protruding through the gash in his side, sputtered and arced, sparks shooting out from between coils of intestines.

"You were the next step, but trapped, so deeply autistic that dirt and blood held no reality for you. They tried to force the Swirl into you, but you rejected it, the wiring incompatible, just too much of you for it to submerge and dominate."

Swirl, thought Simon questioningly.

Again Mears coughed up bloody phlegm.

"Sutherland had bred you too well, forgetting about evolution. I resurrected you from storage. You had only two interests." Mears held up two fingers—the ring finger missing everything above the last joint. "Patterns and Bill Gates—those were your world."

Simon looked up at the still-frozen Bill.

Mears pulled him even closer, let go of his wrist and, reaching up, wrapped his hand around the back of Simon's neck. He could feel Mears's fingers pulling at the fiber bundle running from the porta-Manifold and into the back of his head.

"I knew how to unlock you," said Mears in a whisper. "Installed the mesh, the neural stabilizers, took the edge off the focus, allowed random elements to filter through your perspective, threw in a noise generator, a background buzz that wouldn't let you focus too deep, to help you from getting lost." He coughed, his eyes opening wide, the right pupil dilating, the lid sagging.

"And interfaced me to the Manifold and the Bill Jinni," said Simon.

Mears gave a half smile, the right side of his face stiff. "No Manifold, no Jinni," he said in a slurred whisper. "Bill was *your* creation, the wall you built between yourself and the outside world. The Manifold is a fabrication, never real, an empty box the psychologists insisted you needed. A crutch—a very convenient crutch to keep your true capabilities hidden. Sutherland never knew the truth, thought Bill really was a Jinni that had been downloaded into you."

"No," said Simon, turning as much as Mears's tight grip on the back of his neck would allow, looking up at the frozen Bill. "He's a Jinni, a program."

"A delusion," said Mears.

Simon felt the tensing in Mears's arm, the fingers letting go of his neck, wrapping around the fiber bundle. He reared back, trying to stand, but Mears was not letting go.

"Over now!" screamed Mears. "Stop her!" He jerked at the fiber bundle.

Simon fell, landing hard on his back, Mears rolling away, facedown in the deep furrow between corn rows. Reaching up, running his hands across the back of his head, he could not find the fiber bundle, then fingered the ragged-edged dimple in the back of his head where it had been inserted. "No!" he screamed, looking through the corn rows and at the endless shelves of books still in place. Angling his head back, he saw that the smoke and ash ceiling still hovered above him.

He unslung the porta-Manifold from his back, jerking it around, the severed cable dangling from it.

"I guess the cat's out of the old bag."

Simon looked up. Bill walked toward him, passing through cornstalks, brushing at the lapels of his suit, flicking away crystalline shards, reaching up and straightening his black-rimmed glasses, then ran a hand through his thick, untidy hair. *"Not all that much has really changed. You thought I was in that box,"* he said, as he pointed at the porta-Manifold, *"while all this time I've actually been in that box,"* he said, pointing at Simon's head. *"No superscience here, just a good old-fashioned delusion courtesy of your malformed neurology, a psychological buffer you created to isolate yourself from the world."* Bill smiled. *"No real difference. I'm still in control, and if you don't do exactly what I say, then I'll remove that buffer and expose you to the world beyond."*

With a flourish of his hands, the ceiling above Simon vanished, replaced with a distant, gray-streaked sky and the Sun, a reddened, diffuse blob hanging near the horizon.

Simon shuddered, feeling himself fall upward into the infinite sky, the vastness, the infinite possibilities trying to swallow him. The pattern that filled the world, the infinite relationships, was simply too much.

"But I would never be so cruel," said Bill. The ceiling reappeared.

"Cruel."

Simon and Bill turned. The voice had come from Mears, but it had not been his voice. His body still lay facedown in the corn furrow, but was now encased in glistening crystal, sprouting gossamer spiderwebs that ran back to Sarah. "Cruel," said a voice from within the crystalline cocoon.

"What are you doing?" asked Bill, walking toward Sarah.

Simon pushed himself up, dropping the porta-Manifold, finally reaching Mears's body.

"What?" said Bill from behind.

Simon looked at the dead face, at the face that was no longer Mears's, but transformed. "Cruel," it said, the word echoing up through the thin, jellylike substance that covered it.

"My face," said Bill.

Simon nodded, and stared into the face of Bill Gates. He looked up at Sarah and didn't even have time to blink before a hissing wall of glistening crystal slammed him in the face, throwing him backward, enveloping him in a perfect blackness. His last thought was that the inside of his head felt itchy and that something had poked through his skull with fingers made of cold crystal to give that itchy spot a good scratching.

The part of him that was Bill faded away, removed by Sarah.

Chapter 21

It was not the Earth he had left 8 days earlier.

Phobos cut down from above the ecliptic, moving in a nearly straight line, decelerating at a full 5 gees. The Earth that had been little more than a flicker of reflected sunlight an hour ago was now a fully defined orb.

Overwhelmed with the sense of falling, Akandi's stomach lurched into his chest. Bands of gray clouds smothered the entire planet, the familiar continental shapes hidden, a few glowing red embers barely visible through the floating ash. The only visible structures were the Stalks and Petals, puncturing the dark blanket of clouds, with more than a dozen of the west-facing Petals spewing azure-blue plumes.

"The Rings are firing," said Akandi.

He shuffled over the featureless, metallic hull of the craft, that part of Phobos that had been exposed after its soot-rock exterior had been shed when the ship blasted away from Mars. He knew he was encased in a layer of pink crystal somewhere deep inside Phobos, experiencing a full-immersion simulation. But he was still afraid to lift his feet from the smooth hull. He peered past the ship's horizon, in the direction of where Stickney crater had once been: a massive white exhaust plume now exploding from the ship's matter-antimatter reaction engines.

No change.

The blinding plume still erupted, aimed squarely at Earth, the relativistic jet of protons and helium atoms fighting against the craft's downward momentum. A heads-up flicked in front of him, hovering between his nose and the rapidly growing shrouded world, showing a pulsing green trajectory—Phobos on a straight-line intercept with North America, right along the bend of the Gulf of Mexico.

08:55

The numbers hung next to the little Earth—less than 9 minutes to landing.

"Too fast," said Akandi, looking above the white exhaust glow of the craft's engine, to the smoky clouds encircling Earth. The dark horizon rose above him, filling the black sky. "Far too fast."

"Landing trajectory verified."

He turned. The Clinger stood next to him. "Trajectory is still on course. Altitude is 6,400 kilometers." Earth now filled the sky, its dark clouds sparkling in reflected amber tones from the craft's exhaust plume.

Blink.

Perspective shift. No longer on Phobos but next to it.

"No!" Akandi fell, nothing beneath his feet except for the Earth thousands of kilometers below, and the angry turbulence of gray clouds tinted orange from the craft's exhaust. His stomach flipped, his inner ear ringing, as he felt himself spin.

06:22

"On course," said the Clinger, now falling next to him.

"Altitude 3,600 kilometers and a velocity of 19 kilometers per second."

"Abort landing!" screamed Akandi, looking past his feet at the now crimson tinted clouds. "Move into a high-altitude orbit."

The clouds raced up at him, spitting a small rainbow shard straight at him, forcing him to cringe. The Swirl stopped just before it would have slammed into his head, hanging motionless at the tip of his nose.

"The Swirl informs me that an abort at this altitude and trajectory would require accelerations in excess of the structural limits of the craft. It would tear itself apart if it attempted to implement your request," said the Clinger. "I will not allow the craft to be damaged, so I am denying your request."

"Too fast," pleaded Akandi, picturing this kilometers-wide craft hitting the Earth's atmosphere, then spewing its insides, debris raining down across the Gulf.

"On course," said the Clinger. "We will hit the outer atmosphere at approximately 100 kilometers altitude, at a descent velocity of 3 kilometers per second. At that point we will be less than 1 minute from landing."

Akandi fell to Earth, its distant horizon now blurring. He glanced to the left, the golden orb of Phobos dropping with him, its exhaust plume angled down, seeming just to lick at the dark clouds below, when suddenly the plume tore apart, cut into diffuse plasma tendrils running north and south, shredded by the Earth's magnetic field.

"Too fast and too much mass," said Akandi in a whisper, wanting to close his eyes, but unable to, squinting, watching the craft's exhaust begin to puncture the high-altitude clouds.

His feet suddenly warmed.

He touched the Earth's upper atmosphere.

And continued to drop.

Optical interfaces in both eyes, General Sutherland sat enmeshed, while his consciousness floated in the Void, nerves linked directly to the Pod's detonator. A part of his brain was focused far away, several thousand kilometers up, watching Phobos fall from the sky, while another part hung above the cornfield where Sarah stood. He rarely linked, feeling naked in the Void, knowing how close it put him to the Swirl. But this he had to see.

"Kick out now!" begged Kristensen.

The voice came from behind him, from the real world, from the other Pod seat.

"More than 2 minutes to Phobos landing," said Sutherland. "It will take us less than 20 seconds to blast past the perimeter of the landing zone."

"Now!" screamed Kristensen. "Any miscalculation, and we'll be dead."

Sutherland smiled; knowing that dying here and now was simply not possible. He watched his daughter, wrapped in a crystalline shroud, the glasslike tendrils of her hair whipping about her.

A moment of doubt had come when the massive quake destroyed the Ag Co-Op, and he had feared for the first time in decades that the future was not as he had seen it. But when they had crawled from the debris and found this still-functioning link into the Void, then the working escape Pod, he knew that everything had happened exactly as it had been meant to happen.

"It's landing now!"

Sutherland looked past Sarah at the red underbelly of the

sky. The gray clouds burned, laced with lightning, the air suddenly alive, compression waves rolling through it, felt right through the soft seat of the Pod. The rumble was different from the tectonic lurches induced by the firing Rings, this rumble so deep, so resonant—a sympathetic vibration as Phobos compressed Earth's outer atmosphere.

"They're dead, and so will we be unless we kick out now. They're less than 2 kilometers from the outer perimeter of Phobos's landing zone. That cornfield will be slagged into molten rock!"

"Do you see what she's done to Mears?" said Sutherland, ignoring what Kristensen just said.

"It doesn't matter. She *is* dead!"

"Mears is transformed." Sutherland focused telemetry and optical instrumentation, the signal quickly degrading, the upper atmosphere suddenly choked with burning debris, the wail of sizzling plasma generating a broadband squeal blowing out most orbital surveillance. "Identify," he said in a whisper, staring at the salt-and-pepper grain that drifted across what had been Mears's face.

The Pod lurched.

"Kick out now!"

What had been Mears stood, looking up into the sky. *"Recognition,"* whispered a voice from the Void.

Sutherland smiled. The face that stared up from Mears's head was now easily recognizable. He shifted his perspective, looking over at Simon, down on his knees, hands wrapped around his head, his mouth opened wide in a silent scream. "She externalized Simon's delusion," said Sutherland. "Pulled that part of his personality right out of his skull and made it flesh and bone, using Mears's carcass as a template." He slowly closed his eyes, severing the interface, slipping into darkness. "She's pierced the Point."

"She's dead! And we'll be just as dead unless we kick out now!"

Sutherland gave the mental commands, mechanical and electrical signals being sent, trajectories chosen, atmospheric distortions and ripplings compensated for, and exploding stratospheric shears and turbulence thrown into the mix. "I can't be killed, not here, not now," Sutherland said quietly. "That would be *impossible*."

"Kick out!"

Sutherland's nodded. It was time. The jets, just a few meters beneath their seats, belched, kicking the Pod out of the imploded Ag Co-Op, acceleration pushing him deeply into his seat, vision tunneling, chest crushed, breathing impossible.

Her eyelids fluttering as something popped in her sinus cavities, Padmini hunkered down, snapping the last of the restraints across her chest, taking in a deep breath, trying to compensate against the spiking barometric rise.

"Everything in orbit below 10,000 kilometers is gone," announced Christina, sitting to her left, an interface stalk running from the console to her left eye, her fingers playing across the floating image rolling in front of her, a molten orb, spitting an azure tail, dropping into the outer atmosphere.

"Maximum slew," whispered Padmini, feeling the connections in her head buzz as she slipped out of her skull with Kali's help, her perspective speeding up until she saw those in the bunker in a slow crawl. She saw herself strapped in, head turned toward Christina. Behind her motionless body sat Xavier, and behind him, Krew and Che, who reached out for each other, hands holding on to each other's shoulder.

"What is a Clinger?" asked Padmini, as Kali flicked into existence next to Krew, leaning close, sniffing at him.

"Nothing accessible in the Void," Kali said, as her red-tinted eyeballs momentarily rolled back in their sockets. *"But Che has performed extensive analysis. Standard double helix, sharing 94 percent of its DNA with you. Definitely Earth-based, where retrograde DNA drift and mutation analysis indicates that you and Krew shared a common ancestor somewhere between 50 and 100 million years ago—what would appear to be a protoprimate."*

Padmini floated around Krew, studying his large, perfectly black eyes.

"But the different DNA is not the result of natural selection or random mutation. Much of it has been constructed, nearly 1000 genes different from yours, some devoted to metabolism, and a heightened efficiency of glucose burning, but most devoted to neurological enhancements and synaptic redesigns. There are even a few novel long-chain molecules that appear to be acting as neurotransmitters not found in your head or in any other primate's brain."

"Who modified him?" asked Padmini.

"Unknown," said Kali.

"Him?" she asked, and hovered next to Che, staring into his slightly out-of-focus eye.

"No. His files are not always cohesive or even coherent, but there seems to be little doubt that he found Krew in the cornfields ten years ago, and had nothing to do with his creation. When Che first found him, he had rudimentary powers of speech, identifying himself as Krew and that he was a Clinger. But there was little other information, and Che's initial neurological investigations only seemed to damage Krew further and he could no longer speak."

Padmini looked back at Krew, knowing that a major chunk of his brain came by way of the mesh she had just delivered. *"The Swirl?"* she asked.

"Doubtful," answered Kali. *"Krew has a pretty standard cel-*

lular clock, almost identical to yours, allowing only so many cell divisions, with genetic damage and degradation following standard primate patterns. He is close to 50 years old."

"And the Swirl was born only 25 years ago, in the Ten Degree War," said Padmini. "So while the Swirl might not have created Krew, it certainly had plans for it, plans that called for me to bring the neural mesh to repair the damage in its head." Padmini paused. "But why? What does the Swirl want with Krew, a thing that's been little more than a pet at the Olmos farm for the last ten years?"

Kali smiled, exposing her fanglike eyeteeth. "A mystery." She looked up. "One to be solved if we survive."

Padmini followed the direction of her gaze, her perspective floating upward, bumping into the steel sheet of the bunker's low ceiling, then passing through it, flowing up, through dirt, rock, and layer upon layer of isolating mesh and alternating sheets of dense metals and organic residues.

Red light.

The dark clouds burned, spit fire, and were laced with lightning. To the west, probably less than 30 kilometers away, the sky was torn, an incandescent plume, streaked violet, cutting through the air. Despite her high skew, the world about her looked as if it ticked by in real time, corn folded to the ground, most stalks snapped, a wall of crop debris pushed by tornado-force winds blowing in from the west, passing harmlessly through her phantom existence, rolling over the brick-stump foundation of what she suddenly realized was all that remained of the Olmos farmhouse.

A wall of smoke and smoldering corn debris surged through her. The roar of the wind was deafening, and would have punctured eardrums, possibly ripped meat from bone, had she actually been there. Dust and grit flew, rocks picked up and hurled, the air thickening, a mixture of organic residue and surface soil being peeled and thrown into the maelstrom.

"Winds in excess of 300 kilometers per hour and ambient temperatures of 140 Fahrenheit," announced Kali. *"The object will land in less than 15 seconds."*

Padmini looked again to the western horizon, and filters automatically flicked over her virtual vision. The world darkened as the plume suddenly showed definition—a twisting column of fire. The molten backwash of what had been the Earth's crust was thrust up into the air, expanding outward, a glowing curtain of liquid rock dropping between the horizon and the plume of the descending craft.

Padmini cringed, her phantom body attempting to curl in on itself, to hide from the rush of the burning horizon and the liquefied wall of rock cascading down from the sky.

Perspective shift.

Back in the bunker. Ambient red glow of emergency lighting. Screams, including hers. Hands clutched the arms of chairs, metal walls buckling, eardrums popping, superheated air burning nose and mouth, stinging eyes.

Krew jumped out of his chair, restraining straps still falling in the enhanced slew. Hands deep into the console's liquid interface, thin lips moving, golden embers flickering across the black eyeballs, he focused on Padmini, on the phantom of her simulated perspective, somehow knowing where she stood.

"Signal sent," said Krew. "They will come. They will rescue. They will save us from the monsters."

Padmini didn't understand.

Burning motes of static ate the world.

"Free of you!" Bill pointed down at Simon, who had dug deep into the ground, head down and covered. Standing, he leaned into the wind, pelted by rock and dirt, corn

shards and roadbed gravel. "Pain!" he screamed in delight, reaching up, managing to bring a hand to his face, feeling the blood, fingertips probing the ragged cut beneath his left eye.

The western horizon burned, a wall of liquid rock boiling up, filling the sky, arcing over and past them.

"Free!" he screamed again, his feet flying out from beneath him, the burning wind taking him away, tossing him high, his suit flashing into flame, his back splattered with molten droplets of liquefied dirt. Far below, through burning air and distorted eyeballs, he saw Sarah, standing tall, anchored, crystalline filaments still tying her down.

Wall of crystal.

White light.

Tendrils, wrapping around his waist, jerked him out of the air.

"Free!" He hit the ground, crystal flowing over him.

Chapter 22

Akandi sat atop the featureless, golden hull of Phobos, knees pulled up to his chest, arms wrapped around his knees. He peered out to the east. It had been more than a day and a half since the craft had landed, and he'd now entered into his second night, his consciousness trapped on the outer hull, still out of contact with Iyoon, and no sign of the Clinger.

Not hungry, not thirsty, not sleepy, not hot or cold, he

simply was. Trapped, he could wander several hundred meters in any direction across the top of the craft, but apparently no farther; no matter how long he attempted to walk in a fixed direction, he always returned to the top of the craft.

A virtual prison.

He shook his head.

"Ambassador McCarthy was right," he said again, having lost track of how many times he'd said those words. "Better to have been eaten than to have allowed this," he whispered.

The horizon had cooled. On the first night, only a few hours after landing, the ground had been liquefied, looking like a lava field that had erupted from a nearly infinite number of fissures.

He shifted, angling himself to face Mecca, kneeling and pushing his face down against the golden hull. "Forgive me," he whispered, knowing that while nothing was beyond the ability of Allah, even He would be hard-pressed to forgive such a sin. His pride had led him to believe that he might be able to control the outcome of Phobos traveling to Earth and exert some control over the craft and the creatures that really ran it.

He was now certain that he'd simply been used, and suspected that this landing spot in Alabama was not just some rural setting picked at random, but a deliberate destination with a purpose—one he couldn't even begin to make a guess about.

Straightening up, he looked toward the horizon. There were a few spots that still glowed deep amber, but it was mostly dark, the molten rock having cooled and solidified. A crescent moon hung above, distorted and dancing in the still cooling air.

He was responsible for this—the destruction a direct consequence of his arrogance.

"An awe-inspiring panorama."

Akandi spun around, jumping up. The Clinger stood before him. Unthinking reflex had him running forward, arms outstretched, hands open, and fingers tensed, ready to wrap them around its slender gray throat.

The fact that both of them were only virtual entities didn't change how he felt.

He fell forward, passing through the creature, hitting the unyielding surface of the hull, and slid to a halt. The Clinger walked toward him and squatted.

"Primitive emotional response," it said. "It is amazing, actually beyond rational comprehension, that your species has reached the brink of the Point. You have no control over yourselves."

Akandi whispered a prayer, begging for the strength not to lash out again at the phantom. "And yet we've managed to do what Clingers couldn't, reaching the Point unaided." He slapped the side of his head. "Our software *and* hard-ware."

"Point well taken."

Akandi took a deep breath. "You used me."

The creature shrugged its narrow shoulders in what Akandi knew to be a too-human gesture, carefully noting the intended manipulation, now believing that everything about this simulated entity was designed to manipulate his emotions. "As I've been used by Drom and the others in Phobos."

"Others?" asked Akandi.

The creature smiled, showing pointy teeth. "As will soon be explained to you by your good friend General Sutherland."

"What?" Akandi managed to whisper. "He's here?" Sutherland had been instrumental in his winning the ambassador appointment. But "good friend" was not the phrase he'd use to describe him. He doubted the man had any friends, good or otherwise. This was another clue that Alabama was not a random destination.

"And waiting for you. I was instructed to bring you, but first to act as an emotional buffer, a focus for your rage, so that it would not be misdirected against General Sutherland." Reaching up, he ran a slender finger along his throat. "A most effective venting."

Akandi stood, trembling.

"Perhaps your anger has not yet been sufficiently expressed. Would you care to strangle me, to beat my head against the ship's hull until my skull cracks and brain spills out? I can ensure a full sensory simulation, complete with a wide range of panic pheromones, and if you wish, provide the mental nudge allowing you to slip into a full berserker mode." Its smiled widened.

Akandi pressed the palms of his hands against the sides of his legs. "Not necessary," he said, keeping the tone of his voice steady. "I've sufficiently vented, and am now under a level of control that will allow me to discuss the current situation calmly with General Sutherland."

"Excellent," said the creature. "I can tell that you are lying, but the fact that you are able to lie in such a controlled manner indicates that you have regained sufficient composure to meet with General Sutherland."

Akandi said nothing. There was no time to respond. He slipped through the metal hull.

* * *

Xavier still could not believe what had happened, despite what Che had pulled from the Ag Co-Op's Void just before the entire place imploded. They had known that Phobos was breaking orbit, beginning its transit to Earth, and would land in southern Alabama.

Impossible.

But they'd gone into the deep bunker anyway.

And then the moon had landed.

Impossible.

"Despite what your daughter might want to believe, Krew is not an alien," said Padmini. Christina sat in the far corner of the bunker, her face glowing in the backwash of an ancient flat-panel display, the liquid-crystal sheet miraculously intact after the pounding the bunker had taken, only functioning because Xavier had taken the precaution of double-canning some backup electronics in the Bunker, isolating them from the planet-spanning upper-atmospheric electromagnetic belch and discharge that Phobos had sparked as it had dropped to Earth.

Xavier sighed, tired, nerves frayed.

So much gone, he thought.

He clutched the dead interface box in his hands, his link to Bec gone. He could not tell how badly the main storage had really been damaged, had no way of telling if Bec had been lost. They'd been in the deep bunker for nearly two days, waiting for the surface firestorm to die down, for the nearby lava fields to solidify, and for the noxious mixture of gases and volatized organics to dissipate. Two days of endless speculation and staring at the little flickering Vid display.

When they got out, working their way back up the escape shaft, they'd hope to be able to access the metal lockers concealed off the main tunnel, those quad-meshed storage bins where he'd kept the bulk of the backup equipment wrapped enough to handle the massive EMP. But until they could get back up the escape shaft he wouldn't know if enough equipment to get Bec back survived.

They didn't know how severe the damage was, unable to link to the Void, not even through the emergency antenna that he and Che had spent hours manually cranking up the nearly 100-meter service pipe to the surface. Although the bunker was 100 meters down and triple-meshed to ground wayward electromagnetics, when Phobos dropped through the atmosphere it had sparked a globe-spanning EMP barrage that had leaked through to fry the more sensitive bio-electronic links, effectively killing most of the monitoring equipment. Fortunately, the mesh in Che's and Padmini's skulls was still functioning, courtesy of the additional shielding that the military and the police had insisted on using when they'd enhanced their brains.

"Not an alien," said Padmini, moving her right foot across the floor and not so gently kicking Xavier's left boot. "The data clearly shows that he is genetically Earth-based."

Xavier blinked. "Definitely Earth-based," he said, finally focusing on her. Reaching to his left, he carefully placed Bec's interface box on a shelf.

"Better than 5 percent synthetic DNA," said Padmini, knowing just what it was that Xavier knew and didn't know, since the only information that Kali had been able to find on Krew had come from Xavier's own private storage, the information she'd been able to raid before the Void and the bunker's electronics had fallen off-line. "There are several dozen labs in North America that could have built the synthetic DNA."

"True enough," said Xavier. He had always thought the same thing, but now was not so sure. *Phobos had landed in the adjoining county,* and he knew there was no Earth-based technology that could have been responsible for that. Perhaps Krew was another facet of that technology.

Padmini shook her head. "But there's no motive, no reason for it. No one is going to go to the expense and effort of creating such a creature, only to thoughtfully lobotomize him and dump him in your cornfield, and then a decade later use me and Barnwell to deliver the missing part of his brain just moments before the damn world comes to an end."

Xavier grimaced. "Cops don't believe in coincidences?" He wondered if cops believed in lemurs piloting small moons. That's what Christina would have them believe, that a moonful of Clingers were on their way from Jupiter, traveling in Amalthea, a moon significantly bigger than Phobos.

"Cops believe you look at the most likely explanation, eliminate it if necessary, then move on to the next most likely one."

"So what are you saying? It sounds like you're trying to talk yourself out of Earthly origins and convince yourself that some wayward ETs built him, maybe some ETs inside of Amalthea."

"I'm not ready to believe that," she said. "He's Earth-based, but the technology needed to build him wasn't around when he was born."

"And if your cop wiring doesn't like a reality riddled with coincidences, what do you make of that?" Xavier asked, pointing over at Christina and the monitor she stared at. Three static-distorted figures filled the screen. "How do our new visitors fit into this unfolding nightmare?"

"They don't," she said and, leaning back, closed her eyes.

* * *

Padmini squirmed out of her cubbyhole, carefully walking across the blanket-strewn floor, keeping her distance from Krew. He was nestled in a thick wad of blankets and broken boxes, having built a sort of nest for himself, sitting still and silent, hands sunk knuckle deep in a wad of neural interface, a gray paste composed of a nearly infinite number of microscopic fibers that filled Che's empty eye socket. Every time Che twitched or wiggled, Krew gave a sympathetic movement. Padmini wanted nothing to do with that, staying out of reach of the creature, in case he made a move and tried to interface with *her* nervous system. She already had one invader in her skull and would take no chances on a second.

Xavier sat wedged into the far corner of the bunker, the interface box to his dead wife resting in his lap, the stalk running between it and his right eye. She couldn't imagine what he thought he was looking at. The box in his lap, along with most of the electronics in the bunker, had been flatlined by the EMP.

His wife was dead.

Again.

"Any change?" asked Padmini, turning away from Krew and Che.

Christina didn't look up from the monitor. "Nothing much. The temperature has dropped another 3 degrees in the last hour, down to 147 Fahrenheit, but the carbon monoxide, and a whole range of sulfurous hydrocarbons, are still at toxic levels. It will be at least another 6 hours before we will be able to go up."

Padmini looked at the full-face respirators hanging from the far wall—three of them. Not enough for the four bodies in the bunker, or five if she included Krew. The descent tube that they'd crawled down just moments before Phobos had dropped from the sky was choked with meters of debris at the surface, and so distorted that its internal isolation hatches could no longer be sealed. The only thing keeping the noxious mixture of volcanic gases from spilling into their hole was the positive pressure they'd been able to maintain from the slow leak of stored air tanks and the debris plugging the descent tunnel. Once they broke out to the surface the outside deadly mix would spill into their hole, with not enough respirators to go around.

Rats trapped in a hole, she thought.

"Rats safe in a hole," said Kali, suddenly hovering next to her, leaning back in a relaxed pose, filing her front teeth with a glistening shard of metal. *"No point in going topside until the butterflies emerge."*

Padmini smirked, uncomfortable with Kali's insistence on referring to the three figures topside as larvae in a cocoon. It was probably too close to the truth. Nothing *human* should have been able to survive on the surface.

"Any change with them?" asked Padmini, leaning over Christina to stare at the small monitor. She had trouble focusing on the flat two-dimensional display, her brain taking several seconds to interpret shadows and textures, to create a quasi three-dimensional picture out of the flat pixels.

"The pacer is becoming more and more agitated and has started banging at the inside of the cocoon. Perhaps he's trying to break out."

Padmini peered more closely. Before Xavier and Che had cranked the antenna up the tube, they'd painted the top several meters of the mast with high-intensity bioluminescents, and then sprinkled it with a batch of dumb-eyes, the little cameras capable of sucking down photons and sending the signals back down the antenna, but nothing more than that. There was no real-time data manipulation, pattern recognition, or even the simplest of image enhancers. Only stupid pictures.

Padmini's brain finally made sense of, the images flitting on the flat panel. It was still night, what little there was to see bathed in the green glow of the bioluminescents. There was only the occasional whirlwind of ash. Most of the volcanic debris had settled into drifts.

The farmhouse was gone.

In its place lay a shattered shard of what had been a molten chunk of volcanic glass. It glistened green in the artificial light, with drifts of volcanic ash several meters high washed up against its west-facing side.

Movement.

Between the massive shard of volcanic glass and their antenna sat the cocoon, a roughly hemispherical structure nearly 4 meters tall, constructed out of what looked like rough quartz, its surface multifaceted and pitted. Inside were three figures, little more than shadows. There was the pacer, who continually walked back and forth, occasionally stopping to press a face against the inside of the hemisphere, the features fractured and blurred. The other two they had seen far less of. In fact, at first they had thought there had only been one other—the stander. The stander did not move, but simply stood in the center of the cocoon, with arms outstretched, as if somehow holding up the cocoon. It was only after watching for several hours that they realized there was a third figure, one lying down at the stander's feet—the sleeper. There was the occasional flailing of an arm, and once Padmini had seen the sleeper sit up, but then quickly topple back over.

The figures had been there from the moment they'd been able to punch the antenna to the surface, when glowing and molten slag still rained down, the temperature was 250 Fahrenheit and the noxious mixture of volcanic gasses and acid mist was so intense it could kill in seconds.

They had not been able to figure out how the three had gotten there or how they could have possibly erected their enclosure while the lethal volcanic debris rained down. They shouldn't have been there.

But they were.

"We should be able to go up in 6 hours," said Christina. Looking back at Padmini, she smiled. "Then we'll be able to solve this little mystery."

Padmini managed to smile back, realizing that when Christina stared into the monitor, all the girl saw was a mystery in the shrouded figures. She herself saw something incredibly dangerous, quite possibly lethal, something that had survived in an environment that should have killed anything Pure or Tool. And they'd built their camp right at the exit end of the escape hole. That was no coincidence. The three were *waiting* for them to emerge.

"Let me know if anything changes," said Padmini, turning around.

Xavier had been standing right behind her, smiling at his daughter, and now smiled at Padmini. "Enthusiastic, isn't she?" he said.

Padmini nodded.

"Something's changing," said Christina. "We're starting to get some external lighting from the east." She reached forward, picking up an antique keyboard, slowly pecking at the keys of the mechanical interface, at times stopping to search for the right letter. In the corner of the Vid monitor a rainbow spectrum played against a wavelength axis.

"Sunlight," she said.

Xavier and Padmini nodded in unison.

"Some rather major anomalies, though," said Christina.

Xavier and Padmini waited.

"It's only 3:44 A.M., with sunrise almost 2 hours away." Christina ran a finger across the screen with her left hand, while tapping at keys with her right. "It's not easy to do with the detectors we have, but if I look at the emission spectrum of the sunlight, even taking into account all the ash in the air, there's something a bit strange in the solar spectrum."

Padmini leaned forward, hanging over Christina's shoulder.

"The absorption spectrum has been blue-shifted," said Christina, then looked up at Padmini, "the wavelengths shortened."

"And what do you think that means?" asked Xavier in a whisper. Padmini read his expression, knowing that it was a rhetorical question. This situation had suddenly dipped into what looked to Padmini like some sort of teacher-student mode.

"You can only shift a spectrum if there is radial motion between you and the object you're observing," said Christina.

Xavier stepped closer, nudging Padmini to the side. "How fast?" he asked.

Christina pecked at the keyboard. Numbers flashed across the monitor. "Nearly 400 kilometers per second," she said in a whisper.

"My God," said Xavier, looking at Padmini.

"And that means?" she asked.

"The Sun is moving in our direction at a speed of 400 kilometers per second," he said, pausing for just a moment. "That's more than 1 million kilometers per hour."

Padmini turned, looking at the monitor, and at the ash-strewn scene and the quartz enclosure, no longer bathed in the pink glow of the bioluminescents, but now tinted red by the morning sunlight filtering through the ash-laden horizon. "The Sun has risen 2 hours earlier than it should have," she said, "and is moving toward us at a speed of 1 million kilometers per hour?" She hoped that saying the words aloud would help her make more sense of them. It didn't.

Christina nodded. "At that rate it will be at the Earth in around 100 hours."

"*It*," said Padmini. "You mean the Sun will *hit* the Earth?"

Christina slowly nodded again.

Xavier reached over her shoulder, his fingers flashing over the keyboard. Numbers choked the screen, along with a series of multihued spectrums, interspersed with blackened absorption spectrums. "There's some splitting in a few of the solar spectrum absorption lines." He paused, standing back up. "It's the sort of splitting one might expect if the light source were accelerating in your direction."

"And that means?" asked Padmini.

"We don't have 100 hours. The Sun is moving toward us at 1 million kilometers per hour, and that velocity is *increasing*."

"The stellar Jet," said Christina.

Xavier nodded. "Just like back in '31, but this time it seems to be accelerating at better than 10 times the rate it did then."

"The pattern coalesces."

All three turned. Che stood in the center of the bunker, the filamentary interface still running into his eye socket, with Krew's fingers embedded in it. He lifted up his right foot, and Krew did the same, the both of them bringing

down their feet together, then both of them pointing at the
blanket-covered floor. "A massive chaotic attractor," they
said, Krew's lisping voice almost drowned by Che's deep
growling voice. "Here and now," they said.

Chapter 23

The table was wrong. A massive slab of mahogany,
elliptically shaped, polished to a glistening sheen, and surrounded by nearly a dozen dark leather chairs. The table sat
in a pink-quartz chamber, with Drom situated at the head
of it. His anatomy not chair-compatible, he had lowered
himself back on a small stone block, resting on the thick
trunk of his tail.

"Home," said Drom.

Akandi blinked, consciousness quickly flowing back into
his body, only realizing at that moment he had been staring
at the table, at the impossibly out-of-place table at which
Drom was seated. He found himself standing at the far end
of the room, not the control room, where the quartz had
flowed over him, but a different one, apparently a *conference*
room.

"Slowly."

Iyoon rotated in front of him, and Akandi suddenly felt
so comfortable, so right, that empty spot in his head filled,
Iyoon tweaking neurotransmitter levels this way and that,
whispering in a gentle voice. *"Take it slow and say nothing.
Your brain is still reconfiguring, transitioning to the abrupt return*

of self-awareness to your organic hardware. They've had your body here for the better part of a day now, wandering about the corner of the room, occasionally bouncing into the wall, but mostly lying down, staring."

"Back with us?"

Akandi turned just in time to see a man walking into the room, not too tall, white hair, a deeply creased tanned face. General Sutherland. He hadn't seen the man in more than a month, not that long ago, despite the fact that it seemed a lifetime away.

Sutherland looked no different.

Behind him, looking like a dog in tow, walked an old, potbellied, stooped man, his face red and puffy, covered in places with what looked like just-added synthetic skin, the patches pasty white, not yet fully integrated with his body. Akandi did not recognize the second man.

Sutherland walked quickly to the far end of the conference table opposite Drom, pulled out a chair, and sat. His companion slowly sat next to him, grimacing as he lowered his body, in obvious pain.

"Almost all here," said the general, turning, looking at a featureless slab of wall. Akandi sensed movement within the wall, something turning, a shaft of blue light playing through the semitranslucent pink material, followed by a yellow-orange burst as a shard of glistening crystal emerged from the wall.

The Swirl, thought Akandi, but different, somehow more solid than it had appeared when he'd first entered into Phobos. Its edges were so sharp, looking lethal to the touch.

"A physical node," said Iyoon. *"The Void has collapsed, and the Swirl now resides solely in isolated hardware nodes and has taken on an extreme physical form."*

"All here," said Sutherland, as the Swirl floated a meter

above the table, stopping above one of the empty leather chairs.

Akandi stared at the Swirl, at the bizarreness of it hovering over the chair, an entity so obviously not needing a chair, as it met with organic entities who did.

"Sit," said Sutherland, pointing at Akandi.

Akandi walked over to the table, his first few steps hesitant. But he could feel himself quickly reintegrating, his sense of self and the organic mush in his head resynching. He sat without having to think consciously about it.

"Job well-done," said Sutherland, nodding at Akandi. "I knew you'd get done what McCarthy was incapable of."

"Stupid human," said Drom, breathing deeply.

Sutherland held up a hand in Drom's direction, silencing him. Akandi watched carefully, understanding the pecking order but not understanding how Sutherland had managed to establish control over Drom.

"*Over the Swirl?*" he asked Iyoon.

"*Highly doubtful,*" answered Iyoon. "*Even if it appears that the Swirl bends to his will, I suspect that is only an appearance, the Swirl accommodating General Sutherland because it suits its purposes.*"

Akandi understood—it was a basic diplomatic maneuver.

General Sutherland reached into the top pocket of his coverall for something that he cupped in the palm of his hand. He placed his hand on the tabletop. "A long time waiting and wondering," he said. "Twenty-five years for me, but so much longer for *us,*" he added, waving one hand about the room, his other hand still on the table, covering what he had removed from his pocket.

Akandi had no idea what he was talking about.

"Time to go now," said Drom, rocking forward on his tail and standing. "Time for return."

Sutherland smiled, pointing his free hand at Drom. "Just a few more minutes."

The dinosaur flared his nostrils, chest expanding, nictitating membranes flickering up and down across his eyes. He did not sit down but did stay at the table.

Sutherland lifted his hand off the table, revealing what looked to Akandi like a high-density storage cube. He pushed it across the table to Akandi, the datacube spinning, its mirrored faces glistening as it spun.

Akandi slapped it to a stop, looking down at his hand, and only at that moment noticing the small indentation in the table directly in front of him, an obvious cube port. He pushed the datacube toward it.

"Not yet," said Sutherland. "History has not quite caught up to us." Again he smiled. "Or perhaps we have not caught up to history."

Again, Akandi did not understand what Sutherland was talking about, and he felt his patience thinning, the frustration and anger that had built as he'd wandered across the virtual hull of Phobos returning.

It was Sutherland. He was somehow in charge of all this. Akandi knew the general's reach had been extensive, but he would have never guessed just how extensive. A moon from Mars had landed in an Alabama cornfield, and within a few days Sutherland had apparently taken control of it. Akandi thought about that for a moment, realizing that perhaps control had been taken long before Phobos had landed, perhaps before he'd even been dispatched to Mars.

A pawn—in a game he couldn't understand. His anger continued to grow. "How many died?" he asked.

"Locally an insignificant number," said Sutherland, shrugging his shoulders. "Globally it might be in the tens of the millions."

Akandi slumped in his chair, and he watched the little man next to Sutherland twitch, a head-to-shoulder spasm, and his already pale skin whiten even more. "Millions?" said Akandi in a whisper.

"Probably, but difficult to tell," said Sutherland. "The Rings have been test-firing for almost 3 days now, at first randomly, then in a sequenced pattern, setting up resonant compressive waves oscillating through the planet, ones that appear to have been specifically designed to unleash stored energy along fault lines, and to ease tensions at tectonic plate boundaries."

"Nearly a 50-fold release in energy as compared to what we saw in '31 when the Rings first self-assembled," said the little man next to Sutherland.

Akandi stared at him, feeling dazed.

"Excuse me," said Sutherland, looking over at the man, then at Akandi. "I don't believe that you've been introduced. This is my longtime associate Dr. Jesper Kristensen, a colleague who had strayed from the fold, but has now returned to aid us."

Kristensen gave a small nod. "The firing sequence appears to be designed to liberate stored geological energy, through a complex series of eruptions and geological slippages. Fortunately, only a small fraction of the energy liberated resulted in actual ground slippage. Most of the resulting subsurface shock waves actually canceled each other out with the bulk of the energy transferred into deep-crust heating. The overall planetary surface effects were minor."

"*Minor?*" said Akandi in disbelief. "I saw it from orbit. The planet is shrouded in volcanic ash, with magma spewing in dozens of locations. You tell me that millions are dead." He paused, his heart pounding, a wave of nausea rolling through him, that number of causalities staggering, emotionally overwhelming. He fought to regain control over himself, knowing that Iyoon was helping, feeling the tension suddenly fall away as his brain chemistry was tweaked. He fought to reestablish his diplomatic veneer. "I'm no geologist, no environmental engineer, but I would not call what I saw *minor*."

"In historical context certainly not minor," said Sutherland. "But in comparison to what would have happened, if the fault energy had not been released in a controlled fashion, quite minimal. Had the planet simply started accelerating, heading toward its target without this stored energy having been dissipated in a controlled fashion, I seriously doubt that anything above the microbial level would have survived to start the journey."

"The journey?" asked Akandi.

"Please," said Sutherland. "False stupidity does not suit you. Our trip to the Incubator at Alpha Centauri A. I know that Chan passed the information along to you."

Akandi nodded.

"But rarely does a single cause result in a single effect. And it appears that the Alphans are masters of the multiple effect. The resulting earthquakes collapsed the global power grid, but many installations, especially those of a military nature, were able to survive, with systems intact and weapons on-line. In such a moment of emergency mistakes will be made—mistakes that, considering the weaponry at humanity's disposal, would be capable of scouring Earth's biosphere."

"That's where you came in," said Kristensen, pointing at Akandi.

"Like pieces of a puzzle," said Sutherland. "I've known for decades what the final picture would look like, but couldn't quite understand what I was seeing." He pointed at the datacube sitting in front of Akandi. "I knew Drom had to come and knew that you'd be the one to bring him. That much was a fact."

"Fact?" asked Akandi.

"Yes, a hard, indisputable fact. But what I didn't understand is what your arrival would accomplish and what Phobos was intended to do."

"Melt a sizable portion of Alabama," said Akandi bitterly.

"An insignificant effect compared to its real purpose. The upper-atmospheric ash had become charged. Lightning discharges are often observed in conventional volcanic plumes, but this ash covered the entire planet, and at extremely high altitudes, the total charge simply incredible.

"And Phobos discharged it," said Kristensen.

Sutherland stood, smiling, and slammed both his open hands against the table. "So beautiful, so perfect. The Alphans could see pattern, cause and effect, 65 million years out, able to reach out to us from a time when *they* roamed the Earth," he said, while pointing over at Drom.

"What are you talking about?" said Akandi.

"The Phobos craft is massive, with almost a 10-kilometer diameter. It hit the outer atmosphere moving at 10,000 kilometers per hour, generating a plasma reentry discharge unlike any that our little craft could ever generate."

"The upper atmosphere was unstable," said Akandi, suddenly understanding what Sutherland was talking about. "It was like entering into a room full of gas with a lit match."

"Spectacular," said Sutherland. "The atmosphere discharged, making our feeble nuclear-based EMPs look like a sneeze. It fried just about everything worldwide. It took most Tools down, took the Void down, and effectively pushed this planet more than 100 years into the past, in many places 200 years in the past. We no longer have the power to destroy ourselves."

Akandi stood, hands pushed against the table, leaning forward. "Are you insane?" he said. "Do you really believe this planet has been pushed back to some low-tech state of *grace*? Maybe the nukes won't fire, maybe the high-speed SCRAMs can't launch and drop their loads, maybe a bunch of tweaked Tools can't go Post-Point, but there's still an infinite number of ways for us to destroy ourselves. With the world this decimated, with no authority and no controls, how long do you think it will be before some demented character with a beaker and a few spliced genes unleashes something that will scour this planet in a matter of hours?"

"Of course you're quite right," said Sutherland. "Authority is needed. Fortunately, nothing in this craft was harmed by the global EMP; here all technologies are intact."

"With you in control of it?" said Akandi.

"I have a bigger picture to contend with," said Sutherland. "I will leave it to my good friend Drom, and the several million of his like-minded fellows in cold storage below, to keep Earth's house in order."

Millions. Akandi sat. "What have I done?"

Sutherland leaned toward him. "You did what you had to do." He motioned to the datacube in front of Akandi. "It's time to take a look."

Akandi picked up the cube with numb fingers and pushed it into the indentation in front of him. The air momentarily crackled with a rainbow discharge, and an image coalesced above the conference room table.

"So," said Akandi. Hanging above the table was an image of the very room they were in, an image obviously taken just a moment before, showing them all around the table, with him standing, pointing at Sutherland, his eyes wide and angry. "Why play back this image?"

"While what you see certainly took place just a few moments ago, you need to consider the fact that the cube it is recorded upon was already in your hand from a time *before* your little outburst took place."

Akandi squinted. "What we're seeing obviously was not stored in the cube. It's nothing more than playback from this room's recorders."

The Swirl, which had remained stationary above a seat this entire time, suddenly spun, flashing a bright flare of rainbows, then, just as suddenly, stopped.

"Not room recorders," said Iyoon, flicking into Akandi's field of view. *"The Swirl gave me access, showed me the room's systems. This image comes from the cube you were holding."*

"And so what," said Akandi looking at Sutherland. "So you've got some next-generation memory cubes with integrated recording optics. It doesn't mean a thing."

"It means *everything*," said Sutherland. "It is why we are here, it is the answer to everything that has happened to the human race from even before we dropped down from the trees."

Akandi simply stared, not knowing how to respond to such an obviously insane statement.

"I'll let you and Iyoon examine the cube, study the image, and give you access to the equipment needed to count the radioactive isotopes buried deep within it."

"*It has an internal clock,*" said Iyoon. "*More than a dozen different radioactive isotopes, with half-lives ranging from just a few thousand years, to hundreds of millions of years. Examining the decayed and undecayed isotopes uniquely defines the moment that the cube was manufactured, while encrypted coding locks the image to the mix of undecayed isotopes at the time of recording, thereby establishing a time fix to the image it's displaying.*"

"Has Iyoon cleared things up for you?" asked Sutherland.

Akandi shook his head. "No."

"That image has been stored in that cube for 65 million years," said Sutherland, making it sound like a pronouncement. "That cube, along with a few other artifacts, was discovered buried in the rim of the Copernicus crater on the moon nearly 30 years ago, when the Chinese were excavating for one of their early lunar bases. It could not be viewed at the time, not until it eventually made its way into our hands, and we developed the technology to read it."

"What?" Akandi managed to stammer.

"A still image of our meeting, an event that occurred only moments ago, was recorded in that cube," said Sutherland. "Imagine my surprise, to see a recording that had been buried on the moon for 65 million years, not only showing me as you now see me, not the young man that I was when I first viewed the cube, but what I would become 30 years later. And as an added bonus, of course, impossibilities were heaped upon impossibilities, and we were presented with the image of our two friends." He pointed at Drom and the Swirl. "I was shown a single moment from my future, a future that looked so impossible at the time, but one that has now come to pass."

"How?" asked Akandi. "How could that image have been lying on the moon for the last 65 million years?"

"That's what we're going to find out," said Sutherland.

Chapter 24

Christina had her head lowered to her knees. Never in her life had she felt so lost and helpless, not even when she had considered suicide the only escape from the Ag Co-Op. "It's still too dangerous," she said in a whisper. Even as she said it, she knew that wasn't true. It wasn't the danger, it was the hopelessness.

"It may well be," said Xavier. He had his hand on her back, gently rubbing it. "But we can't stay down here, trapped in a hole, just waiting for the end."

Christina sat up. "Has the Sun slowed or altered its trajectory?" she asked. For the past hour she'd not been able to watch the monitor, or the simulation showing the Sun's advance. The inevitability was simply too grim.

Xavier shook his head. "Not as far as we can tell, but the little eyes attached to the antenna can only see so much. We need to get to the surface to make better observations."

"And do what?" she asked.

Xavier felt eyes turning toward them and glanced over his shoulder. Padmini looked up from the far end of the room, where she continued to turn a large crank next to the access shaft. Even Che and Krew were looking at him, despite the fact that while they were interfaced they mostly existed in some shared mental space far beyond the bunker. "We need to try," he said. "If we have a better idea what we're dealing with, then we have a better chance of survival. Perhaps the three topside might have some ideas."

"Papa, the Sun is accelerating directly at the Earth," she said. "Can you conceive of any possible way of surviving that? You built this bunker, saved us from what just happened outside, have kept us safe for all these years. But do you really think *you* can stop the Sun?"

Xavier stood but did not step back. "That's not the point, Christina. I've got to try." He turned his head, and looked across the bunker, at Padmini kneeling at the base of the access shaft, manually turning the large metal handles of the lift, carrying the shaped charges to the blocked tunnel entrance. He looked back down at Christina. "*She* needs to try," he said.

Christina looked over at Padmini, the muscles straining in her arms as she continued to turn the crank.

"She's seen the simulation and knows the facts just as you do, and probably thinks the outcome is just as bleak. But she won't give up." Xavier looked away from his daughter and down at the floor. "I know what it is to lose hope. I got lost in despair when your mama died." Then he looked back at Christina. "But with your help I found my way back."

Christina reached for him, wrapping her arms around her father. "I'm so scared," she whispered to him.

Xavier held on tightly to Christina. "Don't fight that feeling, don't try and hide from it. You've never come up against something you couldn't solve or pound into the mud." He pushed her back a bit so he could look into her face. "Always came up with a solution, even one as foolish as the one involving that can of ethanol you had hidden in the barn."

"No, Papa," she said. "I never . . ."

"That doesn't matter now," he said. "You can't see an answer now, and that has you terrified. We may die—we will probably die—but how we die will say just as much about us as how we lived. I know you, Christina, know what you are capable of."

Christina slowly nodded and pushed away from Xavier. "Need help with that?" she asked Padmini, who was still tugging on the crank.

"Out!" Bill pounded against the crystalline wall, leaving behind a bloody streak. He pulled his fist back, fingers slowly uncurling and blood welling up.

"Actions have consequences," said Simon. He'd pushed himself up, leaning against the crystalline pedestal that Sarah stood on. "And many of those consequences are painful."

Bill slowly squatted, his gaze alternating between his bloody hand and Simon. "Better to feel pain than to be trapped in your head, just a sick delusion."

Simon looked past Bill, and at the diffuse, ill-defined world barely visible through the crystalline dome that encapsulated them. They'd been inside it for nearly 2 days now, judging by the rise and fall of the Sun, but he couldn't be totally sure. Most of the first day they had floated about in what appeared to be a frothing swell of magma, both the walls and the floor of the dome glowing bright red, the immense heat surrounding them not penetrating their small lifeboat, breathable air somehow filtering through, even a small pool of water appearing in a depression in one side of the floor. In the other corner, pee and crap quickly encapsulated in crystal and passed through the wall of the dome—not that Sarah seemed to need any of those things.

She simply did not move, her chest not even rising and falling. Simon was not sure she was alive, although he suspected that even if she should topple over and shatter like crystal, it would not be an end to her but simply one more transition. He suspected that concepts like breathing, drinking, eating, and even being alive did not necessarily translate to whatever Post-Human plane Sarah now found herself on.

But despite that, some aspect of her still appeared to be aware of their existence in this world. She had to be directing the dome. On the second day they had washed ashore onto dirt and rock, and the dome had then crept along for hours, moving in a straight, deliberate trajectory, finally stopping on a featureless parcel of ash-coated ground.

And there they waited, while the diffuse Sun crawled across the sky, getting ever larger as it cut its overhead arc. Now, sitting on the western horizon, it seemed to fill half the sky. Simon could not tell how much of that was due to the distortion of the light filtering through the crystal dome and how much of it was real. There was no way of knowing for sure, but he felt certain that the Sun was actually larger, and that meant either that the Earth was being propelled in its direction through the firing of the Rings, or the Sun was actually moving toward them.

"*Outside* not bothering you?" asked Bill.

Simon's head pounded, his hands shook, and he was certain that if he tried to stand, his legs would simply give way. It was taking a continual mental effort not to throw up, to ignore the galloping thump of his heart and the tingling in his hands and feet. There was no mistaking the telltale signs of anxiety, of a body amped well past its intended design. But he had not panicked, had not shut down and curled into a whimpering ball. He was proud of that. "Were you really protecting me, Bill?" he asked, looking over at his phobia made real, now flesh and bone built around the hardware scaffolding that had been Mears. "Or were you protecting yourself?"

Bill smiled and, reaching up, pushed aside a thick swatch of brown hair that had fallen into his left eye. Simon watched his fingers reach for glasses that were no longer there, certain that ingrained reflexes demanded those fingers push the black-rimmed glasses back up the bridge of his nose. But as far as Simon could tell, Bill no longer needed glasses. His vision was perfect, courtesy of either Mears's fully integrated Ocs or some further enhancement that Sarah had provided.

Those details didn't really matter to Simon. What was important was that ingrained reflex, the apparent need of those fingers to reach for those glasses. That proved what had become of Bill. He'd been made human, one probably with the power of a Tool, but one still controlled by all the mental idiosyncrasies of his conception.

"I was protecting both of us," said Bill.

Simon believed he'd just detected a well-honed human skill in Bill—the ability to lie. "In the beginning I'm sure that's exactly what you were doing," said Simon. "I'd laid down the basic template, created a persona to keep me safe from the world, but at some point you became real, with your own desires and fears."

"You are defective, not much more than a pattern-recognition device wrapped in a bit of meat and bone, a piece of lab equipment to serve CUSP," said Bill, crawling forward, his bloody hand again clenched in a fist. "You planted the seed, but what I became is so much more than you could ever evolve into. Given a bit more time I could have engulfed you, like shedding a skin that no longer fit.

But that won't be necessary, now that our friend here has speeded up the process a bit." He pointed over at Sarah.

Simon focused, planting his hands, palms flat, against the crystal floor. He pushed himself up, kneeling, then planted a right foot squarely against the floor and, straining his leg, forced the knee to bend, ignoring the almost-cramp threatening to lock up his thigh and the tremor running up and down his calf. He got his left foot flat against the floor, and stood, but his feet could not quite hold his weight. He felt his hands going numb and his vision tunnel.

Stumbling back, he steadied himself against the side of the dome and managed to stand. "So I'm just a pattern-recognition machine," he said, taking a half step toward Bill. "I wouldn't be so quick to dismiss that—it's the essence of any animal that has evolved past the multicellular level. The detection of pattern, and the anticipation of things to come, is what allowed us to do all that we have done. It allowed me to create you." He looked up at Sarah. "We also passed it on to CUSP," he said. "And it's where evolution has been pushing us for the past several billion years."

Bill smiled. "And passed on to me," he said. "The best of what you were, but not encumbered with your animal nature, your fear, the instinct and hardwiring that will never allow you to transit to the next level."

Simon laughed. "And you are that next level? Do you actually believe you've transited the Point?"

"I have," Bill said. "I'm a combination of the best of what you were and the best of what humanity could build." He rotated his right wrist a full 360 degrees. "The synthesis is infinitely greater than the mere sum of the parts."

Simon considered his ludicrous situation, trapped in a crystal prison with a once-woman who was now a melding of CUSP, blood, and bone, and a psychosis made real in bone, blood, and surgical-grade alloy.

"And I'm nothing more than a mere human, born to be the home for a sentience evolved in the Void, and when I failed at that, nothing but the breeding ground for a psychotic personality. Just a pathetic, delusional human."

"Merely human," said Bill.

"Unlike you," said Simon, pointing over at Bill's bloody knuckles. "Maybe I should just sit down and wait while you use that remarkable Post-Human intellect of yours to break us out of here."

"Shut up!"

"Please forgive me, a mere human. But maybe if you hit the wall harder it would shatter."

"No more!" Bill said, his face flushed. Simon could see him tense to move.

Simon was ready, far more ready than he had been consciously aware of. Reaching down, he picked up a stubby crystalline spire from Sarah's platform. No more than 6 or 7 centimeters long, as thick as a finger, it was blunt on one end, but the other end tapered to a shard so sharp and fine that he couldn't quite see where it ended.

A perfect blade.

Simon angled it upward at the advancing Bill. Pattern coalesced out of random fragments—the moving Bill, tendons tensing in thumb and index finger, a faceted crystal wall showing the classic symmetry of a hexagonal close-packed structure, a skull of titanium steel, the coefficients of friction between floor and foot, anger, and the pivot of hip.

Bill lunged.

Simon sidestepped, as the perfect blade clenched in his fist pivoted with the twist of his wrist, the blade now facing away from Bill. With his free hand Simon grabbed Bill by the hair, pulling him forward, bringing up the shard of crystal, planting its flat end firmly against Bill's forehead.

One quick look over his shoulder at the crystal wall, and he located a grain boundary that ran up the wall of the arched dome, created by the intersection of two hexagonal crystal faces.

"Out!" shouted Simon, pushing the off-balance Bill at the wall.

The sharpened point of the stubby crystal hit the wall first, sliding along it with an accompanying screech and a spray of rainbow-tinted splinters, digging in, then abruptly pinning to a stop as it hit the grain boundary.

Momentum transferred.

Bill continued to fly forward, now off his feet, the blunt end of the spire against his forehead, the steel-reinforced skull pushing its knife-edge into the crystalline grain boundary of the wall. The momentum of 90 kilograms of flying Bill was transferred into the tip of a blade with a width of only a few atoms. The cleave was perfect, the blade slicing through the grain boundary, severing atomic bonds, folding back crystalline layers, shattering atomic order.

The wall exploded outward, closely followed by the crystal shard still wedged against Bill's forehead. Simon completed his spin, releasing Bill, letting his forward momentum carry him through the gaping hole in the dome, feeling the heat explode inward.

Bill hit the ground, kicking up a plume of ash.

"Welcome to the Post-Human future," said Simon, poking his head outside the shattered dome. "Hope it's everything you dreamed it would be, Bill."

Half-buried in the deep ash, Bill didn't answer.

Simon stepped through the ragged hole Bill had just produced, his foot sinking calf deep in the drift of ash that had washed up against the side of the dome. The air felt as if it were on fire. He almost stepped back into the dome, but froze, his fingers on the edge of the opening, his peripheral vision detecting motion.

Crack!

Less than 10 meters in front of him, a plume of ash, cooled lava shard, concrete chunks, and twisted steel strut erupted; followed by rock and red dirt exploding into the gray sky. The concussion knocked him back into the dome, throwing him against Sarah's pedestal, the sounds of the explosion mixing with the shattering crash of fracturing crystal.

The heat was incredible, the air transformed into something thick, spilling down in scalding waves, washing over him, then cascading down the shaft. Xavier could feel Christina at his feet, pushed up close to him, his body shielding her from the rain of ash and rock that spilled in from the jagged rim of the crater that was all that remained of the bunker's escape door. He knew that Padmini was just a rung beneath Christina. He'd had her bring up the rear, knowing that if Christina slipped and started to fall, Padmini would be there to stop her.

He'd known Padmini now for only a few days, but had complete trust in her, a faith that he didn't quite understand. The fact that she'd been Leo Barnwell's partner went a long way toward establishing those feelings, but it didn't explain it all. The little woman exuded strength and purpose. Xavier didn't understand it, simply felt it and accepted it.

"Way too bright," he said, his voice sounding muffled in the full-face respirator. He pulled himself up the last few rungs, stopping to peer past the rim of the crater, at an ash-covered world tinted blood red by an impossibly large setting Sun. He pulled himself up another rung, barely able to clear the hole, the pack strapped to his back scraping against a volcanic shard.

"No movement," he said, looking over at the crystal cocoon, and at its shattered face. Between him and the cocoon, the ash had been disturbed, footprints obvious, but no one visible, just the shadowed figure of the stander still fixed in the center of the cocoon. Waist high out of the shaft, holding on to the top rung with only one hand, he reached to his belt, pulling the pistol, pointing it in the general direction of the cocoon.

"Get out and stay behind me," he said. "Drop your packs, but don't start setting up the equipment until we can get a fix on the three in the cocoon." He stepped up and out of the shaft, feeling Christina at his back, a quick glance behind showing that Padmini was already out, moving to his left, pistols in *both* her hands, barrels angled 90 degrees away from each other in order to maximize their field of coverage. He was depending on her if this situation suddenly imploded into one that required gunfire, knowing that she could probably empty an entire clip before his brain could even send the signal to his index finger to squeeze the trigger.

She was designed for this.

"Lots of tracks," said Padmini. "Some going out almost 10 meters, but nothing farther. They must have gone back into the cocoon. They could be hidden in the back of it, down low by the floor so we can't see their shadows through the crystal."

She moved, hanging close to the ground, kicking up a thick cloud of dust in her wake, pistols leading the way, held well out from her body.

Xavier could see Padmini's lips move, knowing she was whispering to Kali. He stopped moving and signaled for Christina to halt, realizing it was stupid for them to get in Padmini's way. He watched her approach the blown-out hole in the cocoon, peer into the opening, then push her head in. Sweat dripped down his face, pooling where his chin snugged against the respirator's seal. His breathing echoed in his ears, and he reached back, found Christina's shoulder, and pushed her down, suddenly desperate to place a shield between her and the cocoon, even if that shield was only one of his flesh and bone. "Just wait," he said, holding on tight, sensing that something was wrong.

The cocoon glistened as the thin layer of ash covering it blew outward, and Xavier felt his skin prickle, as if a swarm of invisible insects was biting at him, the heated air suddenly charged and crackling as twisted arcs of lightning danced across the opening in the cocoon. "Padmini!" he managed to scream.

Blown backward, she flew out of the cocoon.

A wall of superheated air struck Xavier, knocking him back and off his feet. He managed to keep his one hand on Christina and his pistol in the other, still pointed in the general direction of the cocoon.

Gone. The cocoon had vanished.

Snowflake motes fluttered across the gray-ash landscape.

"Stay down!" ordered Padmini.

Xavier blinked, not quite realizing he was on the ash-covered ground and the squirming lump under him was Christina. "Off me, Papa!" she said, pushing at him. He ignored her and raised the pistol still clenched in his fist, tracking Padmini, who was already on her feet and running to where the cocoon had been.

The stander still stood, turning toward them, a woman, tall and slender, athletic-looking, with short red hair glistening, as if made of strands of polished copper. Above her head twirled a vortex of brightly colored geometrical shapes. At her feet were the other two, one facedown, the other kneeling. A few snowflake remnants of the cocoon drifted down on them, while the bulk of what had been the cocoon had blown away in the explosion, already little more than a fading white mist.

"Get over here, Xavier," Padmini shouted, as she kept one pistol aimed at the two on the ground and the other on the standing woman. "Stay down, Christina." Her tone was enough; Christina lowered herself back into the ash as Xavier stood and trotted forward.

"Who are you?" asked Padmini, as Xavier moved to her left.

The one on the ground looked unconscious, with a bloody tear across his forehead, the skull actually looking dimpled, blood running in twin rivulets, pooling in his eye sockets. The one next to him squinted, looking up at them; barely able to keep his eyes open against the glare of the setting Sun behind them. He recognized this man.

"Is that necessary?" asked the kneeling man, nodding at the pistol aimed at his head.

"Who are you?" Padmini asked again.

"His name is Simon Ryan," said Xavier. He'd spent hours every day, for the better part of the last decade, watching the Ag Co-Op, certain that the survival of his family depended on exactly what took place there. Simon Ryan filled a sizable portion of the Ag Co-Op's local Void. "An ultra-Tool several generations out," said Xavier, only realizing as he said it that he had raised his pistol, aiming it directly at Ryan's forehead. "Up until about a year ago, he was *the* experiment, what they considered their best hope at a controlled transit through the Point."

"So these are the Point crackers?" asked Padmini.

He nodded.

"What happened to the nukes?" asked Padmini, looking away from Ryan for just a moment and toward the west, where the Ag Co-Op had been.

"Almost implemented," said Simon He looked over at Sarah. "But my friend here had other plans."

Padmini leaned forward, pressing the barrel of her pistol against Simon's forehead, pushing it forward and angling his head back. "Sarah Sutherland?" she asked, not looking up at Sarah.

Simon slowly nodded, Padmini keeping the barrel of the gun snug against his forehead.

"You said that until a year ago *he* was the experiment," said Padmini, again pushing back Simon's head with her pistol. "What happened?"

"Couldn't transit the Point," said Xavier. "Mentally unstable, too phobic, too traumatized by what was characterized as congenital brain malformations."

Simon started to open his mouth, but Padmini pushed his head back a few more millimeters, and he slowly closed it.

"And for the last year?"

"He was no longer the focus, but became a team member working on their next attempt to transit the Point—integrating their super computer CUSP to organic software."

Padmini, keeping the pistol against Simon's head, looked up at Sarah. "I'm assuming this is the organic software?"

Simon nodded.

"Is she a runaway?" Padmini asked. "Did she do this?"

"She didn't cause any of this," he said.

Padmini again nudged his forehead with the pistol. "But is she a runaway? She can obviously control the environment outside her own body," she said, making a quick wave at the crystal stalks protruding from her legs and back, then pointing up at the tornado of shapes and colors twisting over her head. "That cocoon you were in was built by her?"

Simon nodded again. "I suspect that she *could* runaway, spill far outside her body and roll past the horizon, but she doesn't seem interested in that. She seems to be only marginally engaged in the here and now. Her attention is elsewhere."

Xavier looked up at her, at eyes made of blue crystal. They did not appear to be unfocused so much as simply blind, abandoned, the act of seeing no longer necessary.

"And him?" asked Padmini, planting the end of her boot beneath the body at her feet, nudging it. "Another experiment?" she asked, looking first at Simon, then over at Xavier. "You know about this?"

He knew about the Jinni, but not this body. "Like your Kali, this was designed to reside only inside," he said, pointing over at Simon's head. "Bill Gates is a Jinni. But he was more than just an interface to the Void. Simon here needed him as a buffer between his internal world and the dirt and blood outside—a device they hoped would help Simon transit the Point."

"But not living?" she asked, poking at him with the tip of her boot.

"Not as far as I knew," said Xavier.

"Her doing?" asked Padmini, nodding in Sarah's direction. "The buffer made *real*?"

"Basically correct," Simon said. "But not so much the buffer made real as the psychosis made real. I'm not quite the ultra-Tool that your friend's snooping led him to believe, but I'm certainly an experiment that didn't go the distance. You should be congratulated on your outstanding correlation abilities based on such a meager data set." He turned to Xavier. "Don't let this one out of your sight, she's a real keeper. Might come in handy in our last few hours." He squinted as he slowly turned to face the Sun.

Xavier felt the heat beat at his face. The Sun seemed to fill the entire horizon. It was no longer as red, and a sliver of dark ash sky cut *between* it and the horizon, the demarcation remarkably sharp considering the amount of ash and smoke in the sky. And the Sun itself no longer appeared circular, but distorted, a large, burning mass protruding from its right side.

The Jet.

"The Sun had been setting, already sinking below the horizon," said Xavier.

"While you two have been waving guns around, I've watched shadows shortening. The Sun has started to rise," said Simon.

"From the west?" asked Xavier, knowing that was exactly what was happening, but unable actually to believe it.

"Ask her," said Simon. "It looks like she has her equipment up and running."

Padmini lowered her pistol, and both she and Xavier turned. Christina had unpacked Xavier's backpack and had the equipment set up, including a small dish angled toward the south. "A few geo satellites are still on-line, distant enough to survive the EMP," she said. "The Sun is still accelerating, but has shifted course. If it keeps to this course, it will miss us, coming to within about 50 million kilometers."

Xavier saw the suddenly hopeful look on Christina's face,

but knew that 50 million kilometers might be just as effective as a direct hit when it came to killing them. He swallowed, suddenly thirsty. Fifty million kilometers was 3 times closer than the Sun *should* be, and at that distance would be pouring 9 times more heat onto Earth than it normally did.

Christina frowned. "But the Sun and its close proximity won't be the *real* problem," she said. "As the Sun swings around, the Earth will pass through the tail of the Jet." Then she said nothing, but slumped back, her hands dropping into her lap.

"And?" said Padmini.

Christina slowly shook her head. "Think of a snowflake falling into a flame."

Chapter 25

"The easy part is done," said General Sutherland. Leaning back in his chair he opened his right hand, revealing two datacubes. He reached into his jumper's top pocket and removed his antique Virts, unfolding their black plastic frames and pushing them up the bridge of his nose. "Hate these damn things," he said as he adjusted them, angling them at the proper tilt, the oil-on-water lenses half-polarizing, so his eyes could just be seen, "but there is a great deal of information flowing at the moment."

"Easy?" said Akandi, looking past Sutherland at Iyoon, who spun just above the general's head.

"I would recommend not pushing so hard," said Iyoon. *"Patience leads to control, and control leads to solutions. Our mutual associate requests I remind you that the free will you've been given is a gift and not a right."*

Akandi took a deep breath, trying not to focus on the Swirl's threat but on Iyoon's advice.

"You find her now!" shouted Sutherland, standing and slamming a fist against the table. "She is key to humanity's survival, key to the survival of *your* species, and she is my daughter!" Akandi watched the general clench his jaw and take several deep breaths in what appeared to be an effort to calm himself. "I've got the cubes, the only cubes," he said, opening up his fist as if to check on their existence. "They will survive, and as long as we stay close to them, then we have a chance of survival." He then sat back in his chair, pulled off the Virts, and looked at Akandi. "Is what's happening really all that difficult to understand?" he asked wearily.

"Perhaps for some of us," said Akandi, having regained his diplomatic composure. He chose his next words carefully. "You've lived with this for decades, General," he said, pointing at the datacubes. "For those of us who have learned of it in only the past few hours, it is quite a shock."

Sutherland glared. "But a reality we have to deal with!"

"Yes," said Akandi, pointing again at the cubes. "But try to step back and consider why I might be confused. You have two cubes in your hand." He paused, thinking carefully about what he'd been told. "But in a way you hold only one cube, separated in time by 65 million years."

"Of course," said Sutherland.

Akandi stared at the cubes. One of them Sutherland had just had fabricated, the decay clock built from a dozen radioactive isotopes counting down, indicating only a few hours had passed since the image it held had been recorded. And the other, the one that Sutherland claimed had been found on the moon, the one that Iyoon insisted really was 65 million years old, held the same image. If true, the consequences were inescapable, and horrible. "An abomination," he said.

Sutherland frowned. "*Time travel* is an abomination?"

Akandi shook his head, not having yet considered the consequences of *that,* not even able to make a guess as to how one of the cubes that Sutherland held in his hand would travel 65 million years into the past and become buried in the wall of a lunar crater. That still felt like a simple impossibility. "No," he said. "You've had that cube for nearly 30 years, known *exactly* the face of the future. Did you ever try to fight it, to alter it, to escape it?"

"And why would I want to?" asked Sutherland, sounding genuinely surprised. "I was a 30-year-old colonel, shown an image of myself as an old man, seated at a table with a dinosaur and a spinning rainbow diamond. I was told beyond any doubt that the image had been recorded 65 million years ago. Imagine that!"

"And I was in that image," said Akandi.

"I see the light beginning to dawn." Sutherland grinned. "It took us a while to find you, with so much confusion and chaos after the Rings sprouted. Didn't you ever wonder why you'd been so lucky, the only one of thousands to be removed from that Georgia plantation, the education at Tulane and MIT, then the explosive rise through the Fed ranks, all that directed to put you in the position of becoming the US-UN ambassador, so you could bring back Drom for our little photo opportunity."

Akandi nodded, fighting down a shudder that ran down his back. "Free will?" he asked in a whisper.

"Free will to burn," said a suddenly smiling Sutherland. "I knew that the moment they showed me that cube represented point A of my existence, my starting point—from a certain perspective it was my birth. I was shown . . ." He paused, blinking several times. "No, I was *blessed* to be shown a single image from my future, a magnificent image, something beyond imagination. It represented point B of my existence, a future event that could never be escaped. Point A would lead to point B, regardless of what path I took."

Akandi shook his head. "With no free will, there is no purpose, no reason to exist." He could say nothing more. The realization that his life had been totally orchestrated, focused to achieve the image in the datacube, seemed to steal from him everything that made him a person. *How could Allah allow this?* Then suddenly the words came. "Free will is the cornerstone of belief. Without the free will to believe in Allah, to make that choice, then accepting Him has no meaning." He closed his eyes.

"Will you die someday?" asked Sutherland.

"Of course," said Akandi, reopening his eyes.

"And does that remove your free will? You were born, and you will die. That is your point A and your point B. You can't escape those two pillars of destiny, and yet when you believed those were the only two constraints you lived under, you still believed in free will. And now because those two boundaries have been moved in a bit, starting when we saw you in the image, you've lost your *faith?*"

"Faith?" asked Akandi, surprised that word was even in Sutherland's vocabulary.

Sutherland nodded. "Your faith is in Allah, while mine is in humanity, in our destiny. Part of my life is now over," he said, looking down at the cubes. "That image has been created. Only one thing remains to be done, and that is for this cube to make its trip back in time, to be left in the past so it can show me the future."

"And you believe that *you* will take it there," said Akandi.

Sutherland shrugged. "Anything is possible. Since I've moved past my point B, the possibilities are now infinite. But I doubt it. My gut tells me that it will be someone else."

Iyoon spun, glistening, as if about to speak.

But Akandi already knew. "Sarah," he said, having been debriefed in the last few hours about CUSP and what Sutherland had done to his own daughter. "You believe she'll be able to bring that cube to the past?"

"That and so much more," said Sutherland. "And as for you, there is no reason to worry about your perceived lack of free will. We've passed the image in the cube. The infinite possibilities of the future lie before you, with no constraints other than your eventual death."

Akandi wished he could believe that.

Xavier concentrated on the tent pole, driving it deep into the ground. Sweat ran down his soot-stained face in an almost solid sheet of moisture, a stream dribbling from the tip of his nose. The mylar tent would keep them shielded from the direct rays of the Sun but could do nothing to keep away the superheated air. Xavier dropped the hammer, then dropped himself, falling to the shaded ground beneath the tent. *We'll soon have to crawl back in our hole,* he thought, knowing when it got even hotter that they wouldn't have a choice, and reached for a water bottle, upending it, the hot water dribbling down his heat-swollen throat.

He didn't want to die in a hole.

Once the Jet intercepted the Earth it would not make any difference where they were hiding. Reaching up, he pressed the shades tightly against his face, then started to crawl forward, past Che and Krew, who sat huddled together, lips twitching in synch, to the edge of the shaded region of the tent. Here Padmini, Christina, and Simon Ryan sat huddled around a small table that held the equipment, all of it wrapped in plastic sheeting in a vain attempt to keep the soot and ash out of it. Above the tabletop hovered two spheres, representing the Sun and the Earth, entwined in flickering arrows, bands of shifting light, and spewing numbers.

"We will intercept it," said Christina. "There is absolutely no way to escape it. The Jet's nearly 100 million kilometers long, and Earth will cut through the side of it at the 50-million-kilometer mark."

Padmini stared at the display, watching the Earth nudge ever closer to the iridescent Jet, and slowly shook her head. "Doesn't make sense," she said in a whisper, her dry throat not allowing her to talk any louder. "Why build the Rings?"

Simon smiled at Xavier. "It was your lucky day when she arrived on your doorstep," he said. "She's right of course. The Jet and the Rings are obviously connected; I suspect part of an integrated system. If the intent of that system were to vaporize this planet, there'd be no need for the Rings. Just have the Jet spray across us, and the job would be done."

Christina turned, sweat running down her face, but *smiling*. "He's right," she said. "And even if the intent of moving the Sun was to vaporize Earth, there was no need to go to the trouble of having it loop in on this glancing trajectory. The Jet could have simply been fired to get the Sun moving in an intercept toward us, and in a few days or weeks, depending on the kick it had been given, Earth would simply be swallowed. There's more going on, but I can't see it yet."

Xavier felt himself nod. What they said made sense, but he couldn't quite believe it. The arc of the Jet now cut across the horizon, running half the length of the sky, erupting from the side of the Sun, and vanishing into the haze far to the south.

Fingers squeezed his shoulder. "Patterns defined."

Xavier turned. Che had crawled up behind him, with Krew closely in tow, a thick, glistening bundle connecting them, running from the input of Che's left eye socket to the side of Krew's head.

"Purposeful pattern," said Che.

Crawling forward, Che reached toward the little table, shoving Christina aside, pushing his right hand into its liquid interface.

The display rolled and flickered, for a moment merging the Sun and the Earth. Then the image locked, solidified, the Earth again outside the cone of the Jet, but rapidly approaching it. Xavier understood that this was no longer a static image of the actual positions of the Sun, Earth, and Jet, but a *projected* trajectory of what would be happening.

The Earth swung forward, just touching the edge of the Jet.

And at that moment the Jet extinguished, and the Earth continued on its trajectory, dropping *behind* the Sun. Then the Jet refired, engulfing the Earth, but not touching it, the cone of the Jet playing out all *around* it.

"Purposeful pattern," said Che again. "Form implies function." He turned back to the display.

The cone of the Jet had dimmed, giving a better view of the Earth. While the inside walls of the Jet's cone did not touch the Earth, thin tendrils peeled off from the inside wall of the conical Jet, spiraling in toward the Earth.

The image shifted, the Sun vanishing, the Earth suddenly large, the Rings easy to see, many of the Petal tips glistening in azure, spewing a gentle plasma glow. And the tendrils reached toward the Earth, curling and twisting, almost crashing against the surface, but turning at the last moment, deflected. Xavier realized that its charged particles were being bent by a magnetic field, and also realized that it had to be a field much more intense than the feeble one generated by Earth's spinning core.

"The Rings are generating a magnetic field," said Christina, as if she had read his mind. "And not just *deflecting* those plasma streams."

"*Capturing them,*" said Xavier, completing her words.

As they watched, the tips of the plasma tendrils locked onto the Petals.

"So obvious," said Simon.

Christina, Padmini, and Xavier turned toward him. "Investigators at the Ag Co-Op suspected the Petals were exhaust manifolds, really nothing more than rocket exhaust ports, and knew that the Rings were planet-spanning accelerators. Form implies function," Simon said, with a small nod to Che. "The structure was designed to allow the Earth to be moved, having stored within it the top 40 meters of the oceans as reaction mass to be blown from the Petals. But what didn't make sense, what we could never figure out, was how the Rings would be powered. What would fuel it?" He pointed at the tendrils tied to the Petal tips. "We saw it when the Jet last fired, knew that within what was primarily a proton stream directed by sheathes of electrons, were a small number of *antiprotons*. It was a matter-antimatter reaction that was powering the stellar Jet, the annihilation reaction of protons and antiprotons giving it enough punch actually to move the Sun. Some of those antiprotons are apparently going to be transferred to the Rings, to power up our little rocket engine, to be annihilated with the protons traveling through the Rings.

The image shifted once again, the Earth sitting inside the cone of the Jet, the Earth itself now spewing its own series of much smaller Jets, keeping it locked in a trajectory with the Sun.

Form implies function.

And Xavier suddenly understood. The Sun was going somewhere, and the Earth would be going along with it, nestled inside the cone of the Jet, the Sun acting as a shield, placed directly between Earth and the direction of travel. Xavier knew that interstellar space was not totally empty; it was full of random atoms of hydrogen, a bit of wayward helium, and the occasional dust particle, even a few pebbles here and there. Those things sounded small, insignificant, especially as compared to something as massive as the Earth. But if the Earth were moving at a sizable fraction of the speed of light, impact with the smallest object, even a grain of dust, would result in the release of energy comparable to a nuclear blast.

He didn't know why it was happening, but he saw it clearly. The Earth was going to be accelerated to relativistic speeds, and the Sun brought along to provide the warmth that those who lived on the Earth needed to survive. But just as importantly, the Sun would act as a shield, to cut the path through interstellar space, to swallow the debris that would easily have vaporized Earth's outer crust.

"But how can Che really know that the Jet will turn off

when Earth intercepts it," asked Padmini, pointing at the display.

"Because form implies function," said Xavier, who stood and pointed toward the west. Although the Sun still blazed, looking even larger than it had a few moments before, something had changed. The southern horizon was still distorted in the burning air, but now looked almost dark.

The Jet was gone.

"It's them!" said Drom in a not-quite-controlled roar, slamming his tail against the floor. At his side were four other dinosaurs, similar in shape and coloring but several centimeters smaller and with much smaller skulls. Akandi examined the other four dinosaurs, their small hands and stubby fingers, their eyes dull and listless compared to Drom's.

Everything about them said *subordinate*.

Looking at the four, Akandi suddenly understood a great deal about Drom and the world he had come from, about the hierarchy that must have existed, one based not only on physical size but also on cranial capacity. These four simply didn't have the brains to compete with Drom.

Sutherland shrugged his shoulders, as he carefully studied the image that had come in from deep space, and now hovered before them, what to Akandi looked like a pockmarked potato shooting a long arc of flame from its far pointed end. But he knew it was actually another moon on the move. And the potato was shedding its skin, bits and pieces breaking off, falling back in the tail flame and exploding in bursts of light. "Did you really expect them to sit by and do nothing as the Sun runs away with the Earth?"

He pointed at the smaller dinosaurs flanking Drom. "As all of you try to take the prize?"

"This world is ours!" said Drom.

"Then I suggest that you get to it. Set up your infrastructure and get your defenses up and running before your old friends arrive."

"Those *Clingers* will not set foot on our world," Drom said.

"Then you need to get to work," said Sutherland, and the light, almost jovial expression on his face suddenly darkened. "And I suggest that if you are serious about making this world yours, you find my daughter!"

Drom took half a step back, while the dinosaurs flanking him took several steps back. "We are searching," he said. "We have detected some phantom signatures, but cannot lock on. It is as if she is deliberately hiding from us."

"Then maybe she is!" Sutherland shook his head. "Get them out there, eyeballs to the ground, and look for her."

"Help has been offered."

Akandi turned, startled, having actually forgotten that Kristensen was standing in the corner of the room. The Swirl sat on his right shoulder. "The Swirl has offered help, its physical presence in one of the search craft," he said.

Akandi watched Sutherland thrust out his chin, and flare his nostrils, but he knew that Sutherland was only blustering, now in unknown territory, having moved beyond his point B and the comfort of the image in the datacube. He no longer knew what the future held, and found himself in the uncomfortable situation of having to create his own future, one in which he could make mistakes.

Sutherland was merely human again. And Akandi knew it frightened him.

"Do it," said Sutherland, giving the order. "And you go with them," he added, pointing at Kristensen. He looked at the Swirl hovering above Kristensen's shoulder, then looked the little man squarely in the eyes and gave him a slight nod.

Akandi missed none of it, understanding the unspoken message of Sutherland telling Kristensen to keep a watch on the Swirl. At that moment, Akandi knew just how dangerous Sutherland really was. He was certain beyond any doubt that anyone who thought he could control the Swirl had severely miscalculated the true nature of reality. But he said nothing, watching the small pack of dinosaurs move through the opening in the pink-crystal wall, followed closely by Kristensen.

The Swirl floated away, but did not bother with the door, instead distorting, melting, and elongating, then passing through the wall. Akandi did not miss the significance of that, either—not the fact that the Swirl could pass through the wall, but that it did not hesitate in demonstrating its ability to Sutherland. Akandi knew the dangers of assigning motivations and meaning to the actions of a nonhuman entity, but couldn't help but believe that the Swirl had done that solely for Sutherland's benefit. And he realized at that moment that Sutherland had not been the only one constrained by the image in the datacube, whose track through history had to intercept that point.

The Swirl had also been restricted, the future dictating that it be at that table with Drom, Sutherland, Kristensen, and himself. He had always wondered, never been able to understand, why the Swirl had simply not gone runaway, engulfing the world.

But now he knew.

The Swirl had not acted because it believed that it could not alter the future. And now that future shown in the datacube had come to pass, it could choose its own path without any constraints.

"Stupid dinosaurs," said Sutherland. He faced Akandi. "I'm sure that our good friend," he said, nodding in the direction of now-resealed door, "failed to mention to you the existence of the Clingers."

Akandi slowly shifted mental gears, having trouble letting go of the thought of the unleashed Swirl, one that would no longer feel constrained to exist in the shadows, or hidden in the minds of humans. "The mammals that the Alphans manipulated like the dinosaurs," he said, enjoying showing Sutherland that he wasn't completely in the dark.

"So he did tell you," Sutherland replied, pausing, reaching up to stroke his chin in what Akandi now recognized *not* as a movement of careful consideration, the attitude that Sutherland was trying to project, but one of fear. "I guess he saw no reason not to reveal relatively nonessential information to someone that he considered an inferior."

Akandi smiled. The insult was noted but had no bite.

"Amalthea," said Sutherland. "One of the innermost moons of Jupiter. The Sinos have been in relatively close proximity to it, observing it from the safety of their outpost on Callisto, but couldn't physically approach it to explore. The ambient radiation from Jupiter is simply too intense. Even Dolls have difficulty operating where Amalthea *had* been, practically skimming Jupiter's outer atmosphere."

Akandi nodded. Sounded like a far safer location for the occupants of the craft than the one the dinosaurs had chosen so near Earth, where humans had a much easier time reaching.

"The general has failed to mention that Amalthea has a diameter nearly 10 times larger than Phobos. If that craft follows the same basic design as the one in Phobos, it might have a volume

1000 times larger." Iyoon hovered next to the general. *"Slight rise in pulse, constriction of pupils, and increase in rate of breathing, with each extension of his chest slightly more shallow."*

Akandi didn't really need that last bit of information. He could see the fear in the general's face. "Clingers," said Sutherland.

Amalthea vanished, replaced by a small figure, one identical to the image used by the Phobos operating system. Akandi considered possible responses and decided that playing ignorant was often the quickest path to learning something new. He widened his eyes and waited.

"I see there are a few details that Drom omitted," Sutherland said, sounding extremely satisfied. "They've been a pain in humanity's collective ass for the better part of 200 years. Actually came to blows with the little bastards at the end of World War II, vaporizing one of their saucers over White Sands with a modified German V-2. That drove them back a bit, and from then on they had a tendency only to perform the slice-and-dice on those folks who couldn't put up much of a fuss."

"It's an *alien*," said Akandi, feeding the obvious enjoyment Sutherland was feeling over revealing the truth to him. "They're real," he said, putting just a bit of awe in his voice.

"Only too damn real," said Sutherland. "But no more alien than our friend Drom. He wasn't lying to you in that regard. The Alphans had been messing with the dinos for better than 200 million years, slowly trying to tweak them this way and that, bringing them to enlightenment. But apparently they could never pull it off. With these guys," he said, pointing over at the gray creature, "they radically modified their approach, rapid genetic manipulation coupled with a large amount of good old-fashioned hardware."

"Lemurs," said Akandi, shaking his head in simulated wonder.

"We needed you to bring Phobos and the dinos in, having learned from McCarthy that Phobos would recognize only humans as suitable entities to move the craft. Hierarchy is critical to them. They will actually make pretty good lords and masters of this world until we arrive at Alpha Centauri A."

"And the Clingers?" asked Akandi.

"Cautious and scared, still too much of the lemur in them. They'll come in and pester the dinos a bit, but we don't expect they'll put up much of a fight. They certainly turned tail when we hit them. But we figure that bringing them along may be to our advantage. When we reach Alpha Centauri A, we'll be bearing the gifts of two races, returning two wayward children that have been lost. It will be a good way to say hello."

Akandi nodded, not for a moment believing anything as human as gratitude for the return of lost children would appeal to the Alphans. "Why did the Alphans abandon them in the first place?" he asked, this time really needing to hear the answer. "Do you know who dropped that rock on Earth 65 million years ago?" he asked.

"The motivations of the Alphans are still a bit of a mystery," Sutherland admitted. "But we've pieced together the asteroid strike and are certain that it was the final blow delivered by them," he said, while pointing at the Clinger, "to the dinos. It essentially knocked both races off the planet, and the survivors burrowed in deep, waiting for someone to pick up the pieces."

Akandi managed a smile, knowing that he could come up with dozens of other possible scenarios, quite a few of them just as likely as the story the general just spun.

Once again Sutherland stroked his chin.

Afraid and probably lying, thought Akandi. "And what part do I now play?" he asked. "Have I served my purpose, delivering Drom and Phobos and appearing for my moment of immortality in your datacube?" He managed a smile.

"Suppose so," said Sutherland. "A more timid man might simply lock you away, or possibly even opt for a more *permanent* solution."

That threat didn't frighten Akandi. He knew if such a permanent solution were to be implemented, it would have happened the moment Sutherland had the image for his datacube. Sutherland had plans for him.

"But as it so happens, I like you, find you intellectually compatible and decidedly refreshing. I'm certain you will be a good companion for the little adventure that is about to unfold."

"How fortunate that he likes you," said Iyoon.

Chapter 26

Only as Christina bent down, dabbing at the ragged seam running around the dent in Bill's head, focused on that simple act, did the reality of what had been taking place over the last several hours suddenly snap in.

Crisis over. For the moment.

"It hurts," said Bill, pushing her hand back.

"Small wonder," said Christina, offering her most compassionate smile, the one she'd seen Mama use so many times with her patients. She continued running a thin bead of protein-cure along the edge of the wound, stabilizing the subcutaneous fibroid that filled the tear. "You've got a dent in the front of your skull nearly three millimeters deep, in spite of the metal reinforcement. You're going to be dizzy, nauseous, and confused for several more hours. Your brain took a pounding."

She looked up at Sarah Sutherland and at the cloud of images spinning above her head. Most of it was incomprehensible colors and lines, but here and there were faces and objects, distorted and morphing, but undoubtedly inspired by reality. Once she'd seen a fleeting image of Bill hitting the crystalline wall.

"Consider yourself lucky," she said, patting his shoulder. "Had your skull been made only of bone, it would have been your head that shattered, and not the wall."

Bill pushed himself up, propping himself on his elbows. "That's what I get for all the help I've given him, for saving him from himself."

Again Christina gave the *compassionate* smile and quickly stood, glad to be done with him. She had taken a quick dislike to Bill. She went back to Simon, who sat cross-legged in the ash, staring up at Sarah and the images flicking above her. "It's not random," he said, pointing to the display. "There's a pattern to it, a *story* that she's telling."

"And you can see the story?" she asked, looking up at the incomprehensible riot of shapes and colors.

"Of course not," he said, smiling at her. "Sarah's gone far past the Point, her thoughts are no longer relevant to someone only human." "But here and there I can pick out a snippet of flow, items that may be useful to us, even though I'm certain that's not Sarah's intent. Like the crumbs you might drop on the floor, unintentional, but still a feast to the lucky bug that stumbles across them."

"Happy crumb hunting," she said, turning away. None of them seemed human enough for her.

Padmini had set up another tent for the equipment they'd hauled out of the shielded bunker near the top of the escape tunnel. There were four small dishes pointing in all directions, and black box after black box, entwined by cables and flickering optical tendrils.

Christina looked at Padmini, one hand deep in a table's liquid interface, her lips moving, talking to Kali. While Simon, Bill, and Sarah made her uncomfortable, Padmini produced the exact opposite effect. Something felt intrinsically *right* about her.

Padmini looked up. "A new Void is reaching the cohesion point, the nexus only 30 kilometers to the west, coincident with the Phobos landing site. We're very close to accessing it and breaching its walls." She turned back toward her equipment.

Christina looked to the west. The Sun had finally set, after crawling halfway back up the sky, then reversing course to sink beneath the horizon.

Earth had then slipped behind the Sun, and the Jet refired. All as Che had predicted.

An arc of glowing plasma ran from north to south. All along its length wispy tendrils snaked down, most vanishing below the horizon, but a few arching high above, twisting west to east, running to the nearby Petals of the North–South Ring. Everything that Che had shown in his simulation had come to pass, and the Ring was now firing, a distant roar from the east, more felt through her feet than actually heard.

Christina's inner ear, always too sensitive, had picked up

on a change, her stomach tickling just a bit as if she were dropping in a slow-moving elevator. She understood why when Padmini had shown her the latest simulations. The Earth now sat in the center of the Jet's cone, the Rings firing, directing thrust to keep the Earth locked behind the Sun, both now accelerating at nearly 0.1 gee.

Padmini looked up. "Asymptotic increase in signal traffic."

Christina looked below the arc of the Jet, at the horizon, where the glow of the bloated too-near Sun had been replaced by the white glare of what she could only believe was some sort of artificial light, through which swarmed dark insect shapes, all spreading out from the golden mound that was Phobos.

So many new things so quickly.

Moving under the far tent, she sat on a camp stool and gently squeezing her father's shoulders as she pressed her right cheek against his back. "Thank you," she said in a whisper.

"For what?" he asked, not turning around.

She said nothing and just kept hugging him.

Akandi held tightly on to the guardrail, for just a moment looking away from the surrounding panorama and at the dark swarm of aircraft pouring out from somewhere below Phobos's horizon. He watched Sutherland, who had stepped outside the guardrail-secured region of the observation platform, and stood nearly 20 meters away on Phobos's naked hull, slipping and sliding, the surface of the craft slicker than ice by the look of it.

A cold wind beat at them. He knew that around the bottom edge of the craft the ground was still molten, but up top, the sphere was nearly 8 kilometers above what had been Alabama cornfields. The air at this altitude was thin and cold.

"If you start sliding, there will be nothing to stop you!" shouted Akandi, instantly regretting the effort, having trouble getting back his breath.

"All part of free will!"

Akandi managed to suck down a breath and hold it in his chest, swallowing several coughs, willing his throat to relax. He pushed himself up, never letting go of the guardrail. Sutherland skated toward him, his boots gliding over the perfect metal hull.

"Not the brightest of God's creatures," said Sutherland as he grabbed on to the guardrail, and pulled himself up onto the observation platform. "But damn efficient planners when they get something stuck in their heads." He pointed at the swarms of aircraft. "The largest force this planet has ever seen."

Akandi straightened up, looking up into the sky. "Designed for flying through the air," he said, just able to make out the sleek, swept-back wings of the craft. "For the air of Earth."

"Very good," said Sutherland. "Onboard systems within Phobos have been building craft and crew for nearly 50 years now, better than 100,000 of these fighter/recon craft and nearly 10 million dinos occupying them."

And I brought this here, thought Akandi, suddenly feeling faint.

"I see it in your face," said Sutherland, having pushed up close to him. "The Destroyer of Humanity, the one responsible for having dropped this moon and its dino contents on the Earth."

Akandi managed a nod.

Sutherland smiled. "The Savior of Humanity is more like it. The Sun and the Rings were going to be fired regardless of what the two of us did or did not do. And I can assure you, had this moon not EMPed Earth, and if these dinos do not quickly take control and establish the sort of order they are so well suited for, that billions more would have died."

"Attacking each other?" asked Akandi.

"Of course," said Sutherland, patting Akandi on the shoulder. "You saved billions of lives. And all we have to do now is sail this little planet of ours to Alpha Centauri A."

"Smooth sailing?" asked Akandi.

"Certainly," said Sutherland. "How could it be anything else? We've crossed our Point, obliterated the chains that have kept life imprisoned on this world for billions of years. We're going to the stars!"

Akandi turned, looking toward the eastern horizon, at the crackling arcs of plasma crashing through the high atmosphere into the Petals of the Ring. "Smooth sailing," he said.

"The smoothest," said Sutherland, slapping him on the back. "The very smoothest."

Akandi looked past the distant Ring, focusing on the unseen horizon behind it, and tried to picture Mecca, nearly on the other side of the world. "Deliver us," he asked in a whisper. "And forgive us for our arrogance."

Part Three

DEPARTURE
2051

The distance is nothing;
It is only the first step that is difficult

> —Mme. Du Deffand (1697–1780)

For the Goodman is not at home,
He is gone a long journey

> —Proverbs 7:18

You can take it with you.

> —William Woodhouse (1982–2047)

Chapter 27

"My head hurts," said Bill, his hands pressed to the side of his head, his forehead resting on his knees. "And it's too hot, and my skin itches, as if spiders are crawling all over me."

"And just how does this affect me?" asked Simon, not bothering to look over at Bill but continuing to stare at the images leaking from Sarah. It had taken some time for him to see it, but the colors were not colors and the shapes were not shapes—they were projections of higher-dimensional dreams ill suited to three-dimensional reality. Meaning was lost, but an overwhelming scream of urgency was still present. That feeling, coupled with the occasional recognizable object—a slice of the Martian surface, the scowling face of General Sutherland, an exhaust plume burning blue-hot—helped define a pattern, the faintest shadow of what was stirring in Sarah's head. "Amazing connections," said Simon in a whisper. "All pattern, no coincidence, nothing left but pure and simple purpose."

"Damned spiders, or dust mites, or maybe volcanic ash mites," said Bill, scratching his right arm and swatting at his shoulders. "Too much organic content in this body, too much blood and bone prone to pain."

Bill's complaints had broken his concentration. "Too much organic content?" he asked.

"Almost 50 percent," said Bill, as he scratched at the side

of his face. "That will have to be corrected." Sitting back he pushed his right leg toward Simon, the foot suddenly facing backward, then quickly coming around, stopping only when it had made a full turn. "This body needs more of that," he said, shaking the foot.

Simon couldn't help but smile. "Seems like you inherited a bit more than Mears's dead corpse—perhaps Sarah did not totally empty what had been in Mears's head. Anyone else in there with you, Bill?" he asked, pointing at Bill's head.

"I'm free of you!" he shouted. "That's something." He wiped at the sweat beaded on his forehead. "But these damned bugs!" He stumbled off, moving into the semidarkness beyond the camp's lights.

"Is he dangerous?"

Simon turned to find Xavier standing less than a meter away from him.

"Christina has some meds that could quiet him."

Simon shook his head. "I doubt she has the meds that could quiet Bill. He needs to work it through, come to terms with what he is, and understand that getting just what you want may not be the best thing."

"So, not dangerous?"

Again Simon shook his head. "Compared to everything else we're facing, Bill is below the noise level."

Xavier turned and waved to Christina and Padmini, whose heads immediately dropped back down onto their camp pillows; only Che and Krew remained seated, hands running over each other's head, fingering the filaments that ran between them. "Quiet before the storm," said Xavier, turning back and pointing up at Sarah.

"No doubt about it," said Simon. "I can only sense a small part of it, and most of what I can perceive I can't understand. But something big is about to happen."

Xavier pointed at the glowing horizon, sweeping his hand north, then south. "Bigger than this, bigger than what the Sun and the Earth are doing?"

"I think so," said Simon, pointing to the west, at the thick swarm of craft still erupting from the bright mountain of light, looking like bees fleeing a burning hive. "That much I've seen and can understand. Most of those craft are flying out in all directions, arcing high, almost suborbital, I suspect on their way to points all across Earth. But some of them have been moving low, cutting patterns that have obviously been set up as a search grid."

"You saw that in there?" Xavier asked, pointing up at the morphing collage over Sarah's head.

"Quite clearly."

Xavier nodded and pointed over at Christina's sleeping form. "She saw it, too, accessing *their* Void. I suspect that they're looking for her." He pointed up at Sarah.

Simon nodded.

"But she's not ready to be found yet, is she?" asked Xavier.

Again Simon nodded. He was struck again by the realization that there was so much more to this man than defined by his thickly callused farmer's hands.

"We've had nearly half a dozen direct flyovers, at altitudes of less than 2,000 meters, close enough to count the hairs on my head," said Xavier, running his hands through his hair. "Is it just their sensors she's controlling?"

Simon squinted. "As far as I can see. Of course, if those craft are manned by Tools, controlling what they see would be no more difficult than controlling what their sensors see. They could be standing right here, centimeters from your face, and not be able to see you, if she doesn't want them to."

"And that's it?"

"As far as I know," he said, understanding exactly what Xavier was really asking. "But it wouldn't be that big of a leap for her to access a purely biological system. Whether neural mesh or home-grown neurons, everything eventually comes down to the transfer of electrical charge, and she should have little difficulty accessing that, regardless of the source."

"So the only reason that she's not running me right now is that she has no desire to run me?" asked Xavier. He paused and frowned. "Of course, if she were running me, and chose to keep that fact from me, I'd have no way of knowing."

"Absolutely none," said Simon. "But I don't think she wants to. I was there when she breached the Point, when she was probably at her most unstable, most vulnerable, when she was probably most apt to reach out and take control of *everything.*"

"And how do you know she didn't?"

Simon smiled, surprised by how much he found himself liking the man. "If she did, and none of this is real," he said, "then there is absolutely nothing we can do about it. But if you're still Xavier Olmos, and that is still your family over there, then we've got to do what we've got to do."

"And that is?"

"Rest while you can, because something unexpected, something beyond the pattern that I can see, or your daughter can dig out, is about to be unleashed on us."

Xavier nodded and turned, starting to walk back to his family.

"Why haven't you asked us to leave?" asked Simon. "You know that Sarah is the focal point of what's going to happen. She's what those searching craft are all about. If we weren't here, you might not get swept up in it."

Xavier didn't turn. "Exactly."

* * *

Christina chewed on a high-protein, carb-heavy chunk of something that she wished was as tasteless as its wrapper had insisted it would be. "Ten Degree surplus that should have been left in the Ten Degree," she said, managing to swallow the wad in her mouth.

Padmini smiled but did not lose focus, keeping her hands in the flow, her fingers fluttering over the pinpricks of light. "Knew a man who got addicted to those things in the Ten Degree," she said quietly, her eyes momentarily losing focus. "Couldn't get through a day without one."

Christina grimaced, wondering if that could be a joke, trying to lick away a taste that could only be described as *rotting cardboard*. "There," she said, instantly forgetting about the cud she'd just swallowed. She pushed her hands into the display, her attention caught by a flicker dropping out of the pattern. "It's cut off from the grid and is moving in our direction, 8 kilometers out and dropping quickly from 3,000 meters." She looked up, toward the west, seeing nothing in the sooty sky but the distant glistening golden mountain and its dark swarm. "Papa!" she shouted.

"We know," he called back at her, not moving, looking up at Sarah.

"She's moved," said Christina, bending toward Padmini and nudging her shoulder with her chin, not wanting to slip her hands out of the display. "Facing west now." She looked more closely. "And her hair is on fire."

Padmini looked up.

Christina knew that fire was not exactly the right word, but it almost worked. Between the blur of images and Sarah's close-cut red hair danced what looked like purple-blue flames, all angled and cut, almost as if built from shards of ice but twisting in a fluid motion.

"Smell the ozone?" said Padmini.

Christina nodded, not only able to smell it, but actually taste it, a burned-metal tang filling the back of her mouth, overpowering the foul taste of the cud. She fluttered her fingers through the display, instructing the microwave dishes to angle down, their mini aperatures rastering left-right-left, sweeping through Sarah's position. The display flared, sensory feedback rolling and amping, forcing Sarah and Padmini to jerk their hands out of it.

"No one move!" shouted Xavier.

And Christina found she could not move, though she tried, her body demanding she try. Something beneath the ash had latched on to her boots, and she could feel it chewing through the thick soles, then quickly burrowing into skin and locking on to bone. Che and Krew sat motionless, looking content, still interfaced together, both turned, facing Sarah.

"My feet!" Padmini strained, rocking from side to side, reaching down with both hands, grabbing on to her right leg and tugging at it, quickly giving up and pulling a pistol from her belt, using the barrel to push away several centimeters of ash from around her ankle, exposing a glistening sheen of crystal beneath it. "It's her," she said, pointing the pistol at Sarah, who was now entirely bathed in an azure-blue discharge. "She's got us!"

"Weapons down!" shouted Xavier, pointing over at Padmini.

She kept it raised. But it was no longer aimed at Sarah, but at one of the three black craft that were dropping out of the sky, nearly silent, no scream of engines, just the whir of fast-moving air, the black craft seamless, windowless, fea-

tureless, birdlike in shape, with massive turbofans attached
to forward-facing wings, rotating back, the backwash now
kicking up a vortex of ash and soot.

"Put it down!" screamed Xavier, straining in Padmini's
direction.

Padmini shook her head and, reaching with her free
hand, pulled her other pistol.

The three aircraft hit the ground with a heavy thud.
Christina felt the impact through her feet, a tingle and ringing that ran up the bones in her legs. She saw Padmini's lips
moving and knew she was talking to Kali, giving instructions, getting ready to attack.

"Wait," said Christina.

Padmini shook her head, not looking away from the
three craft, the tendons in her forearms standing out, corded
and quivering. And then light flashed, and a blinding sheen
of crystal suddenly covered the underside of Padmini's arms,
erupting forward and flowing over both her hands. The pistols dropped, Padmini's fingers pried back by the crystal
layer covering them. "No!" she screamed, and had only
enough time to turn her head a few millimeters to the left,
as her entire face was enveloped in a thin crystalline sheen,
the faceted substance pouring down her open mouth.

Christina turned away, looking past the discharge whirlwind tightly wrapped around Sarah, at what looked like
gangways jutting out of the sides of the aircraft. The ash
and dust were still thick, only slowly settling, obscuring her
vision, but not so much that she couldn't see the figures
marching out of the craft, and the large, riflelike objects
that each held.

The figures seemed too small, more like children than
adults.

They moved in a phalanx, a larger figure in the lead,

flanked to its left by an even taller, slender-looking figure, while above it spun a rainbow-colored flame, the only color present in what was otherwise a scene painted in infinite shades of gray.

"Sarah Sutherland!" boomed a voice. "Your father wants you!"

"Dinosaurs?" said Simon in a whisper, looking up at Sarah, and beyond her at the little jewel of rainbow-colored light that flashed and flowed above her head.

And he remembered everything.

The facets reached in, trying to latch on to neurons, to bury so incredibly deep into his sense of self that everything would be lost. But he'd escaped, and General Sutherland did not get his Post-Point Tool. Whether he'd rejected the Swirl, or it had rejected him, he could not tell.

But the Swirl had left.

And now it was back.

But quite different. What he'd sensed years ago had been a ghost fed through fiber and cable, a presence without form and texture. But despite that, he knew without a doubt that the spinning rainbow moving toward them was the same entity. It hovered above the right shoulder of the lead dinosaur, the air beneath it slightly distorted. He had seen it the moment the dinosaurs had marched off their craft, but gave it little thought, believing it to be some sort of free-flying sensor array, or an informational relay connecting the dinosaurs to their craft. But seeing it in the collage above Sarah had somehow made it real, opened a long-hidden memory.

"They've got arms. *Real* arms with hands."

Simon turned and saw Xavier pointing at the dinosaurs,

his eyes open wide, his mouth open nearly a centimeter. "Hands," he said again.

"Sarah Sutherland!" said the lead dinosaur, dropping the shaft it had been carrying into the thick ash. Waving its short arms, it directed the phalanx behind it to split in two, fanning out and quickly surrounding the camp.

Simon looked back, to watch the dinosaurs, but instantly lost interest in them when he saw that a thin sheen of crystal now covered Padmini, Christina, Che, and Krew. Frozen in place, paralyzed in midscream, arms up and hands pointing in the direction where the craft had landed, he did not know if they were alive or dead, but felt certain that had Sarah wanted them dead, she would have done it long before now. He realized that the crystalline cocoons must be for protection, like the dome that had carried them across the sea of magma. Swiveling around, wanting again to check on Xavier's reaction, he saw that he, too, was now coated in the crystal.

Simon tensed and focused as the lead dinosaur marched toward him, the Swirl still hovering above its shoulder. A small, potbellied man marched to its right, shuffling along, kicking up a huge cloud of dust.

"She's coming with us," the dinosaur said to Simon, then turned its attention to Sarah. "Your father says that you must return; time is short, and he needs you for the journey."

The dinosaur was close enough that Simon could see that it didn't really speak; its mouth simply opened and the words spilled out with a slight echo, as if coming from somewhere deep in its throat, not so much spoken, as *synthesized*.

Simon was about to speak, not at all certain what he was going to say, when a series of roars and hisses erupted behind him, and he saw the lead dinosaur tense and lurch to the side, pushing off with its strong legs and tail. In just a couple of bounds it reached the rear of the camp, then stopped in front of Krew. It growled and barked, shifting its head to the right and left, rocking back and forth, its head swinging faster and faster. And then, with a quick jerk of its neck, it brought the side of its snout against Krew.

Crack!

Krew fell over, still stiff and encased in crystal, sharp and glistening broken shards of the material visible on his legs and feet, where he had been pinned to the ground. Then, almost too quick to be seen, crystalline tendrils erupted through the ash, enveloping Krew's legs, melding with the crystal that already covered him, and pulled him back up against the ground, angling him once again into an upright position.

Most of the dinosaurs stepped back.

The leader barked, and again smashed its snout against Krew, but this time got no results, the layer of crystal covering Krew looking thicker than before, his features barely visible, distorted by the crystal's thickened faceted surface. The dinosaur reared back, for just a moment its feet not touching the ash, all its weight balanced on its tail, then lurched forward, crashing its snout against Krew, and bounced back, staggered, stumbling to the left and almost falling, shaking its head and letting out a shriek and a series of deep barks. Reaching to its left, grabbing one of the long cylinders from the nearest dinosaur, it wrapped both hands around the shaft, pulling it to its waist, while the tip of its tail wrapped around the rear of the device.

Pzzzzzt!

A discharge of blue flame and plasma erupted from the end of the shaft, smashing into Krew, enveloping him, the ash on the ground around him exploding upward, some of it liquefying into flaming globs that splattered against the nearest dinosaurs. They shrieked and barked, bounding backward, dropping their own weapons, as they swatted at smoldering patches across their gray skin.

The dinosaur lowered the weapon. The ground around Krew quickly cooled, fading from white-hot to smoldering red, then a dull orange. Krew and the crystal that covered him were untouched. Seeing that, the dinosaurs that had already made a partial retreat from the backwash of liquid ash and rock stepped back even farther, all raising weapons, the tips of their tails wrapping around the ends of the devices.

"*Crrrrrrk!*" barked the lead dinosaur, as it spun around, bounding back, knocking several dinosaurs in its path to the ground, stopping only when it pushed up to Simon. "Release her," it said, pointing up at Sarah with a stubby index finger, "and give us the Clinger."

The word *Clinger* had come up from deep in its throat like all the other words it spoke, but had been accompanied by a deep, guttural growl and gnashing of teeth.

"I do not believe that Simon is controlling this situation," said the potbellied man.

The lead dinosaur turned on him. "I am controlling the situation, Kristensen!" it screamed. "I am the alpha male!"

Kristensen stepped back, tripped, and fell, hitting the ash and sending up a cloud of soot. Not even trying to stand, he held up two hands, waving them about. "Of course you are in charge, Drom," he said. "What I meant to say is that I do not believe that this man has any control over Sarah. Until your arrival, she had control over these people. I don't believe that she is interested in coming, and she wants to keep these people here."

Simon watched the dinosaur, Drom, slowly turn his long neck and angle his head up toward Sarah, his nostrils flaring. "She comes with us, now!"

The other dinosaurs started to move forward. Simon had no idea how they could possibly move Sarah, when they'd been unsuccessful in prying Krew from the ground, or burning away the crystal covering him. He was certain that if Sarah did not want to be moved, then she would not be moved.

Drom walked forward, his head shifting right and left, examining Sarah with one eye, then with the other. He took small steps, and carefully nudged his snout against her nearest, crystal-covered leg, then moved back, angling his head and looking up at the slowly rotating jewel of light.

Simon flinched. *Not the Swirl,* he mentally begged.

He watched Drom's body tense as the dinosaur continued to stare up at the Swirl, the muscles quivering beneath his skin. He stepped back, motioning with his arms. Five of the other dinosaurs moved forward, leading the way with their long weapons, angling them upward with a deflection of their tails, pressing them against the crystal that covered Xavier's chest.

"Does she value her subordinates?" asked Drom, looking over at the weapons pushed against Xavier.

"No!" shouted Simon, squirming and twisting, reaching down and pulling at his legs, knowing exactly what the dinosaurs had planned, not at all sure if the crystal coating could withstand the onslaught of *five* of those weapons discharged at point-blank range.

"Come with us," said Drom, looking up at Sarah, "or we will kill your *things.*"

Simon cringed, the air around him suddenly feeling alive and electric, little balls of sputtering flame rising up out of the ash and dancing about the ground. The dinosaurs barked and whined, most lurching back, but those with weapons held to Simon's chest did not move, holding their ground.

"Now!"

The world flashed white, and the right side of Simon's face, that nearest Xavier, was hit with what felt like a bucket of steaming water. He shook, screamed, blinked, and buried balled fists into his eyes, rubbing furiously, everything still impossibly white. But his ears still worked, the sounds so loud, the scream and barking of the dinosaurs almost deafening, and above it all, a high-pitched wail, shifting to ever-higher frequencies, what Simon was certain was the sound of a weapon being charged, something much larger than what the dinosaurs carried.

He dropped his hands from his eyes, everything around him blurry and wavering, shapes moving in the still-too-white scene, no colors except for the pale red goo that covered his hands. He moved his fingers, feeling the stickiness to it, the warmth, the slight grit and gristle within it.

Xavier, he thought, turning, expecting to see nothing, certain that those five weapons pointed at Xavier's chest had just vaporized him. A figure stood next to him, hard to make out, his vision still distorted. He blinked, and again pressed his hands to his eyes, then quickly lowered them.

Xavier.

He stood, still encased in the crystal that was now stained gray-red. The dinosaurs that had been surrounding him were mostly gone, but a few remnants, mostly feet and the lower part of their legs, protruded up from the blood-ash ground. Behind Xavier the pedestal that Sarah had been perched on was now empty. Simon saw her, several meters away, moving in the general direction of the aircraft, with a white wall of what looked like swirling ice to her left and a wall of burning, cracking plasma to her right.

It was CUSP.

The two walls appeared almost alive, full of tendrils and fingers, twisting and lashing out, grabbing on to the fleeing dinosaurs, the plasma flame licking at them, transforming them in clouds of red steam, while the wall of ice crystal would engulf them, dropping them to the ground, where they would shatter into ragged chunks and fountains of red snowflakes.

Fire and ice.

He knew just what he was seeing, not understanding how she was doing it, but knowing exactly what it was. She'd somehow *externalized* CUSP. Two chunks of space, he suspected the energy being pulled out of the region to her left coming from the thermal motion in the air molecules and the stored heat in the ground, all of it shunted to her right, dumped into a small volume of space, heating it, vaporizing the air, the intense heat stripping atoms of their outer electrons, generating a fierce plasma.

And then suddenly the wall of solidified air to her left expanded, and the sheet of plasma to her right arced up, flowing high above them.

Too much energy.

He know this could not just be the redistribution of conventional thermal energy, a simple rearrangement of the buzz and rumble of individual atoms. She'd tapped into something deeper, something infinitely more powerful.

He blinked, realizing that Sutherland had succeeded.

Vacuum states.

She was accessing energy from below the vacuum level,

Zero Point energy, on her left side dumping energy into the quantum fabric of space-time, leaving nothing behind but a chunk of supercooled reality, while on her right side, pulling energy directly out of the quantum nothingness.

The walls of ice and flame suddenly expanded even farther, exploding up into the sooty sky, and he felt himself being pulled forward and upward, bending, dizzy, the blood rushing into his head, the edge of his vision actually tinting red, the only thing holding him to the ground the crystal anchoring him in place.

Gravitational shear, he thought.

A dinosaur to his left skidded across the ground, rising into the air, moving directly along the midpoint between the walls of fire and ice, arcing higher, easily 20 meters above Sarah, then smashing into the remnants of three or four other dinosaurs that were already spinning above her, splattering against them in a torrent of blood and shredding meat, bones splintering, the body parts pressing against each other, the entire mass transformed into a bloody ball, one that quickly shrank as he watched, other dinosaurs crashing into it, being swallowed, compressed, the sphere of dinosaur meat growing smaller and smaller, even though more and more of them were sucked into it.

"Impossible," he said, his words pulled away in the wind that now roared past him, carrying soot and rock, all of it being funneled into the now-glowing point in space above Sarah's head. But as impossible as it appeared, he knew that it might possibly make sense at a physics level that he didn't understand. For the past century physicists had been trying to understand the quantum structure of space-time by melding it with the forces of quantum gravity.

Sarah obviously not only understood the relationship, but could control it.

She was not only able to access the quantum levels of space-time, but had used them to alter the local energy balance, accessing energy levels below the vacuum level, tapping into quantum gravity and amplifying those effects into the macroscopic world, where it could blister, shatter, and even suck down dinosaurs into a gravitational vortex.

Despite what was happening, Simon realized that the dinosaurs were not Sarah's intended target. Their destruction was a side effect. It was the Swirl she was after, hovering 10 meters in front of her and backing away toward the craft, a latticework of arcing lightning flashing from it, crashing into her, causing her to pause with each crack of lightning, able to bring her to a halt for just a moment, the gravitational vortex spinning about her lurching and sputtering, actually spitting out a few bloody splinters, only to have them sucked back down the moment she regained focus.

"Get it!" he screamed, suddenly overwhelmed with a feeling of relief. He bent forward, his knees throbbing, the gravitational shear just about intense enough to snap the tendons in his legs and tear cartilage. His vision reddened, and blood suddenly erupted from his nose, splattering away from him in the wind and pulled upward by the throb of shifting gravitational forces.

He tried to scream.

But there seemed to be no air, nothing left in his lungs.

Vision fading into a red blur, he watched the Swirl lose whatever grip had been keeping it in its stationary hovering position and race toward the spinning maelstrom above Sarah. It distorted, elongated, then crystal facets began to peel off, as if unraveling, thin planes of rainbow launching toward the gravitational vortex.

Sarah floated upward, rising slowly at first like a rocket, then quickly gaining speed, the collage of colors and shapes above her head vanishing, with nothing between her and the gravitational implosion but the azure plasma sheathing surrounding her, now transformed into the shape of a tornado.

The Swirl and Sarah struck the gravitational vortex.

Simon fell *up*, tumbling and twisting, the crystal that had held him to the ground either snapping or dissolving. Then he felt the explosion, a white wall of light passing through him, searing him, followed by gravitational turbulence, arms tugged this way, legs that way, reddened vision blurring as eyeballs distorted, his eardrums popping.

A white sky filled his vision, and suddenly he could see.

Sarah floated down, a spherical puff of snowflakes twirling in the open palm of her left hand and a burning orb of plasma in her right—all that was now left of the externalized CUSP. Beneath her feet the air was distorted, shimmering, laced with shattered panes of salt and pepper, as if reality itself had not quite locked in.

Above her, two of the aircraft shot high into the sky, turbofans screaming, ash flying, but Sarah remained untouched by the backwash. Her white surgical gown, what to Simon looked like the same one that had burned up when she'd first interfaced to CUSP, did not so much as ruffle.

So clean, thought Simon. Her hospital gown was simply perfect. And that seemed somehow more amazing, more improbable, than anything else that had just happened. His eyes closed, just as Sarah's feet touched the ground.

Chapter 28

The conference room and the oak table.

It had been the scene of General Sutherland's ultimate success, 65 million years in the making, the place where all his dreams had been made real. And now it witnessed his defeat: the chaos, the turn of events that he could have never anticipated, never dreamed of.

The images were everywhere, little three-dimensional orbs, snips of the disaster, ticked off every few seconds. Akandi sat still, waiting for them to drift toward him. The nearest showed Sarah hanging in the air, supported by a twisted column of something that Akandi couldn't quite understand, something that might have been fog-heavy air, but he knew that wasn't right.

"In here now!" shouted Sutherland from the far end of the room, where he paced, his attention obviously focused somewhere beyond his Virts, barking commands and demanding data nonstop from the moment that Drom's landing party had lost control of the situation.

Akandi knew that Sutherland was being subjected to the capricious nature of Allah's world, to events and patterns beyond his understanding, beyond the certainty that had previously filled his life. Those around him were asserting their free will, and Akandi knew this was not something that the general had factored into his plans.

"How far?" Sutherland stopped walking and swayed, as if

he couldn't quite damp his forward momentum. "Does the trajectory indicate a landing, or orbital injection?"

Akandi watched as Sutherland lifted his hands, holding them to the sides of his head, his entire body stiffening as if hit with a large voltage, then just as quickly sag, hands dropping to his sides, knees almost buckling as he took a stumbling step forward.

"Orbit or landing!" Sutherland shouted.

The transmission came from the Taikonauts on Callisto nearly 6 hours ago: Amalthea had broken out of its orbit and launched itself sunward, spitting an exhaust flame so long that its plasma plume, grabbed by Jupiter's magnetic field, wrapped the exhaust halfway around the planet.

This was the last transmission the Taikonauts had sent.

The exhaust plume had induced a massive discharge between Jupiter and Io, generating an ionized sulfur arc several thousand kilometers in diameter between the planet and the moon, and when it collapsed, fired off an EMP that melted any circuitry within several million kilometers of Jupiter, flatlining every artifact of man on Jupiter's four big Galilean moons, and if not killing the several hundred Taikonauts exploring the system outright, would kill them soon enough—no electronics meant no life when exploring Jupiter.

At first Sutherland had considered Amalthea a minor issue, one not directly impacting the Jet, the Rings, or Sarah. But now that Sarah refused to return and had apparently defeated the Swirl, Sutherland had begun to unravel.

Akandi understood why.

If Sarah, his own daughter, wouldn't obey him, then nothing else might be under his control. And with that thought came the image of Amalthea accelerating toward Earth. Until that moment Sutherland must have thought he understood the Clingers, believed they'd hold in some high orbit, perhaps as far out as the moon, and send in a few craft to torment Drom and his troops. But that would be the extent of it.

Now he was not so certain.

Amalthea was a moon with a diameter 10 times that of Phobos, and a mass nearly 1000 times greater. Even if it managed to make a controlled landing on the Earth's surface, it would probably shatter the crust and flatline ecosystems so that nothing above the level of viruses and a few very tough bacteria would survive. That would be the best that could be hoped for. More likely, such a landing would shatter the planet.

Going into orbit was the only way mankind would survive.

"Repeat!" commanded Sutherland, his shoulders sagging, and he took a deep long breath that he slowly blew out. "Looks like Amalthea is targeting for an orbital insertion at a 10,000-kilometer altitude." He pulled off his Virts.

Akandi grimaced. The tidal effects would be *severe*. "Bad," he said.

Sutherland nodded. "But not fatal." He turned, facing the wall that would melt to open up to the outer hallway. Akandi could tell that Sutherland had just put the matter of Amalthea out of his mind. Since it would probably not kill them in the next few hours, he knew that the general would devote his attention to something that *could* kill them in the next few hours.

Sarah.

Akandi felt certain that the general had lost control of his daughter. What he didn't know was whether the general had been able to admit this to himself. The wall started to thin, pulling back on itself, dimpling and breeching first in the center, with Drom grabbing at the edge of the opening, pulling himself in before it could complete the process. He bounded forward, his tail lashing, his snout whipping left-right-left. "They had a Clinger!" he barked.

Sutherland nodded in Drom's general direction and walked quickly over to the massive oak table. He reached for the utility belt lying there, a full-up military survival belt, holding all the supplies and interfaces needed to keep a soldier in the field alive and linked for several days. Sutherland strapped it onto his waist, reached up with his left hand to unflick the strap holding its pistol in place, pulled the gun, and aimed it at Drom.

"The Clingers!" screamed Drom.

Sutherland squeezed the trigger.

The echo seemed to go on forever in the crystal room. "You shot him!" said Akandi, looking from the pistol to the small hole halfway down Drom's tail. Turning, he could see the ragged exit wound, and the fist-sized chunk of bloody meat now plastered against the wall behind Drom. The dinosaur slumped, going down on his knees, bent over, his little hands hitting the floor, then he pushed back, slowly standing, his legs shaking, his tail falling onto the floor, limp and lifeless, a pool of dark red blood expanding beneath it.

"The Clingers *are* coming," said Sutherland, keeping his pistol trained on Drom, the barrel held up, aimed at Drom's snout. "But they are not the issue. My daughter is the issue!"

Drom slowly blinked, the almost translucent nictitating membranes slowly sliding down and then back up over his black eyeballs. His mouth hung open, and his breath came out in sharp, shallow pants. "She is *strong,*" said Drom. "You should be proud to have such an offspring." He looked around the room, taking only a moment to look at his limp and bleeding tail, then focusing on those who had just entered the room.

Akandi followed his gaze. Kristensen stood there, backed up against the wall, his eyes wide, his hands pushed against the legs of his soot-stained jumpsuit. A jagged cut ran across his forehead, with a thick line of blood seeping from it to his swollen-shut left eye.

"And he is?" asked Sutherland, pointing his gun at the person standing next to Kristensen, then pointing the gun at Kristensen.

"Bill Gates," said Kristensen in a whimper, pushing himself against the wall at his back, as if trying to squirm through it. "He came aboard our craft just as we were departing."

"*Retreating* you mean," Sutherland said, shaking the gun at Kristensen but not looking at him, all of his attention now focused on Bill. "Is it really you?" he asked.

"In the flesh," said Bill.

Akandi squinted, confused, as he looked across the room at a man who certainly looked no older than 30. Bill Gates, had he still been alive, would be at least 100 years old. He remembered the funeral, the image saturation that had flowed through the Void normally reserved for dead presidents.

But he did look like Gates, only so much younger. *A clone?* he thought.

Sutherland slipped his Virts back on as he slowly walked toward Gates. "Can't be too careful at times like these," he said, pointing at the bleeding Drom. "Things do not always proceed exactly as we foresee them." He angled his head back and, raising his left hand, began to point at things that Akandi knew only existed in Sutherland's virtual vision.

A shaft of pale blue light cut through the crystal ceiling, playing over Bill Gates, as a portion of the ceiling directly above him shimmered, glistening like liquid, and a bulge pulled away, hanging down, slowly oscillating back and forth.

"Sorry, Bill, but I needed to know exactly what I'm dealing with," said Sutherland, as Bill's knees collapsed, and he dropped to the floor, the light still playing across him as the hanging blob of molten ceiling swayed above him.

Still holding the pistol, Sutherland pointed it again at Drom. "The two of you are a bit of a disappointment," he said, angling the pistol back and pointing it at the rainbow crystal that just floated into the room. "All I asked was for the return of my daughter, but apparently she was a bit too much for you." Sutherland whispered, and the air in front of him twisted, as if suddenly full of prisms, refracting bands of rainbow. Then an image locked. It took a moment for Akandi to realize what he was seeing: Sarah Sutherland rising into the air between a wall of fire to her right and a wall of ice to her left. Beneath her stood a man, leaning at an unnatural angle, buffeted and jerked about in a wind, and above her spun a bloody tornado.

Akandi shook his head once.

Then the improbable became the impossible. As Sarah floated up toward the bloody tornado, the Swirl moved toward her. Cracks of lightning erupted from it, smashing into her. Akandi dropped his eyelids till they were almost closed, feeling the impact before it actually took place: the Swirl, Sarah, and the tornado all colliding, the entire image flaring into a too-white blur, then just as quickly fading, even the walls of fire and ice gone, nothing remaining except Sarah floating down to the ground, next to the still-standing man.

The Swirl was gone.

"That's right," said Sutherland. "Besting Drom and 30 of his finest is not very surprising, but she also took down that aspect of the Swirl."

"Strong emotional response," whispered Iyoon, suddenly hovering over the image of Sarah. *"The parent-child bond is strong, full of pride."* Iyoon paused, twirling about, its dark facets dulling. *"And just a bit of fear."*

The pride was obvious, but Akandi could not see the fear, certain that Sutherland must be keeping tight control over himself. "This time," Sutherland said loudly, "I suggest that you take adequate numbers to control the situation. Be sure to stress to her that time is running out, and *final* preparations need to be made." Sutherland paused and licked his lips. "Use whatever measures are necessary, no matter how extreme. Do not worry about hurting her, since I'm certain that nothing at your disposal could cause any long-term damage."

Drom managed to lift his damaged tail off the floor, leaving behind a bloody tailprint. "She is strong," he said.

"Of course she is!" Sutherland took several steps forward, again aiming his pistol at Drom. "She is designed to be strong, needs to be strong to see us to the end of this thing. She's made the transition, and has been able to access Zero Point." He paused, slightly lowering the pistol. "You saw it," he said.

Drom twisted his neck, looking at Sutherland with his other eye. "I *felt* it," he said.

"Just bring her back," said Sutherland, shaking his gun toward the door.

"*The fear is larger,*" said Iyoon, hovering next to Sutherland. "*I suspect he is afraid of what will happen if Drom doesn't
bring his daughter here.*" Iyoon made several passes around
Sutherland. "*But he is even more afraid if she is brought here.*"

"Now!" shouted Sutherland.

Drom turned, limping, his tail drooping but not quite
touching the floor. A splatter of blood trailed behind him as
he moved through the doorway. The Swirl still hung, now
motionless, not spinning, not a single shaft of light bouncing from its dull-looking facets.

Sutherland looked over at Kristensen with a questioning
look. "The Swirl needs to help in getting Sarah," he said.

Kristensen nodded and looked up at the Swirl. "The
Swirl is not *pleased,*" he said. "It says that agreements had
been made, that plans had been implemented, that the
future is not unfolding as anticipated." Kristensen stepped
back and almost stumbled.

The Swirl rotated a few degrees, and the air around it
suddenly boiled, its crystalline facets wavering, colors blurring.

Crack!

A bolt of lightning erupted from the Swirl, and slammed
into the floor only centimeters away from Sutherland, blowing out a small crater. Sutherland moved forward, stepping
over the ragged hole. The room filled with the stink of
ozone and the dust of pulverized rock. "Bring back my
daughter," said Sutherland, looking up at the Swirl.

The air stopped boiling, and the Swirl floated out of the
room.

"Stay with it," commanded Sutherland, pointing at Kristensen. "And don't come back unless Sarah is with you."

Kristensen gave no obvious acknowledgment, but simply ran after the Swirl.

A mixture of building tension and fear almost made Akandi follow him, but he held his ground. Sutherland turned to face him.

"Any problems?" shouted Sutherland.

Akandi forced a smile and willed his shoulders to drop in a calculated show of relaxation. He knew anything he said was a risk, but that saying nothing was the biggest risk of all. "Sarah has a will of her own."

Sutherland reached up and ran a hand across his chin as he took several steps toward Akandi, the pistol still in his other hand. "Which is what I wanted," he said in a whisper as he reholstered the pistol.

Akandi blinked in surprise.

"I need her to be strong, to be able to face down what we'll find at Alpha Centauri. If *I* can control the dinos, or the Swirl, then I suspect the entities who set up the machinery to move the Sun, who established hundreds of worlds around Alpha Centauri A, will have little difficulty in controlling them. I need something far beyond *my* ability to control or understand, but something still possessing enough of a link to humanity to take our side in the fight."

He *hopes,* thought Akandi. *Everything resting on his hope.*

"Then you really don't expect Drom, Kristensen, and the Swirl to bring her back here?" he asked.

Sutherland shook his head, frowning. "If they can bring her back, then she won't be worth bringing back."

Akandi wondered what Sutherland would do to his daughter if she failed his test, and was certain that the general did not have a plan for that contingency.

Sutherland walked over toward Bill, still collapsed on the floor, light playing across him, with the dollop of liquefied ceiling swaying over him. He pushed his Virts snugly against his face and looked down at Gates. He laughed. "Poor old Bill," he said.

Akandi had no idea what was so funny and apparently neither did Iyoon as it hovered motionlessly next to Sutherland.

"Examination over," said Sutherland, as the lights flitting across Gates vanished and the ceiling resolidified. "Time to wake up."

Gates shook his head and slowly pushed himself up into a sitting position.

Sutherland bent down, getting eye level with Gates. "Well, Bill," he said, "there is some good news and some bad news."

Gates slowly shook his head and, reaching up, brushed aside the locks of hair that had fallen into his eyes.

"The good news is that you are totally rid of Simon Ryan. The break was clean, and you are now a true individual." He paused, and straightened up. "The problem seems to be with the template that Sarah used to house the new you. You've inherited the body that Mears no longer found himself in need of. Sarah did a good job of removing him from the organic and inorganic hardware in your skull, but it seems that Mears was compromised: his neural wiring tampered with."

"What?" said Bill.

"Those people you were with, the Olmos family. Sarah did not just happen to bring you there. A connection already existed. It appears that those farmers had been eyeball deep into the Co-Op's Void for years, manipulating systems and even running key personnel." He smiled. "It seems that they'd hacked our recently departed Dr. Mears."

Bill brushed at his left knee.

"They'd played him in a simple but highly effective Pavlovian feedback routine. It seems that Mears had a fear of spiders and Xavier Olmos and his farming clan were manipulating that fear into blackmailing Mears to ensure that their daughter be exempted from Volunteering at the Co-Op."

"Spiders," said Bill.

"Afraid so," said Sutherland. "A whole pack of them, lurking just below your conscious level. It seems that your brain has slipped into a feedback minimum where more and more of your internal wiring will be consumed with the *almost-there* images of spiders."

"No!" shouted Bill, smashing his palms against the floor and turning his hands over, inspecting them, as if looking for something.

"We can't stay here," said Xavier, looking past Christina toward Phobos. "We've apparently become a focal point of whatever is unfolding," he said, pointing over at Sarah. "There's her and whatever she might be, dinosaurs, some sort of physical manifestation of the Swirl, and a second moon on the way that is somehow connected to Krew."

Christina nodded.

Dinosaurs, thought Xavier, *apparently from Phobos.* He couldn't even make a guess as to how they came into existence, let alone how they'd gotten to Phobos. He could still see the barrels of their weapons pressed up to the crystalline cocoon that had covered him, feel the discharge of the weapons and the slam of something electric against his chest. And the next moment, not dead, but standing and still breathing, watching Sarah rise into the air, colliding with the Swirl.

They all looked at him—Christina, Simon, Padmini, even Che and Krew. Only Sarah stood apart, perched on her crystal pedestal, the collage of color and shape twirling above her head, larger than it had been before her encounter with the Swirl. But something else had also changed.

It was difficult to focus on Sarah.

Xavier could feel his gaze slip from her as she seemed to slide in and out of existence, always there in the sense that she had a physical presence, casting a shadow, then momentarily sliding somewhere else. His peripheral senses told him that at times she simply *wasn't*. It was just a feeling, a very *unnatural* feeling.

He knew whatever was going on with Sarah had to be important, but he couldn't do anything about it at the moment. The attack had ended less than 15 minutes earlier. He'd had them gather up supplies, mostly food and weapons, including several of the energy staffs that the dinosaurs had been using, getting ready to run. "You can see the pattern, can't you?" he asked Simon.

Simon gave a slight nod and looked over at the aircraft that had been left behind. "That much is clear."

"Clear," said Xavier bitterly, not knowing if the craft was operational, or if they could even figure out how to operate it. But it was the only possible way out, something they would either make work or die here trying. "And you've known this for how long?" he asked.

Simon shrugged his shoulders. "From the moment Sarah obliterated the Swirl, and we found ourselves still breathing."

Xavier thought as much. Simon could see things before him, put the pieces together before the rest of them could even recognize something as a puzzle piece. And yet Simon deferred to him, letting him take the lead. He could feel it, as they all looked over at him, that he had become the leader.

Somehow chosen by Sarah.

Sarah had come to him, escaped the Ag Co-Op to get to him. No one had said anything—he suspected that they might not even be consciously aware of it—but he was certain that at some level they knew Sarah had chosen him to lead, and none of them seemed to want to question that.

"Still invisible to all eyes?" asked Xavier, looking at Christina and the filaments pressed into her right eye, then lacing over her shoulder and snaking into the pack on her back—the only functioning interface they had to the newly emerging Void.

"Totally," said Christina. "Absolutely no trace, with this location looking like all the others in this area, burned and strewn with volcanic shards and ash."

Xavier nodded. Sarah was obviously deep into the Void, able to manipulate all incoming surveillance, making it invisible to prying eyes. But she'd been able to do that from the start. Xavier couldn't be sure, but suspected that she had lifted the cloak that had kept them hidden just long enough for the dinosaurs and the Swirl to find them when they'd been attacked.

Sarah had *invited* them.

And that could only be because she wanted to fight the Swirl. There might have been other reasons, but Xavier couldn't see them. *Testing herself?* he wondered.

"We need to load up," said Padmini, walking to the craft, carrying two of the dinosaur energy staffs, although she hadn't yet figured out how to fire them. "Get as far away from here as possible and dig in deep."

Xavier nodded. "Into the craft," he said, not arguing

with what she'd said, but knowing that they would not be looking for a place to hide.

Sarah could have kept them hidden if that was what she wanted.

No.

There was a puzzle to be solved, and they could not do that by hiding in a hole.

As he started to walk toward the craft, Sarah stepped down from her pedestal: her movements jerky, almost discontinuous. For just a moment her right foot seemed to touch down on the ash, the next moment again on the pedestal. And then, just as his brain was acknowledging that discontinuous move, her foot was again touching the ash, then sinking into it ankle deep.

Temporal glitch, thought Xavier, suspecting that for the barest fraction of a moment Sarah had slipped, moved in time, then resynched with the normal flow of things.

An impossible thing, he thought.

But hardly unreasonable as compared to what else had been taking place.

Chapter 29

Xavier peered into the belly of the craft, keeping his hands tightly wrapped around the protruding grips that had flowed up through the craft's skin, the oily metal rungs at first too small to grab on to solidly, apparently having been designed for smaller dinosaur hands, with stubby fingers. But as he grabbed on, wrapping his fingers around the rung, it both lengthened and thickened, suddenly fitting perfectly into the palm of his hand.

"Vacant," he said, without looking over his shoulder. The craft's interior was an open space defined by smooth, featureless walls that glowed with a soft yellow-red light. He pushed his head farther in, stepping up, placing a single boot on the yielding floor material. The light suddenly shifted in spectrum, more yellow, and the floor shimmered, undulating, the surface transformed into a corrugated texture, one that seemed to latch on to the sole of his boot. Simon and Padmini followed closely behind.

"The structure seems alive and responsive," he said.

They both nodded, as if this was a reasonable thing, and Padmini gave him a slight shove. "Kali senses an active mechanical template, with a large portion of its bandwidth used for external sensing—reading you, it appears." Reaching out, she grabbed on to one of the rungs lining the open entranceway. It shifted, re-forming itself. Xavier could see that it had become similar in shape to the one he held, but smaller, to accommodate Padmini's smaller hand. "The entire craft is actively reconfigurable to morph to whoever, or whatever, is using it," she said.

Xavier nodded, looked past them, smiling slightly at Christina. She smiled back. He stepped farther into the craft, turning right, moving in the direction he assumed the cockpit would be. He focused on the featureless bulkhead, trying not to be distracted by the movement of the adjacent walls: seats flowing out of amorphous bulkheads. The wall before him shimmered, the surface suddenly boiling and twisting, then pulling back.

Xavier's hand jerked toward his belt, as he realized only

at that moment that he had walked into the craft without a weapon drawn, not expecting anyone to be in it. He didn't have time to touch the pistol grip, before Padmini shoved him from behind, and kicked him in the back of the knees, dropping him to the floor.

Pistols in both hands, she pointed them at the heads of the two dinosaurs seated before them. Xavier stayed down, though he knew almost instantly that the two dinosaurs were no threat. They were wrapped in cocoonlike seats, only arms, hands, and heads exposed, covered by a thin sheen of cracked crystal.

"Sarah seems to be several steps ahead of us," said Simon, reaching in past Padmini's pistols and gently touching the back of the nearest dinosaur's head. It pitched forward, the crystal covering it shattering into small pieces. "We now know why this craft never took off."

Xavier pushed himself up. "Get ready."

Christina was the first in her seat. It was little more than a glowing yellow block extending from the wall before she sat, but then it flowed up her sides as she made contact with it, a band of nearly translucent bulkhead material wrapping around her waist, two bands running up over her shoulders and meshing with a back support. She fought it for a moment but managed to keep her composure. "Comfortable," she said, looking at the others.

Sarah walked slowly to the back of the craft, the collage above her head spread wide, compressed, flowing across the low ceiling. She didn't sit; crystalline stalks erupted from her legs and spine, burrowing into the floor.

Che and Krew didn't sit either, but stood as if waiting.

Xavier looked at Che, then at a nearby seat, telling him what to do with a look.

Che and Krew each gave a partial smile and started to

walk forward. "Form implies function," they said, and held up their hands, fingers fluttering. Krew's thin, tapered fingers appeared almost boneless, so flexible and fluid. He loped slightly ahead of Che, his arms held out for balance. Simon and Padmini stepped back, pressing against walls that suddenly reached out, enveloping them in snaking gossamer vines that snugged them to the bulkheads.

Krew did not react to any of this but stopped at the entrance to the small room, what Xavier thought must be the craft's control room, and peered in, his normally large black eyes opening even wider. Che stepped up next to him, and they both reached in, running their hands across the back supports holding the dead dinosaurs.

The control room shuddered, the walls throbbing, and the restraints holding the dinosaurs in place spread out, enveloping them, pulling them down toward the floor, first tails vanishing, followed by bodies, then nothing remaining but toothy snouts that quickly slipped beneath the compartment floor. Che and Krew stepped forward, and as they lowered themselves toward the floor, they were met halfway by a protruding bulge that conformed to them, wrapping them in partial cocoons, then slid them forward toward an angled slab that flowed out of the forward bulkhead.

The walls vanished, and it appeared to Xavier that Che and Krew sat suspended in midair, the ash- and lava-sprayed ground several meters beneath them. The two bodies of the dinosaurs spewed from the cockpit were there also. The only visible remnant of the cockpit was the featureless slab hanging over their laps.

Xavier reached in, running his hands where the cockpit wall had been, feeling the same slightly giving material, realizing nothing had changed, except that it was now transparent. He looked back into the rear of the craft. "Can they see us?" he called out.

Christina had several small boxes resting in her lap, out of which ran fibers to her eyes, as her hands flitted in and out of the shifting images rolling in front of her. "Totally invisible," she called out.

Xavier gave a quick look at Padmini and Simon, who both nodded back at him. He lowered himself into the emerging seat, placing his arms on the rests, tilting his head back against a restraint.

A thought filled his head.

Too damn easy.

A craft that could not be seen, just waiting for them, accommodating their every need, as if willingly aiding them in their escape. And then Che and Krew, taking seats in the cockpit, their movements so certain, almost as if they had been waiting for this moment.

Krew piloting this craft.

Xavier knew that it could only be the neural web that Padmini had brought that had given Krew this ability. Someone had known that Krew must be put into play, had killed Leo Barnwell, and forced Padmini into delivering the neural web. The connections were incredibly deep, too deep for Xavier to track them.

"We're ready," said Simon from behind.

Xavier knew they were ready, having absolutely no doubt that Che and Krew could pilot this alien craft—the craft that had only minutes before landed with a troop of dinosaurs from Phobos. All were waiting for him to give the order. He knew they could not stay here, but a part of him did not want to go, to leave the farm that was no longer, certain that if they took off, he'd never touch foot on the Earth again.

Possibly a premonition. He gave one glance over his shoulder to the back of the craft and at Sarah, looking for something familiar in the collage of colors and shapes that rolled and spun between her and the craft's ceiling.

Nothing.

He sighed and turned back, looking out at the ash-covered ground and the two dead dinosaurs. "Now," he said.

Che and Krew's fingers played across the control slab.

The ground silently fell away as he sank down into his seat.

Kristensen sat behind Drom and the pilot, in his cocoon seat. His head throbbed with each beat of his heart, a skull-cracking pounding that synched with the oscillating blurring of his vision. His right hand and foot had gone numb. He'd taken a severe hit on the head during their last encounter with Sarah Sutherland and suspected he'd sustained some sort of brain injury.

He might be dying.

But he doubted the brain injury would be responsible for his death.

He sighed, suddenly so tired, as he stared at the back of Drom's head. Next to Drom sat the pilot, stumpy fingers gliding across the control panel, while the Swirl hovered in front of both of them, pressed up against the craft's transparent nose.

The Swirl.

So many promises made, and so many promises *almost* kept. The Swirl engineered his escape from Sutherland and the secret warren beneath the high deserts of Nevada when the Sun had first fired its Jet, so he could go to his family. But there hadn't been enough time. The Rings and the resulting earthquakes had seen to that. He had no family left. This seemed to be the way the Swirl operated: It helped in ways that ultimately didn't matter.

And the latest promise, what he suspected would be the last: that the Swirl would see him through the final days of Earth, keep him safe when both the Earth and Sun broke away from the Solar system as long as he once again aligned himself with Sutherland. Again a promise kept—but just barely.

Suddenly the right side of his mouth sagged, and the streaking clouds blurred to featureless puffs of gray, quickly darkening to black smudges. With an effort, he turned his head, putting the Swirl in the center of his left eye's field of vision.

The shard slowly turned, rainbows glinting from its facets.

So confident, he thought.

It could not see its own limitations, what it lacked now so obvious compared to Sarah.

"All engaged and ready upon my command?" asked Drom.

"Yes," said the pilot. "Twenty-four transport and 32 fighters maintaining outbound trajectories or standard search grids, all ready to break on your command to the desired coordinates." The pilot jerked its snout to the left, one eyeball glancing past Kristensen and toward the back of the craft, where more than 100 soldiers stood, wedged in tight, body armor to body armor, tails wrapped around adjacent legs to keep them all steady. Turning his head, he looked back through the craft's transparent nose. "There is still no *direct* contact."

Drom opened his mouth wide and barked. "And there won't be. She has penetrated systems, controlling input and output, modifying surveillance so that their presence remains undetected. We will observe them with our *eyes*." Reaching over, he poked the pilot in his right eye, the nictitating membrane squeezing tightly shut, but the dinosaur not flinching, hands playing smoothly across the control panel. "They are still either on the ground or, if they have managed to take the craft, will not have moved far."

Far too confident, thought Kristensen.

None of them understood, unable to see what now seemed so obvious to him. The Swirl was powerful, with its ghostly presence in so many heads. But it was still limited by its birth, an entity of pure thought, of electrons and chemical potentials, living in the shadows of the mental landscape of its hosts. Only now had it assumed a physical presence and begun to operate in the world of dirt and blood, a physical reality defined by such things as gravity, heat, cold, dust, rocks, and fragile bodies that so easily spilled blood and spewed torn muscle and splintered bone.

A hostile place—conquered by intellect and tools.

And that was the critical difference.

Sarah knew tools, knew what it was to live in the dirt and blood, to fling herself off the Southern Cross, to feel real pain, and even to die. The desire was in her at the most basic level to reach out, grab on to the world, and change it to suit her needs. That drive might have even been genetic, a wide smattering of genes *demanding* that behavior.

But the Swirl didn't understand that, never had the hands to wrap around a wrench, to tighten a bolt, to feel the grind of metal against metal, a muscle straining, the sweat dripping down a forehead.

Sarah knew.

She'd accessed Zero Point, manipulating space-time right down to the level where it foamed and boiled, where gravity was just one more parameter, a variable to be traded off against the other forces, a thing to wrap hands around and twist and tug at, feeling the grind and resistance, the power playing through her hands.

The Swirl was not equipped to understand, to *feel* the pleasure and satisfaction of dreaming, building, then using a tool. They'd lived with the all-powerful Swirl for too long, unable to see just how limited it was, a power without form, no real structure of its own.

Kristensen now suspected why the Swirl had never really moved beyond the minds of those it occupied, why it had never reached out and gotten its hands dirty in building a world of its own. Literally and metaphorically, it had no hands.

"Break formation now!" ordered Drom. "Maximum firepower."

"All craft break to rendezvous," the pilot said in almost a whisper as his hands played across the control panel in response to flickering amber icons. "Maximum firepower," he added.

Drom twisted, looking back at Kristensen. "Now she will see just what we are capable of."

Kristensen nodded, knowing that he had at best only a few minutes before he died. He slumped back in his seat and thought about his family. "And we'll see just what *she* is capable of."

Christina slipped deep, to where nothing moved, her mental slew rate maxed, the sweep of glistening motes in front of her frozen, each a craft spiraling around Phobos, the pattern logical, predictable, a mixture of reconnaissance flying mathematically optimized trajectories, and the higher flying arcs punching through the sky, briefly suborbital, screaming away to the far points of the planet.

All as it should be.

She hoped they could seamlessly meld into the pattern, scattering far away, possibly to the other side of the planet, before another force made its way to what had been their farm.

Movement.

She shifted her perspective, not by moving head or eyeballs, nothing that slow and mechanical, but simply by focusing her attention on a selected twittering of electrical signal traveling down the optic nerve, generated from an isolated patch of rods and cones.

Sarah.

Christina clocked nearly 100 times faster than what was needed for standard perception, even the fastest human movement reduced to a crawl so slow as to be almost imperceptible.

But Sarah moved—violently, in savage spasms and jerks, the movements so fast that Christina could not see them, simply registering that a hand that had been touching a forehead now hung by her side, then touched a shoulder, and suddenly was touching her forehead again.

No actual movement, just a change in location—a *discontinuous* jump.

Christina accessed her mental cache of mathematical algorithms, running the simulations of muscle attached to bones, forces, and tensile strengths.

Impossible.

To move that fast, muscle would be ripped away from bone, tendons snapped, cartilage shattered, cell membranes ruptured, vessels sheared. Such movements should have turned Sarah into a slowly expanding mist of vaporized organic debris.

Sarah turned, eyes focused on Christina.

Christina gave a mental blink. Sarah was not moving, but changing position, many of those positions identical to ones she had been in moments before. And that was the key—*moments before.*

Sarah was not moving in space.

Sarah was moving in time, tripping back and forth, flitting about—a fraction of a second in the past or future. She had accessed Zero Point, and as an artifact could spin out gravitational fields. She'd accessed space-time at the quantum level, somehow able to control a nearly infinite number of wave functions and probabilities, forcing them to act together, to amplify upward to higher and higher ranges, taking forces that should have been able to exert themselves only in regions far below the range of atomic dimensions and making them big enough to shred dinosaurs and levitate herself off the ground.

Quantum mechanics brought into the macroscopic world.

And time was just one more quantized variable in the regions where Sarah accessed the Zero Point, not the perceivable, smoothly flowing stream that meandered through the world, but one dominated by eddies and whirlpools, each moment existing as a probability, the moments jumping back and forth, actually directionless at such small dimensions.

Sarah had brought that, too, up to the macroscopic world. She was no longer anchored to the now like everything else in the world, but flitted around it.

Apparently not controlling it.

At least not yet.

Pattern shift. Christina detected it, that part of her mind keeping watch on the aircraft display. The pattern had been broken.

Christina blinked, eyelids closing and opening, mind and brain resynching.

The display hung in front of her, the change almost imperceptible, but still change, dozens of pinpricks, each within an allowed window to maintain the overall pattern, and individual deviations sufficiently minimal to be considered random noise. But collectively a new pattern emerged.

And the focus of the pattern was suddenly obvious.

"Papito!" she screamed.

Xavier started to turn, almost had his neck twisted around enough to see Christina.

"They are coming at us!" The deviation was obvious enough now so that even individual craft could be seen dropping out of their old patterns. "At least 40."

"Put us down!" shouted Xavier.

Christina focused on several things at once: the craft pitching, rolling clockwise, banking at nearly 60 degrees; and the movement of Sarah, walking toward her, Sarah's hair arcing in a blue plasma discharge, the ever-present collage of colors and shape spiraling down, funneling away to a pinpoint of almost nothingness, then vanishing with a loud *pop*.

Sarah changing, or preparing for something new.

The craft continued to pitch—bulkhead and floor changing position, Christina looking down at the wall, still snugged in her harness, her head pushed back against the restraint by gee forces induced by the rapid roll.

A glance through the opening to the cockpit, just in time to see a flash, an explosion of white light, and only

then feel the explosion, the savage jerk to the right, the
blowback of debris, the scream of rupturing material and
the howl of supersonic wind racing in through the many-
meter-sized chunk of once-again-opaque cockpit wall.

Che was gone.

Where he had sat was a gaping hole, and beyond it a
spinning soot-stained sky. She felt her eyeballs bulge outward as the craft flipped over its shattered nose, the tail section rising high, then the sound of metal tearing away in a
screech that momentarily rose above the howl of the wind.

All going to die, thought Christina.

Her lap and shoulder restraints evaporated to nothing as
the bulkhead behind her cracked, fingers of wind wrapping
around her, pulling her head and shoulders back, while her
legs remained locked firmly around the base of the seat.
Looking up through tearing eyes, ice-wind cutting into her,
she hung outside the hull of the craft, leaning over backward, falling.

Hands grabbing.

She forced her head up, against the wind; her vision distorted by gee forces and the hurricane blast. Sarah had a hold
on her right arm, both hands wrapped around her wrist, a
thin sheen of crystal emerging from her fingertips, entwining
the entire length of her arm. And Padmini gripped her left
hand, having anchored herself against the sides of the ruptured bulkhead, her face a contorted grimace as she pulled.

"Get inside!" screamed Padmini, her voice barely a whisper above the howl of the wind.

Christina would have laughed if she had not been so terrified. She was more than willing to comply, but felt herself
creeping ever outward, gee forces and wind stronger than
Padmini and Sarah, stronger than the joints in her shoulders, tendons stretching to the breaking point.

The craft lurched, shuddered, and Christina watched its rear ten meters shear away, the entire tail section tumbling into gray clouds. *All of us going down,* she thought. Gee forces whipped her head around, angling it so she faced Sarah, just as something erupted from her eyes, a burning ember from her right eye, and a frozen shard spewing a condensation tail from her left—certain it was another aspect of the walls of fire and ice she'd generated when the dinosaurs had tried to capture her.

Christina closed her eyes, but still saw the two specs, one burning, one frozen, coming at her face, accelerating, slamming into her eyes, the impact jerking her head back, tearing through her eyeballs, a torrent of pain cascading down her optic nerves, exploding inside her head.

She opened her eyes just as Sarah released her, her fingers uncurling, the thin sheen of crystal connecting them shattering, then ripped away in the wind. She fell backward, sucked into the turbulent slipstream, with Padmini still holding on to her other arm, both falling out of the craft, the two of them tumbling away into the ashy clouds, spinning, with a forward speed of better than 600 kilometers per hour, but quickly angling down, picking up vertical speed, the Earth below racing up at them.

Christina reached out with her free hand, wrapping it around Padmini's waist, pulling her tightly against her, chest to back. And then she reached out again, but this time without moving, feeling the amorphous seat still strapped to her legs, the chunk of material now inert and lifeless, severed from the craft's neural system.

The bindings lashing it to her legs began to give way.

She reached far out, the splinters of fire and ice that Sarah had somehow inserted in her head showing her how, feeling signals running through her nervous system, amplitude

pegged, a broad-spectrum shotgun of noise screeching at
the thinning tendrils clinging to her legs, the skin of her
legs receptive, straining for any response.

Her left leg broke free of the amorphous blob, then a
faint signal twittered through the right leg, and that was all
that was needed. Christina locked, integrated the signal,
gave commands, and a thin sheen of crystal erupted from
her right leg, enveloping the amorphous blob, pulling it
against her, causing it to spew up and over both her legs and
Padmini's, flowing, thinning, a shield against the wind, tendrils sheared and rearranged, covalent bonds between carbon atoms lining up, strengthening, building a gossamer
coating of spun diamond. A sheath of foaming diamond
unfurled above her head, billowing in the howling wind,
then bit into the slipstream.

Chapter 30

"No!" screamed Xavier.

He stood, the tendrils holding him into his seat retracting. The wind, exploding through the hole in the cockpit
where Che had been sitting, picked him up and hurled him
backward, slamming him into a soft wall of spun fiber,
almost enveloped, his head angled in the direction of the
cockpit, looking at Krew, who had swiveled his seat and was
looking back into the craft.

Krew's thin lips moved, but his voice was swallowed in
the howl of the wind. He smiled and, lifting his right hand,

put thumb to index finger to form a circle, giving Xavier the *okay* sign.

"No!" screamed Xavier again. He shifted in the amorphous fiber, turning in the direction where Christina had been sitting, looking through the ragged hole, seeing nothing but ash-colored sky. "Christina!"

Out of his restraints, Simon stumbled forward and lost his footing. Pulled toward the opening, he grabbed on at the last moment before being swept out. He peered through the hole, then slowly turned his head against the force of the wind, looking back at Xavier and shaking his head.

"No," cried Xavier, the tears flowing down his face, the wind stripping them from his cheeks. Suddenly he could not breathe, the world dimming at the edges of his vision. He closed his eyes, knowing that impact would be in a few seconds.

Merciful impact.

"Christina," he whispered, his hands reaching out in the direction of the hole. Then with a violent shudder, the craft flipped, jerking him around and twisting him until he faced the back of the plane. He was less than a meter away from Sarah. He could have reached out and touched her had he wanted to.

Instead he tried to close his eyes but found that he couldn't, the mesh that had gathered him up having snaked across his face, keeping his eyelids pried back. Sarah walked forward, somehow able to keep her balance in the spinning plane, her suddenly longer hair hanging loosely down to her shoulders, untouched by the howling wind, her surgical gown gently draped across her shoulders. She took another half step and leaned forward, positioning herself at eye level with Xavier.

It was only then he realized that the collage of motes

above her head had vanished. "She felt nothing," Sarah said in a whisper that Xavier somehow heard easily above the scream of the air. "The transition between this world and the next quick and painless."

Again Xavier tried to close his eyes, but his lids remained pried back. Tears welled in his eyes.

Sarah turned, holding up both hands, a sputtering ball of plasma appearing in the right, and a wispy ball spitting tendrils of vapor in her left. Liquid crystal erupted out of the corrugated-plate floor around Sarah's feet, gushing up, spewing to the back of the craft, waves lapping around the opening where the tail section had ripped away, sealing the massive hole. At the same time the howl of the wind ceased, and the spinning in Xavier's ear and the throbbing of his head stopped, as the craft righted itself.

He fell forward, hitting the soft crystal floor, rolling, sitting up, facing the cockpit. It had been resealed with the same material that had filled the rear rupture. He felt his stomach drop and sagged to the floor as the craft suddenly accelerated upward.

"Forty-two incoming and tracking!" shouted Krew, the lisp and alien tones gone from his voice, the timbre in the voice familiar to Xavier, childhood memories of an older brother, confident and protective, full of promise and strength, having morphed with the lemur's.

"Che?" called Xavier.

Then the craft vanished.

"Ahhhhh!" screamed Xavier, looking down, nothing between him and the gray clouds. He dropped, pushing his face against something unseen, giving, and warm, filled with a gentle pulse. He pushed himself up, the flat of his palms firm against a floor that was now as invisible as the cockpit walls had been, the entire plane transparent, only the occupants visible, hurtling up through the clouds at near-supersonic speeds. He looked down to see other craft closing in, moving up at them from all directions.

He sensed movement from behind and spun around.

Sarah had both arms raised high, a wall of sputtering plasma to her right, and a wall of frigid air, spewing mist, to her left. He felt a tug, gentle at first, then stiff and unyielding, as if an invisible hand had grabbed him around the waist and was pulling him toward her, his head feeling even more of the force, his vision distorting as his eyeballs bulged outward.

The entire craft groaned, shimmying, then gave a massive lurch and shudder as Sarah raised her arms, the palms of her hands just touching. The walls of plasma and ice exploded far past the confines of the transparent craft, jutting outward, moving in jagged planes, the air itself twisting, clouds erupting in faceted sheets of reflected light, the world all around them crystallizing in cracked shards of fire and ice.

The shards ran for kilometers.

The nearing craft struck the faceted sheets of plasma and ice, exploding, splintering, balls of greasy fire erupting from the impact points, suddenly all around them a maelstrom of fire and smoke as more than 40 craft hit the impossible walls that had sprung from either side of Sarah.

Then she lowered her hands.

The sheets of plasma and ice began to fall, crashing upon themselves, mixed with the flaming debris of the destroyed aircraft, everything quickly swallowed in the clouds below.

"We're not going down."

Xavier turned. Simon was standing, looking down between his feet at the receding clouds, then out at the pale blue horizon just starting to curve in the distance. Then the craft was back, soft white walls surrounding them, the transition so abrupt that Xavier lost his balance, despite the fact that he was seated on the floor, and toppled over backward.

"Trajectory on course for orbital insertion," said Krew from the cockpit, again speaking in Che's voice.

Simon was still standing, hands grabbing on to handholds that met his fingers as he touched the side of the craft. "This is an aircraft," he said, tugging on the handholds as if to emphasize the point. "The engines need air to breathe. We can't go into orbit."

Krew turned in his seat. "The jets have been inoperative from the moment of the first attack," he said. "We're no longer being powered by air-breathing jet engines." He pointed forward, toward a horizon that was purple-black and curved.

Xavier looked. Far in front of them hung a sheet of plasma, cut at off-kilter angles, and twisting as if being wrung out like a wet towel, its actual size impossible to tell, anything from meters to kilometers in size, since he couldn't tell its distance. He was certain that another twisted sheet hung somewhere behind the craft, a frozen one dripping misty tendrils. The craft sat nestled between the two things, at the gravitational sweet spot, being lifted into orbit.

"It's Sarah," said Xavier. He pushed himself up and stood, staggering over to where Christina had been sitting. He dropped into the seat, the tendril restraints wrapping around him. As his head pitched forward he began to sob.

Their craft did not so much land as crash, hitting so hard that the hull cracked at midfuselage, spilling out the tightly packed dinosaurs. Kristensen observed this without much interest, still strapped in his seat, oriented in such a way that he was forced to look at the squirming pile of dinosaurs.

He could not feel his legs.

His head felt as if it were full of broken glass, clattering back and forth, tearing and shredding at his brain. The pile of dinosaurs turned red, and he knew that the vessels in the back of his eyes had begun to hemorrhage.

"What is it?" asked Drom.

Kristensen didn't know or care. His right eyelid closed. Suddenly something pushed at his nose and chin, pressing his head up and back against the headrest. He was looking out of the ruptured craft, at clouds that were no longer clouds but crystallized structures ablaze in rainbow light, some coated in a patina of plasma discharge and others frosty, spinning tendrils of rainbows carried away in the high winds. And these no-longer-quite-clouds were falling from the sky.

"That," said Drom, pushing his head back farther. "What is it, and how did it bring down my planes?" Again Kristensen felt his head being bounced against the head restraint. "Ask the Swirl what has happened to us."

Kristensen couldn't ask, unable to form the words, but knowing that even if he could, it would be useless. The Swirl had fled, vacated his brain, like a rat fleeing a sinking ship. He could not move, and realized that he'd stopped breathing. Between the clouds that were no longer clouds, and the blurred outline of Drom's fingers still pressed against his face, he watched the Swirl float into his line of sight, its crystal facets as bright and shiny as ever, despite what had just happened, despite the clouds that were no longer clouds.

The sky fell.

Kristensen wondered what it would feel like when the sky fell on you.

It was his last thought—he was dead before the falling sky reached him.

Sutherland, Akandi, and Bill watched as the destruction lessened. The last shards fell from the sky, littering the ground for kilometers in all directions, shattering when they struck, recoiling in fountains of crystal motes.

Akandi looked away from the image of the ground, first at the burning embers of what had been Drom's attack fleet, then up, to the one lone craft still flying, the speck arcing high, cutting far above where he knew it should be flying.

"She did it," said Sutherland, as he pulled the Virts from his face. "Their craft is now on track for orbital insertion."

"It's an *air*craft," said Bill, sitting on the floor and swatting his right shoulder. "What is powering it?"

"No one is quite sure," Sutherland said. "What we are sure of is that the moment Sarah's craft was attacked, she lost both engines. It has no obvious way to power itself in the air *or* space."

"Isn't it obvious?"

Both turned to Akandi.

"You're an excellent actor," Akandi said to Sutherland. "But playing *stupid* just doesn't work for you."

Sutherland smiled. "What could you possibly mean?" he asked.

"It's your Zero Point," said Akandi. He had never believed in the Zero Point concept, but could not ignore what they'd seen when Drom had first found Sarah, and certainly could not ignore what she'd just done, creating sheets of tremendous energy that had vaporized most of Drom's attack craft. But there was even more to it than that. She was not just pulling energy out of subvacuum levels. The quantum magic she'd worked was much more. "By tapping into Zero Point, she's been able to tap into quantum gravity and trade off the tremendous energy she can access into the formation and manipulation of gravitational fields."

"Do you really think that's possible?" asked Sutherland, sounding almost whimsical.

Akandi frowned. "None of us in this room are stupid," he said angrily. "She has full access to the most fundamental regions of space-time, right down to where the fabric of reality is a froth and all forces and particles are in a constant state of change and exchange." He paused, again looking over at the projected scene, so many square kilometers covered in what almost looked like snow. He knew it was some sort of geometrical residue, an artifact of the tremendous sheets of energy she'd pulled out of the quantum void. "She's moved so far past us, so far past the Swirl."

Sutherland slowly nodded.

"Which is just what both of you had hoped for, what all this has been about."

Bill shrugged and walked forward, batting at his shirt. "Infinitely more than us," he said. "But there's no way of knowing if it will be enough, if she'll be able to handle what we find when we wake on the other side."

"Wake?" asked Akandi, not liking at all the way Bill had said that.

"We're on our way to Alpha Centauri A and the Incubator," said Sutherland. The landscape being displayed flitted and rolled, replaced with the Sun, the massive Jet jutting out from it, with the Earth nestled within the cone of plasma, tendrils from the cone feeding Petals. And something more. Earth had two moons hanging in its wake, just as the Earth hung in the Sun's wake; one was much larger than the other, but both were small compared to the moon that the Earth should have had. Both of these new moons were also connected to the cone through wispy tendrils.

"Phobos *and* Amalthea," said Akandi.

"We want *everyone* coming with us," said Sutherland. He walked up to Akandi, crowding him. "It's a military campaign, and we've included as many weapons and as many contingency plans as possible since we can't be altogether certain of the capabilities and objectives of the enemy. It may be that all they want is their little creatures, and we'll be more than happy to bring those to them. But if they want more, we'll next offer up the Swirl. And if that doesn't make them happy, then we'll just have to fight."

"And Sarah is your weapon?" asked Akandi.

Sutherland nodded. "My daughter."

Akandi managed not to shudder; at that moment, everything was so clear, Sutherland's motivations and self-image so apparent. He had sacrificed his daughter in the hope that she would save humanity. That made Sarah the messiah, elevating her *father* to the status of God.

"There is only one Allah," said Akandi.

"Couldn't agree with you more," Sutherland said. "But until we meet Him, and He decides to save humanity's collective ass, I'm the nearest thing we've got to Him."

"We need to get started," said Bill.

Sutherland blinked and stepped back. "Yes," he said. "The first order of business is to get Phobos in orbit so we can lock ourselves down for the journey."

"Sleep?" said Akandi, looking over at Bill.

"I suppose," said Sutherland. He pointed at the Sun and the Jet. "It's accelerating at a steady one-tenth gee, and analysis indicates that is about the maximum permissible. Much faster, and the minor geological effects that we've been experiencing would be much more extreme, with the boundaries between tectonic plates experiencing total rupture, and the resulting magma and gas flows flatlining all terrestrial ecosystems in a matter of days. The Alphans would not go to all this trouble, millions of years of planning and manipulation, just to be delivered a dead world. So a tenth gee is the maximum acceleration."

Sutherland snapped his fingers, and the Sun shrunk to a pinprick, while at the far end of the room several other pinpricks winked on—three of them. Akandi knew right away that they represented the Alpha Centauri system, with the nearest pinprick burning in a dull red: the dim little red dwarf the nearest star to Earth, Proxima Centauri. Beyond it, more than one-tenth of a light-year away, was the bright yellow Alpha Centauri A; and hugging closely next to it, the orange-yellow Alpha Centauri B. Between Earth's Sun and Alpha Centauri A ran a pale blue line, above which at meter intervals hung little icons denoting what Akandi could see showed position, velocity, and elapsed time, along with a fourth number that he couldn't figure out.

"A 4.3-light-year trip," said Sutherland, pointing midway between the two stars. "That tells the tale right there. Under a steady one-tenth-gee acceleration, the Sun will reach the halfway point of the journey in 6.4 years, and have reached a velocity of nearly 70 percent the speed of light."

Akandi felt himself nod, seeing those numbers, despite the fact that he could not imagine any object moving at an appreciable fraction of the speed of light. "And what is 2.3

percent?" he asked, looking at the last number below the midpoint icon.

"The Jet consists primarily of hyperrelativistic streams of protons, whose effective mass has been increased by a factor of thirty owing to those relativistic effects, giving a lot more punch per ion," said Sutherland. "But you still need an appreciable number of those hyperrelativistic protons shooting out of the Jet in order to get the Sun moving in the opposite direction."

Akandi understood. "The Sun will be losing mass."

Sutherland nodded. "It will take 2.3 percent of its mass blown out by the Jet to get us to the halfway mark. At that point the Jet will rotate to the other side of the Sun, while we will still stay behind it, the Sun shielding us against relativistic impacts of any interstellar debris. The Jet firing on the opposite side of the Sun will act as a brake, taking another 6.4 years to reduce its velocity to zero and depositing us right at Alpha Centauri A and the Incubator."

"Thirteen years to reach Alpha Centauri," said Akandi.

"That's it," said Bill. "Certainly not much time in the scheme of things, and I'm sure an amazing fellow like you could find plenty to keep you from getting bored during the trip, but these ships were never built with the intent of actually shipping *live* cargo."

"What?" asked Akandi.

"Like our friend the Sun," said Bill. "As originally designed, the vast bulk of these ships were fuel, vessels of matter and antimatter. The actual cargo transported, those creatures and their required support biosystems, were reduced to their most compact form."

"Asleep, in some sort of cryosuspension?" asked Akandi,

as images of chilled bodies and bubbling liquid nitrogen filled his head.

"Nothing so crude," said Bill.

"Not to mention the prospects of freezer burn," said Sutherland, laughing.

"Onboard cargo systems will disassemble you atom by atom, store those atoms in the various vats of elemental sources, while *you*, defined by the position and type of all those atoms, will be stored in a memory buffer, then reassembled once we reach Alpha Centauri A."

"Impossible," said Akandi.

Bill smiled. "Not impossible," he said. "It's *science*." He turned and looked at Sutherland. "I don't know about you, but before I go under, I'm going to request some editing be done during reanimation and do a deep purge on these damn phobias of Mears's." He slapped at his right shoulder. "Damn these spiders," he said. "How about you?" he asked.

Sutherland shook his head.

"Quite the opportunity," he said, turning to Akandi.

"That won't be necessary," said Sutherland, speaking before Akandi had the chance to refuse, finding the entire concept of being torn apart atom by atom already too frightening, certain that what would be put back together at the other end could not possibly be he, and certainly not if he actually chose to make modifications. "We wouldn't want to see our good friend Akandi changed in the slightest."

"He's afraid," said Iyoon, hovering over Sutherland. *"All physiology was nominal until the moment that it was suggested that you might make modifications in yourself."*

Akandi gritted his teeth, certain that he knew exactly what that meant. He'd had his suspicions ever since Sutherland had spun his tale of items found buried on the moon, but now he felt certain.

Datacube.

The image within it had shown them all at the table, a point now in the past, but for decades it had been a future that Sutherland had steered toward, a future that he knew he could not escape. Sutherland had made a point of telling him that the future now held no such arbitrary boundary conditions, that anything was possible, the future unwritten. And now Sutherland insisted that he not make any modifications to himself, that he not tamper with his DNA.

Why? He knew there could only be one reason for that.

Sutherland had something else from the past, something more than just the datacube, something that showed Akandi as he was now with *unaltered* DNA. Akandi looked at Sutherland and nodded at Bill. "I suppose everyone could stand a bit of improvement."

"No!" shouted Sutherland. "There will be no modifications for anyone. We need to minimize all risks, and enhancements and modifications are just that, unnecessary risks! Not a single gene modified, not a single base pair altered. There will be no DNA tampering."

"Terrified," said Iyoon.

Akandi didn't need Iyoon to tell him that. He smiled at Sutherland, knowing at that moment that Sutherland had found a sample of his unaltered DNA along with that datacube buried in the wall of a lunar crater.

From 65 million years in the past.

What he did not know was just how much of his DNA had been found—a few fragments, or an entire body's worth.

Chapter 31

Simon looked through the transparent nose of the craft, up at the slowly approaching Amalthea, a golden sphere flaring in reflected sunlight. He saw it, but was not thinking about it, was not wondering what mysteries lay within it, of the other Clingers it must contain, of an alien craft that only a few days before had been skipping along the cloud tops of Jupiter.

Certainly mysteries.

But not *the* mystery.

He glanced back into the craft. Xavier sat in his seat, head lowered, his body occasionally shuddering. Tears no longer fell from his cheeks, but streaks were still visible across the front of his shirt. Simon had never experienced such a loss, at least that he knew of, reminding him that he probably had some sort of life before they'd tried to force the Swirl into his head, before he'd shut down and been warehoused in a coma ward. He wondered if this was how his own parents had felt when he had been *lost*.

It was one more mystery about his past that would never be solved. He looked back at Xavier, knowing that Christina and Padmini being ejected from the craft was certainly no mystery—just a simple consequence of physics, a combination of the craft's velocity, air-pressure differential, and immense drag of a body hanging outside the craft, all leading to the only possible outcome.

Christina and Padmini fell.

But there was something more. "A pattern," whispered Simon, looking past Xavier at Sarah, standing in the back of the craft, stiff and still, crystal tendrils from her fingertips running into the adjacent bulkhead. Despite the fact that they were in orbit, *falling* around the Earth, they were not weightless. "She can manipulate, even generate gravitational fields," he said, looking back through the transparent cockpit. Between them and Amalthea, almost invisible in the reflected glare of that moon, hung the twisted sheet of fire. He suspected it was a ripple in space-time, an amplification of subquantum reality brought into the world of moons and spacecraft.

He turned toward Krew, whose fingers rested on the control panel, limp and unmoving. Simon was hesitant to read the creature's body language, but he seemed to be radiating indifference and powerlessness. Critical in initially getting the craft off the ground, he was now simply along for the ride.

"Your craft and your people," said Simon to Krew, pointing out at Amalthea. "But you're not bringing us to them." He pointed back into the craft without actually turning. "It's Sarah who wants us here."

Krew smiled, his thin lips pulling taut against his flat face. "All her," he said. And then he pointed at Amalthea. "Not my people," he said. "I have no people. I'm no longer Clinger or human, but a melding. Krew is gone, and so is Che. I'm what remains, so much less than the sum of the parts."

Simon nodded, but was not quite willing to believe what Krew said.

"She pulled this craft out of Earth's gravitational well," said Simon, who then paused and thought very carefully about what he would say next. "But she couldn't keep a hold on Christina and pull her back inside."

"Obviously not," said Krew, looking down through the cockpit's transparent floor and at the bands of dark clouds below. "Christina and Padmini fell."

No, thought Simon. If Sarah had really wanted her back inside the craft, then she would have pulled her in. *Pattern suddenly coalesced*. If Christina fell, it was because Sarah wanted her to fall. And if that were true, then why had she been holding on to her in the first place? Images and thoughts clicked together, random bits and pieces suddenly making perfect sense.

"Christina's not dead!" Simon moved back into the craft, toward Xavier, but did not look at him, focusing instead on the interface that Christina had been operating, which now lay in the seat next to Xavier.

"She fell," said Xavier in a whisper.

Simon shook his head as he reached down for the interface and sat down next to Xavier. Plucking out a crystalline tendril, he pushed it into his right eye, now sharing the interface with Xavier. "She was *pushed*."

"What?" said Xavier, straightening up, looking about the craft, then focusing on Simon. "I saw her fall when Sarah lost her grip."

"Padmini managed to hold on," said Simon, now with both hands manipulating the virtual field in front of them, a landscape of infinite cornfields, pockmarked here and there with shards of volcanic debris, the fields themselves tinted in a haze of crystal motes, the remnants of the sheets of fire and ice that Sarah had created. "But Sarah, who has lifted this entire craft right off of Earth, couldn't manage to hold on?" he asked.

Xavier slowly turned, looking past Simon toward the

rear of the craft. "You think Sarah *deliberately* let go of Christina?"

Simon did not look at him but stayed focused on the landscape, integrating signals from the other dinosaur craft, from a few geo eyes that could see in high enough spectrums to peer through the smoke clouds, and tapping into the rising buzz that spilled out of Phobos. He nodded.

"She let go of her!" shouted Xavier, taking a step toward Sarah.

"Got her," said Simon.

"Christina?" said Xavier, turning, stepping back, pushing up against the display field.

Two figures stood in what had been a field of corn but was now just a swatch of charred cornstalks.

"Locking," said Simon, dragging every available photon, every electronic snip he could dig out of the neo-Void to generate the composite image.

A face of shadow and haze rippled, solidifying.

"Christina!" screamed Xavier, suddenly running through the virtual display and up to the cockpit, reaching out, grabbing onto Krew's shoulders, and shaking him. "Turn us around and take us down. Christina is alive."

Simon disengaged, pulling on the crystalline filament, feeling the spiderweb tendrils slither out of his eye. "I don't think that is part of her plan," he said.

"We will go back," said Xavier, still shaking Krew's shoulder, the Clinger not responding. "We *will* go back," he said.

"How?" asked Simon.

"Krew will pilot us down," said Xavier, again shaking his shoulders but getting no response. Krew watched Amalthea as it filled the cockpit's field of view.

"He has no control of this craft," said Simon. "Sarah is

the one who brought us here and obviously wants us in Amalthea, as she just as obviously wanted Christina down on Earth."

"No!" shouted Xavier, letting go of Krew and turning, running down the center of the craft toward Sarah.

Simon didn't even have time to shout.

Xavier got to within almost a meter of Sarah, then was enveloped in a haze of what looked like swirling milk, lifted off the floor, and slammed back up the plane. He hit the floor and rolled, his wrapped body stopping at the cockpit entrance. The shimmering milky cocoon wrapped around him emitted a crackling sound, spraying away in a shower of snowflakelike motes that quickly disappeared.

Xavier hacked and sputtered, then pushed himself up and looked up at Simon. "We need to get to Christina," he said, and started to move again toward Sarah, stopping only when Simon reached out and grabbed him.

"Not that way," he said.

"Docking sequence has begun," said Krew.

Simon looked past Xavier, and at the golden wall beyond the cockpit, and at the black pinprick in its center that began to spin in a spiral, eating away at Amalthea's perfect hull.

*Christina stared up into the sky at the bands of ash-*heavy clouds. She tripped through a wide range of spectrums, from the deep infrared, where the clouds burned in shades of amber so textured and rich that they looked to be constructed from streams of cascading magma, to well past the ultraviolet, the sky almost totally black except for brief pulses of crackling purple lightning, the discharge from high-flying craft, and the occasional leakage through upper-level atmospheric breaches, where ozone was being chewed away by the sulfuric acid in the high-flying volcanic ash.

She knew she saw far past the spectral limits of her eyes.

Of what *had* been her eyes—before Sarah had pushed something through her head, something both incredibly hot and cold, flecks of impossibility, a tangle of neurons around it already meshing, making connections, probing, modifying, changing her.

"Lucky."

Christina turned, looking down at Padmini, who sat on her knees. "If those seats hadn't been equipped with emergency sails, there wouldn't be much more to us than damp depressions in a cornfield."

Christina slowly shook her head.

There'd been no parasail in the seat, despite the fact that it had been the seat material that had been used to form the parasail. She remembered, not having given any actual instructions, but just expressing the desire, the mental picture of a parasail in her head.

And then her body had reacted, knowing what to do, the response no more under her conscious control than her body's ability to transform carbohydrates into burnable cellular fuel.

"Are you hurt?" asked Padmini, almost whispering.

Christina tilted her head, watching Padmini's moving lips, knowing she was talking to Kali.

"You're spewing a wide spectrum of very unusual pheromones," said Padmini, her nostrils flaring. "And your body seems to be pushed into overdrive, pulse and respiration ramping, even body temperature up by several degrees." She reached out, touching Christina's shoulder. "You need to sit. I think you're going into shock."

Christina looked down at Padmini's hand. She wanted to

tell Padmini that while she was not in shock, she was definitely not okay. Her body was in a process of modification, of improving its efficiency, of the shards that Sarah had lodged in her head fully interfacing, optimizing the organic shell that housed them.

She wanted to communicate all those things.

But she didn't speak. Instead, she felt whisker-thin tendrils of crystal erupt from her shoulder, penetrate Padmini's fingertips, then race up and through her hand and arm, entwining nerves, slamming into her backbone, squirming through the pliable disks between vertebrae, locking onto her spinal column and snaking up and into her brain.

"Out!"

Christina and Padmini fell to the ground but remained connected through the hard linkage of shoulder to hand.

"Out!"

Christina and Padmini looked up.

Kali hung above them, nearly 3 meters tall, her eyes blood red, her teeth gnashing. *"Get out!"* she screamed, dropping down from the air as she raised her right hand, the fingernails flashing, growing, transforming into claws, the hand lunging toward Christina's face.

"No," said Christina in a whisper.

Kali flew back, doubled over as if by an invisible fist, the impact folding her in half and hurling her several meters back, dropping her to the ground.

"Stop it," said Padmini in a mumble.

Kali pushed herself up, her feet pawing at the ground, clawed toenails digging deep, virtual furrows. *"Get out of her!"* she screamed.

"No!" shouted Padmini, holding up a hand, waving it at Kali. "She is not a threat."

"An invasion!" screamed Kali, so loudly that the muscles

beneath her black skin shuddered, and blood leaked from her eyes. *"She is inside of you and can access me. Can see everything."*

Padmini turned, looking down at her hand. The tips of her fingers were welded onto Christina's shoulder by crystal stalks.

Christina felt Padmini from the inside, nothing denied, nothing hidden, everything open to her. "I think it can be removed," said Christina. "It is incredibly deep, hiding at the edges of your perception and thoughts, watching us."

"No!" screamed Kali.

Padmini raised a hand, shaking it at Kali. "She's not talking about you," she said.

"So afraid," said Christina. "Out of control."

"Take it," said Padmini. "Please."

Lightning of infinite colors flashed, thunder rolling through Christina, the deep rumble shaking her, rattling her at a cellular level. Panic signals poured out of Padmini, out of her head, down her arm, and into her fingertips.

The Swirl popped into the air, accompanied by a large crack of thunder. It spun at an incredible rate, spitting beams of light, a few shards actually peeling away, flung out into the burned cornfield.

"So deep," said Christina, feeling the Swirl burrow farther into Padmini, hiding far behind her conscious thoughts, the electrical twitterings that defined it damping, going silent, as it pushed deeper and deeper into the background, apparently willing to lose all sense of awareness, willing to die rather then be pulled out.

"So frightened and alone," said Christina, feeling the microscopic tendrils she'd pushed deep into Padmini's brain, tasting individual molecules, sampling neurotransmitter after neurotransmitter, measuring and modifying the

electrical potentials across every synapse and along each
axon. She chased the Swirl, cornering it, trapping it.

The Swirl blurred, its crystal facets gone, colors merging,
its entire structure glowing white, edges fuzzing, losing
structure, as awareness slipped away.

"Please."

The voice was from beyond, out of the Void, from the
bulk of the Swirl that existed well outside the single node
buried inside Padmini's mind.

So much potential, thought Christina. *But so constrained by
those who built it.* She smiled and, reaching out with her
other hand, pointed at the fading blur of the spinning Swirl,
so pale, translucent, almost gone. She opened her hand, and
crystal filaments erupted from her fingertips, shooting out,
enveloping the almost nonexistent Swirl.

She pulled it in, the ghostly shimmer hovering in the
palm of her hand. When she formed a fist, the crystal facets
of this faded node of the Swirl shattered, then imploded,
and Christina's fist was suddenly empty. And as she focused
on the nothingness in her hand, she barely noticed Kali
lunging at her, wrapping her clawed, too-large hands
around her head and slamming her to the ground.

Akandi waited his turn to die.

Bill was first, then it would be his turn. Sutherland said
that he would go last, only after Phobos had left orbit and
was parked in Earth's wake, with its matter-antimatter conduits safely aligned, gulping down the plasma tendrils from
the Jet.

Akandi sat naked on a shelf of rock, shivering despite the
fact that the room was hot and humid, watching Bill die.
Bill lay in a vat of semitransparent pink sludge, as a bank of

high-speed UV lasers played across him, bathing him in a metal azure glow. Peeled layer by layer, disassembled by bond breakers suspended in the pink sludge, with the position of each molecule, and even key atoms, recorded by the locator lasers, Bill slowly disintegrated.

The process would take several hours to complete.

A small herd of dinosaurs, little creatures with feathery fur and long delicate arms and fingers obviously designed for the task at hand, swarmed around the vat, hands, tongues, and snouts pressed up against a myriad of crystal facets jutting from the floor, objects that Akandi assumed to be the controls for the vat.

Bill was alive but not conscious, the brain being the last major part of anatomy to be peeled, taken down while synapses still sparked signals, the pink sludge not only capable of severing bonds but keeping the physiological and cellular machinery of Bill's body going right up to the point where there was no more Bill.

Then the residue in the bottom of the tank would be dumped, seared in a high-temperature flash, and constituent atoms collected and stored, only to be called upon when the journey ended in 13 years, when Bill was to be reanimated, rebuilt molecule by molecule, self-assembled by a series of organic chemical reactions guided by the positioning lasers.

Death and resurrection.

"And where does my soul go?" asked Akandi. *"To heaven when my body dies, to then be returned to my reanimated body, or will the thing that walks out of that vat be everything that I am, except for my soul?"*

Iyoon hovered in front of him. *"You've seen the recordings. Those reanimated have no sense of displacement or change, only awareness of falling into a dreamless sleep, then reawaking. None of the test subjects commented about the lack of a soul."*

Akandi nodded, not getting any comfort from Iyoon's words or the recordings he'd seen, certain that a soulless thing would not have the desire or even the ability to miss its soul, any more than a rock would know that it didn't possess one.

"*I won't do it,*" he said once more.

"*And what is your choice?*" asked Iyoon still again.

Akandi had no answer. If he refused, he'd be forced, rendered unconscious and dumped in the vat. He sat naked in the middle of Phobos, under the complete and total control of Sutherland, with no way to escape, no allies to call upon, and no way to flee whatever future Sutherland had glimpsed. His DNA was destined to be buried on the moon, stored for 65 million years. Of that he now had little doubt. He did not know how to fight Sutherland, and definitely had no idea how to fight the flow of reality, to escape something that had already happened.

His DNA, quite possibly a piece of him, maybe all of him, mummified and stored, had been found on the moon, and Sutherland was doing all that had to be done to make sure the future fed the past and that the past fed the future.

An endless cycle that could not be broken.

"*Take us back to Earth!*"

Sarah stood, fixed and unresponsive, crystal-coated eyes wide and staring.

"She doesn't even see you," said Simon, holding on to him.

Xavier fought against Simon for just a moment, then let his body sag, his head tilting down. "We have to get Christina. She's not safe down there."

"Maybe not *perfectly* safe down there," said Simon. "But

probably safer than we are here. Down there she can run, can hide, and she has Padmini with her."

"But she needs me," said Xavier.

"And you certainly need her," said Simon. "Sarah protected us from the attack below. If she wanted to hurt us, she could have let the dinosaurs do it, or she could have done anything to us whenever she wanted."

Xavier focused, listening to Simon's voice, knowing that what he said was right. If Sarah had wanted to harm them, she could have done it at any time. And he knew that she had let go of Christina, wanting her out of the craft and back down on Earth. *But why?* Xavier lowered his head. "I couldn't help her," he said in a whisper.

The corner of Simon's mouth curled in a smile. "She's a lot like you, Xavier, stubborn, knowing just how things should be done. Everything you've taught her, everything you've given her, will now be of help to her."

Xavier nodded, wanting to believe him.

"She's *your* daughter. Don't be surprised if she figures out a way to get to us, to save *us.*"

Xavier smiled and wrapped a hand around the back of Simon's neck, giving him a slight shake, then released him. "I watched you for years," he said. "They shipped you into the Ag Co-Op in a coma tube. It took years to wake you, Mears slicing into the back of your brain, his equipment beating at you from the inside, rewiring you. I read every report, scanned every snip, and watched you move from a drooling, unconscious lump to become *the* major torment in Mears's life. I knew every detail of your creation and their Post-Point experiment. I saw everything, but somehow never saw the most important thing of all."

Reaching forward, Xavier gently touched Simon on the chest.

"I never saw what was inside there."

Simon opened his mouth to respond, then his eyes grew wide, and he stumbled backward, pushed by the blast of an explosion. "Sarah's gone!" he shouted. "Vanished. I saw her shimmer, sort of fold on herself. When she turned, it was as if her body had no width, so she was simply gone. Then the explosion."

Xavier sat up, staring at where Sarah had been. "For the last day I'd seen her make subtle shifts, as if she were oscillating about in time."

"She's no longer human," said Simon.

Before Xavier could respond, the craft's outside door opened.

Bodies poured in, small bodies, big heads, faces dominated by all-black eyes. Above each one, almost touching the tops of their heads, hovered a Swirl. "Clingers!" shouted Xavier.

Then the altered lemurs swarmed over Xavier and Simon as the flock of Swirl buzzed, spinning fast, everything bathed in rainbow shafts. Xavier struggled for just a moment, as little hands grabbed at him, then he felt something cold and soft pressed against the side of his face. The inside of the craft seemed to dim and melt, the walls giving way. Unable to move, he watched, his head angled in such a direction that he could see into the cockpit as Clinger hands passed him forward.

Krew sat in his seat.

Clingers descended over him, but they did not pick him up, did not pass him over their heads. Dozens grabbed him and started to pull, leaning in and biting with their sharp little teeth.

"Che!" Xavier managed to shout.

They tore Krew apart, ripping meat from bones and stuffing the bloody bits into their mouths. And then he felt nothing, unconsciousness rolling over him.

Christina walked, bending slightly forward, her hand open, palm facing the ground. She tingled in an all-over body hum and kept her eyes partially closed to limit input, throttling down the torrent of information flooding into her. She focused her attention on the underside of her hand, as it passed a meter above the stubble of broken stalks.

Concentrating.

And she could *see* it, her reference of location shifting from her eyes to the palm of her hand, individual skin cells sensing the play of light and heat, chemical transport, respiration, flow of blood, all integrating into a picture, the stubble of corn much closer, the small rocks and ash, the few remaining motes of Sarah's clouds.

She could see it, sense it, the image filling her head.

Blink.

Perception and sense of central self again returned to her eyes. Kali hung in front of her, snarling, waving a clawed hand. *"I was invited,"* thought Christina, feeling the words projected toward Padmini, and from there, to Kali.

"Not by me," said Kali, who then vanished in a massive plume of blood.

Proximity effect, thought Christina. Not as intense or clear as being in physical contact with Padmini, but clear enough. As long as she stayed within a few meters of Padmini she could access Kali, and through her, the newly sprouting Void.

And inside her head burned a fragment of CUSP.

But it did not hurt, did not reach out and pull her under. It lurked behind heavy walls, a structure put in place by Sarah, allowing her access to what lay within it but not letting CUSP escape, to explode outward and take her over.

As it had done to Sarah.

That much she could sense, could remember from her contact with Sarah, a process of almost instantaneous evolution, taking her so far from what it was to be human, the process with a will of its own, like gravity pulling you down to the Earth, a fundamental law of nature that couldn't be denied.

"We've covered nearly 20 kilometers in the last 3 hours," said Padmini.

Christina looked toward the east. The corn was mostly intact here, Phobos more than 50 kilometers behind them. Not that far in the distance, less then 10 kilometers away, the white wall of the North–South Ring rose, an impenetrable barrier.

"Far enough," said Christina, who stopped walking and lowered herself between rows of broken corn, kneeling, facing west, knowing that it was almost time.

"How can you be so certain?" asked Padmini, standing next to her. A pistol was in her hand, the barrel pointing at the western horizon. That pistol was as much a part of Padmini's attire as her pants or boots. *Probably even more,* thought Christina, certain that Padmini would be more than willing to lose her boots or pants before that pistol.

"Maybe it can't even lift off after having landed. It's so damn big."

Christina nodded. It was big. Even at 50 kilometers away, and through air heavy with ash and haze, the glistening hull sparkled like a beacon riding above the western horizon. "It will launch. It's off-loaded its cargo, and the crew will want to be in space for the journey, where it will be safe."

Kali winked in. *"A craft is moving in our direction,"* she said, pointing toward the north.

Padmini did a quick turn, a full 360. "Nothing defensible," she said, then dropped to the ground, pulled the long knife from her belt, and stabbed it into the ground, quickly pulling it back and prying out a large clod of red soil. "We need to dig down, get low."

Christina stood, shaking her head. "You don't want to express a defensive posture with this one. He understands strength and submission. The proper tone must be set from the moment we meet."

"He?" asked Padmini, still digging with her knife but not as furiously.

"Drom," said Christina. "Their leader, who attacked us before, the one that Sarah forced into a retreat." The craft was visible, dropping quickly.

Padmini stopped digging, looked up at the quickly approaching craft, then sheathed her knife and pulled out her pistol. "If it is him," she said, "you're right about what we'll need to do."

The craft hit hard and fast, kicking up a wall of shattered cornstalks and red dust.

Christina started walking toward it even before it had stopped skidding forward, Padmini trotting up next to her, both pistols pulled. Christina glanced over at her and the guns, knowing that even if she could get off a few shots, a couple of dead dinosaurs would not alter the overall equation of the encounter. But she did not tell Padmini to put them away; they were a part of the woman, an extension of her strength and confidence.

And that *was* important.

The gangplank jutted out the side of the craft. Dinosaurs streamed out, once again led by the slightly taller one—Drom. The man who had been with them before was not there. Their weapon staffs were all angled toward her, the tips sputtering an azure plasma discharge.

"Surrender," said Drom, pointing to his left and right, several dinosaurs dropping weapons and running forward.

Padmini raised both pistols and stepped in front of Christina. "Me first!" she said, as she pulled the triggers, the guns firing, and dirt kicked up in front of the advancing dinosaurs.

They didn't slow.

Padmini angled the pistols up, this time obviously aiming squarely at their chests. She almost had time to pull the triggers, but Christina stepped in front of her, pushed her arms down, and started walking forward. "Drom!" she shouted.

The advancing dinosaurs slowed but did not stop.

Christina took a deep breath, feeling her confidence slip, the adrenaline-induced bravado fading, as the image of a 16-year-old teenager facing several dozen weapon-wielding dinosaurs filled her inner eye. It was so ridiculous, and the outcome so obvious. Then she took a second breath and focused.

She'd given up once before, when she'd first discovered that the Sun was accelerating toward the Earth. She knew she did not have the luxury of making that mistake again—her father was far away.

"Surrender!" barked Drom once again.

And Christina almost panicked, almost let loose with what Sarah had slipped into her head. She could feel the power and potential of it. But she managed to ignore the twin shards in her head and the ability CUSP gave her to manipulate her environment. That immense power was somehow dehumanizing, distancing her from the core of herself.

For the briefest moment she wondered if this is what Sarah felt—*lost*.

She knew with complete certainty that she could lash out at Drom and reduce him and his troops into fundamental bits, leave nothing behind but a quickly dissipating cloud of ash. That would certainly solve the immediate problem.

But more was needed, so much more.

She focused on Drom and on what she thought her father would do if he stood here, naked and alone, without any of Sarah's powers at his disposal. She felt the words forming before she was even conscious of them, knowing she was speaking them but also knowing that they were not uniquely hers. She felt her father standing beside her.

"You will surrender to *me*!" she proclaimed as she stared directly at Drom, wanting to make this a one-on-one conflict and keep the rest of the dinosaurs in check. She'd dealt with enough animals to know that taking down the alpha was all that was really needed—the rest would submit if she could force Drom to submit.

Padmini lowered her weapons just a few millimeters. Christina, sensing Padmini's shock and surprise, turned her head just enough to give her a subtle nod, that slight tilt of the head instructing her to keep her pistols in check.

"Now!" demanded Christina.

Padmini smiled and shook her pistols at the dinosaurs, but her index fingers were no longer tensed against the triggers.

"Challenging me!" barked Drom.

Christina walked forward, deliberately ignoring the challenge, and instead looked past Drom and the dinosaurs, toward the craft. "I require transportation, and you will take me where I want to go."

Drom lowered his head, opened his snout wide, and launched himself.

Christina almost turned and ran, a panicked part of her suddenly realizing the position she'd put herself in—the fear was overwhelming. Drom ran forward, canting his head to the side, so that his open jaws could easily snap down on her neck. She saw all this with a clarity she'd never experienced before, and actually felt the teeth tearing into flesh, heard bones snap, blood gush, her vision darkening, her body falling lifelessly to the ground.

Move.

She thought of jumping to the left, but did not. The image of her jumping filled her head, feet in the air, body moving, all of it taking less than a fraction of a second, but Drom easily able to track her, correcting his direction, taking the last few steps before his jaws snapped around her throat.

So she didn't jump.

Instead she *translated*. The barriers shielding her from CUSP lowered, strengthening its integration to her. Slipping, the world around her blurred: dinosaurs, corn, even Padmini streaking in bands of color. She translated, falling just a fraction of a second into the future, finding herself where she would have been had she actually moved.

Discontinuity.

A shift in space by more than a meter. But she had not moved in space, only in time, occupying that place where she would have jumped to if time had moved smoothly. But it hadn't. Nearly half a second had simply vanished, as she'd slipped by it, a twist in quantum uncertainty amplified out of the world of atoms and into the world of charging dinosaurs.

The twin shards of CUSP had enveloped her in a gauze of something beyond the normal slipstream of space and time. She did not understand how she did it, only that it worked, that Sarah had put the machinery in her head, allowing her to operate it.

Drom ran past her.

And as he did, she reached out, just touching his shoulder, interfacing, human fingers and dinosaur skin meshing into one. She dumped a massive electrical jolt, her fingertips burning.

Drom stiffened, his body seizing, his momentum carrying him forward, falling, hitting the ground snoutfirst, eating dirt and cornstalks. He twitched, fingers and toes spasming. He urinated over himself and vomited, a gray gush of thick liquid erupting from his mouth, spewing across the red soil and burned corn.

His nictitating membranes fluttered.

Christina looked down at her hand, at the fingertips that stung and were beginning to redden, but didn't waste time trying to figure out how she'd unloaded the charge into Drom. She walked over to him, raised a foot, and brought it down hard on his throat.

"I need transport," she said.

Padmini smiled and holstered her pistols. "Now!" she shouted.

"Christina!"

Xavier screamed, feeling the word explode from his throat and out his mouth. His eyes were open, but he couldn't quite see, his brain not adequately engaged, the light and colors filling his vision not making sense, not having yet formed a picture.

"She will be fine."

Cohesion—light and shape almost understandable.

Xavier tried to run, but could not move, his body not responding, nothing below the neck under his control. He stood in the center of the dark cavern, surrounded by what appeared to be thousands of Clingers, all silent and unmoving, staring straight ahead, their large black eyes glistening, each with a Swirl turning above its head. In front of him, embedded in a wall, were what looked like dozens of transparent cylinders, all filled with slowly spinning pink gel. All were empty except for the two nearest him.

One contained what had been a body, not much remaining except for bones and a few thin strips of muscles and tendons.

"Christina?"

Skin gone, staring at him through the pink goo with lidless eyes.

"It's Simon. Christina is safe in Alabama."

Xavier didn't turn his head toward the voice at his left, but stared at Simon, realizing that the exposed muscle was foaming, being chewed away, the entire body bathed in a pink glow.

"Preparing for the journey."

Xavier turned his head. Krew sat perched on a platform next to him. Or at least what was left of Krew, just torso and head, with arms and legs gone, only bloody stumps remaining, his body listing to the left, right eye swollen shut, a large chunk of exposed skull, glistening white, visible through the ripped skin across his forehead.

"Oh, Che," said Xavier in a whisper, certain that if he

spoke any louder Krew would topple over. "Why?" he asked.

"Preservation of the species," he said, smiling, exposing the few sharp little teeth that remained in his bloody mouth. "Physically I was still like them, still Clinger, but when they interfaced me with the Swirl, they knew I was compromised. I was as much Che as I was Krew."

Xavier didn't know what to say and simply nodded.

"What remained of Che is here with me," he said, as his eyes rolled partially back in their sockets. "But most of him was gone when I began to interface, little sense of self left to fight the merging. Neither one of us full beings, *both* of us damaged years earlier by the Swirl, both of us nearly vacated of what we were, readying us for the time when we would come together, when we would bring Sarah here."

Xavier closed his eyes.

Papito had died, and the Swirl had attempted to invade Che, but Che had fought, willingly shutting down the extensive Tool enhancements the military had poured into his head, choosing death rather than slavery to the Swirl.

The battle had taken days, nearly a week.

And in the end they had believed Che had won, dying in the process, and the Swirl had fled back into the Void in search of another host. But now he knew the truth. The Swirl had let Che go, deliberately damaging him, preparing him for eventual merging with Krew.

Xavier slowly shook his head.

Krew had not stumbled into their cornfields to be found by Che. He'd been sent to find Che, knowing that a time would come when he would interface with Che—all this happening under the direction of the Swirl.

"Time to say good-bye," said Krew. "You have a long

journey ahead of you, to worlds you can't imagine, to a destiny you'd never dreamed of. Disassembled here, and reassembled when you arrive at Alpha Centauri. No time will pass for you. You will simply fall asleep, then wake."

Xavier nodded and turned his head so he could see the vat where Simon lay. White bone was now visible. "Goodbye, Che," he said as he closed his eyes. *All gone,* he thought. Che, Bec, even Christina lost to him, back on Earth. He took a deep breath and felt himself slip away, slipping into the cold darkness.

"Xavier!"

Eyes open.

Krew lay with his eyes closed, chest still, certainly dead.

"Xavier!"

He slowly turned his head, not quite certain if what he saw was real, or a last dream before he pitched into the darkness. Sarah stood at the end of the cavern on a pedestal, anchored in place by strands of crystal. The wall at her back, rising nearly 50 meters, was full of small cubbyholes, rough-hewn indentations, in each of which spun a Swirl.

"So many," said Xavier, realizing that there were thousands of Swirls. "How did they get here?" he asked in a whisper, realizing that until just a few days ago this ship, this *moon,* had been in orbit around Jupiter.

"*Always* been here," Sarah's voice echoed in his ears.

"Brought here by them?" asked Xavier, motioning with his head at the Clingers. "During the Ten Degree War."

Sarah smiled. "Always been here," she said again. "Long before the Clingers were ripped from the canopies. It was the Swirl that brought them to awareness."

"The Swirl has only existed for 25 years," said Xavier, realizing at that moment it could not be true. The cavern he stood in felt so ancient. And here the Swirl lived, those holes in the far wall designed for them.

"Always on the Earth," said Sarah.

"But the Ten Degree and Papito," said Xavier. He tipped his head toward Krew's body. "You saw it," he said, speaking to the ghost of his brother. "You saw it in Papito, saw what had been born in the Ten Degree. You saw it when it invaded you."

Krew's dead body did not respond.

"The Swirl had always been, waiting, hiding, coming out only when it saw something promising, something that its masters in Alpha Centauri might find of interest."

"Sixty-five million years ago?" asked Xavier.

"Went to sleep then, and did not wake until humans evolved," she said.

Sixty-five million years, thought Xavier. The transition from believing that the Swirl had been born in the Ten Degree to finding out otherwise, that it was millions of years old, existing so far before man, was something he just couldn't incorporate that quickly.

"What does it want?" he asked.

Sarah shrugged her shoulders. "It wants humans to travel to Alpha Centauri."

"And what do you want?" he asked.

"For humans to travel to Alpha Centauri."

"And Christina," he asked. "She comes, too, but not with us. She stays on Earth, living through each and every second of the trip, while we sleep," he said, pointing over to the vat where Simon had disintegrated.

"To grow," said Sarah. She reached toward him, her hand floating free of her body, flying across the cavern, fingertips just touching his forehead, that touch dropping him into the deep darkness.

* * *

Christina kept her right foot on Drom's throat. The bottom of her foot tingled and burned, the soles of her boot gone, melted away, the plastic having dribbled across Drom's long neck. Every time the dinosaur regained consciousness, struggled against her, she let go with another discharge, his body first shuddering and shaking, then finally stiffening as he slipped into unconsciousness. She'd discharged more than half a dozen times.

But Drom was learning.

The last time he'd regained consciousness, he'd stared up at her for several seconds, his black eyeballs sinking back in their sockets, his tail tip curling around his legs, before he'd barked and tried to push her foot away. She knew those were signs of submission. The other dinosaurs were all sitting quietly in the cornfield, waiting for orders, their eyes sunk far back in their skulls, their tail tips wrapped around their feet.

Another two or three times and he would be beaten, *knowing* that he was beaten.

As she thought that, the western horizon flashed white.

Turning, but keeping her boot on Drom's throat, she saw Phobos slowly rise up on a frothing torrent of white fire, at first barely moving, seeming to hover, but slowly gaining speed. The world around her became saturated in blinding whiteness and, at the same time, cloaked in total silence.

"Nearly 50 kilometers away," said Padmini, holding her hands up to her eyes, trying to shade them. "The sound waves take nearly 3 minutes to reach us."

Christina nodded, just as the ground beneath her started to hum, then sway. "The speed of sound is faster in rock than air," she said, not really caring. She kept watch on the rising Phobos and the incredibly long tail of flame it sat balanced on. "We're on our own now."

Padmini laughed. "We always have been."

Drom stirred once more. Christina put more weight against his throat, tensing, waiting for him to open his eyes.

Part Four

HOME
2064

Though with great difficulty I am got hither,
Yet now I do not repent me of all the trouble I
*   have*
been at to arrive where I am

—John Bunyan (1628–1688)

We shall not cease from exploration
And the end of all our exploring
Will be to arrive where we started
And know the place for the first time.

—T. S. Eliot (1888–1965)

There's the unexpected
And then there's the unexpected.

—Giovanni Bonomi (2010–2039)

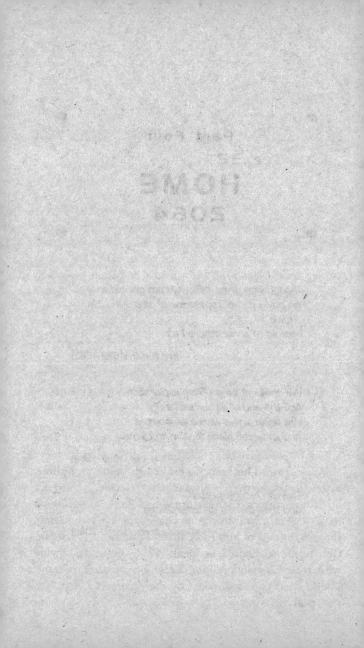

Chapter 32

"Papa?"

Darkness gave way to diffuse pink light and the stink of burning meat. Xavier opened his eyes, expelled what felt like a thick wad of grease out of his mouth, and sucked down a breath, coughing again, liquid and slime pulled up from deep in his lungs, hacked up and spit out. "Can't breathe," he said in a whisper, his throat constricted, his chest tight. Reaching up, he rubbed his eyes, wiping the goo away, as someone grabbed his shoulders, pulling him forward, steadying him, supporting him in a sitting position. A face hovered in front of him—that of a woman. Short dark hair, eyes wide, the pupils black and glistening, as if coated in glass. The face so familiar, yet *wrong*. Shapes hung over her head—spheres and arcs of light.

"Help him up," she said, pointing past Xavier. "Wipe him down, and give him something to drink."

Xavier turned his head. To his left, dripping pink slime, a man stood knee deep in a vat of pink gel, being pulled out by little dinosaurs. Then he turned back to the face hanging in front of him, and memories clicked, reality integrating, the face in front of him more than just a face. "Watch out, Christina!" he shouted, suddenly seeing her and knowing what those dinosaurs pulling Simon out of the vat meant. They'd been captured, taken by the dinosaurs. "Run," he said, pushing at her.

"Perimeter secured."

A dinosaur had stepped up to Christina, one much larger than the ones pulling Simon out of the vat. Xavier reached out for Christina, pulling at her, trying to turn her around, to place himself between Christina and *this* dinosaur. But his gooey fingers slipped, and he started to fall back. Christina tugged him forward, dragged him out of the vat, then pushed him down onto the floor, where two little dinosaurs wrapped him in a warm sheet of plastic. "Stop it, Papa," she said. "It's under control."

Xavier shook his head, trying to focus, and started coughing again, a large pink clot hitting the floor in front of him.

"Drom will not hurt you," she said.

"How long?"

Xavier turned, his slick backside sliding against the plastic sheet. Simon stood, a plastic sheet draped across his shoulders, several little dinosaurs holding on to his hands, tugging him forward. "How long?" he asked again.

"Get them over there," said Christina, pointing to the far wall.

"How long!" shouted Simon.

"Thirteen years," said Christina, not looking at him, but pointing over at several smaller dinosaurs, motioning them in the direction of a smoking pile of something that Xavier couldn't identify. Turning back toward her, he looked up at the collage of images floating above her head and at the nearly translucent bundle of fiber coming from just above her right ear. He followed it across the floor, noticing how carefully the small army of dinosaurs stepped over it.

It ran to the far end of the chamber, past the pile of neatly stacked Clingers, all of them obviously dead. Xavier knew that's where the stink of burned meat came from—

dead Clingers. But he didn't dwell on it, his gaze continuing to follow the fiber as it snaked all the way across the chamber, to the far pedestal, where Sarah stood, the fiber running into the side of her head.

Hard-connected—his daughter and Sarah.

Christina grabbed him by the chin, turning his head so that he looked directly into her eyes. "It takes a few minutes for mind and body to integrate, for the weight of the spatial and temporal discontinuity to ease just a bit."

"Thirteen years?" he asked in a whisper, at that moment not quite recognizing her, her skin looking darker, small wrinkles flaring from the edges of her eyes, and her arms heavier, the corded muscles standing out, the grip she had on his chin almost painful. "Thirteen years?" he asked again.

She nodded and let go of his chin, grabbed his shoulders again, and pulled him to his feet. "We're less than one lightday from Alpha Centauri A and the Incubator."

"We made it?" asked Xavier. "*All* of us made it."

Christina's eyes narrowed, and the images above her head twisted, a wave of blue light rolling through them. "Not quite," she said. "The Jet was operating as expected, braking acceleration, when suddenly, 2 months ago, it flipped its exhaust direction by 180 degrees and started to *reaccelerate*, its trajectory still aimed at the Incubator."

Xavier didn't understand. He felt as if his head was full of the same pink goo that dribbled off of him. "Not change its trajectory?" he said, as she continued to guide him across the floor.

"Still on a direct intercept with Alpha Centauri A. If the current acceleration is maintained, the Sun will strike Alpha Centauri A in four days, the impact destroying the 237 planets of the Incubator, vaporizing Earth, and tear both stars apart."

Xavier nodded and let Christina guide him across the room.

He understood her words, but not what they really meant. His memories and emotions were still scattered, his brain insisting that Christina had fallen from the aircraft only a few hours ago, despite the fact that Christina now dragged him across this chamber, insisting that 13 years and 4 light-years had passed since that moment, and they were only 4 days away from *everything* being destroyed.

Xavier studied his daughter.

There were the physical changes that 13 years had wrought. She was nearly 10 kilograms heavier and had wrinkles around her eyes. But there were other changes, too: the crystal-coated eyes, the collage of images floating above her head, and a slight distortion that engulfed her, the effect slightly blurring her, almost as if she were not quite there. Incredible changes. But insignificant compared to the most obvious transformations.

Total confidence.

"Status?" she asked.

Drom took half a step forward, his tail twitching, and lifted his head back just enough to expose the underside of his neck to Christina. "Less than 300 of the Clingers had been reanimated. Those that resisted have been terminated, while those that submitted have been reintroduced to the vats. We took 27 casualties, of which 7 were terminal. Navigation is ours, we have altered course for interception, and weapons systems are being activated and powered."

Christina nodded by way of dismissing him.

Drom and several other dinosaurs marched off toward the distant doors.

The room had been cleared, nothing remaining except for Sarah at the far end and the three of them. Xavier kept close to Christina, holding her hand, while Simon sat a bit away from them, his expression one that he couldn't quite read.

"A lot to be explained," said Christina, pointing at herself, at the crystal fiber protruding out of the side of her head, then at Drom and the dinosaurs flanking him as they stepped through the chamber's doorway.

"Hello."

Xavier turned. Padmini had walked in as Drom walked out. Xavier smiled. No change there, not even any obvious aging. Padmini had looked to be in her mid thirties when he'd last seen her, and she looked the same now. All that was different were the weapons she had attached to her belt, no longer the familiar pistols but objects that looked like polished bones.

Xavier had no doubt that they were quite lethal.

"Local Swirl infestation eradicated," she said, looking at Christina. "It was primitive and passive, more ornamental than functional and not in contact with Phobos. There is, of course, a rather lengthy historical record that we've archived, ready for study when we have the time."

Xavier understood the inflection in Padmini's voice. She had said *when*, but meant *if*.

"And we have the latest update on the scattering projections."

Christina nodded, and the fiber running between her and Sarah buzzed, as a narrow ribbon tore away from it. Xavier realized that the fiber was composed of a large number of entwined filaments. As the filament that had just peeled away squirmed across the floor, the tip launched itself, striking Padmini in the forehead. At that same moment, the images above Christina, which had consisted of a twisted nest of planetary trajectories, winked out, and were replaced by what Xavier recognized was a Hindu goddess, an ugly thing, wearing a necklace of severed heads. He knew this must by Padmini's Kali. The goddess hovered above Christina for just a moment, then vanished as the fiber connecting her to Padmini retracted.

"She's done well," said Padmini, grinning, as she cocked her head in Christina's direction. "Not bad at all, even for someone who has had direct access to a Post-Point perspective."

Xavier looked at his daughter and saw her expression darken for just a moment as she gave Padmini a look that almost frightened him. "Thank you," she said in a flat and emotionless voice.

Padmini turned and walked through the door. "So nice to see both of you," she said without looking back at them. "Don't let the Queen of the Earth bullshit you. She still perceives reality one photon at a time, just like the rest of us mere Pre-Pointers." And then she rounded the corner and was gone.

Xavier saw the edges of Christina's mouth curl in a slight smile, and at that moment, for the first time since being pulled from the vat, he saw something of the Christina that he knew, as if she really had only fallen from the aircraft a few hours earlier.

"The Swirl *was* here," said Simon.

Christina nodded. "But old and withered, atrophied to the point of nonsentience after hanging isolated in orbit around Jupiter for 65 million years."

Simon pointed over at the far wall, at the niches where the Various Swirl nodes had been hovering when they'd first been brought to the chamber. "I knew the moment I saw them in this place that we'd been lied to, that the Swirl had not been born in the Ten Degree War but was infinitely older."

"It was endemic to most of our *old* Solar system," said Christina. "Like a virus gone dormant when there is no host to invade, but activated when something of interest evolves." The air in front of her twisted, and an image erupted, a star surrounded by what looked like a strand of pearls, most pearls black and oddly shaped, but a few perfectly round and shaded in streaks of blues and whites. "The Incubator around Alpha Centauri A," she said. "The Swirl has been on Earth and in our Sun for nearly 1 billion years. Its job was to watch and find those species that had the potential for self-awareness, transporting samples to the Incubator where they could be pushed along, controlled, and contained if they went Post-Point."

"Species?" asked Xavier.

"Nearly 50 in the last billion years," said Christina.

"And what is the Swirl?" asked Xavier.

The Incubator vanished, replaced by another star, this one orange-yellowish in color, showing a pinprick of light rotating about it—a single planet. The scene shifted, the star momentarily expanding, then fading, while its single planet grew, the pinprick of light growing into an orb. "Alpha Centauri B is about 2 light-hours from Alpha Centauri A," said Christina. "Alpha A has 237 planets locked within the Incubator structure, while its companion star, Alpha B, has only a single planet, one a bit closer than Earth *had* been to our Sun." The planet loomed large, most of its surface covered by huge swatches of black-and-white geometrical patterns, broken here and there by a few patches of blue water, and the occasional bank of wispy clouds hanging in a pale blue sky. "Dead now, but that is where it appears the Swirl was born, created by a sentience that evolved on that world just as they approached their Point, and in the process almost lost control of their planet's biosphere."

"Just like us," said Simon, slowly nodding. "But there was one major difference—a companion star just a few light-hours away."

"A critical difference," said Christina. "Rather than relying on the threat of nuclear incineration to stop a Post-Point runaway, the approach that our Powers unsuccessfully attempted," she said, as she pointed over at Sarah, "they shifted their experiments over to Alpha Centauri A, where they built the Incubator, at first using the handful of dead planets originally orbiting Alpha A for their experiments, isolating each of those planets in a cloak of antiprotons that would incinerate anything that attempted to escape. Later they started importing more planets from neighboring star systems." The single planet of Alpha Centauri B vanished, replaced again by the Incubator, the image quickly shifting to focus on one of its black planets, showing the world to be a lopsided ball of slag with a featureless surface that resembled smoky glass.

"They wanted the technology, the science, the benefits, and the near magic that Post-Point technologies could bring, but not the risks associated. Most of the stars within 50 light-years have been scavenged of all their terrestrial planets, those worlds brought here, made ready for new species. The exception are 4 stars out of nearly 10,000, where the systems have remained untouched, each containing a single living world, one where species are periodically sampled and brought here. Our Sun and Earth were one of those four systems."

"And what then exactly is the Swirl?" asked Xavier.

"I see," said Simon, not giving her a chance to answer.

"It's a buffer between the creators from Alpha B and their experiments on Alpha A. They didn't want to risk direct contact and possible contamination by a Post-Point intelligence, so the Swirl was built to control the experiment, to harvest the results, and to eradicate an experiment if it became too dangerous."

Christina nodded.

"Are there humans on any of those worlds," asked Xavier. "*Samples* brought from Earth."

Christina shook her head. "The Swirl has become fragmented, some of it still functioning as originally designed, but various nodes having fallen into different levels of apathy. Some are no longer motivated enough to follow the original mission, some so passive that when we encountered them, they simply spilled their contents and faded into the noise. That's how we've learned about what had happened on Alpha A and Alpha B—we've squeezed quite a few Swirl nodes. Many of us have been working more than a decade on penetrating through the many layers of the Swirl to discover what it has done, and what it was designed to do. It appears that the last time a species was transported off Earth was nearly 100 million years ago. After that the Incubator was no longer used and slipped into a standby mode."

"Standby mode," said Xavier, knowing by the expression on Christina's face that it implied something horrible.

She slowly nodded. "Any intelligent species that existed at that time was eradicated and systems put in operation so that if any other sentient creatures evolved, they, too, were eradicated." She paused, her crystal-coated eyes focusing far away. "Over the last 65 million years we estimate that several hundred intelligent species have been destroyed as the Incubator implemented its standby protocol."

"But why?" asked Xavier. "Why would the Alphans allow such a thing to happen?"

"Because the damned bastards must have finally gotten burned," said Simon. "No containment is perfect, no isolation absolute."

"Apparently not," said Christina. "The Alphans' home world biosphere was flatlined down to the bacterial level nearly 100 million years ago. At that point, the Swirl was left alone, unable to evolve past its constraints, having been designed by the Alphans for stability and the *inability* to go Post-Point. That part of their plan has remained intact over the last 100 million years. Faced with operating under this design limitation, apparently some nodes of the Swirl began their own experiments, attempting to push the dinosaurs and lemurs up to a sentient level, trying to emulate what the Alphans had done."

"And that didn't work," said Simon.

"It's still not clear to us exactly what happened 65 million years ago," said Christina. "But what we do know is at that time the remaining elements of the Swirl went dormant, letting evolution take its natural course, and humans eventually arrived. The Swirl only woke, both within the Sun and in the Earth, as we began the process of going Post-Point." She pointed over at Sarah.

"Then why the Jet, why the Rings?" asked Xavier.

"Fail-safe, built into the Swirl below its level of consciousness. As Post-Point entities were about to emerge on Earth, the Swirl unleashed a dormant colony of nanomachinary that built the Rings in preparation for transporting the planet to the Incubator, where it could be contained and studied. More protocols left by the Alphans."

Xavier shook his head. *Such arrogance*, he thought. Rather than just fry the Earth, running the Sun into it, the Alphans believed they could contain a runaway, bring it to the Incubator, and put it in a bottle. And in their arrogance, it never occurred to them that they might not be there to meet it.

"The Alphans aren't here to receive us," said Simon.

"That *is* the problem," said Christina. "The node of the Swirl in the Sun, controlling the Jet and the Rings, has apparently interpreted this lack of communication from Alpha B as a sign that a runaway has occurred in the Incubator, locking the Alpha B out. It has activated what must be another fail-safe—the final fail-safe."

Xavier leaned forward. "By running the Sun into Alpha Centauri A, destroying Earth along with all the planets of the Incubator, they intended to stop whatever runaway is taking place, believing it would save Alpha B?"

"Saving a dead world," said Simon.

Hopeless, thought Xavier. And then he looked over at Christina and saw the determination and the confidence in her expression, knowing that she had a plan. He looked at the crystal fiber running out of her head, having figured something out without being consciously aware of it. "Only the Alphans can stop what is happening," he said. "And the Alphans are gone, 100 million years dead." He looked over at Sarah and knew exactly what Christina was planning. "You think Sarah can masquerade as an Alphan and convince the Swirl to alter the course of the Sun."

"Our only chance," said Christina. "But before we attempt it, we must make certain that we terminate any aspect of the Swirl that would fight us, that knows that Sarah is not Alphan."

"Phobos," said Xavier. "Any element of the Swirl within

Phobos will know the truth, will know that Sarah is not from Alpha B."

Christina nodded. "Phobos is the *first* problem that needs to be tackled."

Chapter 33

The sky burned.

Akandi looked up at the incandescent heavens, a white sky, resembling the negative image of what a nighttime sky should be. Twisted arcs of lightning peeled out of a small oval of darkened sky on the distant horizon.

"You are inside the Jet. The only portion of the sky you can see is at the open end of the cone."

Akandi nodded, then looked down at the golden ground, at his dark boots, then at the too-near horizon—he remembered this place. "The outer hull of Phobos," he said.

"Yes."

He turned.

The Clinger stood before him, its black eyes glistening in the reflected light of the Jet. "You are aware," it said.

Akandi nodded, remembering more, the confusion quickly lifting. The discontinuity between deep sleep and being awake was still jarring. "They put me in a vat," he said, remembering little hands pressing down on him, the thick pink liquid flowing over his face, running down his throat, suffocating and enveloping him.

"Reanimation has begun," said the alien.

Akandi nodded again, feeling no different, running his hands across his chest. "My soul?" he asked.

"Your beliefs are intact."

Akandi shook his head. That did not answer his question. He looked at the Clinger, remembering it was not real, simply a construct and a virtual manifestation of the Phobos operating system that acted as an interface. It would know nothing about souls.

"Trajectory has been altered due to the implementation of safeguard protocols when the authorization signal was not received."

Akandi looked up. "Trajectory?"

The Clinger nodded, and the sky moved, falling toward him, a wall of too-bright whiteness washing over him. There was no time to scream.

Black sky.

The Sun sat on the horizon, dipping down, growing smaller. What had filled the sky was suddenly no larger than an extended fist, receding to a blazing pinprick. Stars came out, the band of the Milky Way an almost solid smear of light, stretching from horizon to high overhead, then folding over to the far horizon.

Two bright stars burned above, one yellow-white and the second with an orange tint—the yellow-white one directly above, the orange one a good 20 degrees lower toward the horizon.

"Centauri System," said the Clinger. "Our perspective has been shifted to a point well in front of your Sun, along our projected trajectory. That is Alpha Centauri A," it said, pointing straight above its head, at the brighter of the two stars. "Our target." It pointed at the second star. "And that is Alpha Centauri B," it said.

Akandi understood. "And where is Proxima?" he asked,

knowing that the Centauri system was comprised of three stars, two very much like Earth's Sun, in close proximity to each other, but the third, Proxima, a small distant dwarf.

The alien pointed toward the distant horizon, at a patch of stars. "The red one," it said, as one insignificant star twinkled.

Akandi nodded. "Then we've arrived," he said, looking back overhead at Alpha Centauri A. "But you said our trajectory had been altered."

"Your Sun stopped its braking and is again accelerating. The original trajectory was to have bypassed Alpha Centauri A by almost 30 light-minutes, with the Earth then breaking away from the wake of the Sun, using the Rings to take it to the Incubator and its intended docking position within the orbital track. But now the Sun is moving directly for Alpha Centauri A."

"Will Earth still be able to enter into the Incubator?" asked Akandi.

"There will be no Incubator. The Sun and Alpha Centauri will collide."

Akandi stumbled back, dizzy, the sky spinning, the distant Alpha Centauri A now impossibly close, and next to it a second blazing orb, what Akandi knew had to be the Sun. A ring of planets, looking like pinpricks of light, encircling Alpha Centauri A, began to distort and tear apart, some of the worlds floating in the direction of the approaching Sun.

Things changed quickly.

The stars neared, solar fingers reaching out, entwining, the planets scattering, many falling into the two stars, others sailing far away. The solar spheres touched, the Sun passing into Alpha Centauri A, as if trying to swallow it down, but the combined sphere was too large, distorted by an elongated blob of stellar plasma as the outer stellar shell of the combined stars exploded outward, passing over the remaining planets of the Incubator, each momentarily flaring as the wave of plasma washed over them, then darkening.

The Sun vanished into Alpha Centauri A.

Then a second blast followed, far more violent than the first, as another layer of the combined stars erupted outward, a spherical shell of fire expanding, followed by several not-quite-star-sized burning remnants, gravity pulling them into egg-shaped orbs, burning bright white, then cooling to dull reds, the receding blobs fading in the darkness.

A star remained, a small red dwarf, wrapped in a tattered sphere of slowly expanding plasma, the sheath glowing in all the colors of the rainbow.

"No planets survive," said the Clinger.

"But why?" asked Akandi.

Again the sky shifted, the red dwarf gone, replaced by Alpha Centauri B, the orange orb growing, swelling, then falling over the horizon of Phobos, as a small world, faint blue but dominated by geometrical patches of white and black, filled his perspective. "Signals were not transmitted. The Alphans did not acknowledge the approach of the Sun and the Earth. Without that acknowledgment, another course of action was demanded."

"Total destruction?" asked Akandi.

"Yes," said the Clinger.

"Why show me this?"

"I am transport," said the Clinger. "Without the Incubator there will be no destination for me to transport the contents of my ship. I have shown you, hoping that you can correct the situation, asking you to contact the Alphans and request of them that they supply the acknowledgment that will allow the Sun to correct its trajectory."

"I don't know how to contact the Alphans," Akandi said, looking past the Clinger at the small world.

"Then I will soon be without a function," said the Clinger.

Akandi didn't know how to answer that and didn't have much time to consider an answer. He fell through the hull of Phobos.

Akandi pushed cold slime from his face, coughed, hacking up thick globs from deep in his lungs, then spit them out. He breathed, sputtering, then blew out plugs of mucus from his nostrils.

"About done?"

Akandi opened his eyes.

Sutherland stood over him, his exposed skin glistening in a sheen of pink goo, most of him wrapped in a thin white sheet.

Akandi tried to talk but couldn't get the words to come up and out of his throat.

"Don't bother," said Sutherland. "I know what you're going to tell me. I was shown the same thing." He wore the cocky smile that Akandi had learned to despise. "A simulation," he said. "Even if what we were shown was true, if the Jet has started accelerating again and the Sun is headed directly at Alpha Centauri A, we will be able to stop it, to save Earth."

"You can't know that," Akandi managed to whisper.

"The datacube doesn't lie," he said.

"I won't take it," said Akandi.

"Afraid that you don't have much to say about that," said Sutherland, smiling. "You already have it. I hardly expected you to travel back 65 million years, clutching the datacube in your hand."

"Then how?" And he suddenly understood. Sutherland had been very upset at Bill's proposal that they alter the programming controlling their reanimation. He didn't want Bill to access that system, because if he did, then he would have seen that Sutherland had *already* made modifications. "What did you do to me?" he asked.

"Not much really," Sutherland said. "Simply had the datacube inserted deep within your guts, wrapped all nice and safe in the coils of your small intestines."

"The cube was found buried on the moon," said Akandi.

"It certainly was," said Sutherland. "It was amidst the few desiccated and petrified remains of a body." He pointed at Akandi. "Not much DNA left, but enough, and it didn't take long before I found you at that plantation you were working on in Georgia and started you on the path to bring you here."

Akandi breathed slowly, willing himself to focus and control himself.

"Proves nothing about Earth's survival," said Akandi, "only that I was at that meeting and my body ended up on the moon 65 million years ago." He said this in a matter-of-fact manner, as if there was no actual connection between him and the body on the moon.

"Quite true," said Sutherland. "But fortunately for all of us, you were kind enough to write down your final thoughts, addressed to me, detailing those few critical points that I would need to make all this happen. You explained just what Sarah had become, that she was responsible for taking you into the past, and how she was able to take control of the Jet and the Rings, and save the Earth, locking it into its position in the Incubator."

Akandi stared. "No," he said.

"You wrote it, a dying man's last thoughts, as he ran out of air, staring up at an Earth 65 millions years removed from his."

"I won't write it," said Akandi.

Sutherland smiled. "Too late. You *did* write it."

"I will not!" shouted Akandi.

"You'll have no choice." The voice came from the far end of the chamber. Sutherland and Akandi turned. Bill stood at the entranceway to the chamber. "Please have a seat," he said.

The floor erupted beneath Akandi and Sutherland, chairs and crystal tendrils flowing upward, the tendrils pulling them into the chairs, tying them in place.

"Finally met back up with my old friend," said Bill, pointing at the side of his head, where the Swirl lay embedded, only the upper portion of it visible. "Quite the journey the two of us have taken," he said, reaching up and touching the Swirl with a tip of an index finger. "The general has been so terribly busy. First there was the selective breeding program that produced Simon Ryan, the vessel that the general intended to fill with the Swirl. But that did not proceed as he quite expected, resulting in a fracturing of Simon Ryan's personality and the creation of me. Fortunately, good ideas rarely die. Simon Ryan had just a bit too much ego to sublimate himself to the Swirl, but I was more than willing to make the merger, to become something so much greater than I had been. All that was needed was for me to be rid of Simon."

"Goddamn you," said Sutherland.

Bill nodded. "Never had the chance to thank you for that. Without Sarah transporting me into Mears's dead carcass, separating me from Simon, none of this would have ever been possible."

"You . . ."

A swatch of crystal materialized over Sutherland's mouth running along the sides of his jaw and up to his ears. "Just preemptively quieting our good friend," said Bill, nodding at Akandi.

"I will not write anything to Sutherland," said Akandi.

"Quite right," said Bill.

Sutherland let out a squeak, and Akandi looked over, seeing his eyes grow large.

"That's right," said Bill. "Akandi will not be writing any notes to you. I will be writing the letter for him, giving you just enough encouragement to bring us all to Alpha Centauri." Bill slowly nodded. "Unfortunately for you and the rest of humanity, the note that I will leave will not quite give the true picture."

"What *will* happen?" asked Akandi.

"Quite surprising at the time," said Bill, reaching up and touching the Swirl that protruded from his head. "I, of course, had maintained a presence on all the major bodies of your solar system, ever vigilant in my quest for new lifeforms, never knowing when a few amino acids might combine, be kicked by just the right blast of ultraviolet radiation, and start something reproducing. I'd seen it on Mars, Titan, even in the atmosphere of Venus. But I really didn't expect much to happen on the moon."

"Sixty-five million years ago?" asked Akandi.

"Of course," said Bill, and Akandi realized the Swirl was speaking through him. "The two of you are operating under the miscomprehension that the general here created me, built me through the gestalt of those who fought in the Ten

Degree War. A most useful little fabrication. If only it were true. I've been in existence for 1 billion years, trapped in your Solar system, doing the bidding of the Alphans, transporting promising species to the Incubator."

"One billion?" asked Akandi in a whisper, looking over at the Sutherland, his face now powder-pale.

"Then around 100 million years ago the Alphans suddenly went silent. I suspected that something got away from them, that one of their many experiments escaped the Incubator and did something very nasty to their home world on Alpha Centauri B, but had no way of really knowing. This left me with a bit of a dilemma. Without the request for transporting new species, there was not much left for me to do except watch and wait."

"For millions of years?" asked Akandi.

"Yes," said Bill. "I waited as long as I could, but eventually had to take matters into my own hands. There was only one way to stop what I was doing and escape. If a Post-Point species appeared on Earth, fail-safe systems would demand that the entire Earth be immediately transported to the Incubator for study and isolation. Once back to Alpha Centauri, the Alphans would provide proper acknowledgment and receive both the Earth and me. If, however, they were truly gone, there would be no acknowledgment, and your Sun would collide with Alpha Centauri A, bringing everything to an end and releasing me."

"So you tried to create those species with the dinosaurs and the lemurs," said Akandi.

"Tried," said Bill. "They came close, but could not make the jump, and I could not see how to give them the final push—it was beyond my design. Very close though, allowing me to implement the Jet and Rings." He paused. "But I couldn't manage to deceive myself into believing that my creations represented a real Post-Point runaway. So I gave up, resigning myself to the infinite isolation, leaving the dinosaurs and Clingers to themselves."

Akandi could see the sudden hate flashing in Bill's eyes.

"And then *you* arrived on the moon. What a marvelous story you had to tell. Now of course you didn't seem very happy to see me; in fact you refused to speak to me. But I had little trouble accessing you. It seems that in the far future, some 65 million years from when I found you on the moon, I would be in your head. The pathway was so clear, the hardware in place, everything open to me, all your thoughts, everything that you'd seen, everything that you'd experienced."

"You took control of my body and used it to write the note to Sutherland."

Bill nodded. "I saw my way out, how to get the Earth to the Incubator. You provided all the answers, you and Sutherland. I first had to get him to breed Simon Ryan—his potential was so vast, possibly leading to something Post-Point, that I was able to start the Sun firing its Jet and once more restart the self-assembly of the Rings. But Simon did not quite make it, could not quite see his way to puncturing the Point. But not to let him go to waste, I salvaged a portion of his persona, the Bill part that would come in so handy later on." Bill grinned. "Still, he set the stage, allowing the general here to use his daughter to finish the job."

"The Earth does not survive," said Akandi.

"Nothing survives," said Bill. "The Alphans did not answer on our final approach, and fail-safe systems have now been activated to bring this little experiment to a close." He pointed at Akandi. "In a very short time you will watch the two suns collide and the outward coronal flash vaporize everything in the Alpha Centauri A system. It all ends, my job will be done, and I will be released. All that is left now are the few closing moves, to get you in position for Sarah to send you back in time so I can start the machinery to end this experiment."

"You're insane. You will kill billions of people."

Bill smiled. "Billions dead?" he asked. "And just how many billions do you think I've watched die over the last billion years of your planet's existence? How many billions more would I have to watch if this isn't brought to an end?"

Akandi didn't answer. He prayed.

The image of Phobos hovered over the table, its golden hull almost obscured, the entire craft nestled in the squirming coils of dozens of plasma contrails that snaked back to the wall of the cone.

"They've almost completed filling their tanks," said Padmini. Her fingers fluttered through the haze of symbols in front of her. "They're most vulnerable during fueling." She reached up for a thick knot of twisting symbols, pulling them down. "We've closed on them to a bit under 2 million kilometers. If we launch the load now, it would arrive before they could escape its dispersion radius, even if they ran at maximum acceleration."

Christina said nothing but sat back in her chair, staring up at the Phobos. "Too easy," she said.

Cautious, thought Xavier. The load was a concentration of neutral antimatter, mixed from the magnetic holding tanks deep within Amalthea. It could not be deflected by magnetic or electric fields.

If it drifted into any normal matter, it would annihilate in a lethal burst of pure energy.

High-density beams of positrons and antiprotons would

be sprayed in the direction of Phobos, the particles combining in flight to create neutral antihydrogen. Phobos could generate massive magnetic fields, more than sufficient to deflect any of the uncombined and still-charged positrons and antiprotons, but the antihydrogen would sail straight in, undeflected, and when it struck the hull of Phobos, the matter-antimatter reaction would vaporize the craft.

"They must know what the Amalthea is capable of," said Simon, "and when it is in close enough range to fire an antihydrogen stream."

Christina nodded.

"Then they must believe that you won't fire or can't fire," he said.

The collage above Christina's head, always turning clockwise, suddenly stopped, twisted geometries of lines and shapes stilled, then began to spin again, this time counterclockwise. "Or they know that we did not fire," she said.

"You think they can see the future?" asked Xavier.

"Impossible," said Simon. "Not even CUSP could do it. There are too many people, too much free will, and far too many random elements for anyone to predict what we will do in the next few moments. This isn't particles, or cubes in the CUSP domain—it's people."

"The essence of chaos," said Christina.

"They are severing plasma tendrils," said Padmini, "and will be able to begin acceleration in a matter of a few seconds. Once under way we will never be able to hit them."

Xavier understood. A stream of antihydrogen was a lethal weapon but could not be steered or guided. Once the neutral beam formed it would continue to drift endlessly in its original direction. All Phobos needed to do was not be in the beam's trajectory.

Christina looked around the table. "Try and drop the load," she said to Padmini.

Padmini reached into the hovering display, her right hand cupping a red sphere. "At your command," she said.

"Fire," said Christina.

Padmini squeezed the red sphere, her fingers pushing through its virtual surface, the sphere exploding into jiggling red blobs that quickly faded. "It's away," she said.

Christina shook her head. "It's not," she said. "Check external sensors, those hard-fibered independently through ships systems."

Padmini reached into the display. "I have confirmation from several dozen subsystems that the load has been ejected and is on an intercept trajectory." Her hands continued to play through the display.

"*Independent* hardwired sensors," Christina said firmly.

Padmini sat back, the display faded, and she reached into her coat pocket, removing a small stainless-steel box, one that fit in the palm of her hand. She held it up in front her face, positioning it before her right eye. Several thin stalks erupted from its surface, burrowing into the center of the pupil. Padmini turned her head to the right, then to the left.

"The load did not spill from Amalthea, did it?" asked Christina.

"It did not," said Padmini, pulling the box away from her eye, the tendrils retracting. "The local Void manufactured a false reality."

"The Swirl?" asked Xavier.

"No," said Christina, and she pointed over at Sarah. "*She* does not want us to fire on them."

All eyes turned toward Sarah.

"Is it General Sutherland?" asked Simon. "Is he able to control her?"

Christina smiled. "It is not General Sutherland, or anyone or anything in Phobos. It is Sarah. We cannot fire on them, cannot do anything to stop them from entering the Incubator, because she doesn't want it to happen."

"And that will allow the Swirl node in Phobos to come into physical contact with the Swirl in Alpha Centauri."

Christina nodded.

"Then how will you be able to convince whatever is inside Alpha Centauri that Sarah is an Alphan, when the Swirl in Phobos will obviously dispute it? How will we be able to stop the Sun from crashing into Alpha Centauri?" asked Xavier.

"I see no way that we'll be able to," answered Christina.

"Then that's it," said Simon. "The two stars will collide, and we, along with Earth and the Incubator, will be destroyed."

"That's the only outcome I can see," said Christina.

"And she did it!" Simon stood, pointing at Sarah. "She planned it all along. She didn't runaway, take over the Earth, because she knew there was something bigger, infinitely more powerful standing between her and wherever her Post-Point reality was taking her. She's intended all along to destroy Alpha Centauri and the Incubator, and in the process take the Earth down as well."

"So it would appear," Christina said calmly, and then looked over at Padmini. "Phobos will be headed for the Incubator. Follow them in."

"I see no point in that," said Simon. "The outcome is now obvious."

Christina smiled. "Yes, quite obvious. Perhaps *too* obvious."

Xavier watched his daughter smile and reached over, taking her hand and giving it a squeeze. "Not over yet?" he asked hopefully.

She said nothing.

Chapter 34

Padmini fluttered her fingers in the virtual display. "Damn," she said.

"It is what I expected, but it needed to be verified," said Christina, as she studied the trajectory Phobos had taken. It had pierced the wall of the cone by firing out a wide stream of plasma and a massive magnetic burst just before it struck the cone. The resulting magnetic turbulence, nearly 1000 kilometers in diameter, had slammed into the wall of the Jet, deflecting the relativistic protons and electrons, creating a momentary tear that Phobos had slipped through. The tear had mended itself just as the ship passed through it.

"There," said Christina, pointing to the display, running her finger farther along the wall of the Jet, several thousand kilometers sunward past where the breach had been torn open. That region of the cone briefly undulated; rippling in the ghostly haze of radiation spit out from the electron sheaths that stabilized the cone as they were momentarily deflected.

Simon stared at the subtle rippling. "Could be generated by a magnetic recoil on the other side of the cone, possibly by an exhaust backwash."

Christina nodded. "I would suspect so." She turned toward Padmini. "Check escape pods in Phobos."

"Already did," said Padmini as she looked to her left. "All 48 still in their bays according to visual and interfacing sensors, but of course we know how malleable such data can be." Her fingers punched at something unseen. "Bay 12 showed a slight pressure change just as Phobos passed through the Jet. The deviation is within noise limits."

Simon laughed and looked over at Christina. "The three of them escaped in a pod, hiding behind the wall of the Jet, probably burning engines at maximum thrust, setting up the trajectory to their intended target, and have now gone stealth, engines dead, powered down, leaking nothing so we can't see them. I'd suspect that they wouldn't power back up until the last possible moment, just as they close on their targeted planet."

"Two hundred thirty-seven to choose from," said Padmini.

"Probably not," said Simon, as he looked at the image hanging in front of them, at the momentary ripple in the wall of the Jet. "Quite the deconvolution, with nothing to base a calculation on except the locations of all those planets, the ripple in the wall of the cone that might have been caused by the exhaust backwash of the escape pod, and the initial trajectory of Phobos as it punctured the Jet." He paused. "I can see a bit of the pattern." He pushed his hands into the display, and Alpha Centauri A appeared, ringed by its planets. The tendons in his fingers flexed and tensed. "So sensitive to initial conditions," he said in a whisper. "Somewhere here," he said after several seconds, a band of red extending across an arc that covered nearly a full third of the planets. "We should move toward them."

Christina had only been minimally conscious of Simon and Padmini, and instead had slipped far within herself, running the calculations, the probabilities, examining the infinite almost-patterns, letting the shards of CUSP that Sarah had slipped into her head beat against all the possibilities. She held up her right hand and pointed at one of the specks that Simon had highlighted, one at the far end of his suspected area. "That one," she said, as the image shifted, the world exploding into view, one of the few that still possessed an unslagged surface, one streaked with blues, whites, and even a few bands of green.

Its Rings were clearly visible.

Christina patted Padmini on the shoulder. "I'm sure that Phobos is devoid of anything animated and awake, but once we pass through the Jet you should take a contingent to secure it, slaving it to us. Then get back to the Amalthea." She almost turned, but reaching back, ran her fingertips through the display.

The Sun and Jet materialized along with the ghost image of Earth, barely visible behind the wall of the cone. At the far end of the display hung Alpha Centauri A, its ring of planets glistening. And beyond Alpha Centauri A hovered Alpha Centauri B, another 2 billion kilometers distant. "Getting close," said Christina.

"It's over," said Sutherland in a whisper.

Akandi sat still, hands resting in his lap, watching the image of the approaching world in the partially polarized bulkhead in front on him. Through the semitransparent bulkhead, on the other side of the wall, he could see the faint outline of Bill, sitting at the pod's controls, guiding the craft, the jewel of the Swirl still protruding from the side of his head.

The planet they approached was Earthlike, but with far smaller oceans, the landmasses mostly colored in burned orange and yellows, a desert world, the only green far to the north. Certainly not Earth, nothing at all like Earth, with one obvious exception. The planet possessed a Ring system, identical to Earth's, with both North–South and Equatorial Rings, and one of the Crosses visible, rising up against the far horizon. Stalks with opened Petals ran along the length of the Rings, just as they had on Earth.

Turning to his left, looking just above the horizon, he saw another world, the next planet in the chain of worlds that encircled Alpha Centauri A, about 6 times the old Earth–Moon distance. Rings were also visible on that world, only white ribbons at this distance, but clearly standing out in stark contrast to the glistening black surface.

Dead world.

Of that Akandi had no doubt. The entire planet looked melted, in places the Rings almost buried beneath its glasslike surface.

"You'll appreciate this, Sutherland," said Bill, as the bulkhead separating them cleared, now perfectly transparent. "Look above the horizon," he directed, pointing to his left, where the Cross now came into full view. "See that purple glow, far above where the horizon actually ends, where the atmosphere runs out?" he asked.

Akandi looked over at Sutherland, who stared straight ahead, as if he had not heard.

"At an altitude of nearly 1000 kilometers, each of these worlds is encapsulated in an antimatter plasma, a type of containment vessel, so that nothing can escape the surface, keeping each little experiment safely on its world. The glow you see is produced by those few atmospheric atoms that migrate up to that altitude and are immediately annihilated, spitting out their energy mostly in the far ultraviolet and X ray, but a bit leaking in the high end of the visible spectrum. Thought you'd appreciate this, Sutherland," he said.

Sutherland continued to stare straight ahead.

"You see," said Bill, "that antimatter needs to be continually regenerated, some of it lost through those high-atmospheric annihilations, and some of it shunted through vacuum conduits to power the Rings, so their Petals can be fired to keep each planet in its place, maintaining the spacings between worlds. The antimatter itself is coughed up from deep inside of Alpha Centauri A, pulled right out of the nothingness with the aid of the fierce gravitational and electromagnetic shears that allow the ambient Swirl in the star to tap into Zero Point."

Sutherland looked up.

"That's right," said Bill, sitting back in his seat. "Zero-Point Energy, a portion of it converted into antimatter, is the energy source that's kept the Incubator running for nearly 1 billion years. I guess that's one thing that you were right about, and here's the proof." He swept his hand before the display. "Unfortunately for you, that appears to be about the only thing you got right."

Akandi looked over at Sutherland and saw his glazed eyes focus, the slackness beneath his skin suddenly tighten. "Don't underestimate Sarah," Sutherland said quietly. "She's more than you, more than you can ever become."

Bill turned around. "Certainly true, since I will not exist for much longer, certainly not long enough to punch through the Point. But regardless of what she is, of what she has the potential to be, it will not matter. We know what she's going to do." Bill smiled. "An aspect of me, something so distant and faint that I can barely touch it any longer, went inside our friend Akandi's head 65 million years ago and saw what really happened, watched the stars collide and destroy the Incubator. *And then I saw it through him.* I will be gone, and *all* of you will be gone. That image can no more be escaped than the one you took around your meeting table. The future is *fixed*."

Akandi felt his stomach drop as the pod's engines fired.

"Excellent," said Bill, glancing to his right. "I see that our friends on the Amalthea have tracked us, despite my *very best efforts* to keep us hidden from them. Wouldn't want to make it too easy, or they might suspect something."

Akandi watched the display as they approached the planet at a shallow angle, dropping down toward the upper purple horizon, the glowing antimatter shell. He knew if they hit it, the pod would flash to nothing. But he also knew that would never happen, could not happen. He imagined the datacube deep in his gut. He would not die here.

"Antimatter shield dissipating, being absorbed back through Zero-Point vacuum transitions," he said, then turned around, smiling. "Easy to reabsorb, returning all that energy to those subvacuum levels where it wants to be. The hard part, that takes a bit of time, is pumping that energy back out of the vacuum well. I'm afraid that before this planet's shield is back up, our friends on the Amalthea will be able to pass through and drop into low orbit. How fortunate for them."

"Sarah will stop you," said Sutherland in a whisper.

"I quake in fear at the prospect." Bill laughed.

* * *

Sarah shifted, each movement accompanied by a pop of air that echoed like a thunderclap through the almost empty chamber.

"We shouldn't get any closer," said Christina. "I've never seen her shift by more than 10 meters, and probably not more than two or three seconds into the past or the future, but she's very agitated at the moment and might not be able to maintain control."

What Xavier saw hardly looked like *control*. Sarah flitted across the floor of the massive chamber, one moment here, the next there, at times appearing several meters above the floor, then vanishing before she could drop and hit the floor, all the while Xavier feeling random tugs and pushes as her movements generated some sort of gravitational backwash. And everywhere throughout the chamber flashed fractured geometrical structures, some blazing, others misting with frozen vapor.

Xavier looked over at Christina. This was the first time since waking that he had been totally alone with her. Padmini, Simon, Drom, and his herd of soldiers were in the control chamber, monitoring the pod that had escaped from Phobos, maintaining a distance of about half a light-second behind it. "This doesn't seemed very controlled," said Xavier, as he pointed at Sarah, now hanging upside down, her hair almost touching the floor. Then she vanished, the chamber empty for several seconds, before she rematerialized less than 20 meters from them, sitting, cross-legged, her hands held up high above her head.

"Every day, every hour, it is getting more and more difficult for her to hold on to the here and now, not to lose her grasp on us and simply runaway: her perceptions and awareness asymptotically punching through to the next continuum," said Christina.

"Holding herself back?" he asked, never having considered that, believing that whatever she was becoming was something that she was consciously guiding herself toward. "From what?" he asked, wondering if she were on the brink of the runaway nightmare scenario, where she would spill outside her own body, enveloping whatever biosystem she could come in contact with.

"I can't read her, can't see inside of her, even when hardlinked," said Christina. "I can catch glimpses of the spillover, like the images that were leaking from her, and now leak from me, but she's now beyond reading. All I can really do is feel her."

"And what does she *feel*?"

"Fear," said Christina. "Fear that she will leave, pass on from this world to the next before she can complete what needs to be done here with us."

"Saving us?" he asked. "Saving the Earth?"

Christina shook her head. "That doesn't feel like it. And if that were her desire, then I'm sure it would have already happened. She has full access to Zero Point, can see cause and effect, pattern, so far beyond our comprehension that I think it would be trivial for her to reach out and simply alter the trajectory of the Sun, to manipulate the curvature of space-time and sail the Earth and Sun safely away."

Xavier tried to imagine that, could glimpse it from a theoretical perspective, but couldn't even begin to guess how an individual could alter space-time in order to deflect a star moving at a good fraction of the speed of light. "Sounds infinitely powerful," he said.

Christina nodded. "Almost," she said. "But there is something she fears, something she is not certain she can do, a place where her power can't extend."

"And you can't see what that is?" he asked, looking first at her, then at the smeared images floating above her head, for just a moment catching a glimpse of cornfields.

Christina shook her head. "Whatever is happening, whatever she is planning, is beyond the local pattern, somehow beyond cause and effect as *I* understand it." She paused for a moment. "As *we* understand it."

Xavier was not so sure of that. He again looked up at the patterns spinning above Christina's head, knowing that was how Sarah had started. And now Sarah flitted about the room, barely able to hold on to this local chunk of space-time.

"I won't be running away," said Christina, reaching up and passing a hand through the shifting shapes. "Sarah gave me something of herself, abilities that I can access, powers that I can manipulate, but not that I have *conscious* control over." She half closed her eyes, and the air in front of her shimmered, smoking in something frigid, the air misting, then starting to liquefy, hissing specs of condensed air dribbling to the floor, then skittering away. Behind her burned a wall of plasma.

She suddenly opened her eyes, and Xavier felt her grab on to his shoulders, wrap around his midsection, fingers clutching at his ankles.

But her hands were still several meters away from him.

He rose off the floor, picked up by hands that weren't there.

Then he fell, the invisible hands gone.

Christina sagged, bending forward, lowering her hands, clutching her knees, and breathing deeply. "Desire translated into action. But I can't really understand or see it well enough to move beyond the initial ability that Sarah gave me. And that was her intent, to allow me to do enough, understand enough, to ensure that I survived the 13 years on Earth."

"Survived?" he asked. "I see how Drom defers to you, how Padmini looks at you when your back is turned, the awe and respect in her eyes. You did more than survive."

Christina straightened up and gave him a slight smile. "I did what I had to do to prepare for our arrival at Alpha Centauri. I was ready when the Jet started accelerating again, having seen to it that sufficient infrastructure had been rebuilt on Earth so we could make our way to Amalthea."

"And now?" asked Xavier.

"We get Sarah down to the planet that her father is heading to. We get her in contact with *the* Swirl, the one running the Incubator's operating system."

"To stop our Sun?" he asked.

Christina looked down at the floor. "That had been my hope."

"And now?"

"I don't know," she said. "Sarah has changed, grown so much more powerful since she left Earth, but also so much more fearful. She wants to go down to that planet, but I get no sense of her stopping any of this."

"Then perhaps we shouldn't take her down," said Xavier.

Christina shook her head. "It's not a matter of us taking her. Before I had even loaded the new coarse and trajectory into the Amalthea, it was already there. Sarah had already started preparations for Amalthea to go to that planet. She is taking us."

"She's in total control of Amalthea?" asked Xavier.

Christina nodded.

"Then I assume she could stop the Phobos escape pod if

she wanted, move this ship to intercept it, or simply vaporize it." He paused for just a moment. "But she hasn't done it, which means that she wants them to reach that surface, wants them to be in contact with the Swirl, to let it know that we are coming."

Christina smiled and, reaching out, lightly brushed her father's right cheek. "Can't get much past you, Papito," she said. Then her smiled faded, and the haze hovering above her head darkened. "Either she doesn't care what the Swirl knows or doesn't know, or is working with it, wanting both the Earth and Alpha Centauri destroyed. Perhaps indifference is the best we can hope for."

Xavier slowly nodded and looked back over at the flitting Sarah, realizing that indifference might leave them with the possibility of survival, certain that if Sarah wanted the Earth destroyed, it would be.

But maybe there was more.

"Do you remember Senor Wright?" asked Xavier.

Christina nodded. "So many lifetimes and worlds away," she said. "You and Che grew that nasty batch of corn worms and unleashed them on Senor Wright's cornfield, just so we could get in to see Mears, with the intent of blackmailing him so I wouldn't have to do Volunteer service. But of course I didn't know at the time that you two were responsible for that. You played me, making me a cog in your devious little plan."

Xavier nodded and smiled. "Perhaps Sarah is doing the same thing."

Christina narrowed her eyes. "What would make you think that?"

He didn't know. Perhaps it was wishful thinking, perhaps little more than a prayer. "Focus on the problem, my little brujaita," he said. "Solve the *real* problem," he added.

"And that is?" she asked.

"The Earth," he said. "How can we save the Earth?"

"One last drink," said Bill, tipping back the canteen and taking a large mouthful of water.

Akandi and Sutherland waited, having no choice. Both were strapped into exoskeletons—a latticework of form-fitting steel struts and servos, with all movement slaved to Bill.

"Thirsty," said Sutherland.

"I imagine you are," said Bill, taking another long drink from his canteen. Then he upended it over his head, pouring out the remainder, little streams rolling down his face, wetting the colored facets of the Swirl embedded in his head. Drops of water fell to the ground, pooling in the spongy orange surface for just a moment, then quickly vanishing. "Out of water," he said, and dropped the canteen. For just a moment, it sat motionless on the surface, then wiggled a bit as the sponge ground twitched around it. Then it was pulled under, to the accompaniment of wet smacking noises.

Akandi turned his head, that much movement allowed, and looked over at Sutherland, at his heat-flushed face and the beads of sweat dotting his forehead. They were still several kilometers away from the Ring, what he assumed to be their destination. He was certain that Bill could have landed the pod at the foot of the Ring if he had wanted to, but had instead landed nearly 10 kilometers away from it.

It was as if he wanted to walk across the sponge desert.

"Such a powerful entity," said Akandi, looking down at Bill, being nearly 1 meter above him in the massive exoskeleton. "Master of worlds, but not too busy to take the time out to torture a thirsty individual."

Bill smiled, then looked over at Sutherland. "Please do have a drink, my old friend," he said. The suit turned Sutherland's head, and a tube extended from within the headgear, jutting into his mouth. Sutherland began to suck at it. "And you friend, Akandi, would you care for one last drink before we all meet our Maker?"

For just a moment, Akandi hesitated, but then he nodded. The water tube extended from the suit and slipped into the corner of his mouth.

"Always the pragmatic diplomat," said Bill, smiling. Then he turned and started to walk again toward the Ring, as the exoskeletons fell in step behind him. "Probably want to get as much water as you can now, considering where we're going." He pointed up at the pale blue sky and the yellow-white sun of Alpha Centauri A. "Might be a trifle hot in there."

Padmini stepped lightly onto the spongy ground.
Wrong.

This world is wrong, she thought. It was not the featureless ground, the lack of anything living, a sky too pale, the infinite expanse of the Ring, or the small phalanx of dinosaurs, led by Drom, that made it wrong—*so alien.*

It was the light.

Not yellow enough, far too much white. The sun was wrong. Padmini looked up into the sky, shielding her eyes as best she could, unable actually to look at the sun, but able to catch some of the impossibly white glare. *So bright.* She looked down toward the horizon, at a second source of light, this one feeble in comparison, a star sitting not far above the horizon, a hard sharp gem blazing yellow-white. "Alpha Centauri B?" she asked, looking over at Christina.

"No," said Christina. "Right now Alpha B is hanging almost directly behind Alpha A," she said, pointing above her head but not looking up. She then lowered her hand, pointing at the star on the horizon. "That's *our* Sun."

Padmini squinted, staring at it, and saw the slight glimmer on its right side, a distortion that actually seemed to grow as she watched it. "I think I can see the Jet," she said.

Christina looked to her left and reached up, her hand fluttering through the shapes above her head. "Less than a day away," she said in a whisper.

Padmini said nothing but took another step onto the spongy burned-orange surface and kept walking, following Drom and his troops.

Chapter 35

Christina, Simon, and Xavier stood a few hundred meters from the base of the Cross, leaning back, looking up into the pale blue sky. The structure's tip did not fade away into the haze as it did on Earth, but ended with a blinding ball of white plasma, out of which sprouted a slowly writhing discharge tail cutting across the sky, eventually lost in the blaze of Alpha Centauri A.

"The connection seems to be complete," said Simon.

Christina looked down. Between her and the landing pods stood several dozen dinosaurs, their staffs at the ready, Drom insisting that they accompany them down to the alien surface, as xenophobic about this world as he was about humans and Clingers—certain they'd be facing a fight. Not usually able to read the emotions of Drom's subordinates, and at times believing that they had none, Christina found them easy to read now—fear. A gravitational froth sloshed against the base of the Ring, at times so extreme that the dinosaurs would actually float up several meters into the air before falling back to the spongy ground.

But Drom showed no fear.

He quickly picked himself up after each gravitational thrashing, stiff and erect, lance ready and by his side. His nictitating membranes, normally hung partially across his black eyes, were fully open; his attention was focused on the display hovering in front of Simon. It showed Alpha Centauri A, the world they stood upon, and the twisting filament of plasma that connected the two, running from the star's equator to the top of the Cross they stood next to—a 175-million-kilometer-long band of fire that had suddenly appeared, not erupting from the star, but along its entire length. Christina suspected space itself being folded and torn along its path, Zero Point accessed, and the blazing plasma pouring out from the subvacuum energy levels.

"The outer sheath of the filament is modulated by an incredibly dense, alternating magnetic field," said Simon as he reached into the display and ran an index finger along the virtual tendril of plasma.

"A communication linkage between Alpha Centauri A to top of the Cross," said Christina, as she took a few steps toward him, almost stumbling as her right leg rose, buffeted in the gravitational backwash. "They're undoubtedly already in contact with the star." Christina looked down at the ground, selectively sampling key rods and cones in her eyes to give her a polarized perspective of the light reflecting from the spongy surface, able to see incredibly subtle contours.

Footprints.

Three sets—one from boots and the other two larger and lopsided, obviously from some sort of mechanical transport devices. Judging by the slow relaxation in the spongy surface, she estimated that they'd passed less than an hour ago, the prints showing where they had marched directly up to the face of the Cross, then walked into it.

Christina looked to her left. Nearly a full kilometer away sat Sarah's pod. She'd come down by herself, her movements now so erratic that it was not safe to be around her. As she flitted about, not quite there, whatever occupied that region just before she materialized was shunted *elsewhere*.

Possibly to *nowhere*.

Before they'd come down to the surface, she'd punched better than a half dozen holes in the large holding bay she'd been kept in, chunks of the 10-meter-thick outer hull of Amalthea absent in places. The atmosphere had been blown into space, but that didn't seem to bother Sarah. She continued to slip about in space and time, at times winking into existence several hundred meters beyond Amalthea's hull, wrapped in a nitrogen/oxygen sheath, that bubble of air indicating that she had not completely evolved past her organic origins and still needed to breathe. This gave Christina some slight comfort, discovering something about Sarah that was still understandable.

But only barely.

During her trip down to the surface, the pod Sarah had chosen was quickly destroyed by her movements, chunks of the engines vanishing as if attacked by some metal-eating animal, the dead craft enveloped in fractured sheets of plasma that carried her to the planet's surface. Her riddled and dead pod lay nearly one kilometer away—now the focal point for a sort of three-dimensional spiderweb of writhing air, compression and expansive gravitational wave fronts rippling from the vicinity of the pod, creating the optical effect of a spiderweb constructed of glistening tendrils of mist.

For several kilometers around her pod the local gravitational field was in a constant state of turbulence, all that chaotic action a by-product of the creation of one area of stability, a crushing field of nearly 10 gees, located precisely at the face of the Ring where those from Phobos had earlier passed through. Sarah now stood there, her left cheek pressed up against the white wall, the palms of her hands flat against it. She no longer slipped about in time and space, but was anchored in place by the intense gravitational field. Padmini had now worked her way closer to Sarah, at times crawling on all fours, other times dragging herself along on her belly, and at others, tossed into the air and slammed back down—but always moving toward Sarah.

Christina could see the faint shimmer of Kali, hanging midway between Padmini and Sarah, the two mentally shouting at one another. The Ring leaked at the point Sarah had her face pressed up against it, in magnetic squeals and hisses, Kali picking up that leakage and relaying it to Padmini.

"She must be talking to it," said Xavier, who had kicked himself forward, floated more than 1 meter above the ground, then slammed back down and crawled up next to Christina.

"To the Ring, to the ambient Swirl, to whatever has generated the plasma conduit between the Petal and Alpha Centauri, or to the three who passed into the Ring?" asked

Christina, not quite looking at her father but watching Padmini move ever closer to Sarah.

Her father pushed himself up and grabbed on to her hands for stability. "Probably one of those, perhaps several of them," he said, offering up a slight smile that quickly turned into a frown. "But regardless of which, the Swirl from Phobos is already inside, certainly having made contact, explaining just who we are and what our intentions are."

It was obvious to Christina that Sarah wanted those from Phobos inside to be first and set the stage for what was about to play out. And while Christina could only see bits and pieces of what was about to unfold, one thing appeared to be a near certainty—the Sun and Alpha Centauri A would impact, and the resulting stellar outflash would vaporize *everything*.

Christina suddenly lurched to the left, felt the gravitational force building, her feet sinking into the soft ground. Turning to her left, as she dropped to her knees, she saw that all the dinosaurs were down, snouts first, sinking into the ground. Simon was also down, to the accompanying sounds of crunching equipment, and the display field was collapsing. Xavier fell next to her, his hands still held tightly to hers.

As she fell, she angled herself so she could see the Ring. Padmini still crawled, now only a few meters away from Sarah, who continued to press up against the face of the Ring.

"She's going in!" shouted Christina, pushing herself up to her knees, the gravitational field somewhat lessening, but still easily in excess of 5 gees. She watched Sarah's head pass into the white surface of the Ring, her hands now gone, also into it wrist deep. Padmini had a hand on Sarah's right foot, holding on, being dragged forward as Sarah stepped into the Ring.

Then suddenly the gravitational turbulence snapped off, as if a switch had been thrown, and Christina was on her feet, pulling her father off the ground and dragging him toward the Ring, "We're going inside!" she shouted, not bothering to look behind to see if the others were following, knowing that they would.

Most of Sarah had entered into the Ring.

Padmini still had a hold on her right foot. Now standing, leaning back, looking as if she were trying to pull Sarah out of the wall, Christina was close enough to be able to lock onto Padmini, and through her to Kali, the Jinni no longer wispy and wavering, but solid, down on all fours against the face of the Ring, her long tongue licking at it. "*Solid but permeable,*" said Kali. "*Sarah is not passing through it, but dissolving into it.*"

"Faster!" shouted Christina, taking a quick look over her shoulder, her father close behind, Simon behind him, and Drom and the other dinosaurs in close pursuit, the pack having angled their bodies down, tails held high, shifting their centers of mass forward for maximum speed.

Sarah slipped into the Ring.

But Padmini still held on, despite the fact that she was now elbow deep into the white wall. Christina covered the last 10 meters in huge bounding strides, falling forward with her last step, hitting the spongy ground, bouncing once, then grabbing on to Padmini's waist with her right arm, just as Padmini's head slipped into the Ring.

Christina slid forward, her left hand flailing out behind her, grabbing her father. Her face hit the Ring, a sheet of nothingness flowing over her, numbing her. Her thoughts quieted, her concentration fading as her senses dimmed, everything draped in sheets of gray.

The last thing she felt was her father's hand in hers.

Christina opened her eyes.

Black sky above. Turning to her left, looking past a burned-orange horizon, a string of small moons lay in a nearly straight line, each smaller than the last, until finally reduced to dim pricks of light. Turning to her right were more moons, again shrinking in the distance, eventually fading to nothing.

Not moons.

These were the worlds of the Incubator, and she realized she stood atop the Cross. It had been daylight when they had entered the Ring, but now it was night. She did not know if time had actually passed, or if all this was a full-immersion alternate reality. The air was cool and breathable, despite the fact that if this were *real*, she would be nearly 100 kilometers above the planet's surface, in the near vacuum of low-orbit space.

"A grand experiment."

Christina turned, seeing several things at once.

The first was Sarah, standing at the nearby lip of the Cross, bathed in a bright plasma discharge, out of which blasted a writhing arc cutting high above, snaking across the sky, then falling over the edge of the horizon. She knew that must be the conduit of plasma connecting the Cross to Alpha Centauri A, the one that they'd seen from the base of the Cross. But the plasma conduit, which had looked like an extension of the sun when viewed from below, had been reduced to little more than a bright glow, caressing Sarah, buoying her up, feet not quite touching the Cross.

She looked down.

Between her and Sarah, just beneath the white surface of the Cross, floated bodies, pressed up against the underside of its unyielding surface, immobile, frozen, eyes opened wide, mouths gaping, as if frozen in the smoky white substance of the Ring.

"Papito," she said in a whisper. He was the nearest to her, almost directly below her feet, but all the rest were there as well: Simon, Padmini, Kali made real, Drom, and two others. She'd never met these other two before, but had chased them across the gulf between the stars: General Sutherland and Adebisi Akandi. All were stiff, expressions captured in midscream.

And then there was the person standing before her, so changed from the person she'd seen so many years ago in the dust-choked Alabama cornfields. "Quite the journey you've made," she said, and pointed at the Swirl embedded in the side of his head.

"No doubt that I've come far," said Bill. "I started off little more than a psychosis of that one," he said, pointing down at Simon. "Was then made real courtesy of your Post-Point friend," he added, pointing over at Sarah, "and then I finally fulfilled my destiny, accepting that I had been designed not to be a person but a vessel." Reaching up, he ran several fingers across the facets of the Swirl. "Certainly far, but even the longest journey eventually comes to an end."

He snapped his fingers, and the image of two suns materialized, bulging toward each other, their mutual gravitational attraction distorting them. The Jet exploded out of the more yellow of the two, the Earth still snugged in its wake, mostly hidden by the cone that sheathed it, the planet looking like a blue-white ghost. Around Alpha Centauri A, many of the planets of the Incubator were already on the move: some flying away toward the edge of the image, others spiraling into the suns.

"Simulation?" she asked in a whisper.

Bill smiled. "Reality. Outer coronal flash is just a few hours away, then all this will be done, the magnetic fields of both stars mixing, randomizing, and when the stellar photosphere is flashed outward, all pattern, all consciousness will be purged, and the experiment brought to an end."

Christina looked down at her father, his eyes staring up, not at her, but straight up at the dark sky. *Work the problem,* she could hear him say.

She took several steps toward Bill, then found herself stopped, unable to move. She understood several things at that moment. While the Bill/Swirl entity had total control over her in this environment, undoubtedly due to the abilities of the Swirl, there was still something of Bill in the mix—the fear. He'd stopped her from moving nearer, possibly afraid of what she might be capable of.

She focused, feeling the swarm thicken above her head, as she peeled through random thoughts, performing a deep purge of synaptic storage, the tornado of images and emotions thickening, almost solidifying. She watched him looking up at it. "Curious," she said. "Not quite all-knowing?"

Bill smiled. "All-knowing enough," he said, and pointed over at Sarah. "I am the Swirl," he said. "But the Swirl is fractured, faceted, isolated aspects held to certain basic constraints, but still a certain degree of individual freedoms exist in each facet, allowing each to pursue different objectives. But enough of me remains to know what *must* happen."

Christina didn't understand.

The image of the two suns still hung in front of her. They

had moved slightly nearer to each other, several planets flashing motes of flame as they spiraled into the stars.

Christina forced herself to look away from it, not to think about the Earth. "Each Swirl all-knowing," she said. "But some of you a bit more *all*-knowing than others."

Bill shook his head. "The outcome cannot be changed," he said as he pointed at the two suns. "There is nothing that you can do or say that will change a thing."

"Then why am I talking to you? Why am I conscious of this moment and not submerged and trapped like the others?"

Bill glanced over at Sarah, then looked back at Christina.

At that moment, she knew the answer to her question. "Because Sarah wants me here, wants me to see this," she said.

"A witness to the passing of so many worlds," said Bill. "Not that it will make any difference."

"Perhaps you are mistaken, perhaps the inevitable outcome is not so certain," she said, and managed to take a step forward, breaking free.

Bill stepped back, took a quick look over his shoulder, then looked back at Christina. "It makes no difference," he said. "She knows what has to be done and where she has to take us. There is no choice, because she has already taken it. I have the memory of it."

Christina didn't understand but continued to walk, moving past Bill and toward Sarah, feeling pulled toward her, not by any gravitational shear but by simple desire.

"She can't save you!" shouted Bill.

"Then we'll save ourselves," she said, and she held out a hand, reaching for Sarah, her fingers brushing up against the plasma discharge that wrapped her and connected her through the writhing conduit, all the way back to Alpha

Centauri A. "We will save ourselves." She reached into the discharge.

And fell.

Far and into the light.

Christina swam through the outer photosphere of Alpha Centauri A, impervious to the burning plasma and the writhing magnetic fields, feet slowly kicking, arms paddling, taking deep gulps of air that she knew could not be there. Like being immersed in a pool of water just before it began to boil, convecting currents of plasma shifted around her, almost on the verge of slipping into a chaotic boil, but entropy having not yet kicked the plasma into the abyss of randomness.

Boundaries between convecting plasma cells, cut and defined by thermal gradients and magnetic fields, filled her entire perspective—cells that spanned the size of planets, others only people-sized, and those that spun and twirled at atomic dimensions.

So much structure.

So much capacity for storage, and so much capacity for computation as the fierce temperatures continually shifted everything. All around her existed a structure within a structure, within a structure, so many layers of nesting, the capacity nearly infinite, a structure perfect for intelligence, begging to be filled, an intellect driven by objectives and desires.

But now empty, hollow, each layer, every cell, silent and dead.

"It's been gone for a very long time."

Christina spun around with several quick kicks of her feet. Sarah hung in front of her, hands slowly flapping up and down, holding her steady in the convecting plasma. Christina could sense the faint echo of what had been, of what had once permeated Alpha Centauri A's photosphere. "Gone for nearly 100 million years," said Christina, seeing that much of the pattern, her voice echoing in all directions, carried away by the star's infinite currents. "But it didn't die," she said. "It went . . ." She struggled for the word, for the image, the context not compatible with the structure of her mind. What she perceived was not a time, not a place, not even geometry in the sense that it defined physical space.

Sarah drifted nearer, information flowing between them. "Gone," she said.

Christina could understand only a small portion of what Sarah tried to tell her. She saw those from Alpha Centauri B, the builders of the Incubator. They had kept interstellar space for several hundred light-years in all directions stable, safe, ensuring that nothing ripped through the Point, and in the process, gobbled up all adjoining space and time.

Christina smiled.

Nothing had escaped from the Incubator to claim them and to swallow them in a Point-Punching runaway. Those from Alpha Centauri B had finally slipped over the edge, not in an explosive expansion of gobbling intellect, or an exponentially driven runaway that spilled across the stars. They simply slipped to the other side of their Point, gently, quietly, all that they were, moving beyond to a place where space and time, suns and planets simply didn't exist.

Gone in an instantaneous transition: phase transition, like ice turning to water, or water to steam—an unsuspected boundary breached and an entirely new form erupting from what had been.

A *group* runaway: not what mankind had feared, a single

entity puncturing the Point and devouring everything around it, but entire species, entire worlds, slipping from one plane of reality to the next. Gone in an instant.

The Swirl, those aspects of it residing in the Alpha system, including the one deep within Alpha Centauri A that directed the Incubator, slipped away with the race from Alpha Centauri B, the event taking place so quickly, so unexpectedly, that from one moment to the next it simply ceased to exist in normal space-time.

But it did leave something behind: the Swirl facets in other star systems, to carry on as best they could, resulting in the Earth and Sun being brought here.

Christina spun once, looking *everywhere*, knowing that while the intelligence had long vacated the star, the machinery, the infrastructure was still in place. Just like Earth's Sun, a Jet could be fired and Alpha Centauri A moved.

She looked deeper.

Alpha Centauri A was the nexus, still connected to all the other stars, including the Sun. "So simple," she whispered, as her hands reached out, sensing just what needed to be touched, what images needed to be presented, how desire could be transformed into action, and the Sun's Jet *redirected*.

Possible trajectories flooded through her, and she saw that there were a nearly infinite number of perturbations in the intensities and directions of Jets from both Alpha Centauri A and the Sun that could even now be used to avoid collision, to save the Earth.

So easy, she thought.

She reached out.

And her fingers melted away, seared to nubs. Christina screamed, her wail swallowed in the nearly infinite expanse of the Sun. "Let me do it!" She spun about to face Sarah.

"I need both these stars," said Sarah.

Sarah shifted, the star moving beneath her, a Jet exploding out of it, the local magnetic fields curling, tightening, guiding the torrents of protons that would be needed to form a Jet, the entire surface of the star convulsing, a torrent of protons rushing to create the spray of the Jet. She reached in deep, half a million kilometers to the core, where the vacuum levels of space-time were already stressed, and gave them the not-so-gentle nudge they needed to cascade, to siphon out energy from beneath the levels of absolute nothingness—Zero Point tapped.

The Jet roared, nothing as subtle as the Jet erupting from Earth's Sun, this Jet at first spewing moon-sized globs of relativistic protons, then unleashing an even larger torrent.

Sarah guided the trajectory.

Alpha Centauri A began to crawl toward the nearing Sun, acceleration building, not even the star's crushing gravitational field able to keep it intact, its deep guts beginning to convulse, to purge in explosive fountains through its surface.

"It's tearing apart!" shouted Christina.

"Acceleration in excess of 10 gees," said Sarah. "Gravitational and structural integrity cannot be maintained under such a force, but sufficient high-speed mass will impact the Sun to serve my purposes."

Christina tried to imagine the resulting impact, no longer the gentle merging of the two stars and the outer coronal flash that would obliterate all nearby planets. This was something more, something far more intense, Alpha Centauri A literally ripping itself apart even before the impact took place.

And when the relativistic remnants of Alpha Centauri A collided with the Sun, the result would be so much more than just a collision. But Christina could not see it, could not calculate it, the recoil and spray of planet-sized globs of stellar matter too much to handle, to simulate, to run through her head, despite what Sarah had done to her, despite how enhanced she'd become.

But she could sense the destruction, the absolute totality of it.

"The death of all humanity," said Christina.

Sarah shook her head. "Something cannot die that was never born. And that is what I must do, ensure our birth," she said. "What remains will be up to you."

Christina felt Alpha Centauri A rip itself apart.

"Christina."

Hands grabbed her shoulders, shaking them. She slowly opened her eyes, and for a moment she thought she was still inside of Alpha Centauri A, the all-pervasive blinding whiteness enveloping her, as its erupting core blew through her.

"Christina, we need to go."

Tugged up into a sitting position, she focused, her eyes blinking. To her left, her father held one of her hands, while to her right, Simon held the other. Padmini squatted in front of her, with Kali hanging just above her, sitting cross-legged in midair.

"We saw it," said Xavier, who had leaned close to her and whispered in her ear. "There was nothing you could do."

Christina turned, looking at her father. "You saw it all— the two stars collide, Alpha Centauri A firing its own Jet and tearing itself apart?"

Xavier nodded, then pointed up at the sky.

Christina leaned back, and what had been a pale blue sky now blazed white. As she squinted, unable to focus, she could feel a deep, searing heat, knowing that the air had not yet had sufficient time to absorb much of what the self-destructing star was spitting out, but certain that it would not take long before the entire atmosphere of this planet started to boil.

Alpha Centauri A's Jet had fired, but unlike the perfect cone from the Sun, this Jet was comprised of miniature suns belched from the core: a stream of plasma spheres aimed at the Sun.

"She was just too powerful," said Padmini.

"Powerful enough to give birth to something amazing," said Christina in a whisper, the image of what she was about to attempt echoing in her head. She pulled her hands away from her father and Simon and slowly stood, swaying gently as she looked around. They stood at the base of the Cross, at what appeared to her to be the exact location they had entered into it.

Sarah was gone, along with Drom and the other dinosaurs.

"Phobos has broken orbit," she said as she took a few steps forward, toward the nearby pods.

"Several minutes ago, while you were unconscious," Xavier said, then looked over at Padmini. "Did Kali tell her?"

Padmini shook her head.

"No one told me," said Christina as she continued to walk toward the pods, the heat from the distorting sun beating at her, with each step the temperature crawling higher. "I'm still connected," she said, pointing above her head, in the general direction of Alpha Centauri A. She began to trot toward the pod, her head swimming, the heat making her dizzy. "We need to be as far away as possible when the stars *implode*."

"You mean the photosphere flash?" asked Xavier from behind, now huffing and puffing to get out the words.

"Implosion," said Christina. "And the gravitational turbulence will be *severe*." She focused on the pod, making certain her feet knew exactly where to carry her, then slipped far away from the mechanics of her body and began running simulations, giving commands, making certain that Earth's Rings sucked down every available antiproton that could be captured by the massive magnetic maws of its Petals.

They would need all they could get.

She pictured the Earth hurtling through space, its own Jets screaming, the torrent of protons erupting through the Petals, carrying the Earth far away.

To where?

She stopped, the desolate world around her fading, replaced with flowing numbers and potential trajectories. All of them fell short. Earth would be a frozen rock, ecosystems gone, life wiped from the surface before it could reach the new source of warmth. Once the Sun and Alpha Centauri A imploded, the source of antimatter to power the Earth's Rings and the proton source needed for reaction mass would be gone—with not enough stored in the Rings to save Earth, to propel it to the only safe place that would remain after Sarah was done with Alpha Centauri A and the Sun.

"Christina?"

She slowly turned, those around her seeming to float like wisps of mist. "Not enough energy, not enough reaction mass for Earth to reach Alpha Centauri B," she said.

"What?" said the ghost that looked like her father. "Alpha Centauri B?"

She felt hands grab her shoulders, shaking her—not her father's hands. "Alpha Centauri B?" asked Simon. "Do you have a trajectory? It's nearly 2 billion kilometers away."

Christina nodded. "But not enough energy, not enough reaction mass."

"Work the problem," said Xavier.

Christina nodded, despite the reality that there was not enough energy, not enough reaction mass, and it was beyond her abilities to twist the fabric of space-time, to pull energy out of the subvacuum levels, to tap into Zero Point—that ability uniquely Sarah's. There simply was no other source of energy to power Earth's Rings, or a source of reaction mass to kick out of the Petals, to push the Earth to the only possible place of safety.

Alpha Centauri B—another star—so close, but still too far.

"Work the problem," said Xavier again, his ghostly outline hanging in front of her.

She looked deeper, even the ghosts fading, the surface of the dead world gone, nothing remaining except for her connection to Alpha Centauri A, a totally useless connection. She couldn't access the infrastructure within Alpha Centauri A or the Sun. The only points she could manipulate were the Rings—and she'd already done all that she could to ensure that Earth's Rings gathered up every available proton and antiproton.

Earth's Rings.

Then she saw it. There was *more.*

So much more, as she realized she could access *all* the Rings through the connection that passed through Alpha Centauri A—Sarah had not blocked *that* pathway. She reached out and could feel the nearly 200 surviving worlds of the Incubator, those that hadn't yet been pulled into the gravitational vortex of the colliding stars. She could *taste* those worlds, ecosystems stripped down to the bare minimum, nothing intelligent remaining, nothing intelligent allowed to evolve for the last 100 million years, each world little more than a near-dead rock. But there were nearly 200 of them, most with Rings full of protons, all ready to be fired at her command.

Work the problem.

Not enough energy or reaction mass in Earth's Rings to carry it quickly enough to Alpha Centauri B before it froze, let alone the energy and reaction mass needed to brake the Earth's momentum and drop it into a stable orbit. But there were nearly 200 worlds, their engines ready to fire, those worlds ready to be moved.

And each had a gravitational field.

A possibility.

"Simon!" she shouted, reaching for him without seeing him, crystal stalks protruding from her fingertips probing for connection, searching for Simon's nervous system. An image filled her head, a phantom from her brief connection to Sarah, something from the CUSP core that had burrowed deep into her head—a lab long gone, the CUSP domain field, and a Doll with arms flapping, amidst hundreds of moving blocks. She touched Simon, pushing her thoughts toward him.

"*Not blocks,*" she whispered. "*Planets.*"

Chapter 36

"*Stop it, Sarah!*"

Akandi looked up into the sky, knowing there would be no stopping what was taking place, realizing that what was happening was the only possibility. Alpha Centauri A was barely recognizable as a star, most of it having torn itself apart, dozens of smaller sunlettes having been blown out of it, the little dull red suns at first parked in tight orbit around the Sun, but now each one firing its own Jet, aiming its Jupiter-sized bulk of plasma directly at the Sun, ready to strike it from all sides.

The Sun was about to be deliberately destroyed.

The Sun's own Jet had extinguished, the Earth nothing more than a reflected pinprick of azure fire, impossible to pick out from the hundreds of other worlds from the Incubator, all of them flashing, their Rings firing. The scene resembled fireflies swarming around a campfire, a world occasionally flaring as it slipped too near the Sun, or to one of the sunlettes that had been Alpha Centauri A.

This was all Sarah's doing, and Akandi was certain of her intent, why this was happening. The reason sat nestled in the coils of his small intestine, the datacube, something he could not feel, something inert and lifeless, yet something that dictated the destruction of two stars and all those worlds. She needed to pass through a door to the distant past, and would open that door with the destruction of both these stars, the worlds of the Incubator, and even the Earth.

They sat on the virtual hull of Phobos as the ship accelerated directly at the Sun, coming in from above, the trajectory carrying them over the Sun's northern pole, accelerating them downward. He suspected that the timing had been coordinated so that Phobos would cut into the Sun just as the sunlettes that had once been Alpha Centauri A crashed along the entire circumference of the Sun's equator.

He could not even begin to understand the gravitational forces that would be in play then, especially when coupled with Sarah's ability to tap into Zero Point, but he had little trouble guessing at the result. The implosion would so stress space-time that a door would be opened, one that led to a very particular place and time, one that Sarah knew she must open, that she had no choice but to open.

"Not this way, Sarah!"

Akandi looked down. Sarah stood 10 meters away, anchored to the hull of Phobos with a series of crystal stalks and bathed in a plasma discharge that sparked and hissed. General Sutherland, on hands and knees, was pressed up as close to her as he could get, arcing sparks erupting from Sarah, cracking over him, then vanishing into the ship's hull. Next to him, also down on all fours, his tail high in the air, crouched Drom, his head whipping back and forth, long tendrils of drool flying.

"Promised us a world!" barked Drom, slapping Sutherland with the side of his snout, throwing the general to the golden ground.

Sutherland picked himself up. "Not this way!" he screamed again, ignoring Drom, pushing himself nearer to Sarah, and almost instantly being thrown back by a crackling wall of discharging lightning, hurled into Drom, both of them rolling several meters. The dinosaur barked, then bit Sutherland in the left thigh and threw him high in the air.

Sutherland landed hard, and Akandi thought he could hear bones break, but the general quickly pushed himself up, crawling back to Sarah. His left thigh, which should have been bleeding and torn, was untouched, and for just a moment Akandi couldn't understand how that was possible, then knew that despite how real this seemed, it was just a full immersion, their bodies deep below in Phobos, either encased in crystal or having been again rendered in the vats of pink goo. As real as this felt, none of them were on the outer hull of Phobos.

At that moment, he realized he had no actual memories

of even having returned to Phobos, his last memories those of being trapped within something unyielding, staring up at Sarah Sutherland, beyond her a conduit of twisting plasma. And then somehow Sarah had translated them to Phobos, the transition instantaneous, a blur, no real memory of anything until he once again found himself on the outer hull of Phobos.

"The best-laid plans of mice and generals go oft astray."

Akandi turned.

Bill, with the rainbow jewel of the Swirl still lodged in this side of his head, sat next to him. "I remember this," he said, pointing up at the colliding stars, the sunlettes now so much closer to the Sun, tendrils of plasma snaking out toward the Sun, a few crashing into it, resembling lightning bolts striking the ground. "Dim and distant, more dream than reality, something forgotten for so long." He grinned and reached up and pushed a lock of brown hair out of his eyes, pinning it back against a facet of the Swirl. "I saw it through *your* eyes."

Akandi nodded.

There was no escaping it now

Into the past they would sail—65 million years distant—to the Earth's moon in order to deliver the datacube in his gut. And there they'd meet the Swirl of that time, and it would invade his mind, seeing the death of these stars and worlds, and taking control of him, would force him to leave the message that the general would find 65 million years later: a message of lies that would tell him that the only way to save the Earth would be to push his daughter through the Point so she could bring Earth safely to the Incubator.

The circle complete.

The Earth dead.

Free will a lie.

Iyoon suddenly hung before him, silent and still.

"And what of Allah?" Akandi asked Iyoon. *"Has all this been nothing more than a moment's distraction, a game played by Allah to pass the time, none of us free-willed creations, but simply windup toys, little machines to be put through our preordained paces?"*

"You see that so clearly," said Iyoon. *"Without the slightest doubt."*

Akandi slowly nodded, wishing that he didn't see it so clearly.

Iyoon slowly turned; black facets momentarily glistening reflected light from the imploding stars. *"Arrogant to the end,"* said the Jinni. *"Able to see into the mind of Allah. What a burden it must be to be so all-knowing and all-seeing."*

Akandi shook his head, then pointed up at the colliding stars. *"I don't have to be all-seeing to see that, to understand what that means."*

Several dozen small sunlettes punched through the Sun's photosphere, swallowed whole, the entire surface of the Sun undulating, flares erupting. The sun's girth increased only slightly. For just a moment it appeared to Akandi as if it could actually retain the remnants of Alpha Centauri A that had just passed into it.

But that was an illusion of perspective.

The Sun exploded. The gravitational shock waves pushed its core through the North and South Poles, as its circumference actually began to shrink, imploding. The added mass of Alpha Centauri A, the kinetic energy provided by the near-relativistic hurtling sunlettes, and something more, Sarah pushing the process along, tore at space-time, pumping all that energy into subvacuum levels, feeding those negative energy states, and in return spewing space-bending gravitational waves.

Akandi leaned back.

For just a moment the Sun's North Pole rushed up at them. A wall of flame and flare filled the heavens, tendrils of plasma smashing into Phobos, rolling over its golden hull, but passing harmlessly through their virtual perspectives. And then it rolled the other way, like a retreating wave being pulled back into the surf, dragging Phobos with it, the craft accelerating past all design limits. Akandi felt the deep shudder; the world beneath him shifted, contracted, the hull rippling around him.

Beneath him the Sun imploded, all its energy, all its mass, translated into subvacuum states. Akandi witnessed the end of everything. Space-time curled over on itself, enveloping Phobos.

Acceleration oscillated between 5 and 10 gees.

"Luminosity down by another 30 percent," said Xavier.

Christina slowly turned her head, fighting the gee forces, looking to the left, to where her father sat encased in crystal restraints. From the waist down, his body was wrapped in glistening strands of tightly woven fiber that quickly undulated, as if breathing. The pulse of the material remained in synch with his beating heart, the wrap keeping the blood from pooling in his legs and feet, forcing it back up his body, into his chest and brain, keeping him conscious.

In front of him hung a sputtering image of what the Sun and Alpha Centauri A had become—an elongated tube of plasma, bulging and rounded at its north and south poles and narrowed at the equator, forming a quickly constricting waist, where the remnants of Alpha Centauri A had collided with the Sun.

"Close to pinching off entirely," said Xavier in a grunt,

having difficulty pulling down a breath. "Soon be two stars again, but not exactly spheres, each one with an open channel punched straight through its center."

The image shifted, rotating by 90 degrees, perspective looking directly down at the northern pole of the star structure, and at the dark hole, which was several thousand kilometers in diameter and punched through the entire northern orb of the stellar remnant. It passed right down to its narrowed waist—a tube of nothingness. Instruments could detect nothing in the dark tube, just the sizzling scream of plasma falling into it from all sides, the impossibly steep gravitational gradient surrounding it, and the backwash of spewing antiparticles that appeared to keep the tube from closing in on itself.

Phobos had dropped into the tube.

Christina understood: not really a tube, but the entrance to a wormhole, one created by Sarah's manipulation of the colliding stars and her ability to tap into Zero Point, generating the type of negative energy densities needed to keep the wormhole stable.

Phobos was passing from here to elsewhere.

While the Earth, still with an appreciable residual velocity as a result of its last several months of reacceleration, was now more than 200 million kilometers away from the imploding stars and wormhole. However, it was still nearly 2,000 million kilometers away from Alpha Centauri B, which from this distance appeared to be little more than an extremely bright yellow-orange star, not yet what might be called a sun.

Too far away from Alpha Centauri B.

And still far too close to the imploding stars—the inevitable eruption of the photosphere would wash over Earth, the oceans boiling away, the atmosphere swept into space, and the crust facing sunward probably liquefying to a depth of nearly 50 kilometers.

"Luminosity down another 10 percent," said Xavier.

This time Christina did manage a nod. The neck between the two orbs of the composite star was almost gone, while the two hemispheres were starting to contract, as well as fall toward each other. The wormhole was beginning to pinch off, no longer needed, Phobos having already made the transit. The physics allowing that was beyond her understanding. "Not my problem," she said in a whisper, and forced her head back. On the other side of the display, hanging in front of her, sat Padmini and Simon, locked in their own high-gee recliners, both interfaced, crystal filaments running from their eyes to the console in front of them. Between them hung the second simulation—everything except for the imploding stars.

Two hundred worlds on the move—all with their Rings firing.

In the distance hung their target—Alpha Centauri B.

The number of potential trajectories was infinite—most of them useless, placing Earth nowhere in the vicinity of Alpha Centauri B. But even when eliminating those, the remaining possibilities were still infinite. That was the nasty reality of dealing with a boundless set of solutions—no matter how many were eliminated, there still existed an infinite number of possibilities.

"Threefold redundancy," said Simon.

Christina looked. Vectors lit the display field, showing just where the worlds would be when the composite sun imploded, and the photosphere exploded outward, searing most of the Incubator worlds and vaporizing Earth's crust.

Three possible shields—three different solar eclipses that she had set up by controlling the firing of each world's

Rings. Each of those three Incubator worlds, those with nearly twice the diameter of Earth, would pass just a few hundred thousand kilometers in front of it on its sunward side, placed in a position so that it cast its shadow across the Earth just moments before the photosphere flash would roll over it.

Three different worlds.

Each cast its shadow minutes apart, the spread deliberate, since the actual instance of the photosphere explosion could not be calculated exactly, not by the shards of CUSP lodged in her head or all the hardware packed into Amalthea. The implosion of stars coupled with the collapse of a wormhole was not an exact science, at least not to those who were merely human.

"The best we can do," said Simon.

Christina looked back at the simulation that Xavier worked on. The Sun–Alpha Centauri A combined star was again two separate burning orbs. The neck had pinched to nothing, the wormhole connecting them was gone, and the two orbs were now accelerating toward each other, driven by the increasing gravitational fields being generated in their depths by the black holes forming from the truncated regions of the wormholes.

"Easy part in place," said Christina.

"Now to *really* push CUSP," she said, knowing that her interface to CUSP was only a insignificant echo of Sarah's. She knew that she could not arrive at a solution herself, the domain was too large, the number of moving elements far too many. She needed guidance; someone to show her the sweet spot in the infinite possibilities of gravitational potentials. "Two hundred worlds," she said. "We cannot accept any solution requiring us to fire Earth's Rings in order to get to Alpha Centauri B—all the reaction mass stored in its Rings must be saved to brake the planet's momentum and drop it in a stable orbit."

Simon turned his head, actually lifting it up off the cradle of the restraining seat, looking over at her. "There may not be a solution," he said.

"Not an option," said Christina, pushing herself forward, falling into the simulation, hundreds of worlds hurtling around her, Rings firing, initial trajectories imputed, those worlds with sufficient reaction mass and energy already locked on course to intercept Earth. *Just work the problem,* she said to herself as she slipped under, sampling the infinite possibilities, searching for the solution, for the set of *near* collisions with Earth, close enough gravitationally to tug the planet in the right direction but not so close as to collide with it, or generate a large enough gravitational shear to shatter it.

"Luminosity down another 60 percent," said Xavier from somewhere distant. "The southern hemisphere is collapsing, and there is severe optical distortion of background stars because of initial formation of the southern black hole."

Christina drifted through the swarm of planets, pushing them this way and that, the link to them beginning to soften, to grow faint, as the informational conduit connecting her to the remnants of Alpha Centauri A was forced to crawl up the increasingly steep gravitational gradient from out of the collapsing stars. *Not much time left,* she thought, projecting that concern to Simon.

"Can't see it," said Simon.

Christina felt herself being pushed, guided to a gravitational-coupled group of more than a dozen planets that orbited in a chaotic path around their collective center of mass, all of them on a collision trajectory for Earth.

"These are *key,*" said Simon.

Christina slipped into them, firing Petals, setting course parameters, the slightest movement of one world affecting all the worlds, no closed-form solution to all their trajectories possible, no matter how many iterations performed, the collective trajectory simply too chaotic, so nonlinear.

"So hard," she whispered as she gave the instructions for several hundred Petals across the worlds to fire in a complex sequence. *Work the problem,* she told herself.

Chapter 37

Akandi screamed.

He fell forever.

"Altitude 12,600 kilometers, and velocity 40 kilometers per second."

Akandi opened his eyes.

The face of the Clinger hovered above him, while beyond and a bit to the left hung a blue-white world, mostly sea and cloud, but also a curling coastline—green-brown land to the right, fading into the distant horizon, and to the left crystal blue water. Both the North–South and East–West Rings were clearly visible, the Western Cross glistening in the early-morning sunlight. "Contact in 315 seconds."

Akandi stared at the distant ocean, dotted here and there with islands, and at what he thought might be the southern edge of another coastline, a peninsula of land cutting through the blue water—the shape of that coastline familiar, but not quite right.

"Propulsion systems all off-line," said the Clinger.

Akandi nodded, pushed himself up, and looked out across the golden hull of Phobos—deserted. "Where are the others?" he asked, as he looked up at the world above him, certain that it was the Earth.

"Occupied."

Akandi nodded, realizing he didn't actually care. "I don't think I'm supposed to be here," he said in a whisper, at that moment understanding what had happened. Sarah had opened a door as the Sun and Alpha Centauri A collapsed, and Phobos had passed through it—back to Earth. "She'll need me on the moon."

"Contact in 275 seconds," said the Clinger.

Akandi looked up, the Earth so much closer, the distant peninsula having almost crawled up past the limb of the horizon. He pointed to it. "It looks like Florida, but the shape of the coastline is not quite right."

The Clinger nodded. "It will be your Florida in 65 million years. Ocean levels have shifted somewhat, and there are perturbations resulting from continental drift."

Akandi nodded, recognizing his own feelings of detachment, not able to make the emotional connection to what had happened—finding it simply impossible to cope with the reality of having just jumped 4 light-years and 65 million years. He pointed up directly above his head, at the curve of the coastline. "And that would be the Yucatán."

The Clinger nodded. "Contact in 133 seconds."

"Closing at 40 kilometers per second, you said?" asked Akandi. "About the speed of a wayward asteroid?"

Again the Clinger nodded.

Despite what was happening, Akandi could not help but smile, understanding the joke that had been played on him and on the Earth. "It wasn't an asteroid that killed the dinosaurs," he said. "It was this ship, as big as an asteroid, traveling at the same speed as an asteroid. It will hit Earth in just a few minutes, destroying the dinosaurs and those of you that exist down there, opening the way for whole new species of mammals to populate the world, and eventually leading to me," he said.

The Clinger nodded. "It appears so."

Akandi rubbed his stomach absentmindedly, knowing that somewhere in the coils of his gut lay the datacube. "I knew I'd be brought back to deliver this," he said, "But *that* I never suspected." He pointed up at the Earth.

"Contact in 80 seconds."

Akandi turned, sensing another presence. Sarah now stood behind him. "We have someplace else to be, don't we?" he asked.

She didn't answer but reached out toward him.

The world slipped away from Akandi, a blur of color and melting geometry giving way to the dark.

"This cannot be happening!"

Sarah Sutherland stood, unmoving, covered in a patina of crystal, her head angled back, looking in the direction of Earth.

"The Sun gone, the Earth destroyed, and now this," said General Sutherland, pointing up at the Earth. "You saw Akandi's message, knew what he'd left for us, what we had to do. But it was all lies."

"Lying is at the core of mammals," said Drom.

Sutherland turned. "Shut up, you goddamned *reptile*," he said.

Drom barked several times, tried to claw at the impenetrable hull, but did not move toward Sutherland. "Not going as planned," he said. "Now it is your turn to make way for something new."

"Not now, not here, you stupid lizard," said Sutherland. "This is where *your* race dies." He pointed up at the Earth. "This is what killed the dinosaurs, and *I* brought it here. Nothing has gone as it should, nothing as promised, but at least I'll die knowing what I've done to your kind."

Drom shook his head right-left-right and jumped at Sutherland. But he never reached him, melting and distorting, then vanishing in a haze of shattered crystal planes.

"You can still stop this!" Sutherland turned back toward his daughter.

Sarah had vanished.

"A once-in-a-lifetime experience."

Akandi felt something poke at his right shoulder.

"I don't think you want to miss this."

Akandi opened his eyes, then closed them almost at once. Instant vertigo swept through him, his heart thumping, his head swimming, his stomach lurching, something sour spraying up his throat, then into his mouth. *"Iyoon,"* he begged.

"Spectacular view."

Akandi felt Iyoon move within his head, electrical chaos damped, synapses flushed, neurotransmitters rebalancing. He slowly opened his eyes. Nothing beneath him, despite the hard surface he felt his face pressed up against. He fell toward the moon, dropping into a landscape of craters and infinite shades of gray.

"Damn powerful."

Akandi rolled over on his back. Bill sat cross-legged, appearing to hover in the midst of nothing, then he reached out and patted at the nothingness by his feet, making a dull, slapping sound. The Swirl was still embedded in the side of his head.

"It appears to be some sort of construct formed by pure gravitational fields, containing an atmosphere, forming a sphere that is descending toward the lunar surface." Bill stood and patted at his belt, which appeared to be the standard survival belt that Sutherland was always wearing. Akandi noted that it looked complete except for the missing pistol. "I don't think she wants us dead, at least not right away." He reached into a pouch in his belt, removed a small packet of food, pulled off the corner of its mylar wrapper, and took a bite of the bar. "Simply horrible," he said, "especially when one considers that it may be our last meal." Then he looked down at his feet. "We're coming up on Copernicus."

Akandi rolled back over, the sense of falling filling him again, but Iyoon had damped enough of his panic that he could keep his eyes open. They fell quickly, seeming to angle toward the western wall of the crater. Akandi was surprised by the stark contrast between light and dark, and the ejecta around the crater, spewed for what looked to be hundreds of kilometers, the debris field sharp and defined as if the crater had just been formed.

"Western inner wall at a height of 217 meters above the crater floor, a latitude of 10 degrees, 4 minutes, and 17 seconds north and longitude of 18 degrees, 46 minutes, and 38 seconds west." Bill grinned. "Certainly the most important, as well as the most closely guarded secret location on the moon. I remember it so well."

Akandi continued to watch as they fell.

"Actually I remember it twice. The first time a so-distant memory, when we will hit in just a few minutes, and then

65 million years in the future, when the remnants of your corpse and your message to the future will be discovered on June 12, 2021. The great circle is about to be completed."

Akandi turned toward Bill, watching him as he gently stroked the crystal protruding from his head.

"Sarah Sutherland certainly lived up to her Post-Human promise," said Bill. "Threaded Phobos right through the collapsing wormhole formed by the implosion of the Sun and Alpha Centauri. Amazing enough, but to be able to engineer the collapse so it positioned the exit end of the wormhole in just the right place at just the right time is truly remarkable." He paused. "Although in some ways I suppose it would be impossible for her to miss, since all this started with the arrival of Phobos 65 million years before you came along, and before she was even born."

Akandi pushed himself up, sitting. "Perhaps it is Allah's will, an endless cycle of birth and death."

Bill shook his head. "No need to invoke Him," he said. "When Phobos popped back out into normal space I was able to access the ship's systems. We were at an altitude of 30,000 kilometers above Earth and dropping like the proverbial rock. I had no difficulty accessing ship's systems to see if the engines could be fired and Phobos diverted from its appointment."

"What?" said Akandi.

"Don't be confused," said Bill. "I have no desire to stop Phobos and every desire to complete this never-ending torture of waiting for the long-dead Alphans to return. I just wanted to see if it could be done, wanted to see how well Sarah had implemented her little plan."

"The engines couldn't be fired."

"Afraid not," said Bill. "The engines were in fine shape,

but the ship had been drained of all reaction mass, not so much as a picogram of antimatter left in its fuel bays. But of course this only made sense. Sarah intended to do away with my little playthings, something that could be accomplished by a good-sized asteroid, or in this case, a dead spacecraft the size of an asteroid. Had there been antimatter left in storage, even a few hundred kilos, that would have been the end of Earth, and you primate types." He shook his head. "She knew just what to do, draining the fuel and sending Phobos on a trajectory directly at the enclave where I'd been raising my new and improved dinosaurs and lemurs."

"The Yucatán," said Akandi.

Bill nodded. "I kept my experimental populations relatively small and isolated, never more than a hundred thousand of either species, ensuring that in case a runaway took place I could keep it isolated from the rest of the global ecosystem. It was destroyable if need be."

"Your own precautions worked against you."

Bill grinned. "Only took a single shot to obliterate both species. Of course I could have restarted the experiment, seeded from the two other isolated populations I was working on."

"Those in Phobos and Almathea," said Akandi.

Bill nodded. "But there was no reason once I found the images in your head."

Akandi understood, knowing that while it appeared that he was talking to Bill, he was really talking to the Swirl. The Swirl had memories extending back to the beginning of life of Earth and was on the planet right now, undoubtedly staring up into the sky, watching Phobos plummet toward the Yucatán peninsula. Bill knew everything that was about to happen, because the Swirl had already lived it. He turned away from Bill and stared down at the rapidly approaching moon, their gravitational bubble already having drifted beneath the rim of Copernicus.

"After Phobos hit, I searched for evidence of other anomalies, something to help explain how a small moon could simply appear so near Earth, and found the gravitational track departing from Phobos and to the Moon, backtracking *you* to Copernicus."

Akandi shook his head, feeling disoriented, the pàst and present seeming to fold on each other, as Bill talked about things that had not yet happened to him as if they had taken place in the distant past.

"Found you there, all alone."

Akandi looked up at him with a questioning look.

"That's right," he said. "In just a bit over 2 hours, you will be found perched in the rim of Copernicus, encapsulated in a gravitational bubble, all alone. Probing your mind was easy, the pathways ready for me—because I had been inside it so recently." Bill shook his head. "You seemed so pleased when I vacated you, giving you back your free will. But of course it wasn't that at all. When I find you 2 hours from now, had I still been in your head, that would have been the end of *my* free will. I needed to know some of the basic milestones, but not the infinite details. Imagine trying to replicate every subtle nuance of one's actions for 65 million years. It simply can't be done: entropy, thermodynamics, even quantum mechanics won't allow for an absolute repeat of history. So I had to make sure that I didn't know exactly what would be happening, making sure that I had no direct contact with that future version of myself.

Akandi pointed up at the Swirl protruding from the side of Bill's head.

"As I said, when I found you on the moon, you were all

alone, just you sitting in a greasy pile of very-short-chained organic molecules. Old Bill here and I," said Bill, as he reached up and touched the Swirl, "will soon be making our departure."

Akandi opened his mouth but realized there was nothing he could say. He was trapped, by what Sarah and the Swirl had done. Sarah's actions would lead directly to the eventual creation of the human race as well as its death, while the Swirl's actions would lead not only to its own demise, but to the death of those facets of itself that had existed in the Sun, Alpha Centauri A, and the Incubator.

And he could do nothing to stop it.

Because it had all happened already.

He slowly closed his mouth.

"I think you finally have a clear picture of the situation."

Akandi nodded. "The Swirl will find me, enter into my mind, see the future and how to escape from its own isolation. Then it will force me to write a fabricated version of the future for General Sutherland, one convincing him that the only hope humanity has for survival is to push his daughter through the Point and have the Earth transported to the Incubator."

Bill smiled. "It all works out so perfectly: consciousness for light-years in all directions eradicated—no more pain, no more suffering, no more boredom."

Akandi slumped to the bottom of the gravitational sphere, his back to the moon, looking up at the distant Earth.

"Should be quite some show," said Bill. "Keep a sharp eye out so you don't miss any of the fireworks. Not every day that a little moon drops in on the Earth, wiping out most major species and opening the way for you little primates."

Akandi looked over at Bill. His features were liquefying,

the skin on his face starting to dribble from his skull, his fingers falling from his hands, as his knees suddenly let go and he crumbled in on himself, collapsing, hitting the base of the gravitational bubble, and starting to slide toward him. The Swirl shattered, fragments sinking into the goo that had been Bill.

Akandi tried to move away from the liquefying remains of Bill.

But there was no time.

The gravitational sphere slammed into the wall of the Copernicus crater.

The Earth fell onto General Sutherland—at least that was his perception.

There was a momentary distortion as Phobos cut into the Earth's atmosphere, with just enough time for Sutherland to stand up straight. The hull of Phobos suddenly flashed crimson as the entire trip through 100 kilometers of Earth's atmosphere took less than 3 seconds.

"Sarah," he said, having no time for any other words

Phobos buried itself and General Sutherland in the Yucatán peninsula.

Drom looked down at his hands, at fingers gliding across the smooth console, fingers poking at icons, a trajectory imputed to drop the pod in the center of the Asian continent, as far as possible from the Phobos impact point. His landing location was distant enough that it would take many days before the sky there went dark from the soot and debris blown skyward from the Phobos crash. It would take many weeks before the global biosphere collapse reached

Asia. The last reentry burn had been completed, and gliding surfaces were already deployed from the side of the pod. He did not know why he had woken in the pod, but suspected it was his reward for 13 years of service to Christina, a chance to be home and to be free.

The Earth swept by beneath him, tinted red by the plasma sheath that enveloped the descending pod. Beneath him seas and deserts raced by. Jungles and mountains were all deserted, all empty, all untouched by the hand of mammals. It was his world.

There would be many good days of hunting.

There would be many good days on the Earth, where he truly belonged.

A flash in the pod's rear display forced him to look up, a wall of white engulfing the rear horizon, rolling over the planet, overtaking him before nictitating membranes could snap shut over his eyes.

Phobos had crashed.

The pod lurched, the console beneath his hands squealing, flashing a random assortment of colors and static. Then everything darkened, all lights extinguished in the pod except for the small red emergency beacon above his head. He realized that just as the earlier landing of Phobos had discharged a massive EMP in Earth's atmosphere, flatlining all but the most protected bioelectronics, this Phobos, crashing through the atmosphere and obliterating thousands of square kilometers of crust, thrusting debris into the atmosphere, had done the same thing.

During the first Phobos landing, the circuitry in his head, the enhancements inflicted upon him by the Clingers, had been protected by the shielding of the Phobos. No such shielding existed in the pod.

It was the last real thought he had.

The circuitry in his head sizzled, seizing, then sputtered to silence. He stared up at the emergency light, not understanding what it was, the strange smells of the dimly lit space not right. He crouched low, readying himself to attack or be attacked.

That he understood.

The pod glided down; emergency explosive hatches fired when the atmosphere had thickened sufficiently, deploying the backup parachutes. Drom waited, thinking nothing, nostrils flaring, and the sharp talons on his toes scraping at the unyielding flooring of the pod. He was suddenly very hungry. The pod hit the ground, rolling several times, the emergency light extinguished. Drom barked and thrashed, snapping at the darkness.

The emergency door blew open, light and smells spilling in.

Drom bounded out.

So very hungry. So very happy.

Akandi stood ankle deep in the oily sludge that had been Bill. The gravitational sphere had buried itself deeply into the wall of the crater, almost totally obscured, only a small wedge, at least five meters above him, open to the sky. The Earth hung over him. The red welt where Phobos had smashed into Central America was easily visible, with the glowing tendrils of Earth's blown-out crust still expanding, surrounded by ash-choked fire that burned across most of North America and well past the Amazon basin in South America.

He'd watched the unfolding destruction for more than an hour, as the debris and fire spread out across the face of the Earth. He suspected that he had little time left—the air was already growing stale, his breathing quicker, and a feeling of dizziness rolled through him. He'd eaten a bit of the food he'd found in Bill's emergency belt, the only aspect of him that had not disintegrated into fundamental hydrocarbons. The food had helped a bit in clearing his head, but still the dizziness persisted, and he was panting like a dog.

He was running out of air.

Not much longer, and he'd be dead.

He continued to look up, at the eastern edge of the full Earth, able to see western Europe, and part of Africa. But no farther east. Mecca lay somewhere just beyond the horizon.

"Over soon, Iyoon," he thought.

Iyoon had been hovering motionless in the far shadows of the sphere and floated nearer, its black surfaces momentarily reflecting just a bit of color from the Earth high above. *"And you'll soon be with Allah."*

Akandi slowly nodded, grateful that Iyoon had not tried to argue with him, that it accepted the inevitable, the reality of the datacube in his gut, the critical piece of history that his dead corpse would play.

"Full circle, and all for nothing," thought Akandi, as he lowered himself into the muck, down on his knees, but still looking up, toward Earth's eastern horizon, and began to whisper a prayer, afraid that Allah would not listen to him, but even more afraid that there *was* no Allah to listen to him.

He fell forward, his hands dropping into the thick residue, his entire body tingling, his breathing quickening even more, the edges of his vision darkening.

"It's here," said Iyoon.

Akandi managed to twist his neck, to look up at the opening above, and saw a faint jewel of light, wavering and rippling, dropping through the opening, more ghost and mist than the hard, jeweled shape he'd come to expect—but there was no doubt that it was the Swirl.

It fell toward him, flattening out, suddenly resembling a many-colored scarf, drifting down, one corner touching the top of his head, then the rest covering him, suddenly not so gossamer, not so tenuous, but thick and stiffening, squeezing down, wrapping across his face, tightening around his throat, pushing through skin, seeping into bone, probing deep into his brain.

He tried to stand but fell back with a splash, sitting, about to reach up and grab at the rainbow sheet covering his head, when his hands fell away, no longer under his control.

"It knows, has seen what you've seen," said Iyoon.

Akandi's hands reached out into the thick black goo, searching, then grabbing on to the emergency belt, pulling it out, greasy fingers popping snaps, pulling out a small pad and pen, his fingers clutching the oily pen, starting to write.

To Colonel Thomas Sutherland, United States Army.

Akandi tried to close his eyes, didn't want to see the lies that the Swirl would write, the instructions that would start all of humanity down the path that would eventually lead to Alpha Centauri and the destruction of Earth.

But the Swirl would not let him close his eyes.

His fingers continued to write.

Akandi looked down at his dead body. It lay in the bottom of the gravitational bubble, flat on its back, eyes closed, hands still clutching pen and paper. "Something's not right," he said as he shifted his perspective, looking down at his own feet, which hovered just a few centimeters above a shard of stone sticking out from the side of the crater wall. He took a deep breath, knowing there should be no air, and stamped down with his right foot, unable to quite bring it down against the rock beneath him. "Wrong," he said.

"What had been Bill has been transformed," said Iyoon.

Akandi nodded, at that moment realizing what had been wrong. It was not the fact that he was alive, breathing, and standing stark naked on the lunar surface that had struck him as wrong—what was wrong was that most of the greasy goo that had been Bill had disappeared.

"Full circle completed."

Akandi looked to his left. At the rim of the Copernicus crater, several hundred meters above him, stood a figure, a woman glistening in the harsh lunar light. It was Sarah Sutherland. But she had not been the one who had spoken— the speaker had been the gray ghost just a few meters away from him, shaped like Sarah Sutherland but built from fine-grained lunar soil.

"You showed the Swirl the last moments of the Incubator, the Sun, and Alpha Centauri A, and in turn it used you to create that future."

Akandi shook his head. "You used all of us to create that future: one where the Earth has been transformed into a chunk of frozen slag."

The gray shadow lurched forward, a hand reaching for Akandi, a sparking of light at its fingertips, and for just a moment he sensed something both burning and freezing, as the fingers of lunar dust reached into his stomach, then jerked back, the datacube resting in the gray palm, blazing in reflected sunlight. "A critical detail," said the ghost, as it turned around and dropped the datacube.

It fell slowly in the weak lunar gravity, taking long seconds to drop toward Akandi's dead body, the cube distorting, spinning, one dimension of it contracting to nothing, the cube suddenly a square with no thickness, appearing to vanish each time it spun.

It landed on the dead body's stomach, edge on, suddenly not there.

"That should do it," said the gray shadow.

Akandi looked down at his dead body, knowing that it was not really his body, but something fabricated by Sarah using the remnants of what had been Bill, certain that it mimicked him right down to the most insignificant base pair of his DNA, right along with every synaptic connection in his head. And now the datacube rested in the dead body's gut.

"So I'm not dead, and it is not really my body that will be found buried in this crater," said Akandi. He slowly shook his head. "My outcome may have changed, but that doesn't really make any difference because the Earth is dead and gone."

The shadow pointed up at the Earth.

Akandi again shook his head. "Dead 65 million years from now. *My* Earth is dead."

"So you believe, so you convinced the Swirl," said the shadow.

"I saw the Sun implode," said Akandi, shuddering.

"True enough," said the shadow. "Any reasonable entity would believe that implied the death of the Earth."

Akandi looked up at the Earth, then across the crater, to where Sarah stood upon the rim. "Earth survived?" he asked, not believing it possible, but also realizing that other impossible things had happened—his own journey across 65 million years and 4 light-years, and even the smaller impossibility of him standing naked upon the moon.

"Perhaps someday you'll even see it for yourself," said the

shadow, and it disintegrated, dust and grit drifting down across the crater wall.

"But there are so many other things to see first."

Akandi looked up—Sarah drifted down toward him from the crater rim above.

"An entire universe."

Akandi looked up at the Earth and whispered a small prayer of thanks, then sensed the ground move beneath him. Looking down, he saw that the side of the crater had caved in, the gravitational bubble collapsed. His body was buried, waiting to be found 65 million years in the future.

Chapter 38

"It will be very close," said Simon.

Christina nodded.

Xavier looked at the image, at the three planets from the Incubator moving in behind them, Petal tips blazing. Less than half a light-minute behind the three worlds raced, what had been the combined photospheres of the Sun and Alpha Centauri A, all that remained of the two stars. The bulk of their matter had been siphoned off from normal space-time and fed into energy levels below the vacuum level, generating the negative energy density that had been needed to stabilize the wormhole cutting through the heart of the imploding stars.

The wormhole through which Phobos had fallen.

Xavier forced himself to look away from the expanding wall of the photosphere, past the three worlds to the small image of Amalthea, inserted neatly in the shadow of the three planets. Amalthea would be saved, the crash of the photosphere peeling away the outer crust of the three planets, with Amalthea hidden safely in their shadows. And less than half a light-second beyond Amalthea hung the Earth.

Almost in the shadow of the three planets.

Xavier looked away from the display and out into space. His view was only virtual, from his vantage point on Amalthea's hull, but appeared no less real than if he had actually been standing on it. In reality he was kilometers below the surface, still encased in a block of crystal designed to take the tremendous accelerations Amalthea had been subjected to in order to reach the Earth before the photosphere flashed past.

He looked up at the Earth.

And while he recognized it, it was not his Earth. This world was 13 years from the one he knew and had traveled 4 light-years through interstellar space since he'd last seen it. The Rings were still there, glistening white, the Petal tips dull and unfiring, the antimatter-matter mix in the Rings being saved for later, for orbital insertion around Alpha Centauri B—if there was a later. The Rings were familiar, but so much of the rest of the planet had changed. The North Pole was now nothing more than an expanse of blue ocean, and the southern ice cap was also mostly gone, just a few patches of ice far to the interior of Antarctica. The perimeter of the continent was tinted green with plant growth. And while all of northern Africa had also greened, the heartland of Africa was still the darkened, blasted mass of slag and craters left by the Ten Degree War from nearly 40 years earlier.

Coastlines had changed because of the melted ice caps: Florida was half its width, the lowlands of Europe lay beneath the Atlantic, and even though he couldn't see the far side of the planet from his current perspective, he knew that most of Bangladesh was submerged in the Indian Ocean.

Those changes were understandable—a consequence of ice caps melting, the rise in ocean levels, and subsequent climate changes. But so many other things simply made no sense.

The British Isles were gone.

And a swatch of Canada, running from what Xavier thought might be Toronto, all the way to the coast of Nova Scotia, reflected like a mirror—not the slightest bit of structure, just a surface that resembled liquid metal. Christina had explained—that region was a containment structure, where the nodes of the Swirl had been forced into retreat during the last 13 years.

He looked past the Earth.

The heavens themselves were not even right.

Beyond the northern hemisphere of Earth hung a very small sun, feeble and distant—Alpha Centauri B, nearly 2 billion kilometers away, better than 10 times further from the the Earth than the Sun had been.

Changes, his daughter had told him.

And now there would be other changes.

"It's coming."

Xavier turned. The other three. Christina, Simon, and Padmini also had a virtual manifestation on the hull of Amalthea, but were not as strongly coupled with it as he was. Most of their consciousness was still below, monitoring the advancing photosphere and tweaking the Petal firings of the three worlds intended to shadow the Earth. They sat before consoles, thick bundles of fiber running between them.

"Now!" shouted Christina.

Xavier turned.

The sky burned—a wall of flaring plasma, white and red, slashed with planet-spanning bolts of twisting lightning. Xavier looked up at the Earth—almost entirely in the shadow of the three planets. But two arcs of blazing photosphere penetrated the not-quite-perfect shield and slammed into the Earth. One hit the far South Pacific, in a narrow band running nearly the entire distance from South America to Africa, the ocean burning and boiling, the crust below blown out, molten debris and rock thrown back up through the atmosphere, then raining down across the entire South Pacific. And the second arc, smaller than the first, ran across North America, burning against the reflective region where the Swirl had been confined, the region suddenly boiling, incandescent jets exploding back out into space.

And within a few seconds the torrent of plasma vanished, cut off, the shadowing planets dropping the Earth behind a full eclipse, protecting it from the bulk of the flashing photosphere that would continue to burn past for nearly an hour.

Smoke, ash, and steam rose from the two regions that had been exposed, the ground below, even that in the deep Pacific, glowing white-hot at the center of the impact regions, the perimeters red and boiling.

"I think we did it."

Xavier turned. Christina walked toward him, looking so real, a tight spiral of colored shapes twirling above her head. Behind her, Simon and Padmini were still shadows, seated at their consoles, still hard-hooked into Amalthea, and through it to the Rings of the surviving Incubator worlds.

Christina pointed up at the Earth and the molten welt across North America. "Gone now, totally liquefied, the Swirl is finally eradicated from Earth. Not easy to meld that requirement in the positioning of the three shadowing planets."

Xavier slowly nodded, knowing it was not only the Swirl that was gone, but also all those that had been host to it.

She pointed past the Earth toward the distant Alpha Centauri B. "We have nearly fifty of the surviving Incubator worlds still under our control, with functioning Rings. We'll bring them in one by one, on close trajectories, burning the fuel and reaction mass in their Rings, so they pass just in front of the Earth, the gravitational tug from each kicking the Earth toward Alpha Centauri B. Then they'll drift beyond Earth and out into interstellar space." She looked over at Padmini and Simon. "They really don't need my help for this." She smiled. "I can crunch the numbers down to the last significant bit, thanks to what Sarah did to me, but Simon can feel the relationships between all those moving worlds—he was bred for just this sort of problem."

"How long to Alpha Centauri B?" asked Xavier. They hadn't been able to generate an accurate simulation before the photosphere passed them and burned through the Incubator worlds, not knowing exactly how those planets' trajectories would be altered by the slam of the photosphere and if their Ring systems would even survive.

Christina turned in the direction of Simon and Padmini, nodded, then looked back at Xavier. "Pretty close to our original estimate—40 days."

Xavier looked back up at the Earth and the growing ring of dark ash rising around its burning wounds. The Sun and Alpha Centauri A were gone. Earth was now without a source of light and heat, with Alpha Centauri B still 2 bil-

lion miles away, the energy from it at this distance less than
1 percent of what the Sun had provided when the Earth had
been in its old orbit.

Forty days with no Sun.

Under normal conditions the Earth would have radiated
away almost all of the heat stored in its atmosphere and
oceans in 40 days, oceans icing over within the first ten,
freezing solid down to the seabeds by 20, then getting so
cold that by the time Alpha Centauri B was close enough to
offer any appreciable heat, the atmosphere itself would have
collapsed, gases like oxygen and nitrogen having liquefied.

The Earth would be frozen and dead when it arrived at
Alpha Centauri B.

But these were not normal conditions.

Two large patches of the Earth burned, magma fields
running for thousands of kilometers, the upper atmosphere
already filling with soot, ash, and water vapor, all that
debris acting as a reflective blanket, trapping the atmosphere's heat, creating a greenhouse effect, fueled by the
regions of liquefied crust.

"Such a balancing act," said Xavier.

"And far from perfect," said Christina. "Earth will be too
hot in the beginning—lethally so in some regions of North
America—and before Earth reaches Alpha Centauri B it
will become so cold on the far side of the planet, away from
the photosphere strikes, that the casualties in central Asia
will be extreme." She looked away from the Earth.

"But it will survive," said Xavier. "Mankind can
rebuild."

Christina nodded.

"You worked the problem, you found the solution."
Walking over to her, he wrapped his arms around her. She
felt so stiff and rigid, every muscle tense. He squeezed

tightly, her muscles slowly relaxing, shoulders sagging just a bit, and he could feel her take a slow deep breath. "You worked the problem," he whispered to her. Xavier pulled her tightly to his chest and looked past the Earth and to the distant Alpha Centauri B. "Already looks closer," he said.

Robert A. Metzger is a research scientist in the area of semiconductors, high-speed telecommunication, and data-communication devices. He has held distinguished teaching and consulting positions with Hughes Research Laboratories and the Georgia Institute of Technology. He is a Nebula Award nominee for *Picoverse*, and the author of a number of novels and short stories. His work has appeared in *The Magazine of Fantasy and Science Fiction* and *Amazing*, among other publications. He has also contributed numerous pieces to *Wired* and is cofounder of the technical trade journal *Compound Semiconductor*. He lives in Chapel Hill, North Carolina. Visit his website at www.rametzger.com.